J

/

MANY A TEAR HAS TO FALL

Also by Joan Jonker

When One Door Closes
Man Of The House
Home Is Where The Heart Is
Stay In Your Own Back Yard
Last Tram To Lime Street
Sweet Rosie O'Grady
The Pride Of Polly Perkins
Sadie Was A Lady
Walking My Baby Back Home
Try A Little Tenderness
Stay As Sweet As You Are
Down Our Street
Dream A Little Dream

MANY A TEAR
HAS TO FALL

Joan Jonker

HEADLINE

First published in 2000
by HEADLINE BOOK PUBLISHING

10 9 8 7 6 5 4 3 2 1

British Library Cataloguir

Jonker, Joan
Many a tea
I. Title
823.9'14 [F]

ISBN 0 7472 7249 2

Typeset by
CBS, Martlesham Heath, Ipswich, Suffolk

Printed and bound in Great Britain by
Mackays of Chatham plc, Chatham, Kent

HEADLINE BOOK PUBLISHING
A division of Hodder Headline
338 Euston Road
London NW1 3BH

www.headline.co.uk
www.hodderheadline.com

To all the readers who have written such lovely letters to me. They are much appreciated.

Dear Readers,
Oh dear, oh dear, oh dear, you'll definitely need two boxes of tissues for this book. I did. But I think you'll love the story and the characters who are warm, friendly and funny, just like yourselves. Happy reading and take care.
Love
Joan

Chapter One

'Only another two weeks and you start your holidays, George.' Ann Richardson rested her knife and fork to glance across the table to where her husband sat. 'I was wondering whether we could afford a few days away? It would be a break for the children, because their seven weeks' holiday from school seems never-ending with them having nothing to fill their time.'

'I think we could manage a few days, love, if we tighten our belts.' George was a handsome man of forty-two. Tall and well built, he had a thick mop of black hair, a moustache that was curled to a point at each end, a strong jaw and a set of even white teeth. He smiled now as he asked, 'Would you like that, girls?'

'Oh, yes, Dad!' Maddy, twelve years of age, bounced up and down on her chair. She had inherited her father's colouring and his enthusiasm for life. 'It would be lovely, wouldn't it, Tess?' She turned in her chair and put a hand on her sister's arm. 'Wouldn't it be exciting?'

Tess nodded, a faint smile covering her thin, pale face. 'Yes, it would be lovely.'

'We could go somewhere in the country, and the fresh air would put some colour in your cheeks.' George looked fondly at the daughter who was a constant source of worry to him and his wife. She'd been sickly since the day she was born, and for years they'd consoled themselves by saying she'd grow out of it. But at ten years of age, she was so small and thin she could be taken for a child of eight. 'You'd enjoy running in the fields and seeing the cows and sheep, wouldn't you?'

'Will Maddy be with me?'

'Of course I will, you daft thing.' Maddy put a protective arm across her sister's shoulders. 'You don't think I'd let you go anywhere without me, do you?'

'Will you eat your dinners before they go cold?' Ann said, putting on a stern expression. 'We can talk when we've finished eating and the dishes are washed.'

'I don't want any more, Mam,' Tess said. 'I'm full up.'

'You've hardly eaten enough to feed a bird, so come on, get it down

1

you.' Ann could feel her husband's eyes on her but didn't look towards him. She knew he would say to leave the child alone if she didn't want any more to eat, but that was the easy way out. If anyone needed feeding up, it was Theresa, and sometimes you had to be cruel to be kind. 'I refuse to throw good food into the midden every night.'

Maddy leaned across to her sister's plate and speared a potato. 'Come on, Tess, eat this to please me.' She held the fork near lips that were clamped tight. 'Please?'

The one person Tess loved most in the whole world was her sister. And she'd do anything to please her. So she opened her mouth and sank her teeth into the potato. But within seconds she was balking, and clamping a hand across her mouth she dashed from the room out into the yard, where they could hear her being sick.

George sighed. 'Why didn't you just let her be? This happens every time you force her to eat more than her stomach can take.'

'She has to eat to live! I will not stand by and watch our daughter starve herself to death. And that's what is happening! Can't you see that?'

'I can see what's happening right now, and vomiting her heart out will not improve her appetite.' George pushed his plate away, his own appetite deserting him. 'Maddy, will you go and see to your sister, please?'

Ann jumped to her feet. 'Will you stop calling her Maddy? Her name is Madelaine. And I will see to Theresa myself.' With a withering look she marched from the room, her back ramrod straight.

George caught the worried expression on his elder daughter's face. 'It's all right, pet, nothing to get upset about.'

'But I do worry about Tess, Dad, she always seems to be sick. She's hardly ever in school and she's miles behind the other children.'

'When she's at home she's still learning, pet. Don't forget your mother was a teacher in an infants' school for three years before we got married. That's many years ago, of course, and much water has flowed under the bridge since then. But when Tess is not at school, your mother does take her for lessons each day.'

Maddy lowered her head. She wouldn't like to be taught by her mother because she was too strict. And the girl often thought the reason for her sister being sick so much was because she was scared. Her mother expected more from her than she was capable of. 'I could help Tess with reading and sums, but I'm not allowed to.'

Her father smiled. 'I'm sure your mother knows you mean well, pet, but she is more experienced than you.'

Maddy would have kept her mouth closed now, believing she'd said enough. But she could hear her mother in the kitchen telling Tess to rinse her mouth out, and the voice sounded more like a teacher's than a mother's. So Maddy dared to say, 'Well, I'd rather be taught by a teacher than my mother. After all, you don't have to live with the teacher.'

George looked surprised, then thoughtful. It was something that had never entered his head, but perhaps the child had a point. So when his wife ushered Tess in, he took more interest in the behaviour of both than he normally would.

'I think the best place for you is bed,' Ann told the shivering girl. And there was no sympathy in her voice, she was just stating what she intended to happen. 'Run upstairs and get undressed. And for heaven's sake, try not to be sick in the bed.'

Perhaps it was Maddy's words that caused George to see his wife through the eyes of her children. She was two years younger than him, of medium height, still quite slim, and she carried herself well, shoulders always squared, never slumped. Her mousy-coloured hair was combed away from her face and plaited into a bun at the nape of her neck. It was a severe style, making her appear haughty, but she'd worn it like that for as long as George had known her, so he couldn't imagine her any other way. She didn't have much sense of humour, nor did a smile come easily to her face, but he was used to that. It hadn't stopped him falling head over heels in love with her all those years ago, and he still loved her dearly. But was it possible that a child as fragile as Tess would feel intimidated by her, even though she was her mother?

'No, leave her be.' George held his arms wide. 'Come here, pet, and I'll give you a cuddle to warm you up.' Holding the girl close, he rocked gently to and fro, until the shivering had stopped. Then he looked up at his wife. 'Make some bread and milk for her, love, with plenty of sugar sprinkled on the top. With a bit of luck she might keep it down.'

There was a hot retort on Ann's lips, but it remained unspoken when she saw the look on her husband's face that told her he would brook no argument.

'You sit on my knee, pet, and I'll feed you like I did when you were a toddler.' Ignoring the disapproving looks thrown his way, George slowly spoon-fed his daughter. And feeling warm, contented and safe in his arms, Tess took in spoonful after spoonful until the dish was empty. 'Well I never!' George feigned surprise. 'Has all that gone down your tummy, sweetheart?'

Tess smiled. She had enjoyed the bread and milk, it had gone down easy. But better still, her father looked really pleased with her. 'I'm a good girl, aren't I, Dad?'

'You're always a good girl, pet.' George kept a smile on his face even though he was feeling sad inside. She was ten years of age, but she didn't speak as a ten-year-old. Like her body, her mind hadn't matured. And it wasn't as though they'd neglected her. Ann had taken her to the doctor's many times, only to be told that while she was a frail child, and probably always would be, the doctor could find nothing wrong with her. No reason for her to be physically or mentally slow. But there had to be a reason, and it was up to him and Ann to find out what it was. 'And you know your mam and dad love you very much.' He caught the sadness in his wife's eyes. 'We do, don't we, love?'

'Of course we do!' Endearments didn't come easy to Ann because she'd grown up in a house where affection was never openly shown. She had been taught to be obedient, never to answer back, and often reminded that children should speak when they were spoken to. Her parents had loved her, she knew that, but words of love were never spoken, hugs and kisses never exchanged. 'We love you dearly.'

'And what about me?' Maddy said, flinging her arms as wide as they'd go. 'That's how much I love you.'

Tess giggled. 'I love you that much, but my arms aren't as long as yours.'

George hugged her to him. 'You can't measure love in inches, pet, it's in your heart. And when you know you're loved, it makes you feel good inside, doesn't it?'

Large hazel eyes stared up at him. 'You won't ever stop loving me, Dad, will you? Even if I can't do my sums or joined-up writing?'

'Scout's honour, pet, I'll never stop loving you, no matter what.'

'You can do sums anyway!' Maddy said with feeling. 'You were watching me doing my homework last week, and you were quick to tell me when I made a mistake in my adding-up. If it hadn't been for you I'd have got a cross by that sum.'

'Is that true, Madelaine, or are you just making it up?' Ann asked. 'You're not helping Theresa by telling lies for her, you know.'

'I'm not telling lies! I was doing my homework at the table and Tess was sitting next to me, watching. You were in the kitchen getting the dinner ready, Mam.' Maddy smiled at her sister. 'I'm not telling lies, am I?'

Tess shook her head before drawing back into her father's arms. She had to tell the truth because she loved her sister dearly and would never let her down. But she waited now for her mother to ask why she could get sums right for her sister but not for her. 'They were only easy sums, though, Maddy, they weren't hard ones.' She was too frightened to add that there was no one standing over her while she did them, no one to reprimand or make her feel guilty if she got them wrong.

'Let's forget all about sums and talk about something more pleasant,' George said. 'Like the Richardson family going on holiday. How about that, eh?'

'It would be great, Dad! All of my friends will be dead jealous.' Maddy's pretty face was agog. They'd never been on holiday before and the prospect was really exciting. 'I won't swank, though, 'cos that wouldn't be nice, would it? So I'll only tell my very best friends.'

'Where would you like to go, the seaside or the country?' George knew it would only be for a few days no matter where they went, because the money wouldn't run to a whole week. But the two girls looked so happy he wasn't going to say anything to take the shine out of their eyes.

'We'll go where Tess wants to go, shall we?' Maddy said. 'What do you think, Mam?'

'I think we should let your father tell us what we could expect from a holiday by the seaside, or one in the country. And then you and Theresa can say which you prefer.'

Maddy's long dark hair fanned her face as she leaned towards her father. 'Go on, Dad, we're all ears.'

He chuckled. How little it took to make children happy. 'Well, you've been to the shore at Waterloo, and all seaside places are the same, with lots of sea and sand. There'd be plenty of fresh air, you could build sandcastles, paddle in the water with your dress tucked into your knickers, or even have a ride on a donkey.'

Maddy was beside herself with excitement. 'That sounds lovely, doesn't it, Tess? Just think, you and me riding on a donkey. We could have a race.'

'Ooh, no, I might fall off.' Tess shuddered at the thought. Then her hazel eyes widened at yet another possible fear. 'And if we were paddling, a big wave might come along and carry us out to sea.'

'You'd have none of those fears in the country, pet,' George said. 'It would be a nice gentle holiday, with plenty of fields and flowers, cows and sheep. And you'd see the high mountains rising up to touch the sky.'

Listening to her husband, Ann marvelled at his gentleness, and the ease with which he talked to their daughters. His childhood had been very different to her own, with easy-going parents who had filled their home with laughter and openly shown their love for their two children. George had never gone home without getting a kiss off his mother, even after he was married. And he treated his daughters as he and his older brother, Ken, had been treated, with love and tenderness. He was stroking Tess's arm now, and although his work-worn hands were the size of shovels, his touch was as light as a feather. And the girl was looking up at him with admiration and love. Ann felt a familiar pang of envy as she wished she could find a way of throwing off the mantle of aloofness which she knew was standing between her and the girls. But the strict discipline with which she'd been reared, from her cradle to the day she'd married, was hard to cast away.

'Ann!' George raised his voice. 'I've been talking to you, but you were miles away.'

'I'm sorry, love, what did you say?'

'I was telling the girls we could go on a picnic. Take some sandwiches and a bottle of lemonade, and find a nice spot where we could watch the sheep and cows grazing.'

'That sounds lovely to me.' Ann put as much enthusiasm into her voice as she could muster. 'With a bit of luck we might even find a quiet spot with a stream running nearby.'

Tess smiled across at her sister. 'That's what I'd like, Maddy, but only if that's what you'd like as well. If you'd rather go to the seaside, I wouldn't mind.'

'Why don't we have a vote on it?' George suggested. 'Hands up those who want to go to the seaside.' When not one hand was raised, he nodded with satisfaction. 'The country wins by an overwhelming majority.'

'Ooh, goody!' Tess sat up straight on his knee. 'When will we be going, Dad?'

'When and where has to be decided yet, pet. I start my holidays in two weeks' time, and I'm off for two weeks. So it will have to be within that time. I'll start making some enquiries tomorrow, see if anyone in work can recommend a decent place. If not, I'll slip down to our Ken's tomorrow night. He and Millicent have been to a place in Wales a few times, and they said it's a pretty village and the two children loved it.'

'I'll go in the morning, if you like,' Ann said. 'I know Ken will be at work, but Millicent should be in. She'll have the name and address to write to, and the sooner it's done the better. With all the factories being on holiday at the same time, chances are most of the bed-and-breakfast places will be booked up. So we don't have a lot of time to spare.'

'That's an idea, love, if you don't mind?'

'It's a good reason to get me out of the house. The weather's so lovely, it's a shame to stay in, and I'm sure Theresa would enjoy the trip out.'

'You lucky thing!' Maddy said. 'I'll be stuck in school all day while you're out gallivanting! Roll on Friday, when we break up.'

'You'll be singing a different tune halfway through the long holiday,' Ann said. 'After a couple of weeks you'll be bored stiff.'

'Not this time, though, Mam, 'cos I've got a holiday to look forward to.' Unlike most of her friends, Maddy loved school. She was popular with all the girls and teachers, and was always near top of the class in every subject except history, which she hated. 'If we take a big bag, we might be able to bring a baa-lamb home with us. You'd like that, wouldn't you, Tess?'

Her sister's eyes rolled. 'Ooh, I don't know about that. I've never seen a lamb, only in books, so I don't know if I'd like one.' Her brows drew together. 'What would we give it to eat, Maddy, and where would it sleep?'

'It would eat all the scraps we leave, and it would sleep in bed with you.'

George's chuckle was hearty when he saw the look on Tess's face. 'She's pulling your leg, pet. Lambs live in fields, not in houses.'

'And they certainly don't sleep in my beds,' Ann said, with mock severity. 'The very idea! I'd spend my life cleaning up after it!'

'That's settled then,' George declared. 'No big bag, no baa-lamb. And I think that's enough talking for tonight, it's time you girls were in bed.'

'Ah, ay, Dad!' Maddy was too excited to go to bed. 'Look how light it is out, we'd never be able to sleep.'

'You heard what your dad said, so do as you're told.' As the words were leaving her lips, Ann was wishing she could take them back. With one sentence, she had wiped the smiles from her daughters' faces. There was no need for it either, as George would have sent them to bed without it sounding like an order. She'd spoken out of habit, but it was a habit she had to get out of if she ever wanted to see the same love and trust in their eyes when they looked at her as there was when they looked at their father. 'You can take your books with you,' she said now, trying to make amends, 'and read for a while.'

'I've got a better idea,' George told them. 'Ask your mam for some paper and you can play teachers. Give each other simple sums to do, then mark them, just like a teacher does. How does that sound?'

Tess didn't look very sure. 'D'you mean Maddy will mark my sums, and no one else will see them?'

George ruffled her hair. 'It's only a game to pass the time, pet, you can tear the paper up afterwards if you like.'

A smile appeared. 'Shall we do that, Maddy? I promise I won't cane you if you get any wrong.'

Her sister nodded. 'I've got a good idea. The one who gets the most sums wrong has to tell a story. It can be a fairy story out of one of our books, or a made-up one. Okay?'

Tess looked at her father and wagged a finger, asking him to lean closer. She whispered in his ear for a while, then George burst out laughing. 'That's very good, sweetheart. If Maddy takes my advice, she'll make sure she wins so she can hear your story.'

'That sounds great!' Maddy's infectious giggle rang out. 'I'll race you to the top of the stairs.'

'Hang on a minute,' George said. 'What about our goodnight kiss?'

Maddy's hand covered her mouth. 'Ooh, er, sorry, Dad. It's just that I can't wait to hear this story.' She hugged her father and kissed him. 'Goodnight and God bless.' Then she moved on to her mother, with Tess following on. 'Goodnight and God bless, Mam.'

'Don't get into bed without washing your hands and faces,' Ann said. 'And fold your clothes neatly on the chair, not on the floor.'

Her words were lost in the mad scramble for the door. At least it appeared to be a mad scramble, but in reality it was Maddy waving her arms and laughing, as she pretended to try and beat Tess through the door. There was never any doubt that she would let her sister win.

'It's a wonder one of them didn't fall and break their neck,' Ann said, when they heard the girls running the water in the bathroom. Then she looked at her husband through narrowed eyes. 'What on earth did Theresa whisper in your ear?'

'Something that surprised me and made me wonder where we are going wrong with her. When she's left to do something off her own bat, she's got as much nous as any ten-year-old girl. I know that she's not strong physically, but there's not much wrong with her mind. If we could only find a way of encouraging her to open up, draw her out of her shell, I'm convinced she'd come on like a house on fire.'

'George, if you tell me what she whispered in your ear, I'd know why you're thinking what you are. So tell me.'

'If she gets her sums wrong, and has to tell a story, she's going to tell one about bringing a lamb home in a big bag. The lamb will be called Curly because all the ones she's seen in books have curly wool. It can sleep on the couch, have its own chair at the table, its own knife and fork, and will be taught to use the toilet so you don't have to clean up after it. And it can be taken for walks with a dog's lead around its neck.'

'That's very good considering she made it up in a matter of minutes.' Ann gazed down at her clasped hands. 'George, am I holding her back? Am I too strict with her? If I am, I don't mean to be. I just want to do what's best for her.'

George patted the space next to him on the couch. 'Come and sit here, love.' When she was settled, he put an arm across her shoulders. 'I know you love her and worry that she'll never live a normal life. And I know you only want what's best for her. But perhaps being a mother *and* a teacher to her isn't the right way forward. You're too close, and when she's not in school, which is more often than not, she never has any time away from you. She worries that she can't meet

8

your expectations of her, and as I've just said, she is never away from you, so the worry is constant. I may be wrong, love, but I think we have to consider Tess's interests and not our own. Let her develop at her own rate and see if that works.'

'But how can she develop if she hasn't any targets to aim for? Every child needs teaching, even if it's only the very basics. She'll never learn if she has nothing to learn from.'

'You've tried the conventional way of teaching, and it hasn't worked. Perhaps it would have done if she'd been attending school every day like Maddy, but there is no point in thinking what might have been. We need to go down every avenue until we find one that suits her. Because there is a way, love, it's just finding it. Perhaps if we try it as a family, or treat it as a game? Anything we can think of, Ann, but we have to find that way. Tess is capable of far more than she's showing at present, of that I'm sure. And I think we should consider allowing Maddy to help her more.'

Ann moved back to meet his eyes. 'George, you can't expect a twelve-year-old to teach a backward ten-year-old, it's out of the question.'

'Nothing is out of the question, love, not where our daughter's concerned. And she'd be more likely to do things for Maddy because she idolises her. But instead of reading stories to her in bed at night, if Maddy set her a couple of easy sums it would be a start. I'm not saying she'd make great strides forward because that would take a miracle. But a couple of sums, getting harder each night, now that would be progress. She wants so much to make us proud of her, and worries because she thinks she's a failure. I believe that is the cause of a lot of her health problems. And why she never has an appetite.' George was conscious his wife might be hurt by what he was saying. She could take his words to mean she had failed their daughter. But it was better to be open than let things carry on as they were. 'I'm not a clever man, love, and I might be talking through my hat. But let's work together on this. Let me have a word with Maddy, and give it a trial for two weeks. Even if she only learns to write a short sentence, and gets a few sums right, it'll be a start. She'll enjoy that, I know she will. And if we find she seems better in herself, and her appetite improves, we can take it from there.' He took her hand in his and gently squeezed it. 'We've got to do what's best for our daughter, love, no matter what it takes.'

'Yes, I know, and I'll go along with what you said. I'll give lessons a miss tomorrow and take Theresa to Millicent's with me. If the weather stays as nice as today, we could walk most of the way and do some window-shopping.' Ann tried to shake off the feeling that she'd in some way let her daughter down. She never shouted at the girl if she got sums or words wrong, but she was strict with her. Lessons were two hours in the morning and two in the afternoon, and after she'd marked the papers, her daughter would be made to sit at the table until she'd corrected any mistakes. And all the time she thought she was doing the best for Theresa, so she could live a normal life, like her sister.

Ann hung her head, seeing herself in her mind's eye standing over the young girl as she struggled with words and figures. Theresa always did as she was told, never answered back, but there was never a smile on her face until her sister or father walked through the door. 'In fact I'll stop the lessons altogether until after the summer holidays. So for seven weeks we'll do as you suggested and see how things work out.' She gazed into her husband's face and he could see the sadness in her eyes. 'I just want Theresa to be like other girls, and have a chance in life.'

'I know that, love, and you've done your best over the years, God knows. So have a break now, relax, and get to know your daughter without worrying about what is going to happen to her in the future. Because I feel it in my bones that everything is going to be all right, and in a few years' time we'll be wondering why we ever thought it wouldn't be.'

While her mother was clearing the breakfast dishes, Tess went to the door with her sister to wave her off to school. 'You'll come straight home, won't you, Maddy?'

'I promise I'll run all the way.' Maddy fell into step with Angie Williams, who lived three doors away and went to the same school. 'Don't forget to tell Auntie Milly I was asking about her and Uncle Ken.'

'I won't!' Tess waited until the two girls turned the corner before going back into the house. 'Shall I help you dry the dishes, Mam, or get my books out?'

'The dishes are almost done,' Ann called from the kitchen. 'And there's no lessons today, we're going to see Auntie Millicent. So go and have a wash and put your nice pink dress on.'

Tess was smiling as she climbed the stairs. The pink dress was her very favourite and she was only allowed to wear it when being taken anywhere. So her mother must think this was an important occasion. The girl didn't spend much time washing, it was just a cat's lick and a promise because she couldn't wait to get dolled up. And as she pulled the dress over her head, she spoke aloud: 'I wonder would me mam get annoyed if I asked her to put a ribbon in my hair?'

Ann was on the landing and heard the words. She quickly turned and went quietly back down the stairs, avoiding the boards that would creak and give her away. In the living room she stood by the table and asked herself was she such an ogre her own daughter was afraid to ask for such a small thing as a ribbon in her hair? Things had come to a pretty pass if that was the case.

Tess flung the door open and rushed in. 'Mam, will you fasten the button at the back, please, I can't reach.' As she turned, her eyes lit on the pink ribbon spread out on the sideboard. 'Ooh, is that for me, Mam?'

'It is, love! You and I are going out of here like a couple of toffs today. When I've combed your hair and put the bow in, I'm going upstairs to put my best dress on. That should give the neighbours something to talk about, shouldn't it?'

Tess giggled, then studied her mother's face. 'Mam, why do you wear your hair like that? You've got lovely hair, much nicer than mine 'cos it's nice and curly. But no one can see the curls the way you've got it.'

'I've always worn it like this, Theresa, because it's easy to manage. And it looks more tidy than hanging about my face and getting in my eyes.'

With no lessons today, and wearing her pink dress, plus the ribbon that would soon be tying her hair back, Tess was feeling on top of the world. And brave enough to talk to her mother as she never had before. 'You'd look much prettier if you wore your hair loose, Mam, honest! And I bet me dad would like it.'

'No, I'd look silly.' Ann the schoolteacher was horrified at the very thought of anything so drastic, but Ann the wife and mother, without knowing, had allowed the seed to be sown. 'Your father would think I'd lost the run of my senses.'

'I bet he wouldn't.' Tess was holding her ground. 'Why don't you let it down tonight and see what he says? I bet he'd love you more than ever, and so would me and Maddy.'

'Nonsense, it's out of the question.' But Ann was not as sure as she sounded. And her daughter looked so crestfallen, she said something she'd really had no intention of saying. 'I'll tell you what, Theresa, so you'll know I'm right, I'll take my hair down this afternoon when we come back from Aunt Millicent's. And you'll see for yourself how stupid I look and never mention it again.'

But as she sat at the table, waiting, Tess was convinced her mother wouldn't look stupid. She'd look as pretty as any of the other women in their street.

'Well, this is a surprise!' Milly Richardson smiled with pleasure as she held the door wide. 'What's brought you down to this neck of the woods?'

Ann ushered Tess ahead of her. 'I've come to ask a favour. We've been talking about having a few days away while George is on holiday, and he said you'd been to Wales a couple of times and might be able to recommend somewhere.'

Milly pulled two chairs from the table and waved a hand. 'Sit yerselves down.' She chucked Tess under the chin before giving her a kiss. 'Ye're looking very pretty today, Tess, a proper little lady.'

The girl was delighted with the compliment. 'Thank you, Auntie Milly, this is my very favourite dress.' Then she remembered what her sister had said. 'Maddy told me to say she was asking about you and Uncle Ken.'

'Tell her we're fine, love, all fit and healthy. Yer Uncle Ken and Billy are at work, and Joyce is at school. They'll be sorry they missed yer.' Milly turned to Ann. 'So, ye're off on a few days' holiday, are yer? Well, I can recommend the place we stayed at in Wales, we've always enjoyed ourselves there. The woman's name is Mrs Owen, first name Gwen, and she does bed and breakfast, or, if yer want, she'll do yer an evening meal as well. Her house is in a little village called Hope, and she's spotlessly clean and a marvellous cook. There's a big back garden full of fruit trees and flowers, and a swing which you'd like, Tess.'

'Does she charge much?' Ann asked. 'We're not exactly flushed with money.'

Milly gazed at her sister-in-law before answering. Although she liked Ann, she couldn't help thinking that if she wasn't such a snob they wouldn't be short of money. A two-up two-down house wasn't good enough for her when she married George, oh no, it had to be a six-roomed in Orrell Park. And she never went to TJ's or the market to buy the girls' school clothes; only Henderson's in Church Street, one of the poshest shops in Liverpool, was good enough for her. George earned the same money as Ken, but with so much extra being spent on rent and clothes, they had nothing over for such luxuries as enjoyment.

Mentally shaking her head, Milly decided she wouldn't change places with Ann for a big clock. It was all well and good living in Orrell Park and shopping at Henderson's if you had the money, but not when you were struggling every week. Still, she thought, we all have different ideas and it wouldn't do for everyone to think alike. 'For bed, breakfast and evening meal, she charges four shillings a day for adults and two bob for children. But yer get yer money's worth because the table's always piled high with good food.'

Ann did a quick calculation. George only went for a pint once a week, and he only smoked five Woodbines a day, but if he did without for the next two weeks, as he'd said he would, they could probably scrape five pounds together with the bit they had saved and his two weeks' holiday pay. Mind you, the rent had to be paid for those two weeks, but that was the only debt they had. 'How do you get there, Millicent? On the train?'

Milly nodded. 'Don't ask me all the travelling details 'cos I can't tell yer. I do know the first time we went, some soft nit told us to get the train from Liverpool and change to another train at some other station. Ken is the best one to tell yer how to get there, I'm hopeless for remembering names. The second time we went was much easier, though. We only had to get the one train, and outside the station there were a line of pony-and-traps waiting to carry people where they wanted to go. It was a fair distance, but the bloke only charged about two bob and we didn't half enjoy the ride through the country.'

Tess was listening wide-eyed. 'I've seen a pony-and-trap in my story book, and the man had a whip to gee the horse up. Did your man have a whip, Auntie Milly?'

'He did, sweetheart, but he didn't need to use it. All he did was click his tongue and the horse knew what he meant.'

'It's such short notice,' Ann said. 'D'you think she'll be all booked up?'

'I couldn't tell yer that, Ann, I've no idea. Drop her a line today and yer'll have an answer in a few days. I've got the address in the drawer somewhere.' Milly left her chair to root in the sideboard drawer. 'I keep saying I'll clear these drawers out, but I never get down to it.' Papers, combs, pencils, curlers and reels of cotton were taken out and plonked on top. 'The trouble is, I did trying clearing out one day, but everything I picked up I decided might come in useful sometime so every single thing was put back. Ken goes mad, calls me a hoarder.' Then she held a piece of crumpled paper in the air. 'Success, at last.'

'Would you write the name and address out for me, please?' Ann asked, smiling at her daughter, who was getting fidgety with excitement. 'I'll write as soon as we get home.'

'I can let yer have some notepaper and an envelope if yer like, then yer can write the letter here and post it on yer way home. Yer'll gain a day by doing that.'

Tess was all for it. 'Yes, go on, Mam, write to the lady now.'

'Are you sure you don't mind, Millicent?' Ann asked. 'I don't want to impose on you.'

'Oh, sod off, Ann, a piece of paper and an envelope is hardly imposing, for God's sake! Yer can buy a stamp at the corner shop, pop the letter in the pillar-box outside and it'll be on its way by dinner time.'

13

Ann opened her handbag and brought out a fountain pen that had been the last present she'd received from her parents before they died. She would never let anyone else use it and carried it with her at all times. Then she sat with the paper in front of her and looked thoughtful. 'I think George said they break up on Saturday the twenty-fourth, so it would be the twenty-sixth on the Monday.'

'That's right,' Milly said, 'Ken breaks up the same time. We're having a week in Blackpool for a change.'

Ann began to write in her neat, precise handwriting, every word correctly spelt and every letter perfectly formed. After reading it through, she folded it neatly and slipped it in the envelope. 'I've asked her to let us know as soon as possible, I hope she won't think that's cheeky of me?'

'No, Gwen won't think that, she's a smashing woman. Never got a smile off her face.'

'I'll make tracks, then, Millicent, and get the letter off by the dinner-time post, like you said. And thanks very much for being so helpful. George will get a pleasant surprise when he knows the wheels are already in motion. If things work out and Mrs Owen can put us up, he'll come and see Ken to get the travel arrangements off him.' Ann pushed her chair under the table, and after pressing the handle of her bag into the crook of her arm, she held out the letter to her daughter. 'You can carry that for luck, Theresa.'

Milly followed them through to the front door. 'Ye're welcome any time, Ann, yer know that. And Tess here, I'd offer to buy her off yer but I know yer'd tell me to get lost.'

Ann waved and set off down the street with her daughter skipping beside her, the precious letter clutched tightly in her hand. And when they had bought a threeha'penny stamp from the corner shop, Tess was allowed to stick it on the envelope.

'Can I put it in the pillar-box, Mam?'

'Of course you can, love.'

The girl put the envelope to her lips. 'I'm kissing it twice for good luck.' Then she slipped it into the pillar-box and listened for the flop as it fell to the bottom before reaching for her mother's hand. It had been a lovely day so far, and she wished every day could be the same. And there was still something to look forward to. 'Mam, you haven't forgot your promise about letting your hair down, have you? And will you let me brush it for you, please?'

'As long as you don't start arguing if I don't think it suits me and I want to put it back before Madelaine and your father come home.'

But Tess had already made up her mind about her mother's hair. She'd seen her so often in her dreams with her hair falling loose about

14

her face, and she'd looked pretty. Not a bit like a teacher. So the girl didn't hesitate to promise. 'I'll be as good as gold, Mam, honest! But I know I'm going to like it, so there!'

Chapter Two

When they got home, Ann made straight for the kitchen. 'I'll make us a pot of tea and some sandwiches. Then I'll have to get the stew on for dinner.'

'Shall I take my best dress off, Mam, in case it gets dirty?' Tess squinted down and was pleased to see there wasn't a mark on the pink cotton. 'I'll put my blue one on, shall I?'

'That's a good idea,' Ann called back. 'If the weather's nice tomorrow we might go to the park for an hour, and you'll have to look respectable.'

'Will I be having lessons tomorrow?'

'We'll talk about that while we're having our sandwiches. Run up and get changed, the kettle's nearly on the boil.'

Tess was down and sitting at the table when Ann came through carrying a tray with cups and saucers on, and a plate of sandwiches. 'That was quick, Theresa, I hope you put your dress away neatly?'

The girl nodded. 'I've hung it up in the wardrobe.' She chewed on a cheese butty while swinging her legs under the chair. 'It's been a nice day, hasn't it, Mam? I like Auntie Milly, she's very kind. And it was good of her to give you the paper and envelope, wasn't it? I mean, if it wasn't for her, the letter wouldn't be on its way. For all we know, it might even be in Wales by now.'

'Not yet, love. Perhaps tomorrow, with a bit of luck.' Ann was leaning her elbows on the table and she smiled across at her daughter. 'You asked were you having lessons tomorrow. Well, your father and I were talking about that very thing last night. We thought you should have a holiday from lessons, like Madelaine does. Not that you shouldn't be learning at all during that time, because I think you understand that with missing school so much you are well behind other children of your age. But your father and I thought perhaps you and your sister could spend some time each day playing school. Make it into a game, but a game in which you learn something. You and Madelaine could take turns in being the teacher and the pupil. Is that something you would like, Theresa?'

Tess laid the sandwich down, her face filled with surprise and pleasure. 'Oh, yes, Mam, I'd love that. Maddy can be the teacher for the first day, so I can see how she does it.' A smile came to the pale face. 'Will we have a cane to smack each other if we get our sums wrong?'

'The last thing your sister would do is raise her voice to you, never mind smacking you. She loves you very much, and would be very proud if she could help you.'

'I love her too, Mam! She's the bestest sister in the whole world. And I'll work very hard so I get a tick by everything.'

'Your father and I don't want you to worry, Theresa, just do your best, that's all we ask. If you find anything difficult, then tell Madelaine and she'll go over it with you until you've got it clear in your mind.' Ann reached across to pat her daughter's hand. 'Why don't you surprise your dad and write him a letter telling him how much you love him?'

'I could write one to you as well, Mam, 'cos I love you too! As long as you wouldn't mind if I made any mistakes. I mean, if I got Maddy to write them for me then that would be cheating, wouldn't it?'

'I would rather have a letter you wrote yourself, even if it was full of mistakes, than one Madelaine wrote for you.' Ann was feeling very emotional. She had never been a loving mother, never shown the two girls any affection because she didn't know how to. But right now she felt like rounding the table and taking her younger daughter in her arms, to cuddle her in a bid to make up for some of the lost time. She reined in her feelings, though, because it would mean mother and daughter ending up in tears. 'I'll really look forward to receiving my first letter from you, Theresa. And I want six big kisses on the bottom.'

'I'll put ten on, 'cos that's how old I am.' Her face was a picture of childlike innocence and it touched Ann's heart. 'Will you write back to me, Mam?'

'Of course I will, by return post. I'll put it through the letter-box myself to save a stamp. We have to watch our pennies now, for when we go on holiday.'

Tess's hazel eyes were like saucers. 'Ooh, yeah! I'll give you my penny pocket money to mind for me, so I can't spend it on sweets. That means I'll have threepence by the time we go to Wales.' Her head wagged from side to side. 'We've got a lot to look forward to, haven't we, Mam? We're very lucky.'

'Yes, we are, love, very lucky. And now I'll have to see to the dinner, otherwise your father won't be feeling very lucky if he comes home and his meal isn't ready.'

'You think I've forgotten, don't you, Mam?'

'Forgotten what, Theresa?'

'The promise you made to take your hair down. See, I haven't forgotten.'

18

Ann glanced at the clock. She should really be getting the stew on now, and peeling the potatoes and veg. But she was feeling closer to her daughter right now than she ever had. On a normal day, she would be in the kitchen while Theresa sat at the table poring over an exercise book with a worried frown on her face. It was time to start making up for those frowns, and she could spare fifteen minutes even though the thought of taking her hair down didn't appeal one bit. 'Come on, then, seeing as you are so determined. I'll let you take the hair clips out, save me stretching my arms.'

In her haste, the young girl pushed her chair back with such force it almost toppled over. She looked afraid for a second, as though expecting a reprimand. When none came she moved to stand behind her mother, her eyes seeking clips in the plaited coil. 'I won't hurt you, taking them out, will I?'

'Not if you don't pull a handful of hair with them. Just take them out slowly, one at a time. And don't forget I warned you that you wouldn't like my hair loose. If that is the case, it goes right back into a bun.'

Tess didn't answer. With her tongue sticking out of the side of her mouth, deep concentration on her face, she drew one of the clips. It came out smoothly and she was delighted. Very soon all the clips were out and her mother's hair was hanging over her shoulders. 'Ooh, you haven't half got a lot of hair, Mam! You've got ten times more than me. If I had pulled a handful out, you wouldn't have missed it and I could have stuck it on my head. It's nearly the same colour as mine.'

'Except you don't have any grey in yours, love.' Ann could feel the hair on her shoulders and it felt strange. She couldn't wear it like this all the time, it would get on her nerves. 'Well,' she turned to face her daughter, 'are you satisfied?'

Tess tilted her head. 'Can I comb it, Mam, please?'

'Just for a couple of minutes, Theresa, because I'll have to make a start preparing dinner. You'll find a comb in the left-hand drawer.'

Tess was delighted as she gently combed the long hair, which was falling into soft waves. Her mother had never let her do anything like this before and she felt really grown-up. She could see grey hairs now, but there weren't that many. 'How is it that you and Maddy have wavy hair, Mam, and I haven't?'

Ann had her eyes closed, finding the gentle combing very soothing. 'My mother had wavy hair, so I suppose I get it from her. But I don't know why it hasn't been passed on to you. Perhaps your hair isn't in very good condition because you haven't been in the best of health. When you get stronger, your hair might grow stronger too.'

'I hope so.' The girl was speaking the thoughts that were running through her head. 'I'd be made up if I had long hair like Maddy's, and

I could put it in rags every night to make it curly. Then I might get to be as pretty as her.'

Ann turned and caught her daughter's hand. 'Why do you say that? You are every bit as pretty as Madelaine. You have different colouring, but that doesn't stop you being as pretty. What about Nita and Letty next door? They have different-coloured hair and eyes, but they are just as pretty as each other.'

Tess gave that some consideration. 'Yes, they are, I never thought of that. But they haven't got thin faces like me. And they're not skinny, either.'

'You won't always be skinny, love, I promise. One of these days you will blossom, like a flower does, and you'll be beautiful. But you do need to put on some weight. To do that you have to eat more. And you know what is the best thing to give you an appetite? Fresh air, and plenty of it. So tomorrow we're going to the park for an hour or so, and you can play on the swings while you breathe in the summer air.'

Tess cocked her head to one side and pursed her lips. 'I think you're right, Mam, 'cos I feel hungry today, and I never have before. It must have been that walk to Auntie Milly's.' Nodding to show her mind agreed with her words, she said, 'I must have breathed in gallons of fresh air today.'

Ann grinned. 'I don't know whether you can measure air in gallons, love, because you can't get hold of it to weigh. It's very elusive, is fresh air.'

'What does that word mean, Mam? I've never heard it before.'

'It means something hard to find or get hold of.'

'Like money? That's hard to find, isn't it?'

Ann got to her feet and put a finger under her daughter's chin so their eyes met. 'I'm beginning to think you know a lot more than you let on, Theresa. That was a very good answer you gave, one I wouldn't have thought of. It wouldn't surprise me in the least if one of these days you are teaching me.'

'I'll never be that clever, Mam.' Tess was feeling very light-hearted. It had been a lovely day, one of the best she could remember. 'Perhaps as clever as Nita next door.'

The clock on the mantelpiece chimed the half-hour, and Ann rolled her eyes. 'I'm going to have to leave my hair looking a mess, I'm afraid. When I've got the stew on we'll see what we're going to do with it.'

'I can peel the potatoes for you,' Tess said. 'I promise I won't cut the peel an inch thick and I won't cut myself with the knife. I'll be very careful.'

Ann was doubtful, but a voice in her head asked her how she could expect the girl to come on when she kept her wrapped in cotton wool.

'All right, but be very careful. Your father would blame me if you cut yourself.'

Tess made a cross on her chest. 'Scout's honour, Mam.'

So mother and daughter stood together in the kitchen, working in an atmosphere that was light, and enjoying being in each other's company. Ann kept her eyes on Tess because the potato peeler was very sharp. And she smiled to herself when her daughter's tongue came out of the side of her mouth and her brow creased in concentration. No potatoes had ever received such attention, or had their peel removed with such care.

'There you are, Mam!' Tess put down the knife and peered into the pan. 'Have I done enough, or d'you want me to peel any more?'

'That's fine, love, there's enough there to feed an army. You've done very well, and I'm really pleased with you. Your father's in for a few surprises when he gets home. We've written away about the holiday, and you've helped me make the dinner! I bet he'll think we're pulling his leg when we tell him.'

'And Maddy! She'll get the shock of her life.'

'She'll get a pleasant surprise, love, not a shock. You see, when you get a shock, it's usually something unpleasant.'

'I'm learning a lot today, aren't I, Mam?'

'You're not the only one, Theresa, because I'm learning a lot too! And it's all about you! I'm finding out that you are far more clever than you let us think. And I wouldn't be in the least surprised if you aren't back at school in the near future. And able to keep up with the other girls. Please God, eh, love?'

Ann was taken aback when Tess threw her arms around her waist. Her own arms held away from her, she looked down on her daughter's head, surprised by the unusual and impulsive show of affection. Her husband was greeted like this every night when he came in from work, but never before had it happened to her. But then, perhaps she hadn't earned the child's trust and affection.

She put her arms around her daughter, tentatively at first, then she hugged her tight. 'We make a good team, you and me, Theresa. We'll have to have more days like this, eh?'

A smiling face looked up at her. 'I don't think we could write off to Wales every day, Mam, to book a holiday. You see, money is elusive. Hard to get your hands on.'

It wasn't often that Ann laughed aloud, but she did now as she ruffled her daughter's hair. 'I've got a feeling I'm going to have a hard job keeping up with you, young lady. You seem to be picking things up very fast.'

'I'm happy today, Mam, that's why.'

'Well, you can tell your father and Madelaine all about it and they'll be happy as well. And then you can eat all your dinner, like a good girl.' Ann took her daughter's arms from around her waist. 'In the meanwhile, what about my hair? Just take a good look at me, love, and be truthful. Don't I look like the witch in your story book?'

Tess rested her chin on a hand and studied the hair in question. 'You don't look like a witch, Mam, but it is too long to wear loose. None of the women in the street have hair this long. You could get it cut, though, and then you'd look nice.'

'Get my hair cut! Whatever next! No, love, that I will never do.' Ann was horrified at the very idea. 'So now you can plait it into a bun again.' She lifted the lid on the pan of stew, and when she saw it bubbling, she lowered the gas and left it to simmer. 'Come on, I've got half an hour to spare before I need to put the carrots and potatoes on. Let's see if you can learn to plait in that time.'

'Will you show me, Mam?'

'Of course I'll show you. And there's method in my madness, love, because when you're good at it you can have the job every morning.'

'Only until I'm well enough to go back to school, Mam.'

'Yes, sweetheart, only until you're well enough to go back to school.'

There was much talk and laughter around the dinner table that night. The two girls were making the most noise, their father the least. George was quite content to sit and watch his family being more animated than he'd ever seen them. Under normal circumstances his wife would have put a stop to the chatter, by telling them they couldn't talk and eat at the same time. But tonight she was as excited as they were. And according to what Tess had said, it wasn't only the holiday that had brought about the change. His younger daughter had been in high spirits, the words tumbling from her mouth, when she told of the trip to her Auntie Milly's, the peeling of potatoes and the plaiting of her mother's hair. He wouldn't have thought these things possible even yesterday. There had been a definite change in the relationship between mother and daughter, a closeness that had been missing before. And it could be seen in Tess's face as she chattered fifteen to the dozen, in between eating her dinner.

'You're very quiet, George,' Ann said. 'Or is it us being too noisy and not letting you get a word in edgeways?'

'Ann, it's lovely to see so much happiness around the table and I'm more than content to sit and take it all in.'

'Maddy, do you know what elusive is?' Tess asked, her eyes bright and her usually pale cheeks showing some colour. 'D'you know what it means?'

Her sister pulled a face. 'I've heard it, but I couldn't explain what it means. Why?'

'I know what it means,' Tess grinned, 'and I know three things what are elusive.'

Ann shook her head. 'No, love, it's "I know three things *that* are elusive."'

Tess lowered her head so they couldn't see the devilment in her eyes. 'Oh, you know three things as well, do you, Mam?'

George chuckled. He couldn't get over the change in his daughter. He hoped it wasn't a flash in the pan, but a real sign that Tess was at last going forward. 'If I didn't know better, I'd think that you and your mam had been drinking on the sly. Auntie Milly didn't give you a bottle of milk stout, did she?'

'Don't be silly, Dad! It was two bottles, wasn't it, Mam?'

Maddy feigned disgust. 'I don't know, here's me doing my ten times table, and you're out having the time of your life. I think I'll give school a miss tomorrow and go to the park with you.'

'You've only got two more days to go, Madelaine, then you're off for seven weeks. There'll be plenty of time for visits to the park.' Out of the corner of her eye, Ann saw Tess lay down her knife and fork and push the plate away. She'd eaten three quarters of her dinner, which was unheard of. 'You've done well, Theresa, and I'm pleased with you. What say you, George?'

'I'm beginning to think I'm in the wrong house! My younger daughter doesn't drink milk stout, and she doesn't know three things that are elusive! Ann, are you sure you brought the right girl home with you?'

Ann went along with him. 'Well, she had Theresa's dress on. But there could be another girl with a dress that looks the same. It's possible my mind was distracted and I took hold of the wrong hand outside the butcher's.'

'And what was I doing while you did that, Mam?' Tess asked, looking very serious. 'I might be slow, but I'm not so slow I'd let a strange girl walk off with my mother.' A pink tongue appeared for a second. 'So there!'

Maddy didn't care how the change had come about, all she knew was that her sister had colour in her cheeks, her nose wasn't running and she was happy. That was enough for Maddy. 'Ay, when we're playing schools, I'm going to be the pupil and you can be the teacher. Then you can teach me the three elusive things you have in your head.'

'I'd like to know them now,' George said. 'If you won't tell me, Tess, I'll have to get them off your mother.'

'You'd have a job, love, 'cos I don't know them.' Ann gave him a gentle kick under the table to warn him not to ask. 'Well, I know one, but the other two are in Theresa's head.'

'I'll tell you, Dad, but you'll kick yourself, 'cos they're easy. The first one is fresh air, and we all know you can't get hold of that. And when your purse is empty and you're skint, money is very elusive then. The last one you gave me yourself when you said about the happiness around the table. You can feel it and you know it's there, but you can't touch it.'

George rubbed his forehead, his emotions running high. This was the girl who the headmistress of the local school had said was too backward to be in the juniors, she would have to go with the infants. In his mind, it was the headmistress who was backward for not seeing the potential in his daughter and helping her to develop it. Yes, she was slow with writing and arithmetic, and she couldn't put down how she felt. But her mind was quick and active, she'd just proved that. Her dreams and hopes were all there, she just wasn't capable of putting them on paper. 'Sweetheart, shall I tell you something? One day you'll be so clever you'll knock spots off everyone.'

'I keep telling her that!' Maddy had her arm across her sister's shoulders. 'She's a marvellous story-teller, Dad, honest! She can make up better stories than I can.'

'Then you must help her write those stories down, Madelaine,' Ann said. 'Who knows, we might have an author in the family.'

Tess giggled. 'If I did make any money, Mam, d'you know the first thing I'd buy with it?'

'No, love, I don't. And don't ask me to guess because you know I'm hopeless at guessing games.'

'I'd buy a cot for the lamb we're going to pinch when we go to Wales.'

While George and Maddy doubled up with laughter, Ann was soft enough to walk into a trap. 'Not the lamb we're going to pinch, Theresa, the lamb we're going to *steal*.'

'That's naughty, that is, Mam.' The girl's face was as innocent as a babe's. 'You've always told us it's a sin to steal.'

Ann spread out her hands. 'I give up! Outsmarted by my own daughter.'

'I wasn't being cheeky, Mam, I only wanted to make you laugh.' Tess picked up her sister's plate and put it on top of her own. 'I'll help clear the table and me and Maddy will do the washing-up.'

'No, I'll do it, love. You go upstairs with Madelaine and practise how to play school. There's a notebook in the drawer.'

There was a mad scramble for the door. 'I bags being teacher first,' Tess called, elbowing her sister out of the way. 'And our mam said as we haven't got a cane, I can use the poker. So you'd better get your sums right.'

Ann's mouth gaped. 'Did you hear that, George? I never said any such thing!'

They could hear shrieks of laughter coming from upstairs and exchanged smiles. 'That is the best tonic she can have,' George said. Then, twirling the ends of his moustache, he asked, 'Did you really let her take your hair down?'

Ann nodded. 'And a right mess I looked. I asked Theresa if I reminded her of the witch in her book, and, God love her, she said I didn't look like a witch but I could do with a haircut.'

'You should have left it down, I would have liked to have seen it.'

'Oh, don't you start, love, it's bad enough my daughter being at me. I like my hair the way it is, neat and tidy.'

'And I like it when you take it down at night to go to bed. So I'm on Tess's side on the subject of your hair.'

Ann tutted. 'George, the bun and the hair clips stay. I refuse to wear it long or to have it cut.' Then she softened. 'For the time being, anyway.'

'Good morning, Ann!' Next-door neighbour Maisie Wilkins was on her knees scrubbing the front step when Ann closed the door behind her and Tess. 'Taking advantage of the nice weather, are yer?'

'Yes, we're going to the park for an hour. It's too nice to stay indoors.'

'Ye're not kidding, it's sweltering! I should have done this earlier before it got so warm, the sweat's pouring off me.' Maisie pushed back the mobcap which had slipped down to her eyebrows. 'The flaming elastic has gone on this and I keep forgetting to see to it.' She grinned at Tess. 'And how are you today, love?'

'I'm fine, Mrs Wilkins. Coming on like a house on fire.'

Maisie sat back on her heels and threw the scrubbing brush into the bucket of water. 'I'm glad to hear it. I just wish I could say the same about my two. Holy terrors they are, always in trouble. The only thing that stops me from strangling them is the thought that I've put up with them at their worst, I may as well hang on until they both leave school and start work.'

'Nita is thirteen next month, isn't she?' Ann asked. 'The same as Madelaine?'

'Yeah, they'll both be leaving school next summer.' Maisie, fair-haired and blue-eyed, was a friendly woman, and a good neighbour. Many was the time Ann was glad of her help when Tess wasn't well enough for her to leave and her neighbour was only too willing to get her shopping in. 'I've been scrubbing away here, consoling myself with the thought that in one year and two days Nita will be leaving school and getting herself a job. As I've said to my Will, I won't know meself with a few extra bob a week coming in.' When Maisie laughed, the whole street knew about it. 'I might even get meself a maid, instead of getting housemaid's knees.'

'I don't know why you have to scrub the step every morning,' Ann said. 'I don't, and neither do any of the other neighbours. Once a week is plenty.'

'I have thought of that, Ann, but if I don't do it, what the hell am I going to moan about to my feller? He thinks I work me fingers to the bone, scrubbing the step, washing the windowsills down, dolly tub of washing every day and slaving over a hot stove.' Again her laugh echoed down the street. 'He's very sympathetic, is my Will. He insists I put me feet up for an hour on the couch every night while he brings me a cup of tea. Now, I'd have to want me bumps feeling to tell him I go to a matinée at the Carlton twice a week, wouldn't I?'

'Will's not only sympathetic, he must be generous as well,' Ann said. 'I couldn't afford to go to a matinée at the Carlton twice a week.'

'It's only tuppence, I don't go in the best specks. And Will has his pleasures, so why shouldn't I? He wouldn't miss his Friday and Saturday pint for all the tea in China. And I'm damned sure he doesn't only have the one pint either. Yer know what men are like if they're with mates, they have to buy a round each. And yer can't tell me that that doesn't cost more than my fourpence a week for the flicks.'

Ann grinned and reached for her daughter's hand. 'You keep telling yourself that, Maisie, and you won't feel guilty.'

Tess had a view on this, and as her mother began walking away she said, 'And you don't tell Mr Wilkins that you *don't* go to the pictures, so you haven't told any fibs.'

'My sentiments exactly, love,' Maisie called. 'Enjoy yerself at the park and make sure yer have a few turns on the swings, because yer won't get near them next week with all the kids being on holiday.'

Tess turned and waved. 'I'll have three turns on the swings, and three on the seesaw.'

With their hands joined and swinging between them, mother and daughter reached the end of the road. 'Let's go to Aintree Park, shall we?' Ann asked. 'And we can look in the shop windows along Walton Vale.'

The lovely weather had brought people out and the Vale was bustling with activity. It was a good shopping area at any time, but with the good weather the shops seemed to be doing a roaring trade. But there were many who had come out to feel the sunshine on their faces as they window-shopped. It wasn't a pastime that Ann enjoyed, believing

26

if you didn't have the money to buy there was no point in looking. But she allowed her daughter to pull her to a halt at the various toy shops, and windows where women's clothes or shoes were on display.

'Look at the heels on those shoes, Mam.' Tess had her nose pressed against the window and was pointing to a pair of black patent-leather court shoes with very high heels. 'When I'm grown up, I'm going to wear shoes like that.' She sighed. 'Aren't they lovely?'

'Yes, they are,' Ann agreed, while thinking privately she wouldn't be seen dead in them. 'But I wouldn't wear them because I'd be afraid of falling over.'

'No you wouldn't, Mam! Look at Elsie Parson in our road, she wears heels that high.'

'Elsie doesn't walk, love, she totters. Whenever I see her I hold my breath, thinking she's going to fall flat on her face any minute.' Ann felt herself being pulled to the next window where ladies' dresses and blouses were on display, and she made all the suitable noises when Tess went into raptures over a pink blouse. 'I think we'd better put a move on, love, otherwise it'll be time to go home before we get to the park.'

They carried on walking until they came to the confectioner's shop, which was noted for its home-made bread and pies. The mouth-watering smells had Tess sniffing up and rubbing her tummy. 'Yum, yum, that smell doesn't half make you feel hungry.'

Ann took her arm and pulled her on. 'We'll have some sandwiches when we get home. That's if we ever get home, the rate we're going.'

'It's not far to the park, now, Mam, and I'll be glad to get there 'cos my legs are beginning to feel tired.'

'That's because it's so hot.' Ann put a hand to her daughter's forehead and was concerned when it felt clammy. 'There's nowhere to sit until we get there, so no more window-shopping, love, let's go straight there and find a tree we can sit under until you cool down and feel better.'

There weren't many people in the park, just a few mothers pushing their toddlers on the baby swings. 'There's an empty bench under a tree, let's sit there until we cool down.' Ann, always concerned about her daughter's health, led her to the iron bench. 'There, that's better, isn't it?'

Tess nodded. 'It is cooler, but I shouldn't have put my singlet on, Mam, 'cos that's making me sweat.'

'That's my fault, I told you to put it on. But you know our house never gets the sun, it's always dark and you can't tell what it's like outside.'

They sat in silence watching the young children in the baby swings being pushed by their mothers. Their chuckles carried on the air and brought a smile to Tess's face. 'Babies are lovely, aren't they, Mam? Was I lovely when I was a baby?'

'You were lovely then, and you're lovely now. Your father and I have always been very proud of you. I can remember when you were a baby, your dad used to wheel you to the park, with Madelaine toddling beside him holding on to his jacket. And when she was tired, he used to sit her up in the front of the pram, making sure she was well away from your feet and fussing over you both like a mother hen.'

Tess began to swing her legs under the bench, her face alive with pleasure. 'Me and Maddy are lucky, aren't we, having such a lovely dad?'

Ann knew her husband came first in the girls' affections; she'd always known that. But it was only now she realised why. George spent his time giving them the attention they needed, showing how much he loved them, and was openly affectionate. While she'd been busy making sure they didn't get their clothes dirty, that they never sat at the table without washing their hands first, that they knew the alphabet off by heart and spoke correctly. No slang words were allowed in her presence. So she had clean, well-mannered daughters who always treated her with respect. But recently she'd been craving more than that. She wanted to share her husband's place in their hearts.

'I'm the lucky one, with a husband and two daughters I love very dearly.'

Tess stopped swinging her legs, and tilting her head she gazed at her mother. The one person who had not been mentioned in the talk of love. And her caring nature made her ask herself how she would like it if she'd been the one left out. 'We all love you, Mam, you know that, don't you?'

'Of course I do!' Ann gave her a hug. 'Now how about a swing? Do you feel up to it?'

'Just the one, then can we go home?' Tess rubbed her tummy. 'I'm all right, but if I have too many swings it might make me sick.'

Because her daughter didn't often complain about feeling sick, Ann didn't linger after Tess had been on the swing for a few minutes. Holding on to each other's hand, and keeping to a leisurely pace, they began the walk home. It was when they reached the confectioner's that Ann came to a halt. 'I'll get you a pie for your dinner, love, you'd like that, wouldn't you?'

'Mam, I'll have what everyone else is having.'

But Ann had made up her mind. If it was a pie the girl fancied, it would do her more good than eating something she had no appetite for. 'You stand here, I won't be a minute.'

There was steam coming from the bag when Ann stepped down on to the pavement. 'This is lovely and hot, so you can have it instead of sandwiches.' She glanced at her daughter's pale face. 'If you find yourself running out of puff, let me know and we'll stop until you get your breath back.'

Tess walked with her head down, determined to get home without stopping. She had pains in her chest and her legs felt wobbly, but she kept on. She hated being like this but couldn't help it. She'd do anything to be able to play rounders with the other girls in the road without losing her breath after two runs. But they wouldn't let her play with them now because no one would have her on their team. So she had to stand and watch.

Ann slid the key into the lock. 'You go and change your dress while I put the kettle on and make you a round of bread and butter to eat with the pie.'

Tess didn't think she was hungry, but when the plate was put in front of her and the smell wafted up her nose, she smiled with pleasure. 'Mam, can I eat it in my hand? If I cut it, all the juice will run on to the plate and be wasted.'

'It isn't good manners to eat with your fingers, Theresa, but I'll let you off this once because I want you to get every bit of goodness out of it.'

There was a look of bliss on the girl's face when she bit into the pie. And any juice that threatened to escape and run down her chin was quickly licked by a darting tongue. She ate with gusto, and Ann told herself it had been worth the few coppers to see her daughter enjoying it so much. George had been right all along, saying a little of what she fancied would do her more good than something she had no appetite for.

'Mmm, that was good!' Tess had her head turned towards the window and her brows drew together. 'Mam, look! Old Mrs Critchley's standing at her door and she's got a funny look on her face.'

Ann went towards the window and pulled back the net curtain. 'She's looking up and down the road as though she's expecting someone, but I've never known her to do that before. I think I'd better nip across and make sure everything's all right.'

Freda and Arthur Critchley had lived in Hanford Avenue for as long as any could remember. They were a nice couple, always pleasant, never bothered anyone and as quiet as mice. They were both in their mid-seventies, Arthur having retired from his job as an insurance clerk ten years ago. They were a devoted couple, and since Arthur had retired you never saw one without the other.

'Is everything all right, Mrs Critchley?' Ann crossed the cobbled road. 'Are you expecting visitors?'

The old lady was small and slim, with pure white hair and a face lined with age. Right now she was wringing her hands and looking greatly distressed. 'I'm glad to see you, Ann, I don't know which way to turn. It's Arthur, he's not well.'

'What's wrong with him?' Ann asked, putting a hand on an arm that was shaking with fear. 'Do you want me to come in and see if there's anything I can do?'

'Would you? He took a funny turn about half an hour ago, then he seemed to come round. But he's got a hand to his chest now, as though he's in pain. He told me he wasn't, but I think he's only saying that so as not to worry me.'

'I'll come in with you and see what I think. It might be nothing, but best to make sure.'

Arthur Critchley had been a fine-looking man when he was younger. Tall, broad shoulders and a healthy complexion. And always a natty dresser. He'd shrunk in size now, through age, but even at seventy-five he kept himself smartly dressed and his snow-white hair was always neatly combed. But when Ann walked into the living room, it was to find him slumped sideways in a fireside chair, with a hand pressed to his chest. It was obvious he was in great discomfort, but when he saw his neighbour he tried to sit up straight. 'It's nothing, Ann, a bit of indigestion, that's all. The wife's making a mountain out of a molehill.'

'Best to be sure than sorry, Arthur.' Ann didn't like his colour; his face was grey. 'Perhaps you should have the doctor, to be on the safe side.'

His wife, Freda, hovering in the background, said, 'I told him he should have the doctor, but he won't hear of it. Here's me worrying meself sick, and he's as stubborn as a mule. But perhaps he'll take notice of you.'

'Have you got pains in your chest, Arthur?' Ann didn't want to push for something the old man might later hold against her. And she really wasn't qualified when it came to pains and sickness. 'It's no good shaking your head when I can see you are in pain. That attitude won't do you any good. But as I'm hopeless when it comes to a situation like this, I wonder if you'd mind me asking Maisie to come over? She's got more nous than I have.'

Freda ignored the warning in her husband's eyes. 'If you wouldn't mind, Ann, me and Arthur would be grateful. I know he says it's nothing, and perhaps he's right. But he's never had indigestion like this in the fifty-odd years I've known him. And as you say, it's best to be sure than sorry.'

'I'll be back in a tick.' Ann fled from the house and ran to her neighbour's. It was a quarter to two, so even if it was one of Maisie's afternoons for the pictures, she wouldn't have left the house yet.

'I was in the parlour and saw yer running across the cobbles like a bat out of hell.' Maisie had opened the door before the sound of the knocker had died away. 'What's the rush for?'

'Arthur Critchley's not well, and I think he might be having a heart attack. I'm useless, Maisie, so would you come over and see what you think?'

'Yeah, of course I will. I'll just get me door key.'

Maisie didn't mess around when she entered the house opposite with Ann hot on her heels. She took one look at Arthur and said, 'You need a doctor, and pronto. To save time running to his surgery, I'll ask the woman in the chippy to ring up and say it's urgent. I know you're with Dr Greenshields, same as us, and I've got his telephone number at home. If he hasn't left on his rounds yet, he could be here in no time.' She was running down the hall when she called, 'I'll be back in a few minutes.'

Freda started pacing the floor, her eyes never leaving her husband. 'Shall I make you a cup of tea, love?'

'Oh, I don't think that's wise,' Ann told her. 'Let's just wait until the doctor comes.'

True to her word, Maisie was back within five minutes. Gasping for breath, she said, 'We caught him at home, he's on his way.'

'Oh dear.' Freda's hands fluttered like a bird's wings. 'The place is not very tidy.'

Maisie, never one to mince words, laughed. 'What are yer worrying about, missus, yer could eat yer dinner off the ruddy floor! There's only one place I know as clean as this, and it's my front path!'

31

Chapter Three

Dr Greenshields was a very well-known figure in the area. To the people on his panel he was greatly respected and trusted as a doctor, and they swore by him. He was devoted to his profession, his one aim to help people whether they be rich or poor. No sick person was ever turned away from his surgery because they had no money, nor would they be refused a home visit. But to those who didn't know him, he was a figure of fun, an eccentric because of the clothes he wore, which were reminiscent of the garb worn by doctors fifty years ago. Black trousers, flared three-quarter frock coat, stiff stand-up narrow collar with wings and a gold pin in a cravat of muted colours. And on his head was a hard high hat with a narrow brim. Rumour had it that his parents had been wealthy and he was comfortably off. He lived with his sister, also a doctor, in a big rambling house in Orrell Lane. Half of the house was their living quarters, the rest served as waiting rooms and surgeries. Both had brilliant minds, but his sister was very religious and word was spreading that she was now getting people to kneel down in her surgery and say a prayer before they left. Women would go along with her even though they thought she was crazy, but not so the menfolk. They called her a religious maniac and switched over to her brother.

Maisie opened the door to him. 'Good afternoon, Doctor. I'm the one what called yer out, 'cos I thought yer should see Arthur. If there's nowt wrong with him he'll never speak to me again.'

The doctor inclined his head and walked past her into the living room. After placing his well-worn bag on the couch, he laced his fingers across his tummy and stood in front of his patient. Seconds ticked by without a word, then he leaned forward and gently pulled Arthur's hand away from his chest. 'Have you any chest pains, Mr Critchley? No, I thought not. Well, tell me exactly what happened and how you feel. Then I'll examine you.'

Speaking slowly, with a slight slur, Arthur said, 'I just went funny all of a sudden, Doctor. Didn't have no warning, nothing.'

'Is it a heart attack, Dr Greenshields?' Freda asked, imagining the worst. 'He didn't half give me a fright.'

'It isn't a heart attack, I'm sure of that. I believe your husband has had a slight stroke. But I'll know more when I've given him a good examination.'

'We'll get out of your way for ten minutes, then,' Maisie said. 'Me and Mrs Richardson will just be over the road if yer want us.' She glanced at Freda. 'Would yer like to come with us?'

'Oh no, I'll stay with Arthur.' Wild horses wouldn't have dragged her away from her husband of more than fifty years. 'But you will come back, won't yer?'

'Of course we will.' The two women left the house, and when they were standing outside Maisie said, 'Come to mine and I'll make us a cuppa.'

Ann shook her head. 'No, I've left Theresa and she'll be wondering what's happening. You come to ours, instead.'

Tess had been sitting at the window since her mother left, an exercise book on her knee. In between keeping an eye on the house opposite, she was writing an account of the walk she'd had this morning for her dad to read. But since she'd seen the doctor arrive, her pencil had been still. 'Is Mr Critchley going to die, Mam?'

'Certainly not! Whatever gave you that idea? We came out while the doctor examines him, but I don't think it's serious.' Ann walked through to the kitchen. 'I'll put the kettle on.'

'Come to think of it, Ann, it's not worth making a cuppa, we'd never have time to drink it. I'll bet Freda comes knocking for us in a few minutes.'

Maisie wasn't far out; it was ten minutes before Freda came running across the cobbles. 'Will yer both come over, please, and hear what the doctor's got to say? I can't think straight at the moment, my head's just going round and round.'

Dr Greenshields was putting his stethoscope back in his bag. A man of few words, he came straight to the point. 'Mr Critchley has had a mild stroke which has affected him down his right side. But he's very lucky because it hasn't caused a lot of damage. His speech was affected for a while and the side of his face was numb, which is why he felt funny. But that is practically back to normal and he just needs complete rest for a few days. This has been a warning to him that he needs to take life easy, he is no longer a young man.' He picked up his bag and donned his hat. 'Call me if you think it necessary.'

While Freda was showing the good doctor out, Arthur was offering his thanks and apologies. 'Thank you for your help, ladies. I won't say I wasn't worried, 'cos I'm no hero and I was scared. You were right, Maisie, and in future I'll do as I'm told.'

'No need to thank me, all I've done is harmless,' Ann said. 'I was only here to make the numbers up. I'm hopeless when it comes to sickness, that's why I went for Maisie.' Freda came back after seeing the doctor out and Ann told her, 'If you want any shopping, washing or ironing doing, you only have to ask. And if you're worried during the night, don't hesitate to knock.' She grinned and jerked her head at Maisie. 'I might not be able to do anything for you, but I know someone who will.'

'I don't think yer've anything to worry about, Freda,' Maisie said. 'Arthur's looking a lot better. But is there anything yer'd like me and Ann to do before we go?'

'No thank you, yer've done enough.' The old lady, still as white as a sheet, followed them to the door. 'I really don't know what I'd have done without the pair of yer. I'll be all right now, but I've got to say, he gave me the fright of me life.'

'Go in and make a nice pot of tea for the two of yer,' Maisie said. 'And sit and relax until yer nerves are back to normal. That's what I'm going to do, make a pot of tea for me and Ann.'

But Ann declined. 'No, we'll have to leave that for another time, Maisie, I'll get home and see to the dinner. But I'll take you up on the offer when we've both got an hour to spare. And thanks for having a good head on your shoulders. If you hadn't been in, me and Freda would still have been standing there biting our nails. Hopeless and helpless, that's me.'

'I'm not surprised Freda was upset,' George said, over the dinner table. 'When you get to their age you can't stand shocks or cope like you could when you were younger. How is Arthur now?'

'I went over just before you came in and he doesn't seem so bad. His speech is a bit slurred, and he keeps holding his right hand as though it hasn't any life in it, but he's not grey like he was this afternoon. Me and Maisie are taking turns keeping an eye on him for a week or so, just to make sure.'

'You never know the minute, do you, love? Especially at their age; they've both turned their three score years and ten.'

Maddy stood up her knife and fork either side of her plate like soldiers on guard. 'What does that mean, Dad? Their three score years and ten?'

George cursed himself for not thinking before he spoke. The girls were very fond of the old couple opposite and the slightest hint they might be ill would bring on nightmares. 'It's just an old wives' tale, pet. You know, a silly superstition, like it being bad luck to walk under a ladder. Or spilling salt.'

'Or walking across the path of a black cat,' Tess said. 'That's supposed to bring bad luck. We saw a black cat today, sitting in the

35

sunshine outside the greengrocer's shop. We walked past it, but I don't think that's the same as crossing its path. I hope not, anyway, 'cos I don't want any bad luck.'

'You've been out today, have you?' George asked, glad to change the subject. 'Where did you go to?'

'I'm not telling, 'cos while Mam was out I wrote it down for you.' Tess wagged her shoulders, feeling pleased with her achievement. 'You can all read it when we've finished our meal and give me marks out of ten for it.'

George speared the last piece of bacon and popped it in his mouth. 'I'm the first to finish, so it's only fair I get first chance to read your masterpiece.'

'Oh no you don't!' Ann said. 'We'll wait until the table is cleared and then you can read it out to us.'

It wasn't until the green chenille cloth was back on the table and they were all seated that Tess, with an air of superiority, handed two pages over to her father. 'I know I've made some spelling mistakes, but ignore those, Dad.'

Maddy leaned her elbows on the table and cupped her face in both her hands. 'I can't wait to hear what you've been up to today.'

George coughed to clear his throat before starting to read aloud how Tess and her mother had gone for a walk to Walton Vale. In great detail she told of the sunshine, the masses of people, how she'd admired the shoes with high heels and was going to get a pair just like them when she was older. And a pink blouse she'd fallen for. The park, the children on the swings, the smell from the cake shop, all were written down. And lastly, the pie, which had been delicious. There were a couple of spelling mistakes, but apart from that George thought his daughter had done very well. Better than he'd ever thought her capable of.

He held the pages up and looked at his wife. 'Tess wrote this without your help?'

Ann nodded. 'I wasn't even here, George, I was over the road. And when I came back I had to see to the dinner. No, I didn't ask her to do it, she did it off her own bat.'

Maddy was hugging her sister. 'You did well, kid, I couldn't have done better myself.'

'Ah, but you wouldn't have made any mistakes, I bet I made a lot.'

'Only three, pet and that's very good,' George told her, passing the pages over to his wife. He was really amazed, he hadn't expected anything so well written and interesting. 'You've spelled "bought" incorrectly, and you've put "to" instead of "too".'

Tess began to giggle. 'It would have been one more, 'cos I didn't

36

fancy trying to spell "confectioner's", so I put "cake shop" instead.'

George reclaimed the pages from his wife's hand. 'This is marvellous, Tess, as good as you'd get from any ten-year-old. You've made me very pleased and proud.' His eyes ran along the lines of words and he chuckled a couple of times. 'I can remember having to get a dictionary out once to see how to spell "delicious".'

Ann looked at him as though he'd said something of great importance. Then, in a gesture never seen before by her two daughters, she cupped her husband's face and kissed him full on the lips. 'Thank you for being a poor speller when you were young, love. You see, I would never have thought of a dictionary, but it's just the thing for Theresa!'

George was taken aback by the open show of affection, but quietly pleased. It seemed that Tess wasn't the only one learning. His younger daughter was bringing about a change in his wife. And in such a short time. 'Well, you have a dictionary, love, so lend it to Tess so she can look up any words she's not sure of.'

Ann was off her chair like a shot to bring the rather worn book to the table. She slid it across to her daughter. 'Take it upstairs with you later, and Madelaine will show you how to look up words like "delicious" and "confectioner's".'

Tess picked up the book with its well-thumbed pages, held it to her chest and looked pleadingly at her sister. 'Come up with me now, Maddy, please? I just want you to show me how to find those two words.'

'We can do it here,' Maddy said, before catching the disappointed look on Tess's face. 'Come on then, we'll go upstairs.'

When they were alone, George took his wife's hand in his. 'It seems to me that if Tess isn't pushed, allowed to work at her own speed, she does far better. Knowing there's no one looking over her shoulder, and she won't be told off if she gets things wrong, she'll try harder and come on better.'

They both looked to the ceiling when they heard loud laughter, and Maddy's voice saying, 'Go on, you soft nit!' Normally Ann would have frowned at the expression, but not tonight. Not when it brought such laughter from her two daughters. 'They seem to be enjoying themselves.'

George patted her hand. 'That's what I like to hear, Ann. There's nothing as sweet to my ears as the sound of childish laughter. There should be a law that says all children must have a happy childhood because it will stand them in good stead when they grow up and have problems.' He chortled when he heard the bed springs twanging overhead and Maddy's infectious laugh. 'We are very fortunate to have Maddy. Most other girls would be jealous of Tess getting so much attention, but not her. She loves her sister and is very patient with her.

But I think it's important that Maddy knows we love her as much as we do Tess.'

'Oh, Madelaine knows that, George, I tell her very often. In fact I had a word with her this morning while she was having her breakfast. I told her how much we appreciate her helping her sister, and explained why it was natural for us to make a fuss of Theresa, but that she must never feel left out because we love both of our daughters dearly.'

'And did she understand?'

'Madelaine is very grown up and understanding. She said she knows we love her, and she doesn't mind if Theresa gets all the attention because she loves her sister and will do anything for her. She looked me straight in the eyes, George, and said, "She will get better, you know, Mam, I know she will." '

George squeezed her hand. 'She'll be thirteen in a couple of weeks, but it doesn't seem any time since she was a baby and I was bouncing her up and down on my knee.'

'And bragging about her taking after you. I remember you saying she had your dark hair and brown eyes. I was quite jealous because she bore no resemblance to me.'

High-pitched young voices and a clattering on the stairs heralded the entrance of the two girls. Pink-cheeked and bright-eyed, they scrambled for their chairs. 'Now, before you ask, I didn't help Tess with the writing,' Maddy said. 'All I did was show her how to look a word up in the dictionary. And I explained that you have to know the first few letters of a word before you can do that. Anyway, what she's written is all her own work, scout's honour.'

Tess was flushed with excitement and pleasure as she held a piece of paper aloft. 'Who wants to read it first?'

Ann held out her hand. 'So there's no favouritism, your dad and I will read it together.'

George leaned towards his wife and put an arm across her shoulders. Their heads close together, they read the revised edition of their daughter's morning activities.

'Excellent!' George looked up to see Tess with a hand covering her mouth to stifle a giggle. 'What are you laughing at?'

'I want you and Mam to mark it, like they do in school.'

Ann tapped her chin, pretending to give it some thought. 'Well, you made three mistakes in your last effort, and there's only one in this.' She turned to her husband. 'What do you think, George? Eight out of ten?'

'Oh, I think so. She's worked hard getting her spelling right, and she now knows the difference between "to" and "too". A very good effort, I should say.'

'Right, young lady, eight out of ten. And I'll underline the word you've spelt incorrectly.'

'I know which word it is, Mam, our Maddy told me. But she wouldn't tell me how it should be spelt because she said that would be cheating.'

'I'll write it at the side and you can study it when you're in bed.' Ann passed the paper back. 'And you do know the difference between "to" and "too"?'

The shoulders of the two girls shook with laughter. 'Go on,' Maddy said, 'tell them how you learned the difference.'

'I will if you start.'

'Oh, all right. Are you coming to bed?'

'I will if you're coming too!'

Their laughter was infectious, and when they were joined by their mother and father, the rafters rang as never before. And while George was thinking how much younger and prettier his wife looked when she was happy, Ann was thinking of all that she'd missed over the years. But she made a vow to make up for it. From now on there'd be much more laughter in this house.

When Maddy came home from school on the Friday, she was grinning from ear to ear. 'No more school until the beginning of September, Tess.' Rubbing her hands together she made for the kitchen, where she could hear her mother pottering about. 'You've not heard from Wales yet, Mam?'

'No, love.' Ann ran her hands down the sides of her pinny. 'I did tell you it would probably be Saturday before we heard, so we'll keep our fingers crossed that it comes in the post tomorrow.'

'I hope she says we can go, I'm not half looking forward to it.'

·'Yes, we all are.' Ann lifted the lid on the pan to make sure the potatoes were simmering. It was Friday, fish day, and they were having mashed potatoes with poached cod. 'I'll come and sit down for fifteen minutes, and explain to you and Theresa what we'll be doing if Mrs Owen can't take us.' Her hands on her daughter's shoulders, she propelled her into the living room. 'We'll sit at the table so we can see each other. Come on, Theresa.'

'I don't want to go anywhere else, Mam, I want to go to Wales.' Tess was in one of her stubborn moods. 'I want to see the cows and sheep.'

'Oh well, I can't do anything about it if the woman is already booked up.' Ann thought giving in to her mood wasn't the answer. If she was too soft with her daughter, she wouldn't be doing her any favours. It was a big world out there and with so many people out of work it was every man for himself. Life, and people, could sometimes be cruel.

'You needn't listen if you're not interested, love, you carry on reading your book. But I'm sure Madelaine would like to know what your father and I decided we'd do for treats if Wales falls through.'

Her words had the desired effect and Tess linked arms with her sister. 'I'll listen with Maddy. I'm not having her knowing something I don't.'

'Your father and I are as eager as you to go to Wales, but in the event it doesn't happen we thought we'd find other things to do so you wouldn't be disappointed. Days out wouldn't be the same as going away on holiday, but at least it would be something for you to look forward to. We thought we could go on the ferry to Seacombe one day, and walk from there to New Brighton. There's plenty to do and see there, like paddling in the sea or looking around the fairground. You could have a ride on the bobby-horses, that would be nice.'

'You and me could sit on the same horse, Maddy,' Tess said, appearing a little more cheerful. 'I could sit on the back and put my arm around you so I wouldn't fall off.'

'I think you'd be safer sitting in front,' Maddy told her, 'then I could keep tight hold of you. And you could hold the reins and gee the horse up to go faster.'

'They don't go very fast,' Ann said, smiling. 'But they do go up and down.'

'Did you and my dad think of somewhere else we could go another day?' Maddy asked, crossing her fingers and hoping it was the place she would most like to go.

'Yes, we thought Southport would be nice. We could take sandwiches and have a picnic on the sands.'

Maddy grinned. 'I was hoping you would say that. We've only been to Southport once, and that was years ago. But I remember it was nice there.'

'I'd still rather go to Wales, though,' Tess said. 'But I won't cry if we can't.'

'I should hope not!' her mother said. 'You are too old to cry because things don't go your way, Theresa. Especially when you are offered something in its place.'

'What time does the postman come, Mam?' Maddy asked. 'Is it before Dad goes out to work?'

'He's usually in the street about seven o'clock, so he could be here before your father has to leave.'

'I'll be awake by then, I know I will. My tummy is doing somersaults now, so as sure as eggs are eggs, it will have me awake early.'

'And me!' Tess said. The sisters slept together from choice. There was a spare bedroom, but apart from a cot it had never been furnished, because when she was little, Tess was terrified of the dark, and Ann had agreed she could sleep with her sister as a temporary measure. But when the time came to separate them, both girls refused to be parted and all attempts to do so ended in tears. 'My tummy's like yours, Maddy, it's going up and down and round and round. It's bound to wake me up early.'

'If you are awake, you must not get out of bed.' Ann pointed a stiffened finger. 'I don't want either of you wandering about the house at seven in the morning. If the postman brings a letter, your father will let you know. Whether it's good news or bad, you will be told right away. And as the eldest, Madelaine, I expect you to heed what I say.'

Tess tilted her head and looked into her sister's face. 'That's what you get for being the eldest, Maddy. There's no fun in it, is there?'

'It has its good points,' Maddy said. 'It means I get to leave school two years before you and that is the best part about it.' She looked across at her mother. 'Anyway, we'll all be happy tomorrow because I know the letter will bring good news.'

'I hope so, love, I really do.' Ann got to her feet and pushed the chair back under the table. 'Don't forget, your father and I are looking forward to a holiday as much as you are.'

'I know that, Mam. And you both deserve one more than me and Tess because you work so hard. But cheer up, because I've got this nice feeling that tells me we will get our holiday. I bet any money that this time tomorrow we'll be sitting here all excited and talking about which clothes we're taking away with us.'

Tess found this very interesting. 'Maddy, what does this nice feeling feel like? And how do you know it's about the holiday?'

'I can't explain the feeling, Tess, it's just there. And I know it's about the holiday because that is the thing I want most.'

Ann stood with her hands on the back of the chair and watched the faces of her two daughters as they talked. Theresa so innocent and trusting, Madelaine so kind and patient. They were more than just sisters, they were friends as well. And their love for each other ran deep. No harm would come to Theresa while Madelaine was around to protect her, and Ann thanked God for that. For her younger daughter would always need protecting.

Tess didn't know how long she'd been waiting for her sister to stir, but it seemed ages. And she could tell by the lightness in the bedroom that it was broad daylight out, so it must be nearly time for getting up. 'Maddy?' She gently nudged her sister. 'Maddy, are you awake?'

After a few seconds there was a movement under the bedclothes, and a sleepy voice asked, 'What time is it?'

'I don't know, but it must be getting on 'cos it's really light outside.'

Maddy rubbed her eyes before raising herself on one elbow. 'Is Dad up yet?' She kept her voice to a whisper. 'Have you heard him moving around?'

'Not yet. But he might be up and keeping quiet so he won't wake us.'

Maddy giggled. 'He needn't bother being quiet, seeing as we're both awake now.' Then she put a finger to her lips. 'Shush, I've just heard their bedroom door open. Not a word now, Tess, just lie nice and still.'

The creaking stairs told them their father was on his way down, and soon after they heard more creaking as their mother followed to see to his breakfast. 'It must be a quarter to seven,' Maddy whispered. 'That means the postman could be here any time.'

'Ooh, isn't it exciting?' Tess took hold of her sister's hand and placed it on her chest. 'Can you feel my heart thumping?'

'Don't get yourself too excited, Tess, because even if the postman comes, it doesn't mean we are definitely going on holiday. I'm sure the lady would take us if she could, but she might not have any room. And then you'll be so disappointed you'll make yourself ill.'

Tess gave this some thought for a moment, then asked, 'Have you still got the nice feeling you had yesterday, Maddy?'

'I'm not saying, because I don't want you to get your hopes up.'

'Ah, go on, Maddy, please? I promise I won't cry or make myself ill if you're wrong.'

Just at that moment they heard the sound of the flap on their letter-box being lifted, and then the faint plop of a letter falling to the floor. The girls looked at each other, and by silent consent they swivelled their bottoms and slipped their legs over the sides of the bed.

George heard the sound as he was eating his toast, and he called through to the kitchen, 'The postman's been, love.' He reached the hall just seconds ahead of his wife. In his head he was saying a prayer as he bent to pick up the letter. 'Please God, eh, love?' He was straightening up when he spied his two daughters sitting on the top stair and his heart went out to them. 'Come on down, don't sit there in suspense.'

Ann was waiting for them as they scrambled down the stairs, and she put her arms around their shoulders and squeezed. 'Fingers crossed, girls.'

George tore the envelope in his haste, and pulled out a single sheet of paper. He began to read as three pairs of eyes watched his face for a reaction. And when he grinned they all ran to stand near him. 'What does it say, Dad?' Maddy asked. 'Hurry up and tell us.'

George handed the letter to his wife, then held his arms out to gather his daughters to him. 'Mrs Owen will be very pleased to accommodate Mr and Mrs Richardson and their two daughters, and will look forward to welcoming them to Rose Cottage for their five days' holiday.'

There were shrieks of delight from the girls as they clung to his waist. 'Oh, Dad, isn't that marvellous?' Maddy's pretty face was aglow with happiness. 'We're very lucky.'

Tess's happiness threatened to bring on the tears and she sniffed up in an effort to stop them putting in an appearance. After all, she'd promised her sister she wouldn't cry. 'You said everything would be all right, Maddy, didn't you? That nice feeling you had brought us luck.'

'I think you might have brought some luck yourself, love,' Ann said. 'Tell your father and Madelaine what you did before you put the letter in the pillar-box.'

Tess smiled and shyly lowered her head. 'I kissed the envelope.'

'In that case, how could we lose?' George was over the moon. They'd never had a proper holiday before because there was always something more urgent to spend the money on. After they got married, it took a few years of hard saving to furnish the house. And they'd just got it as they wanted it when Maddy came along, and then two years later Tess was born. And with her being sickly, there were doctors to pay and medicine to buy. But now, at last, he was able to take his family on holiday and he was a proud man.

'Rose Cottage in the village of Hope,' Ann said, handing the letter to Maddy. 'With names like that, how could we not have a good holiday?'

'And what a lovely day to get the good news.' George ruffled his daughters' hair before sitting down to finish his breakfast. 'The sky is blue with little white fluffy clouds dancing around, and the sun is getting ready to shine. It puts me in mind of the saying "God's in His heaven, all's right with the world". For all is right in our world today.'

'It certainly is, love,' Ann said. 'But you're going to have to put a move on or you'll be late for work. And you, young ladies, can go back to bed. You may take the letter with you, and I'll bring a drink up after I've seen your father out.'

The girls didn't argue with that. After giving their father a quick hug and kiss, they ran up the stairs with Maddy clutching the precious letter. They climbed into bed and propped the pillows up against the headboard so they could sit in comfort. And as soon as they were settled, Tess said, 'Read it to me, Maddy.'

'Dad told us the main things, which is what we wanted to know, but there's more in the letter than that. Mrs Owen sounds very nice and friendly and I'm sure we're going to like her. She says her visitors usually get there about four o'clock, but to be on the safe side she'll reckon on five o'clock for our dinner. And as we'll be hungry, she'll make sure there's plenty to eat. And she hopes we have a safe journey and is looking forward to meeting us.'

Tess leaned her head on her sister's shoulder. 'We are very lucky girls, aren't we, Maddy?'

'We certainly are, Tess.'

When Ann entered the bedroom twenty minutes later, a cup of tea in each hand, it was to see her daughters sitting up in bed, their heads resting on the pillows and smiles on their faces as they tried to picture what Rose Cottage, in a village called Hope, would look like. Maddy imagined a quaint little cottage with climbing roses covering the front of the house and forming an arch around the door. But Tess saw the cottage in the middle of a field, and there were cows chewing the cud and mooing, and little lambs playfully frisking by their mothers.

'Here you are, girls, and don't spill any on the bedclothes because I only changed the beds on Monday.'

'Thanks, Mam.' Maddy reached for the cup. 'Me and Tess have been wondering what time we'll be leaving here on the Monday morning and will we be going on a train?'

'I'm sorry, love, but we don't know any details yet. We're going down to see Uncle Ken tomorrow and we'll know more then. He and Auntie Milly have stayed with Mrs Owen a few times so he'll tell us how to get there and anything else we want to know.'

In her excitement, Tess leaned forward too quickly and her tea came close to spilling over. But she righted the cup just in time and rolled her eyes. 'Oh dear, oh dear, oh dear! Aren't I a silly girl?'

Ann's lips parted to issue a reprimand, but one look at her daughter's face kept the words back. How could she tell the girl off when she'd not long been given the most exciting news of her life? It would be a miserable soul who spoilt her pleasure.

'Can we come with you to Uncle Ken's, Mam?' Maddy asked. 'I haven't seen Joyce or Billy for ages.'

'Well you don't think we'd go and leave you two in the house on your own, do you? Of course you're coming with us.' Ann turned and put her hand on the door knob. 'That's all the questions for now. I've work to do, and I want it done before you come down. So be good girls and amuse yourselves until I call you.'

'We will, Mam,' Tess said. 'And I'll drink some of my tea now so it won't spill over.' To show she meant it, she lifted the cup to her lips and sipped. 'It's lovely, thank you.'

'If you want something to do to pass the time, Madelaine has the notebook on the tallboy, you could start writing down what you'd like to take on holiday with you.' Ann smiled as she walked through the door. 'That should keep you going for a while.'

She couldn't have given them anything better to amuse themselves with. And when she called them down for their breakfast, both girls had made a long list of things they thought they should take. While Ann read the lists and nodded, she was telling herself they couldn't possibly take half the items listed. They only had one case, and that was one she'd had since before she was married and it was old and battered. It wouldn't hold very much, so things like socks, singlets and knickers would have to go in the large canvas bag which was in the cupboard under the stairs and only came out once in a blue moon. 'On Monday we'll look through your dresses and pick out the three best cotton ones. And we'll do the same with your socks and knickers. Then I can get them washed and ironed ready to pack in the case. That'll be a load off my mind.'

'Mam, I've got a hole in the heel of one of my socks,' Maddy said. 'So will it be all right if I get the sewing box out when the table's clear, and darn it?'

Ann was more than happy to nod her head. Her daughter could do as neat a darn as any woman, far better than she herself could. 'That would be a big help, Madelaine, and if there's time you could do one of your father's for me. I don't think he possesses a sock that doesn't have a hole in.'

Tess wanted to do her bit, so she said, 'I'll help, Maddy, I'll thread the needle for you.'

Her sister chuckled. 'Talk about act daft and I'll buy you a coalyard isn't in it! You're not soft, are you, Theresa Richardson? Thread the needle indeed! You're not getting away with that, you can cut the pieces of wool ready for me as well.'

Tess rested her elbows on the table and cupped her face. 'I'll do that, Maddy, as long as you buy me that coalyard you mentioned.'

'Oh ay! You're getting cheeky, aren't you?' Maddy feigned indignation but was delighted when her sister showed spirit. 'Proper clever clogs, you are.'

'I'll have them as well, please.'

Maddy frowned. 'You'll have what?'

'I'll have the clogs! I'll need them to work in the coalyard you're going to buy me. You never see our coalman without his clogs.'

Ann was smiling when she looked at Maddy. 'That's one in the eye for you, Madelaine. Your sister certainly came out best there.'

Her daughter returned the smile, with her eyes saying she was really happy that her sister seemed lots better these days. 'She's getting too big for her boots.'

'Well, it doesn't matter if my boots don't fit, seeing as I'm getting a

45

pair of clogs.' Tess really was in high spirits. 'At least I won't be going on holiday barefoot.'

Maddy leaned sideways and glared at her sister. She pushed her face close, so their noses were nearly touching. 'Will you forget about your footwear and help clear the table? I've got work to do.'

Tess glared back. 'And so have I. Don't forget, if I don't cut the wool and thread the needle, you won't be able to do anything.' The pink tongue darted out. 'So there!'

As Ann watched the water running from the tap into a bowl in the sink, she was thinking that Madelaine was just the tonic Theresa needed. She didn't talk down to her, but treated her as she would any of her friends. And that was what her sister needed. Her sense of humour was coming out as never before, and though her written words weren't up to her spoken ones, she was coming on in that direction too. Please God the improvement would continue.

Chapter Four

It was young Billy Richardson who opened the door on Sunday afternoon and his eyes widened in surprise. 'Hello, Uncle George, Auntie Ann. I didn't know yer were coming, me mam didn't say.'

'Your mam doesn't know, son,' George said. 'We've come to ask for some advice about our holidays.'

'Come on in.' Billy held the door wide while calling, 'Mam, we've got visitors.' He waited until George and Ann had passed him, then grinned at the girls. 'Hi, you two, I haven't seen yer for donkey's years. Yer've both gone and got bigger since then. Ye're quite the young lady, Maddy, and you, Tess.'

'What about yourself, Billy Richardson?' Maddy jokingly asked. 'I see you've gone into long kecks since you started work.'

The boy's shoulders went back, his chest came out and he seemed to grow six inches in stature. 'Four months I've been in them now.'

'They suit you, Billy,' Tess said. 'You look really nice and I bet all the girls are after you. Have you got a girlfriend yet?'

Blushing to the roots of his hair, Billy closed the door, saying, 'That's for me to know and you to find out. Now get in, 'cos this hall's too small for three people.'

Tess made straight for her father's brother, a great favourite of hers. She flung her arms around his neck and kissed him soundly. 'Hello, Uncle Ken, it's nice to see you.'

'And you, sweetheart.' He smiled into her face. 'Yer get prettier every time I see yer. If I wasn't married to yer Auntie Milly, I'd wait for yer to grow up and marry you instead.'

'Ye're well out of it, Tess,' Milly said, keeping a straight face. 'He's a very fickle man is my husband, and he's got a roving eye.'

'Which one is that, Auntie Milly? His eyes both look the same to me.'

Billy's voice was at the stage where it was starting to break and he found it very embarrassing. One minute he was speaking like a man, the next like a girl. But he couldn't sit with his mouth closed or people would think he was dumb. So he took a chance and was made up when it came out really deep without a single crack in it.

47

'Nice one, Tess! Yer were quick off the mark there!'

Ken's shoulders slumped and he put on a woebegone expression. 'I don't know, me own family ganging up on me. I wouldn't care, but I'm the easiest-going bloke imaginable. And I've never let me eyes stray to another woman since, er, since, er, since yesterday.'

'And I bet that was the brazen hussy in number fifteen,' Milly said knowingly. 'We never see sight nor light of her during the day, but come six o'clock, when most of the men are on their way home from work, she stands on her step as bold as brass and gives the eye to anyone wearing a pair of trousers.'

'Ooh, ay, Billy, you'd better watch out.' There was devilment in Maddy's eyes. 'I'd go back to the short kecks if I were you.'

'That's enough, now,' George said, aware that the conversation would not be to his wife's liking. 'Take your arms from around Uncle Ken's neck and let him come up for air, so I can ask about the travel arrangements for our holidays.'

'So yer've had an answer then, Ann?' Milly looked pleased. 'I told yer she'd let yer know right away.'

Ann nodded. 'She sounds very nice from the letter and we're all delighted. The girls would start packing now if I'd let them, and we'd need a removal van to carry all the stuff they've got down on their lists. By the time a week tomorrow comes, they'll have me motheaten.'

'Yer'll like it there, it's a lovely place.' Ken was older than his brother by two years, but they could be taken for identical twins if it weren't for the moustache sported by George. 'And yer certainly won't go hungry, 'cos the table groans with the weight of the stuff Gwen puts on it. She doesn't half feed yer well. And all the meat and vegetables come from local farms, so everything is fresh.'

'It sounds like heaven,' George said. 'Just give me the details on how to get there. I know Milly told Ann it was one train and then a pony-and-trap, but a train from where, to where?'

Ken tutted. 'Milly told me what she'd said, and I couldn't believe her! Honest to God, she's as thick as two short planks! It's no wonder I've got a roving eye.'

'All right, clever bugger, we've been through this half a dozen times.' Milly's head was shaking from side to side and her eyes were turned to the ceiling. 'Can't yer just tell them how to get there without pulling me to pieces in the process?'

'That's because I like to see yer getting all het up, see, love. When yer face gets red and yer eyes let off sparks I can feel me heart pounding. It reminds me of when we were courting and I'd be late for a date.' He glanced at his brother and winked. 'She used to have a right paddy on her and she'd give me the rounds of the kitchen. Her mam and dad didn't interfere but I think they felt sorry for me on the quiet 'cos she wouldn't shut up long enough for me to explain I'd put in an hour's overtime. And she'd keep it up until we got to the picture house and the big picture started.' His chuckle was deep and rich. 'When I was flushed with money I'd splash out on the back stalls, and if we were lucky enough to get on the back row I had another way of shutting her up.'

His wife was grinning as memories came flooding back. They had a rock-solid marriage and she loved the bones of him. 'Ken, I'm sure everyone is very interested in our courtship, but can yer change the subject and answer George's question? The way you're going on, their holiday will be over before he even knows how to get there.'

Just then the back kitchen door burst open and the daughter of the house came in, puffing and panting. Joyce was thirteen and had her father's colouring. In fact she and her cousin Maddy were very alike, with only six months' difference in their ages. 'Yer didn't tell me we were having visitors, Mam! I bet yer did that on purpose.'

'Excuse me, young lady, but where are yer manners? Aren't yer going to say hello to yer cousins?'

The girl's eyes swept over each of the faces and her greeting came with a big smile. 'Hello, everyone, it's nice to see yer. I hope I haven't missed a cup of tea and a cake?'

'Yer'd have a job to miss a cake, sweetheart, 'cos we haven't got any. I told yer I was cutting everything down to the bone so I could save up for our holidays. Mind you, I would have bought some if I'd known we were going to have guests.'

'Don't worry, Milly, I understand,' Ann said. 'If you came to our house you wouldn't get offered a cake because I'm saving every penny too!'

'We're going to Wales for our holidays, Joyce,' Tess said proudly. 'Where are you going?'

'Blackpool.' Joyce grinned at her before looking Maddy's way. 'My mate's waiting in the entry for me, we're going for a walk. Do you and Tess want to come?'

Tess was off her chair like a shot. 'Ooh, yes, I want to.'

Maddy could see the doubt on her mother's face. 'We wouldn't go far, Mam, and I'd make sure Tess was all right. We don't see Joyce very often and it would be nice to have a natter.'

'They'll be fine, Ann,' George said as his wife hesitated. 'But no longer than half an hour, Maddy, we don't want to have to come looking for you.'

With whoops of delight the three girls made a hasty exit, and their laughter could be heard long after they'd closed the entry door behind them. It was this sound that caused Billy to think he may as well be out in the sunshine instead of sitting there listening to older people. 'I think I'll go down to me mate's, Mam, it's too nice to stay in. I'll be back in time for tea.'

When the four adults found themselves alone, Ken spread his hands and shrugged his shoulders. 'D'yer think they find us dull?'

'Of course they do, yer soft nit,' Milly said, getting to her feet. 'The same as we thought our parents were dull. Now, while I put the kettle on, you can give George whatever help you can regarding the travel arrangements.'

'I'll give you a hand, Milly.' Ann followed her through to the kitchen. 'I can get the cups ready.'

Ken chuckled. 'I don't know whether we smell, George, but something has emptied this room very quickly.'

George raised his brows and said with mock severity, 'I'm beginning to think I'm going to have to drag the information out of you. Don't you want us to have this holiday?'

'Ay, a bit of respect for yer elder brother, if yer don't mind.' Again the hearty chuckle. 'George, yer'll go on this holiday if I have to give yer a piggyback. In fact, if we weren't going away at the same time, I'd ruddy well take yer meself! But yer won't have any trouble, it's easy enough to get there. Yer take the underground from James Street to Birkenhead, and they run every few minutes. Then when yer get off, ask any porter to direct yer to the right platform for the Wrexham train. When yer get off at Wrexham, yer can either take one of the small local trains to Hope, or go by bus. Neither of them run very often, so yer might have a long wait. And when yer get to Hope, just ask anyone the way to Rose Cottage. With a bit of luck yer might get a pony-and-trap to take yer for a few coppers, save yer lugging yer case.'

'I don't suppose you know the times of the trains, do you?'

'I'm sorry, George, but I can't remember the exact times. Yer best bet is for Ann to go down to the station and ask for a timetable. She could even buy the tickets while she's there, save yer rushing on the day and getting all hot and bothered if ye're running late.'

Ann was looking happy when she came into the room carrying a tray. 'I'll go down to the station in the morning.' She put the tray down and surprised both brothers by planting a kiss on George's cheek. 'I wouldn't want you getting all hot and bothered, would I, love?'

This open show of affection surprised Ken so much he was still talking about it as he smoked his last cigarette before going to bed. 'Yer could have knocked me over with a feather! I've never seen anything like it! She's always been so ruddy straitlaced I used to wonder

50

how she came to have two children! And she used to be so strict with the girls, too!'

Milly, her fingers curled around the cup she was holding, nodded. 'I noticed the change in her when she came last week. And I think young Tess has a lot to do with it. That girl would melt a heart of stone.'

The girls were counting the days at first, then as the time drew nearer, they ticked off the hours. And finally the time had come and they were on their way to the first holiday they'd ever had. The travelling wasn't as exciting as they'd thought, the trains were jam-packed and they were tired and hungry when they stepped off the train in the little village of Hope.

Ann cast an anxious eye on Theresa and put an arm across her shoulders and held her back so the other passengers alighting from the carriages could go before them. 'Are you sure you feel able to carry on, love? We can find somewhere to sit for a while if you like.'

The young girl's face was ashen and her breathing laboured. They seemed to have been travelling for ages and ages and she didn't think her legs would hold her up much longer. But it was the first day of their holidays, she didn't want to spoil it for her family. 'I'll be fine, Mam, I'm just a bit tired, that's all.'

George waited his turn to hand in their tickets to the collector, then he glanced back to his daughter. Tess had been fine when they left the house in the morning, full of excitement and expectation. But it must have been too much for her because she didn't look at all well now. 'We're on our way to Rose Cottage, I wonder if you can tell me if it's very far to walk?'

'Going to Gwen Owen's are you, then?' The man who acted as ticket collector, porter and station master at the tiny station spoke with a soft Welsh lilt and sounded very friendly. George had noticed the man had a smile and a joke for everyone who had passed through the gate. 'Then it's a fine holiday you'll have, for Gwen is noted for her hospitality. Feed you up, she will, until you're so full you won't be able to move away from the table.' He turned to smile at the two girls and was quick to notice the pallor of the younger one. 'Are you feeling a bit sick after all the travelling, love?'

'It's more likely the excitement,' Ann said, drawing her daughter closer. 'We've all been looking forward to this holiday but Theresa has got herself in a right state over it.'

The man bent to look into Tess's face. 'If it's sick you're going to be, then you couldn't go to a better house than Gwen Owen's to be made better. As good as any doctor she is, and she'll have you right as rain in no time.'

'We'd like to get there as quickly as possible,' George said, thinking it was nice of the man to take an interest, but Tess did look poorly and the sooner they were able to let her rest, the better. 'Is there any means of transport?'

'There is a bus service, and it would take you right to the gate of Rose Cottage. However, they only run every two hours and you've just missed one. I could get you a pony-and-trap if that's any help? All I need to do is blow on my whistle and there'll be one here before you can blink an eye.'

'Thank you, I would be very grateful.' George transferred the heavy case to his other hand. 'I'm sure my daughter will be fine once we're settled. It's been a bit hectic for all of us, climbing on and off one tram and three trains with all the luggage. It would wear anyone out, and put a strain on their nerves.'

The porter was as good as his word. He walked ahead of them through the small wooden gate, stood in the middle of what appeared to be a country lane, and blew hard on his silver whistle. It was about five minutes before they heard the clip-clop of a horse coming towards them. And what a fine-looking horse it was. Light brown with several patches of white on its back and legs, and a white mane. It was pulling a trap with a man sitting on a seat in the front holding the reins, and there were long seats down either side with a low door and step at the back. The sight of it brought a smile to Tess's face. 'It's just like the one in my book, Mam.'

Maddy, whose concern for her sister had kept her quiet for the latter part of the journey, now clapped her hands in delight. 'Oh, isn't it beautiful, Dad? And look at the way it's holding its head, it looks so proud.'

Without any instruction from its master, the horse came to a stop within a yard of the group. It jerked its head back and whinnied as though welcoming them. And after jumping down from his seat, the driver patted the horse affectionately before smiling at the family. 'Good afternoon. My name's Tom, and this beauty here is Goldie. Now, where would you like me to take you?'

As there wasn't another train due either side of the station for an hour, the porter stayed with them. It was partly for company, but if the truth were known, it was mostly because he didn't want to miss anything. Very little of interest happened in the village and he wasn't going to let a chance slip by of having some news to tell his wife over the dinner table. 'They're going to Rose Cottage. Staying with Gwen for a holiday, they are. The young lass isn't feeling too grand after the long journey, but I've told her Gwen will soon put things right.'

'She will indeed! She has a cure for everything, has Gwen.' Tom reached for the case. 'I'll take that for you.'

George relinquished the case with relief. It hadn't felt so heavy when they'd left home, but it had grown heavier each time he'd had to heave it down from the overhead racks on the trains. Now it seemed to weigh a ton, and he'd swear his arms had been stretched a couple of inches. 'Thank you.' George flexed his right arm a few times to get some feeling back in it, then smiled at the porter. 'And thank you, you've been very helpful.'

'Mr Tom?' Maddy knew she wouldn't sleep tonight if she didn't ask. 'Would it be all right if I stroked Goldie, please?'

'Of course you can! She loves children and likes nothing better than to have her nose rubbed.' He noticed Tess hanging back. 'You don't have to be afraid of her, she's as gentle as a lamb.'

'Here, I'll show you.' George led his daughter forward and took her hand. 'Do it slowly, like this, so we don't frighten her.'

Tess thought her heart was going to burst. 'Wouldn't it be lovely if we had a horse, Maddy?'

'Yes, it would, Tess, but where would we keep it? We couldn't keep it in our yard 'cos horses need plenty of grass to eat. And they need a big field to run around in.'

The case and bags were loaded into the trap by now, and although Tom didn't seem to be in any hurry, George felt uncomfortable keeping him waiting. 'Come on, girls, we really must go now or we'll be late for dinner.'

Ann climbed in first and turned to help Tess up. 'Sit by me, love, and Madelaine can sit opposite with your father.'

When they were settled, and Ann had made sure the small door was safely closed, Tom gave the signal for Goldie to move off. And the whole family turned to wave to the porter until the trap rounded a bend in the lane and he disappeared from view. 'He was a nice man, wasn't he, Mam?'

'Yes, he was very kind, dear.' Ann found the clip-clop of the horse and the gentle swaying of the trap very calming. And all around them was greenery. Hedges with colourful wild flowers growing in abundance, tall stately trees heavy with the leaves of summer, and fields stretching as far as the eye could see. She gave a sigh of contentment. 'It's so peaceful.'

George was also beginning to relax. 'Not a sound nor a house in sight. I could do with five weeks of this, not just five days.'

Tom turned his head. 'The first house we come to is Rose Cottage. Then a bit further on the village starts. It's very pretty, with some really old cottages dating back hundreds of years. And it's colourful at the moment, with flowers everywhere. There's a couple of shops if you run out of anything, a church and a public house.'

'Ooh, look, Mam, there's lambs in that field.' Tess had jumped to her feet, only to be pulled down again by her mother. 'There's baby ones and mother ones.'

'Whoa!' Tom pulled on the reins and brought the horse to a halt. 'That field, and the next, belongs to me. It's grazing land, and I keep sheep in this one and cows in the next. You'll see them as we go past.' He could see the girls' eyes opening wide in wonder and felt a pang of pity for them. Country folk like himself who'd lived with animals all their lives didn't really appreciate how lucky they were. This family probably never saw green fields or even a clear blue sky. He'd been to Liverpool once to visit a brother who'd married a girl from the city, and he couldn't understand how his brother could stand the smoking chimneys and the smell of factories and the gas works. And he'd been horrified at the poverty. Men, women and children looking half starved and dressed in rags. He even saw youngsters without shoes on their feet. Unemployment was rife, and any man with a job was lucky indeed. But the thing that had struck him most, and stayed in his mind, was how friendly the people were. They might not have much in life, but they had warmth and humour in abundance. Life in a city wouldn't suit him, he preferred the fresh air and the open fields, but his brother still lived in Liverpool and wouldn't swap it for farm life. 'I've also got a few pigs and chickens at the farm, and if you're out walking one day, you're more than welcome to call in and see them. It's about a twenty-minute walk from Rose Cottage, but it's a straight road and if Mrs Owen points you in the right direction you can't get lost. I've got a daughter and son about your age and they'd be tickled pink to show you around.'

'Oh, thank you,' Maddy said, thrilled to bits. 'I'd love to come.'

'You will take us, won't you, Mam?' Tess pulled on her mother's arm. 'Tell Mr Tom that you will.' Again she pulled. 'Go on, tell him.'

Tom turned around, his weatherbeaten face split into a wide grin. 'If the lass didn't have the face of an angel, I'd say she was blackmailing you.'

'There's no need for blackmail.' Ann returned his grin. 'It's a very kind offer, and as long as you're sure we won't be in the way we'll take you up on it. I would like to see the chickens and pigs myself, and I'm sure my husband would.'

George nodded enthusiastically. 'It would be a great pleasure. And I know the girls would be over the moon. The animals in their story books would come to life for them once they'd actually seen them in the flesh.'

Before turning his head back to face the road, Tom asked, 'How long are you here for?'

'Only until Friday,' George sighed. 'I wish it was longer.'

'Just three full days, then, that doesn't give you much time to see all there is to see. Why don't you come to the farm tomorrow and give yourself the other two days to see the sights? There's a few streams nearby, and a waterfall. The children mustn't go home without seeing them. But Gwen will set you right, she was born and bred in the village so there isn't a blade of grass she doesn't know. And she's a grand lady, you'll like her.'

Maddy knew she was going to like Mrs Owen, but right now she was more interested in the farm. 'What time can we come tomorrow, Mr Tom?'

'Madelaine!' Ann shook her head. Really, the man would think her children had no manners. 'Please don't be so forward.'

'Say about eleven, and I'll tell the wife and children to expect you.' Tom tightened the reins. 'We're nearly there now. Rose Cottage, Goldie.'

'Can she understand what you say?' Tess was goggle-eyed.

'Every word. And she knows the name of every house in the village and beyond. She also knows every person, and she has her likes and dislikes.' The hedgerow ended and the family got their first sight of Rose Cottage. And it was like something out of a fairy tale. It lived up to its name because there were roses of every colour in the garden and also around the door. It was seconds before anyone spoke.

'It's just like I dreamed it would be,' Maddy said. 'Isn't it lovely, Tess?'

Her sister was too overcome to answer. Her expectations of the holiday had been dimmed by the long, tiring journey. She'd felt sick in the tummy and had a headache with the pushing and shoving to get seats on the train from Liverpool to Wrexham. And when they'd stepped off the last train she'd felt so bad she wished she was back home. But the man at the station had been so nice and friendly, she'd begun to buck up. And when the horse came into view, and she was allowed to stroke it, well, her sick feeling and headache had just faded away. She still felt tired, but it was a happy tiredness. The invitation to visit the farm tomorrow, and the prospect of seeing animals she'd only seen in books, went way beyond her wildest dreams. And now, staring at the fairy-tale house, well, it was hard to believe it was all real.

Tom took the case and bags as George passed them to him, then he helped them down the narrow step. 'I hope you're all hungry, because if I know Gwen, she'll have a feast waiting for you.'

'Are you taking my name in vain, Farmer Thomas?'

At the sound of the voice, they turned as one. And there, plump arms leaning on the wooden gate, was a woman of ample proportions with a bonny face and cheeks like rosy red apples. Her smile was warm, friendly and motherly. Tess, who instinctively knew a kind and sympathetic person when she saw one, was the first to reach her. 'Hello, Mrs Owen, my name's Theresa, but my friends call me Tess.'

'Hello, sweetheart, welcome to Rose Cottage.'

Maddy was close on her sister's heels. 'I'm her big sister, Madelaine. But my friends call me Maddy.'

Gwen Owen liked what she saw, opened the gate and held her arms wide. 'Come here and give me a kiss.' The two girls were soundly kissed and gathered to a bosom that was as soft as a feather pillow and muffled their happy giggling.

Tom, the case in one hand and a bag in the other, looked on with a smile. They were a nice family and he knew they'd be well looked after by Gwen. But time was moving on and he had work to do. 'Come on, out of the way so I can put the luggage inside. I've got cows to milk and pigs to feed.'

'Listen to the man!' Gwen shook hands with George and Ann. 'Anyone would think he was overworked. Get yourself inside and take no notice of him.'

'I'll wait until he comes out,' George told her. 'I need to settle with him and he might find it embarrassing with others present.'

He was alone on the path when Tom came out chuckling. 'You'll need the appetite of a giant to eat what I've seen. Your daughters are standing in front of the table with their eyes popping. I'd stay myself but the wife would see it as an insult to her cooking and she'd come after me with a rolling pin.'

'How much do I owe you, Tom?' George pulled a handful of change from his trouser pocket. 'We all enjoyed the ride, it was a good start to the holiday.'

The farmer held up an open hand. 'I don't need paying, it was a pleasure.' He began to walk down the path, brushing aside the other man's protests. 'I'll look forward to seeing you tomorrow about eleven.'

George was still standing on the path with the coins in his hand, and a look of astonishment on his face, when he saw the back end of the trap as it was turned around in the road. And then he heard the clip-clop as Goldie started back the way they had come.

'I'm sure you can find an empty spot in your tummy for a small piece of apple pie?' Gwen held the plate aloft. 'Just a teeny-weeny piece?'

George groaned and shook his head. 'I don't remember now whether it was the porter at the station, or Tom, but one of them said that after one of your meals we'd be so full we wouldn't be able to move from the table. And whoever it was, they never said a truer word.'

With the weather being so hot, Gwen had decided on a salad for her guests. But it was not an ordinary salad like they had at home, with a few lettuce leaves, a tomato, an egg and a slice of brawn. The Welsh woman's idea of a salad was large meat plates piled with slices of beef, ham, pork and chicken. There were home-made meat pies, and home-baked crusty bread cut into inch-thick slices and tasting delicious spread liberally with real dairy butter from a local farm. And lettuce, tomatoes, beetroot, spring onions and radish added colour to the table.

'Not even a tiny piece?' Gwen asked hopefully. 'You've hardly eaten anything.'

Her husband, Mered, watched as heads were shaken and tummies rubbed. 'They've all had enough, pet, don't force it on them or they'll be sick.' He looked at George, and by way of explanation said, 'I work on a farm all day, out in the fresh air, and by the time I get home I'm famished and eat everything the wife puts before me. And she expects everyone to have as big an appetite as me.'

'We're not used to having so much food,' Ann said, 'because we couldn't afford it. I have never seen a table as heavily laden with food as this one. And everything on it is delicious, Gwen, you really did us proud. Milly said you were a good cook and you fed them well, but I never imagined anything like this. The meal I've just eaten is the best I've ever had in my whole life, and I thank you.'

'And I've eaten a lot, haven't I, Mam?' Tess really had tried to please. She'd taken everything that was offered to her, but her eyes were bigger than her tummy and much of the food was left on her plate.

'Yes, you did very well, love.'

It had only taken one look at the young girl for Gwen to realise that here was a delicate child. And the anxious eyes of the mother and father as they kept glancing at her to see if she was eating confirmed her belief. 'I'm going to watch you, sweetheart, 'cos I think you're the one who's going to eat me out of house and home.'

Tess giggled. 'No, it's Maddy you'll have to watch, she eats like a horse.'

'You cheeky thing!' Her sister gave her a playful push. 'Who is it that pinches chips off my plate when they think I'm not looking?'

'I only pinch little ones, not big ones. So I'm only a little thief, not a big one.'

George sat back in the chair feeling bloated. It was his own fault, he shouldn't have eaten so much. But he'd never tasted such fine fare and he couldn't resist. 'Would anyone object if I undid the top button of my trousers?'

Gwen's laugh was as generous as her well-padded body. 'Oh, Mered is going to love you! He always undoes the top button, but I warned him he hadn't got to do it in front of guests.'

Her husband was quite tall and well built, with receding grey hair and a face tanned from hours in the sun. 'Go on, George, let's make ourselves comfortable.'

Taking a deep breath and holding his tummy in, George quickly undid the troublesome button. 'Ooh, that's better.' He reached sideways to take his wife's hand. 'A month here, love, and I wouldn't be able to get into my clothes.'

'Oh yes you would,' Gwen told him. 'We'd have you out in the fields helping to gather in the hay. That's why Mered can eat as much as he likes and doesn't put any weight on. As fit as a fiddle and as strong as an ox, aren't you, light of my life?'

'If you say so, love.' Mered spoke quietly, but his face expressed the pleasure he felt at the compliment. 'You know I never argue with you.'

'Only since you realised you never win. I think it was the time I hit you over the head with the frying pan that convinced you it was useless to argue.'

Maddy's imagination took over. 'When he saw you were going to hit him, did he run away?'

Gwen's chubby red cheeks moved upwards to narrow her eyes. 'Ran like a bat out of hell, he did, right through the village. Everyone came outside to see what the screaming was about. Mind you, when they saw me with the frying pan they knew better than to interfere and went quietly back indoors.'

Mered was shaking with laughter and went along with the joke. 'Tell them the truth, why don't you? By the time I let you catch up with me you were so out of breath you couldn't lift the heavy frying pan. You had to give up in the end.'

Gwen's mouth turned down at the corners and she put on a sad expression. 'I made a fool of myself. A right laughing stock. It was the talk of the village for weeks and I had to hang my head in shame.'

The large hazel eyes of Tess had been moving from one to the other. 'And what happened after that?'

'Ah, well, sweetheart, I got wise, didn't I? The next time we had a row I used a lighter pan and caught up with him outside the post office. He had a big lump on his head for weeks.'

Maddy was helpless with laughter until she happened to glance at her sister and saw the open mouth and rolling eyes. 'Tess, it's only a joke! It didn't really happen, Mrs Gwen only made it up for a laugh.'

'Of course I did, sweetheart! Me and my Mered seldom have a cross word and I wouldn't hurt a hair on his head. You see, there's only the two of us. We weren't blessed with children, unfortunately, so we only have each other to love.'

Tess found this very sad and tears were quick to spring to her eyes. 'You can love me and Maddy, Mrs Gwen, we'd like that. And we'd love you back, wouldn't we, Maddy?'

Her sister put an arm across her shoulders. 'Of course we would.'

'You're a pair of sweethearts,' Gwen said, very touched. 'Me and Mered would be the happiest people in the world if we had you for our daughters. I'd offer to buy you, but I've got a feeling your mam and dad wouldn't part with you for all the money in the world. So me and my husband will have to be satisfied with our chickens. We don't get hugs and kisses from them, but they show they love us by laying plenty of eggs.'

'Ooh, have you got chickens?' Maddy waited for a nod of confirmation before asking, 'Where do you keep them?'

'In the chicken coop at the bottom of the garden. It's a wonder you didn't hear them when you went to the lavatory.'

Both sisters wriggled to the edge of their chairs. 'Would it be all right if we went to see them?' Maddy was thinking of all the things she'd be able to tell her friends when she got home. 'I promise we wouldn't frighten them.'

'It's their feeding time, so if you ask my husband nicely, he'll take you down and let you feed them.'

Their eyes alight with excitement, the girls rounded the table. 'Please, please, please, Mr Mered.' They stood each side of him and put a hand on his arms. 'We'll be ever so good.'

'I'll be happy to,' he told them, laughing. 'It will get me out of washing the dishes.'

'Don't you kid yourself, light of my life,' Gwen said. 'The dishes will be waiting for you when you get back.'

'They will not!' Ann began to stack the dirty plates. 'Me and George will do the dishes.'

'What! Guests washing dishes!' The very idea was enough to lift Gwen from her chair. 'Not on your life!'

'Well at least let me help?' Ann didn't want to seem pushy. 'I'm not used to sitting on my bottom doing nothing, I'd much rather be on the go. So you'd be doing me a favour. And George can go and see the chickens.'

The Welsh woman curled her fists and leaned on the table. 'If it got about that I'd let paying guests do the washing-up, I'd be the talk of the village. And I'd never live it down.'

'Who would know?' Ann grinned. 'I'm sure the chickens wouldn't snitch on you.'

George pushed his chair back. 'I hope your garden is a mile long, 'cos I could do with walking that dinner down.'

'It's not a mile, I'm afraid,' Mered said. 'But it's a fair size, as you must have noticed. We've got the garden you can see out of the window, with lawn, shrubs and the big swing. Then there's an orchard behind that, and the trees are laden with apples and pears at the moment. Oh, and there's a plum tree, as well, but the plums are not ripe enough for picking yet. So don't eat any of them, girls, because you'll end up with a tummy ache.'

'It sounds just what the doctor ordered.' George held his hands out to the two girls. 'Come on, let's taste the country life.'

When the two women were left alone, Gwen pointed to Ann's chair. 'Sit down again for ten minutes and relax. Once we make a start we can have the table cleared and the dishes washed before they come back.' She sat down heavily and her bonny face beamed when the wooden chair groaned its disapproval. 'One of these days this chair is going to give up on me and I'll end up on my backside. Still, I'm so well padded I wouldn't feel a thing.' When she began to shake with laughter, there came a creak from the chair to remind her it could only take so much. 'It would be the price of me if I went through the floorboards and ended up in the cellar with my legs in the air. It wouldn't be a sight for the faint-hearted, I can tell you.'

'You've got a cellar, then?'

Gwen nodded. 'A big one, and it's very clean and dry. It's a good place for storing fruit, and my jars of home-made jam. I make stacks of it in the summer when the fruit's plentiful, and it lasts through the winter months. And of course we throw all our odds and sods down there out of the way.'

'This cottage is very deceiving from the front,' Ann said. 'You wouldn't dream, standing outside, that it was so spacious.'

'Everyone gets a surprise when they come for the first time. But its size is in depth, not width. There's four bedrooms, all double like the two you and the girls have got. Then there's the front parlour, which is only used by guests. The only time I go in there is to clean it. Me and Mered feel more comfortable in this room, it's easier to keep warm in the winter with a log fire roaring up the chimney. And then there's the decent-sized kitchen with scullery off. The place is more suited to a big family, it's far too big for just me and Mered. We've talked of moving a few times to a smaller place, but we both know we'll never move because it would break his heart. You see, his parents bought Rose Cottage when they got married, and he was born upstairs in the front bedroom. And when we got wed, we lived very happily with his parents for twenty years, until, sadly, they passed away within a short time of each other. That's when I started to take in holidaymakers. It was partly to give me something to do, and partly because we needed a bit extra coming in to help pay the bills.'

'I can understand you not wanting to leave here,' Ann said. 'I know I wouldn't. It's a lovely cottage in beautiful surroundings.' She looked down at her laced hands and began to make circles with her thumbs, while wondering if she would offend if she said what was in her mind. Then she decided Gwen wasn't the type to be easily offended. 'I don't know how you can make money taking guests in. Not if the meal we've had tonight is anything to go by.'

'It's cheaper to live in the country than it is in a big city. I was going to tell you this earlier when you remarked on the amount of food on the table, but I thought it might upset the girls and I didn't want to do that. You see, being surrounded by farms, we get meat very cheaply. When a lamb or a pig is slaughtered, I can buy from the farmer for half the price I'd pay in the shops. And it's the same with potatoes and vegetables. In fact, to be truthful, most of the time I don't have to pay a penny! My hens are such good layers I have more eggs than I need and do a swap with the farmers. But I don't want you to tell your daughters about the animals being slaughtered because it would upset them and spoil their holiday.'

'It would upset Theresa, she's very tender-hearted. She's never been a strong child and we're inclined to keep anything from her that would worry her.'

'She's a lovely girl, and so is Maddy. Polite, friendly and well mannered. You're well blessed, Ann.' Gwen looked around the littered table and pulled a face. 'Better make an effort and get this lot washed and put away.' When she stood up, she cocked an ear. 'There doesn't seem to be anything wrong with Tess now, she's screaming her head off with delight. If she keeps that up, my egg quota should be double tomorrow.'

It had taken some persuasion to get Tess inside the chicken coop. When the hens came running towards the wire netting, anxious for their food and clucking their heads off, the girl got frightened and refused to follow her sister through the gate. Then, when she saw Maddy throwing food from the bucket, and the birds flocking around her, she took her father's hand. 'They're going to like Maddy more than me if I don't give them some food. Will you come in with me, Dad, please?'

Mered handed her a bucket similar to the one her sister had. 'I'll come with you as well. The birds all know me and I know every one of them by name.'

'They've got names?' Tess was stunned. 'Every one of them?'

'Come in if you don't believe me, and I'll call them over by name.' Mered held the gate open to allow George and his daughter through, then quickly closed it behind him. People thought chickens had no brains, but they certainly knew an open gate when they saw one. And he didn't fancy the job of rounding them up.

'Stand there and watch them eat out of my hand.' Mered dipped his hand in the bucket and called, 'Nelson, come on, Nelson.'

When Nelson waddled towards them, followed by half the other birds, George couldn't believe his eyes. He'd never seen such a large chicken in his life. The bird was enormous! And when Tess tightened her grip on his hand he knew she was afraid. But her fear soon turned to wonder as the bird fed from Mered's hand. 'Just look, Dad, isn't Mr Mered brave?'

'I think I'll have a try myself.' George took a handful of seed from the bucket, split it between his two hands and held them out to the birds. He was fully expecting to be bitten when he saw how quickly the birds pecked, but all he felt was the beak lightly touching his hand.

When Maddy saw what was happening she quickly moved closer to them. 'Will it be all right if I try that, Mr Mered?'

'Of course it will. Just keep your hand steady, don't pull it away quickly.'

Maddy was over the moon and her giggle had them all laughing. 'This one's very greedy, Mr Mered, what's his name?'

'It's a she, and her name's Clarissa.'

'Ooh, that's a posh name.' Maddy noticed a small bird standing by her side and making no effort to join the noisy, gobbling, pecking birds. 'Ah, this one isn't getting anything! It seems frightened of the bigger birds. Look, Tess, why don't you feed this poor hen, otherwise it'll end up getting nothing to eat.'

The words had the desired effect, as Maddy knew they would. Her sister would never let the smallest bird in the flock go hungry because it was afraid. And it was that small, quiet bird that took away all Tess's fears by feeding gently from her outstretched hand. And as the girl delved in the bucket for more seeds, her laughter rang out loud and clear. 'This one likes me, Maddy, she's made friends with me.'

'I'm afraid it's not a girl, Tess,' Mered said, his heart lifting at the sheer pleasure on her face. 'His name's Cagney, after James Cagney.'

'You mean the film star?'

'Yes. We thought if we gave him a tough name it might toughen him up.' Mered was thinking he'd never enjoyed feeding the chickens so much. 'The trouble is, we're still waiting for him to stick his chest out and pick a fight with Nelson. Still, there's time yet, he's a few months younger than the others so he's got some growing to do.'

Tess gave this information some consideration before filling her hand with seed and bending down to the bird, which was waiting patiently. 'Now see here, Cagney, you've got to begin sticking up for yourself. Don't let the others bully you. And if Nelson starts throwing his weight around, you just remind him that the last person called Nelson lost an eye. Tell him to put that in his pipe and smoke it.'

While the men roared with laughter, Maddy put her bucket down and put her arms around her sister. They clung together until the tears ran. 'Oh, Tess, that was so funny.'

'Yes, but I meant it. And if Mr Mered will let us feed them again tomorrow, I'm going to make sure Cagney gets more than the others, to fatten him up. And if I've got the nerve to go near Nelson, 'cos he's awful big, I'll tell him to leave my friend alone, otherwise he'll be losing more than an eye.'

The laughter that followed carried to the two women in the kitchen and they smiled at each other. Gwen lifted a hand from the soapy water to scratch her nose. 'Best sound in the world, that of a child laughing.'

Chapter Five

The family were finishing their breakfast when Gwen bustled in carrying a canvas shopping bag. 'I've made some sandwiches, so when you've looked around the farm and seen all the animals, you can find a nice spot somewhere and have a picnic. I've put four slices of apple pie in, well wrapped up, and a Thermos flask of tea. There's two cups on top of the Thermos, and two enamel mugs that have seen better days. But they are clean and you won't get foot and mouth disease.'

'Oh, you shouldn't have gone to all that trouble, Gwen,' Ann said. 'The breakfast we've just eaten will keep us going all day. And if we did feel peckish, we could get a cup of tea somewhere.'

'I had plenty of meat over and it was too good to feed to the chickens. It's only taken me about fifteen minutes to prepare and hasn't cost me a farthing. And on a day like this there's nothing nicer than sitting by a stream, breathing in God's fresh air with the sun shining down on you. It beats sitting in a café any day, and it costs you nowt.'

'You're going to spoil us, Gwen,' George said. 'We won't want to go home.'

As the rosy cheeks moved upwards, chubby arms were folded under a generous bosom. 'You're on your holidays, you're supposed to get spoilt. Otherwise you might just as well stay at home. I'm not having anyone leave here unless they've put a couple of pounds on in weight, it wouldn't be good for business.'

'I've already put on a couple of pounds,' Ann said, her eyes rolling to the ceiling and a hand running over her tummy. 'It's heaven help me by the time Friday comes.'

'Maddy said we'll need a carriage to ourselves on the train. And she said we'll be so fat we'll roll down our road and the neighbours won't know us.' There was merriment in Tess's eyes. 'Nita Wilkins will get her eye wiped, she won't be able to call me Skinny Links any more. And she'll be dead jealous when I tell her my dad's promised to bring us back next year.'

'That would be bragging, Theresa, and nice people don't brag. The Wilkinses went away on holiday last year, and we didn't because we couldn't afford to,' Ann told her daughter. 'But I bet Nita didn't boast about it to you.'

'Yes she did, Mam! Every time I saw her she told me how much fun they'd had paddling in the sea, and how they'd laughed themselves sick at the Punch and Judy shows they watched every day. That went on for weeks until I was fed up listening to her. So that was really bragging, wasn't it?'

'Yes, dear, it was, but that doesn't make it right.'

'No, you mustn't brag, love,' George said, his lips quivering with suppressed laughter. 'The first time you see her, just in the course of conversation, tell her about Cagney and Nelson and how you and Maddy fed them. Then the next day you could casually mention Goldie, and riding in the trap.'

Ann tutted. 'Really, George, you shouldn't encourage her to show off, it's not nice.'

Gwen was leaning on the sideboard, happy to have people in the house for company. And this was a family she'd taken to right away. She was watching Tess, and saw the frown of concentration before a wide smile creased her face. 'I know what I'll do, Mam. I won't say a word to Nita or Letty, not a word. That's if I can take Goldie, Nelson and Cagney home with me. Then I'll wait until they ask me about them. I mean, they're bound to ask 'cos you don't see a horse and two chickens in our road very often, do you? And if I answered their questions I would be being polite, not showing off.'

Maddy's imagination took over as laughter filled the room. 'I know what we can do, Tess. We can put a lead on Nelson and Cagney, and we'll walk down the road first, with Dad riding Goldie behind us. That would be good, wouldn't it? Better than Punch and Judy any day.'

'And what about me, pray?' Ann asked. 'What will I be doing?'

Maddy couldn't answer for laughing. And it was so contagious everyone joined in, even though they had no idea what was in her head. 'You'll be miles behind, Mam, struggling with the case and all the bags.'

Her mother bit on her bottom lip in an effort to keep her face straight. And with mock severity said, 'That is not very ladylike of you, Madelaine. What should happen is that I ride Goldie and your father carries the luggage.'

Tess pursed her lips and shook her head from side to side. 'That wouldn't work, Mam, 'cos how would you cock your leg over the horse?'

'She has a point there, love,' George said. 'I would willingly join my hands to make a step and push you up, but I have a vision of you going right over the horse's back and ending up on the ground.'

Gwen had long since pushed out of her mind the work she had to do. What would it matter if she just flicked a duster over everything for the one day? The work would be here when she was dead and gone. Right now she was enjoying herself, so she might as well make the most of it. 'I've got a suggestion to make. Why not put a saddle on Nelson, he's big enough?'

This brought forth gales of laughter from the two girls. 'Oh, that's good, Mrs Gwen,' Maddy said, pressing at a stitch in her side. 'That's the funniest thing yet.'

George took a hankie from his pocket to wipe his eyes. 'That's all the problems solved except one. How do we get the animals to Hanford Avenue?'

Gwen tapped a chubby finger on a chubby cheek. 'That is a big problem. You could wrap Cagney in a shawl and pretend it was a baby. But the passengers on the train might think it unusual if the baby decided to crow.'

Ann couldn't remember a time when she'd laughed so much her cheeks hurt. 'Oh dear, oh dear, oh dear! Never has a breakfast time been so enjoyable.' She smiled at the Welsh woman, whose rosy cheeks looked as though they'd been highly polished. 'I feel so at home here, as though we've known each other for years.'

'That's the way I feel, Mam!' Maddy said, surprised at her mother's words. 'I was just thinking that when you said it.'

'And me!' Tess said. 'I love being here.'

George cleared his throat. 'I'm not going to be the odd man out. So I'll say quite sincerely that I could easily spend the rest of my life here. Providing, of course, that my family were here with me.'

Praise indeed, Gwen thought as she straightened up and threw out her chest. 'You're all welcome to come whenever you like. And who knows, Ann, but that in the years to come you'll be able to say we *have* been friends for many years.'

'We've certainly been treated like friends, Gwen, and we'll definitely come again,' George told her as he cast an eye on the clock on the sideboard. 'I think we'd better make a move now. Tom said he'd tell the family we'd be there at eleven and we haven't the faintest idea where the farm is, or how long it will take us to get there.'

'Twenty minutes if you walk at a steady gait. The weather's too hot to be rushing, so take it nice and easy. I'll come and show you the road where you turn off, and you just keep on that road until you come to the Thomases' farm. It's the first farm you come to, so you can't get lost.'

George looked puzzled. 'Is his name Thomas Thomas, then?'

Gwen chuckled. 'No, his name's David. But there's quite a few people in and around the village with the surname of Thomas, and so we know who we're talking about, we call them by their jobs. Like Thomas the butcher, Thomas the postman and Thomas the farmer. There's a few more, but that was just to give you an idea. Anyway, when David's parents died years ago and he inherited the farm, he got fed up being called Thomas the farmer and started to refer to himself as Tom. The name stuck, and that's what he's called by most of us. A few of the old folk who knew his parents and grandparents still refer to him as Thomas the farmer, and they'll not change, not at their time of life.'

'You're lucky living here,' Ann told her. 'Away from the hurly-burly of city life. And away from the noise and smells. It must be paradise living in a place like this.'

'I was born and bred here, and I wouldn't want to live anywhere else on earth. But it isn't the paradise you suppose. Being a small community everybody knows everybody else's business and the gossip goes around like wildfire. If I was to sneeze now, they'd know about it on the hill farms before the sound had died down. And if I was to walk with George to show him where the pub is, they'd be out in force to make sure they didn't miss anything. I don't mind really, a bit of gossip gives us something to talk about. As long as it's not hurting anyone. But there's two old biddies in the village that make a career out of it. They're both spinsters and have lived together for as long as I can remember. Me and Mered call them the Sisters Twitter 'cos of the way they talk, and I suppose they do give us a laugh the way they act. Always at the windows, one downstairs and the other upstairs peeking from behind the curtains to make sure nothing escapes their attention. And if they're in one of the shops they'll stand at the back and let everybody else get served first so they can see what they're buying. I bet they know exactly what everyone in the village has for their meals every day, what colour bloomers the women have on, and how many blankets we've all got on our beds.'

Gwen moved away from the sideboard so the impersonation she was about to give would have a greater impact. 'This is them, as alike as two peas in a pod. Both as thin as rakes, with thin face, nose and lips. And their noses and mouths are in constant motion, even when they're not talking.' She joined her hands in front of her, moved her head from side to side in quick jerks, and, with her nose twitching, began to cluck like a chicken. And the sounds of mirth from her audience cheered her on until she couldn't keep her own laughter back any longer. 'May God forgive me for mocking the afflicted, but what makes them so hilarious is that they're so open and obvious, yet don't realise the whole village has got them decked as nosy-pokes. If two women are standing talking outside the post office, the Sisters Twitter will stand as near as possible so they can overhear every word. And if one of the women gives them a dirty look, they walk to the edge of the pavement and look down the road as though expecting a bus, even though there isn't one due for an hour. Then they shake their heads and move back to take up their position even closer to the women. And it serves them right when they overhear a juicy bit of gossip that has just been made up for their benefit. They've caused a few rows in the village between man and wife, I can tell you. But people know what they are so they're daft if they believe a word that comes out of their mouths.'

'Oh dear,' George said, dabbing his eyes, which were now red-rimmed with constant wiping. 'I must keep a look out for them.' Then he chortled. 'Where is the pub, by the way?'

'In the middle of the village, but you're going in the opposite direction this morning. You could go that way tomorrow, because it's a pretty village and well worth seeing. And there's a waterfall quite near, that's worth a visit.'

'So much to see and so little time. We'll have to make the most of what we've got.' Ann swept a hand over the cluttered table. 'I feel a bit mean leaving you with all the washing-up.'

'Don't be daft, I wouldn't let you help if you got down on your knees and begged me. You've only got three days left, so cram as much as you can into them. Now I'll just slip a coat over my pinny and put you on the right road to Tom's. And tell his wife, Brenda, that I was asking after her, and the two children.'

'This is the life, isn't it, love?' George and Ann were walking behind the two girls, who were swinging their hands between them. 'Lovely clean air, green fields all around us, and the sound of birds singing. A far cry from home.'

'Yes,' Ann said, dreamily, 'it is lovely. I can't remember a time when I've felt more relaxed. And the girls are thoroughly enjoying themselves, which is the main thing. But you have to remember we're seeing the countryside at its best. I should imagine it's pretty grim in the winter when the snow comes down.'

'People born to this life probably don't think anything of it. They're made of sterner stuff than us city folk. Certainly Gwen and Mered appear healthy on it. Mered looks as strong as an ox and he's out in all weathers, snow, rain or sunshine. I doubt if we could ever get used to it, not at our time of life.'

'Ay, not so much of the "our time of life"! You make us sound ancient!' Ann squeezed his arm and smiled up at him. 'They say you're as old as you feel, and right now I feel so young I could skip down this road.'

The two girls came running back to them, their voices high with excitement. 'This is the farm, Mam.' Maddy sounded breathless as she pointed to a house which could just be seen over the hedge. 'See, there's the house.'

'Are you sure it's the right one?'

'It must be,' George said. 'Gwen told us it was the first farm and we haven't passed any other on the road.'

Tess was pulling on his arm. 'Dad, they've got pigs, we could hear them grunting. And Goldie is in the field, we saw her.'

'Well, let's not get too excited,' Ann said, inspecting her daughters' appearance. 'Pull your socks up and tidy your hair. And remember your manners.'

The long five-barred gate was closed with a latch on the inside, and George was wondering whether he would be doing right in opening it when two young figures came flying out of the house. 'Hello, we've been waiting for you.' The young girl, who appeared to be around the same age as Maddy, had auburn hair which was tied back with a ribbon, deep brown eyes and a happy, smiling face. As she lifted the latch and pulled the gate open she said, 'My name's Grace, and this is my kid brother, Alan.'

Looking at the boy, with his fair hair, blue eyes and a cleft in his chin, it was easy to see he was Tom's son. Same colouring and same smile. 'My dad said we were to show you the animals and we weren't to play any tricks on you. Oh, and we're to offer you a drink of lemonade.'

Tess was shy and clung to her father's hand. But Maddy was in her element. 'My name's Madelaine, but I get Maddy from my friends. And this is my kid sister, Tess.'

With the gate safely closed, the children led the group towards the house. 'My mam said we were to let her know as soon as you arrived.'

Grace had no sooner got the words out than a woman appeared at the door, wiping her hands on a floral wrap-around pinny. She was tall and slim, with auburn hair, brown eyes, and a ready smile which showed a good strong set of teeth. 'Mr and Mrs Richardson? I'm Brenda Thomas and I'm very pleased to meet you. Won't you come inside?'

'You look as though you're busy, Mrs Thomas, so we won't interrupt you,' Ann said, not wanting to take the woman away from her work. 'Perhaps the children can show us around the farm and then we'll leave you in peace.'

'I'm not doing anything that can't wait, and anyway I'll be glad of a bit of company. We don't get many visitors and it's nice to hear what's happening in the world outside of Hope. Besides, I need to exercise my mouth.' Brenda stood aside and beckoned them in, patting the heads of

70

the girls as they passed. 'Which one is Maddy and which is Tess?'

'I'm Maddy, and the good-looking one is my sister, Tess.'

'Well, how would you girls like a drink of my home-made lemonade?' Brenda's husband had mentioned that one of the girls didn't look very strong, but he hadn't said anything about her being so shy. 'I made it specially for you.'

Tess raised her head. 'Yes please, that's very kind of you.'

Ann was standing on the threshold of the large kitchen, her eyes filled with wonder and delight at what she saw. The floor was stone, with the long wooden table in the centre almost white with constant use and scrubbing. One of the walls was taken up by a Welsh dresser which had a lovely array of willow-patterned plates standing behind sets of cups, saucers, plates and serving dishes. But what Ann found most eye-catching was the huge open fireplace made from slabs of stone. There was no grate; the logs set ready for lighting were criss-crossed on the stone floor, which was blackened with soot. In her mind's eye she could imagine how warm and comforting it would be with the wood crackling and sending flames roaring up the chimney. And on the iron stands either side sat a huge black kettle and a round pot which was shaped like a cauldron. 'That fireplace is amazing, Mrs Thomas, do you do all your cooking on it?'

'No, I only use it for the likes of stew, and keeping the kettle on the boil. We have a wood-burning stove in the small kitchen where I do most of my cooking and baking. I'll show you around when the children have had their drinks. And the name is Brenda, by the way.'

'This is nice, Mrs Thomas,' Tess said, sipping her drink and feeling less nervous with each passing moment. 'There's a slice of lemon floating on the top, and I don't usually like lemon 'cos it's bitter. But this is lovely.'

'I put plenty of sugar in it, pet. My children have a very sweet tooth.'

'Oh, you, Mam!' Her daughter Grace looked flabbergasted. 'It's you who has the sweet tooth, not me or Alan.'

Brenda lifted both hands as in surrender. 'Okay, I own up, I'm a sucker for sweet things. But I'm not the one who sneaks down the stairs when they think everyone is asleep, and pinches biscuits and cakes.'

'I don't do that, Mam, it's our Alan.'

The boy dropped his head to hide a cheeky grin. 'It's not me, I go to sleep as soon as my head hits the pillow. I keep telling you we have a ghost, Mam, but you won't believe me.'

'Well I think it's very queer that the ghost has exactly the same tastes as you.' Brenda saw Tess's eyes widen and gave her a quick wink. 'And I also think it's fishy that he knows when I make my apple

71

and rhubarb pies. Now how would he know that if he didn't have help from one of the family, eh?'

The boy didn't try to hide his grin this time. 'I've told you, he's got a good sense of smell. I mean, the smell of your baking carries as far as our school. And seeing as the ghost lives in our barn, he can smell it dead easy.'

'You've got a ghost living in your barn?' Tess moved closer to her father just in case it wasn't a joke. 'I wouldn't like that.'

'Oh, he's a friendly ghost. He doesn't move things around in the house like other ghosts do. He pinches some of Mam's pies and biscuits, but he never makes a mess. You won't find any crumbs on the floor, nothing like that.'

'He's friendly all right,' Brenda laughed. 'So friendly he sleeps in your bed and leaves all his crumbs there.'

'You tell fibs, Alan Thomas,' Tess said, confident now to move from the safety of her father's arm. 'But you didn't frighten me.'

'Me neither, I was wishing it was true,' Maddy said. 'I've seen haunted houses on the pictures and they're really spooky.'

'Don't believe a word Alan tells you, he's always playing jokes on people. His dad warned him about it but he might as well have been talking to the wall.' Brenda took the empty glass from her son's hand. 'Take the girls to see the animals and behave yourself. Any tricks and I'll scalp you.'

'Madelaine, you look after Theresa, please,' Ann said, fearful that Grace and Alan might not understand her younger daughter was delicate and shouldn't join in any rough games. 'Stay with her and make sure she's all right.'

'I'll look after her,' Alan said, and surprised everyone by holding out his hand. 'Come on, Tess, I'll show you the little piglets. They're only a couple of weeks old and so small they fit in my two hands.'

There was no hesitation on the girl's part. She took his hand and smiled. 'I love pigs, they're my bestest favourite animal.'

When Ann leaned forward with a protest on her lips, George touched her arm. 'Don't spoil it for her, she'll be all right. Maddy will keep an eye on her.'

Grace grabbed Maddy's hand, happy to have a girl her own age to play with. 'Come on, we'll see the pigs and then go and feed Goldie.' Their hands swinging between them, and giggling with pleasure, they ran from the room, followed closely by Alan and Tess.

Brenda noticed Ann rubbing her hands nervously, and she smiled to allay her fears. 'You don't have to worry about Alan, he's very sensible for his age. Oh, he can act daft and is always playing tricks, but there's another side to him. He's a very caring boy, as you would know if you saw how gentle he is with the animals. I've known him sit for hours trying to feed a new-born lamb from a baby's bottle if the mother has rejected it. He's got far more patience than I have. He takes after his dad for that.'

'I know I shouldn't fuss over Theresa so much, but I can't help it,' Ann said. 'She isn't strong and tires very quickly.'

'Well, if it will put your mind at rest, why don't you go and see if she's all right? I'll put the kettle on while you're out and make us a nice cup of tea.'

'No, leave her be, Ann,' George said. 'You can't be by her side for the rest of her life, she has to learn to stand on her own feet sometime. She's nearly eleven years old and will be embarrassed in front of the other children if you act as though she's not capable of looking after herself.'

Brenda could sympathise with Ann, being a mother herself and remembering how she'd walked the floor with both of hers when they were ill. 'Tom gave me strict instructions to show you around the farm, so why don't I do it now and make the tea later? Then you can see for yourselves what the children are up to.'

'Come on, love.' George put a hand under his wife's arm. 'There's no point in you standing there fretting and making me a nervous wreck into the bargain.'

Brenda was leading them around the side of the house when she suddenly put both arms out and halted them in their tracks. With a finger to her lips she whispered, 'Take a look at that happy scene. It's a sight for sore eyes.'

Ann and George popped their heads around the corner and Ann let out a low cry of pleasure. Tess was holding a tiny wriggling pig in her arms, and she looked so happy and animated it was a joy to behold. Alan was standing beside her, his own face alight and his laughter mixing with hers. And Maddy, who would never stray far from her sister, was only feet away, holding a piglet up in the air and talking baby talk to it. 'Oh, George, I wish we had a camera to capture that scene so we could look back on it whenever we wanted.'

'I've got a camera,' Brenda said, already moving away from them. 'Stay where you are until I fetch it. Don't make a sound, because if you break them up you'll never get them back as they are now.'

'You see, you were worrying for nothing, love.' George put his arm across his wife's shoulders. 'I've never seen Maddy or Tess look so happy. They're having the time of their lives, loving every minute of it.'

'I can't help the way I'm made, George.'

'I know, love, and I'd rather you cared too much than too little.'

Brenda had wasted no time and was quickly back with them. 'There's about six snaps left on the roll. I'll take one of the children now, just as they are, then you can decide what to use the others on.'

The photograph taken, they made their presence known. And the first one to see them was Maddy. 'Look, Mam, isn't this lovely? I've christened him Curly because his tail curls over.' Then she lowered her voice. 'Tess has been all right, Mam, you don't have to worry. Alan's been brilliant with her.'

'I can see that,' Ann said. 'But all mothers worry, you know. Wait until you have children of your own and you'll see.'

Tess hurried towards them with Alan so close his arm was touching hers. 'Mam, this is Pinky, 'cos it's pink all over, even its eyes.' The little pig had given up struggling and was nestling in her arms like a baby. 'Isn't he gorgeous, Dad?'

Brenda put a hand to her mouth and gave a slight cough. 'I hate to disillusion you, girls, but animals don't use a lavatory and I'd hate to see you getting those nice dresses dirty. You wouldn't smell very pleasant, either.'

Grace and Alan doubled up at the horror on the two girls' faces. Having been brought up on the farm, they were well used to the ways of animals and thought nothing of pulling on a pair of Wellington boots and walking through all sorts of slop. 'Oh, Maddy,' Grace said, taking the piglet from a pair of hands now eager to part with it. 'You should have seen your face.'

'Why didn't you warn me?' But Maddy could see the funny side. 'I still think he's lovely, but I won't be so quick to pick him up. Next time I'll sit down and play with him.'

'I wouldn't think of sitting in the sty if I were you,' Brenda laughed. 'Pigs are not noted for keeping their houses clean.'

'Come on, Tess,' Alan said, taking the girl's arm. 'Let's put him back with his mother and go and see the lambs.'

'I'll carry him,' Tess said, reluctant to part. 'You can come with me, though.'

'Can we go and see Goldie, as well as the lambs?' Maddy asked, walking back to the sty with Grace. 'I want to see if she remembers me.'

'You take the camera, George.' Brenda passed it over. 'There's five left on the film, so you might as well use them up. I'll have to get something ready for Tom, he comes home for his lunch. But you go with the children and enjoy your visit.'

The surprise appearance of the camera was a delight to Maddy and Tess. And when George told them they'd been snapped with the pigs, they were over the moon. 'Can we have one taken with the lambs, and one with Goldie?' Maddy asked. 'That would leave three, and if you won't think I'm greedy, I'd really love one with me and Tess, and Grace and Alan.'

'Me too!' Tess said, smiling at the boy, who had been really kind to her. She hadn't had much to do with boys before because they played footie and kick-the-can in the entry, and they were too rough for her liking. But Alan was really nice.

'I think that meets with everyone's approval,' Ann said. 'We can ask Mr and Mrs Thomas to come on the other two.'

'That means one of us won't be on them.' Maddy had soon figured this out. 'Someone will have to take the photograph.'

'One of the farm hands comes home with my dad for something to eat, he can take the photographs so we can all be on them.' Grace gave her brother a dig. 'You'll have to turn away from the camera, 'cos if it gets a look at your phisog it'll fall to pieces.'

Alan returned her dig. 'Hey, what about your ugly mug?'

'She didn't mean it, Alan,' said Tess the peacemaker. 'She was only pulling your leg.'

'Shall we make a move,' Ann suggested, 'and see all the things you want to see? We don't want to miss Mr Thomas.'

Grace and Alan looked at each other and burst out laughing. 'Oh, you won't miss Dad, you'll hear him a mile off. He comes home on a tractor and it makes such a noise the whole village knows when he's on his way. If you ask Mrs Owen, she'll tell you they set their clocks by him.'

'Your dad drives a tractor?' Tess was wide-eyed. She was to see another thing she'd only seen in books. Oh, the joy of it all.

'He'd give you a ride in it, if you wanted.' Alan was still standing close to her, drawn by her smile and gentleness. He'd never known anyone like her; most of the local girls were tomboys and could give back as good as they got. 'Mind you, it doesn't half shake and rattles every bone in your body.'

'Don't even think about it, Theresa,' Ann said with a very determined expression. 'You'll have had enough excitement for one day without riding on a tractor. Now, if we don't make a move you won't see all the things you want to see, and then you'll be sorry.'

'When I come back next year I'll ask your dad for a ride on his tractor,' Tess whispered to Alan as they followed her parents. 'I'll be a year older then so Mam won't worry about me so much. I'm eleven in a few weeks, so I'll be nearly twelve next summer.'

'Are you coming back next year, then?'

'Oh yes, my dad has promised. We'll have to, anyway, or we'll never see the photographs.'

'Yes you will! If you leave your address, I'll get Mam to send them to you.'

'That would be lovely. You are kind, Alan, and when we get the photographs I'll write back and thank you.'

The boy smiled and walked with a swagger. 'That would be great. And I'll be nearly thirteen when you come next year.'

They were in the field with Goldie when they heard the tractor. 'We'll stay another ten minutes,' Ann said. 'We don't want to descend on Mr Thomas before he's had time to turn around.'

'Dad's only home for half an hour 'cos it's harvest time, the busiest time of the year for him,' Grace informed them, sounding very knowledgeable. 'Him and Alfie only have a few sandwiches and a couple of cups of tea, then they're off back to the fields again.'

'He'd like to have his photograph taken though,' Alan said, with more hope than certainty. 'Even if he is in all his muck.'

'Let's make our way back then,' George said. 'We might not get another chance to see him before we leave.'

Tom was sitting at the kitchen table facing a man he introduced as Alfie. They each had a plate in front of them piled high with sandwiches, and in the centre of the table was a huge golden-brown apple pie. 'I've heard about the girls falling for the two little pigs.' The farmer grinned, his white teeth standing out against a tanned face. 'The thing is, pigs don't teach their children to use the lavatory.'

Tess digested this piece of information before saying, 'Perhaps the mother pigs weren't taught by their mothers, so you can't really blame them.'

As Tom stared into the big hazel eyes, he told himself that here was a girl who would never think ill of anyone. 'Now why didn't I think of that, Tess?'

'Because you're very busy in the fields and can't be expected to think of everything.'

Ann put her hands on her daughter's shoulders. 'Mr Thomas hasn't got long, so shall we ask if he'd be kind enough to have his photograph taken with us, and then we'll leave him in peace?'

'I'd be delighted, as long as you don't mind me looking like a tramp.'

'You don't look like a tramp,' Maddy told him. 'You look like a farmer should look.'

So with Alfie doing the honours, the two families had their photograph taken outside the farmhouse door, and another standing by the tractor. The last one was a special request from Tess.

'You can stay and have some lunch, surely?' Brenda asked. 'I've plenty of food in.'

'Thank you, you're very kind, but Mrs Owen has prepared a picnic

76

for us.' Ann pointed to the bag standing at the side of her husband's chair. 'She said there's a stream not far from the village, and a waterfall, so we'll go there for our picnic.'

Grace and Alan looked disappointed. 'There's a wood just up the road from here, and there's rabbits and squirrels galore,' Grace said. 'You'd like it, Maddy.'

'I have an idea,' Brenda said, 'if it meets with the approval of Mr and Mrs Richardson. I could prepare a picnic tomorrow and we could all go to the woods. It would make a nice change for me to get out.'

Maddy and Tess spoke in unison. 'Oh, yes, Mam, we'd love that!'

'It would be very nice indeed and I'd like nothing better,' Ann said. 'But we can't keep taking from people and giving nothing back. So perhaps I can contribute towards the food for the picnic tomorrow, Brenda?'

It was Tom who answered. 'The wife would be insulted if you insisted on that. She's got enough food in her larder right now to feed an army. If you don't eat it, the pigs will, and they really don't appreciate her cooking. Not once have they passed her a compliment, even on her delicious apple pies.'

'That's settled then,' Brenda said. 'But tell Gwen tonight, just in case she decides to make you up a picnic in the morning. Don't worry about her taking offence, because we're very good friends. She's one of the nicest people you're ever likely to meet, but don't tell her I said so in case she gets big-headed.'

'Why can't Mrs Gwen come with us tomorrow?' Tess asked. 'That would be nice, wouldn't it? I like Mrs Gwen, she doesn't half make me laugh, and we'd all be friends together having a nice time.'

'I should have thought of that,' Brenda said, fighting back a desire to hug the girl, who had pulled on her heartstrings since the minute she'd set eyes on her. 'I'll walk down later and ask her. I know she'll be pleased because like myself she doesn't have much social life.'

'There you are,' Tess beamed, 'everybody's happy now, except poor Mr Tom.' She put a hand on his arm and sounded as though she really felt for him. 'We're all sorry for you, and if we could help we would. But Mam and Dad don't know anything about being a farmer, and me and Maddy, we'd be in the way. But you have got your tractor to drive, that should make up for some of the fun you'll miss. I know I'd love to drive a tractor when I'm older.'

'And I'd love to teach you, bach, and your sister.' Tom could see there was no envy in Maddy's eyes for the attention her sister was getting, and there weren't many children who wouldn't be jealous and feel left out. She was a very special sister, was Maddy. 'We can't leave the brown-eyed beauty out.'

Maddy's giggle echoed on the stone walls. 'If I was to say the sun must have gone to your head, Mr Tom, my mam would tell me off for being forward, so I won't say it.'

Tess pulled on his arm. 'What did you call me, Mr Tom? It sounded like "bark" and I don't know why you'd call me that.'

'Not bark, Tess, but bach.' Tom repeated the word several times until the girl had got it right. 'It means "dear", or "love", in Welsh.'

'I thought you'd all be speaking in Welsh,' Maddy said. 'I was afraid we wouldn't know what you were saying.'

'We speak it sometimes when we're on our own, but never in company because it's bad manners. Anyway, with living so near the English border we hear more English than Welsh, and we've got lazy about our own language. Go into the heart of Wales, though, in the small villages, and you'll hear nothing but Welsh spoken.'

Tess could see by her mother's darting eyes she was anxious they were being a nuisance and stopping the farmer from eating his lunch, and any minute she'd be saying it was time for them to leave. And the mischief in Tess wanted to leave them with a smile on their faces. So she struck up a posh pose and said, 'Alan, bach, will you carry that bag to the gate for us, please? Thank you, bach, you are very kind.'

She didn't only leave them with a smile on their faces; she left them believing the world wasn't such a bad place after all.

Chapter Six

It was after six o'clock before Brenda found the time to go to Rose Cottage, and knowing the Richardsons would be having their meal, she went down the side of the house to the kitchen. Through the window she could see Gwen standing at the sink up to her elbows in water, and she rapped on the window. 'I know it's a bad time, so I won't hold you up.'

'Five minutes isn't going to make any difference, so sit yourself down.' Gwen reached for a towel to dry her hands. 'I'll pour you a drink, the tea's fresh, it's just been made.'

Brenda sat on the wooden kitchen chair and crossed her legs. 'I won't have a drink, you've enough to do. I only came down to ask about the picnic tomorrow. I suppose they've told you about it?'

'The girls are full of it and I got a big hug when I said I'd love to go with you. But it's quite a walk from here to the woods, Brenda, and I think young Tess would find it a bit too much. She looked worn out and as white as a sheet when they got in before, and I could see Ann was really worried. But, God love the lass, she insisted she was all right and not a bit tired. You could tell she was frightened of the picnic being cancelled.'

'My two would go mad if it was cancelled, they're really looking forward to it.' Brenda changed her mind about a cup of tea and left the chair to reach for one of the cups on the dresser. 'I'll have a drink after all. D'you mind if I pour?'

'It wouldn't make any difference if I did, you'd still go ahead.' Gwen plonked another cup down. 'You may as well do the honours for me while you're at it.'

'Where's Mered?'

'He's having his dinner in the dining room with the family. I made roast beef and Yorkshire pudding today and they're really tucking into it. I had mine earlier so I could wash the dishes as they finished with them, save them piling high out here. I've made trifle for afters, so I'll sit and have some of that with them.' Gwen tried to perch on the end of the table but her bottom slipped off. Not one to give up, she had another go. But when her bottom slipped off again and tea splashed down her

79

pinny, she gave up. 'I'm sure this table has got it in for me. But I'll beat it one of these days, when it's least expecting it.'

Brenda grinned. 'D'you think it's trying to tell you something? Like a table isn't the right place for a backside?'

'Ay, watch it, you! I'll have you know my backside is scrubbed every morning, same as the table. And I put a clean pair of knickers on every day without fail. But leaving my posterior aside for now, what about tomorrow?'

'I've come up with the solution, but don't tell the family, I want it to be a surprise. Grace and Alan can walk to the woods because it's only half the distance from our house it is from here. And I'll bring Goldie with the trap to pick the five of you up from here. How does that sound to you?'

'Brilliant, bloody brilliant! Oh, Maddy and Tess will be thrilled to bits. I won't say a word, I promise, 'cos I want to see their faces when you turn up. Me and Mered have really taken to this family, we get on so well. All the time I've been taking in visitors, we've never laughed as much as we did last night. The two girls are so funny, they had us in stitches.'

'They're lovely girls, both of them.' Brenda crossed to the sink and let her cup fall into the soapy water. 'Tess catches the eye, and the heart, with her pretty face which is so trusting and innocent. But Maddy deserves a lot of praise for the way she looks after her sister. She doesn't resent taking a back seat, and I find that very touching. I bet she's got a good head on her shoulders as well.'

Gwen nodded. 'I believe she does very well at school, always near the top of her class. She must take after her mother, 'cos Ann was a teacher before she got married. She was teaching in an infants' school when she met George and they started courting. He got called up for the army in nineteen fifteen, and apart from one leave she didn't see him again until the war was over in nineteen eighteen. They got married, she gave up teaching and Maddy was born the year after.'

Brenda's mouth gaped. 'In the name of God, do they talk a lot or are you just plain nosy?'

'Neither, my dear, it all came out in the course of conversation. Just being friendly, that's all. You wouldn't expect me to sit with my mouth closed, would you? I find it very interesting discovering how other people live. Particularly if I like the people.'

'Did you find out where George works, and how much a week he gets?'

'Sarcasm doesn't become you, Mrs Thomas.' Gwen's whole body began to shake with laughter. 'I'll find that out tonight when the children are in bed and we're having our night-time cup of cocoa.' She put a hand to her chest and waited for a few seconds to compose herself. 'Joking aside, they're a lovely family but I think they're struggling for money. Listening to the girls, this short holiday is the first they've ever had. So I intend to make it one they'll remember for a long time.'

'You're an old softie at heart, aren't you? But I'll help your cause where I can. They've only got two days left, so together we'll make them a memorable two days. And we can do it without it costing them, or us, a penny.' Brenda gave her a hug. 'You see to your guests and I'll get back home to my lot. Say eleven in the morning, that should give them time to have a leisurely breakfast. And I'll bring the picnic so you don't have to bother.'

Gwen walked behind her. 'Isn't it funny, I've got a feeling you'll be bringing apple and rhubarb pies which are almost as good as mine.'

'Go in before I clock you one, you cheeky devil.' Brenda waved as she walked down the path. 'Ta-ra, bach.'

'Ta-ra, love. Sleep well.'

'What time did Mrs Thomas say she'd be here?' Tess asked for the umpteenth time. 'Was it eleven?'

Before Gwen had time to answer, Maddy said, 'I wonder why she's coming down here? It means she's got to walk all the way back.'

'Perhaps she needs something from a shop in the village. But she'll be here any minute, she won't let you down.' Because she was listening for it, Gwen's quick ear heard the clip-clop of a horse. 'Shall we go outside and wait for her?'

The mad scramble for the door had George laughing and his wife tutting. 'Really, they'd make a holy show of us.'

Gwen stood behind them and put a hand on each of their backs. 'Out you go,' she said, pushing them forward, 'then I can lock the door behind me.'

They were halfway down the hall when they heard the shrieks. 'You'll have to have a word with them, George, they're getting . . .' Ann's words petered out when she saw the rear end of a horse outside the gate. 'That looks like Goldie!'

Gwen herded her and George on to the path before banging the front door and giving it a little push to make sure it was closed properly. And with a proud shake of her head she said, 'It *is* Goldie, we're going to the picnic in style.'

'Oh, isn't that wonderful!' Ann rushed to see her daughters already sitting on one of the side seats of the trap, and the expression on their faces was a joy to behold. 'Good morning, Brenda. This is very kind of you, it's the last thing we expected.'

'I knew about it last night.' Gwen pulled a face at Brenda as much as to say she could keep a secret as good as the next man. 'But we wanted to surprise the girls.'

'You've certainly done that, just look at them.' Ann was feeling very emotional. 'I can't tell you how much me and George appreciate what the Owen and Thomas families are doing to make sure our daughters, and ourselves of course, have a holiday they'll always remember.'

'We're doing ourselves a favour too, don't forget. Gwen and I don't often get the opportunity for a picnic, not with our men working seven days a week through the summer months. So hop on board and let's have a wonderful day out.' Brenda walked to the back door of the trap. 'One of the girls can sit in the front with me, that will give you more room.'

The girls thought their hearts would burst. To ride in the front, behind Goldie, was more than they'd ever dreamed of. But they cared for each other too much to be selfish and try to be first. It was Brenda who solved the problem. 'Maddy's the oldest so she can sit in the front until we get to our farm, which is about halfway. Then she can swap with Tess. And once we get in the country lane, I'll let you hold Goldie's reins.'

'Is Grace at the farm?' Maddy asked.

'No, she's walked on with Alan. They think nothing of walking that distance, they do it every day going to school. And we couldn't fit everyone in the trap anyway, it would be too much for the horse.'

From the moment Brenda told Goldie to 'gee-up', the day became one of excitement, magic and laughter. When they reached a grassy slope on the edge of the woods, Grace and Alan were waiting for them. And no sooner had Maddy climbed down from the trap than her hand was taken by Grace and she was led into the woods. Their voices and laughter could be heard, but it didn't tempt Tess to follow them because it looked dark and eerie and she was afraid of creepy-crawlies. Alan stayed with her, pointing out the rabbits and squirrels that darted between the trees. The grown-ups had found themselves a spot on the grassy slope and were sitting on blankets Brenda had thoughtfully brought along. They found plenty to talk about, and were quite content to laze with the sun shining down on them and listen to the sound of birds singing and the voices of the children.

After a while Maddy came from the shadow of the trees to find out why her sister hadn't followed her. 'Come on, Tess, you don't know what you're missing. There's rabbits, squirrels, birds and even hedgehogs.'

'I've seen forests on the pictures and they are full of wild animals. I don't fancy having my head bitten off by a lion.'

'This isn't a forest, Tess,' Alan said with a grin. 'It's only a small wood and you won't see any lions here.'

The girl was apprehensive, but she didn't want him to think she was a baby. 'If I come in, you won't run off and leave me on my own, will you? And if I get frightened, promise you'll bring me right out again?'

'Have I ever let you be frightened, Tess?' Maddy asked. 'If anything came near you I'd strangle it with my bare hands.'

'What if it's a snake, and it spits poison at me?'

'There's no snakes in there, Tess, I've been here hundreds of times and never seen one. And even if there was, they wouldn't be poisonous. Anyway,' Alan said stoutly, 'I'll break a branch off one of the trees and use it to protect you.'

This seemed to satisfy the girl, and she allowed herself to be led into the wood. And that afternoon, Tess's story books came to life, as though a good fairy had waved a magic wand to make everything perfect. And when they were called to join the picnic, she never stopped talking about the wonders she'd seen.

'You'll have plenty of memories to take home with you, sweetheart,' Gwen said. 'When you and Maddy are cuddled up in bed on dark winter nights, you can relive these days.'

'Oh, we will, Mrs Gwen,' Maddy said, sitting on a corner of the blanket with one of Brenda's meat pies in her hand. 'Tess is a very good story-teller, much better than me.'

'I'm not better than you,' her sister said, 'but I will be one of these days.' With a twinkle in her eye she said, 'And we won't be waiting for the dark winter nights to cuddle up in bed to relive these few days, Mrs Gwen, we'll be doing it on our first night home and all the nights after.'

'Theresa, you should be eating instead of talking,' Ann said. 'Mrs Thomas wants to leave here at four so she's home in time to get a dinner on for her husband. So eat up and then you can play for another hour or so.'

The children quickly finished off their home-made lemonade and scampered back into the woods. And Tess didn't need any coaxing now; she was first there, with Alan close behind her.

The adults were clearing away the plates and wrapping up the leftover food when Grace and Alan came back. 'Mam, it's Maddy and Tess's last day tomorrow, so can they come to the farm?' Grace asked. 'We could take them around the fields where the cows are, they didn't see them yesterday. And they could say goodbye to the pigs, and to Goldie.'

'And see the cows being milked,' Alan said. 'I bet they'd like that.'

Brenda turned her head to hide a smile. Her eleven-year-old son had fallen for a girl! Oh dear, whatever next? 'I think you'll have to ask Mr and Mrs Richardson. They may have something in mind for tomorrow.'

Two pair of eyes, one brown and one blue, fastened on Ann. 'Can they come, Mrs Richardson? Please say they can.'

'I wouldn't like to be parted from the girls for a whole day, I'd worry about them.' Ann then felt guilty because she knew the girls would love a day on the farm. But she'd never rest, wondering what they were doing. 'Besides, your mother has enough to do without two extra to look after.'

'That's no problem,' Brenda said. 'You and George are welcome to come as well. You could lend a hand if you liked. In fact, I could fit you up with Wellingtons and overalls and you could become farmers for a day. You could help feed the pigs and the sheep. And you might even like to try your hand at milking the cows. But that is only a thought, it might not appeal to you at all.'

'Oh, it does!' George was all for it. 'I'd enjoy being a farmer for a day, but I can't speak for the wife.'

To his great surprise, Ann let her head drop back and gave a throaty chuckle. 'I'd love it! If it's not too much for you, Brenda, I'd really love it.'

Grace and Alan took to their heels to tell their new-found friends the good news. 'They're happy, anyway.' There was a hint of conspiracy in the wink Brenda flashed at Gwen as she bent down to put flasks and cups into a large wicker basket. 'It won't be all fun and games, you know. It's hard work, is farming. But you'll be paid for your work with a nice lunch.'

'I'm supposed to be your friend and I'm not even getting a look-in.' Gwen flared her nostrils and feigned disgust. 'You haven't even got the decency to ask if I'd like to come so I'd have the pleasure of refusing.'

'So you don't want to come, then?'

'I can't refuse if I haven't been asked, can I?'

'Mrs Owen, would you like to come to my house tomorrow?'

The chubby face beamed. 'Now that's real nice of you, bach. And the invitation does include lunch, doesn't it?'

'You're not half pushing your luck, Gwen Owen. But the invitation will include lunch if you help me make it. And that's after you've rounded up the cows for milking.'

Gwen put on a sad expression as she glanced from Ann to George. 'She's supposed to be my best friend.' With a hand on her breast, roughly where her heart was, she said, 'I'm cut to the quick, my pride wounded.'

'You're not too wounded to give me a hand to put this stuff in the trap while Ann and George take a walk in the woods. So get cracking.'

Gwen showed more than a few inches of fleecy knickers as she scrambled to her feet. Then she stood to attention and saluted. 'Aye, aye, sir! Three bags full, sir!'

'Those pigs were dirty beggars, weren't they?' George was trying to cheer up his daughters, who were looking really down in the mouth. It was Friday morning and they were having their last breakfast at Rose Cottage. 'When I was a lad there was a woman living in our street whose house, so the neighbours said, was like a pig sty. Now I know what they meant.'

'The pigs can't help it,' Tess said, lifting her head to come to the defence of Pinky. 'I'm sure if they could walk and carry a bucket they'd keep their sty lovely and clean.'

'I'm sure they would, love. I really liked them, particularly Pinky and Curly. I enjoyed being a farmer for a day, and even if I wasn't good at it, at least I looked the part in Wellies, overall and tweed cap.'

'You did very well, Dad!' Maddy told him. 'As Mr Tom said, you can't expect to be able to milk cows on your first attempt.'

George laughed. 'I thought I was doing great and was really pleased with myself, until I saw Grace and Alan. For their age they do extremely well. With the able assistance of Mrs Owen, they'd milked the whole herd between them while I was still on the first cow.'

'I think you did all right,' Ann said. 'And I didn't hear the cow complain.'

Maddy giggled. 'That's because it had gone to sleep on its feet.'

'It wasn't asleep, it was only pretending,' Tess said. 'It kept opening its eye and winking at me.'

'I think yesterday was a lovely day,' Ann said. 'Thanks to the Owens and Thomases, who really went out of their way to make our holiday perfect. I wouldn't mind living here for good if we had the money. Peace and quiet, with plenty of good food and fresh air.'

'You wouldn't last a winter, love!' George shook his head. 'The countryside is at its very best now, but wait until the rain and snow come down, you'd soon change your mind. I know thick snow on the ground looks pretty on Christmas cards, but when you're walking knee deep in it, then that's a different story. For a holiday, though, it's beautiful.'

'Alan's going to be a farmer when he leaves school,' Tess told them. 'He can do all the jobs around the farm, even driving the tractor. I think he's very clever.'

The room door opened and Gwen bustled in. 'Any more toast wanted? Or a fresh pot of tea, perhaps?'

'No thank you,' Ann said. 'As my dear mother used to say, we've had an elegant sufficiency.'

'Are you sure? You've got a long journey in front of you.'

'Don't remind us.' Maddy pulled a face. 'We don't want to leave.'

Gwen pulled a chair out and plonked herself down. 'I might as well have a cuppa with you, seeing as I've got all day to do what I have to. I'm really going to miss you.'

'And we'll miss you.' Ann spoke with sincerity. 'But you will see us again next year, the girls will see to that.'

'Me and Maddy are going to write to you, Mrs Gwen,' Tess said. 'And to Mrs Thomas and Alan when they send the photographs. And I won't forget, 'cos you've been so kind.'

'It's been our pleasure, bach, and next time make it the full week.'

'Oh, my wife and I have had strict instructions from the girls on that subject.' George laughed. 'One full week at least, but two weeks if we can save up enough.'

'You get two weeks' holiday then, George?'

'Yes, the works closes down for the last week in July and the first week in August, same as every other factory in Liverpool.'

Gwen tapped a finger on her chin, telling herself she wasn't being nosy, just interested. And if she didn't ask, Brenda would tell her she was losing her touch. 'What sort of work do you do, George?'

'I work in a storehouse overlooking the River Mersey. It's a granary, for wheat and barley, et cetera. The grain is weighed into sacks and then loaded on to ships which come from every corner of the world. I've been there since I left school at fourteen, and although the job's quite heavy, I enjoy it. The smell of the Mersey is in my blood now and I can't imagine working anywhere else. And I've got a good boss and workmates.'

Tess scraped her chair back. 'Can I go and say goodbye to the chickens? If we leave it any longer we won't have time. Are you coming, Maddy?'

When the girls had left the room George said, 'I'll put the luggage outside the front door for when Brenda comes.'

The two girls' eyes were red-rimmed after an emotional farewell to Gwen. And there were more tears to shed when they arrived at the station and found Alan and Grace had made the journey by foot and were waiting for them. Promises to write were exchanged, Goldie was stroked and hugged, and then the ticket collector came hurrying down the lane, struggling into his porter-cum-station-master's coat. His beaming smile covered the group. 'I hope you enjoyed your holiday at Rose Cottage?' And he nodded with satisfaction when told it had been a wonderful success. 'I'd be getting on the platform now, if I were you. The train will be along any minute. Leave the luggage on the platform and I'll put it in the compartment for you when you're settled in your seats.'

'You're going to write to me, aren't you, Tess?' Alan asked, standing by her side.

'Of course I am. I always keep my promise.'

And close by, Grace was asking, 'You will come back next year, won't you? And write to me with all your news?'

Then they heard the chug-chug of the train and it was time for last farewells. Grace hugged Maddy close, promising eternal friendship, and when Alan hung back, Tess took matters into her own hands. She flung her arms around him and kissed him soundly on both cheeks. The boy went the colour of beetroot, but inside he was delighted. 'Don't forget to write,' he croaked, knowing he'd get his leg pulled by the family for weeks.

'Come on, girls,' George said, taking his wife's arm. 'The train won't wait for us.'

Brenda opened her arms wide and the girls ran into them. 'Thank you for a lovely holiday.' Maddy wasn't far from tears, and neither was her sister as they were hugged and kissed.

'It's been our pleasure having you. Take care and keep in touch.'

The porter found them an empty compartment and lifted their luggage on to the rack before stepping back on to the platform. After making sure all doors were closed, he blew his whistle and signalled to the driver with his flag. And he kept the flag waving, with Brenda and her two children standing beside him, until the train was out of sight.

The platform at Wrexham wasn't as crowded as they'd expected and there was no pushing and shoving to get on the train. They found an empty compartment and the girls settled either side of a window while George stretched out his long legs and gave a sigh of contentment. 'This is just the job. It'll be murder tomorrow with everyone finishing their holidays and making for home.'

The words were no sooner out of his mouth than they heard a commotion in the side corridor which ran the full length of the train. They couldn't see anybody, but they could hear a woman's voice shouting, 'Stop pushing, yer flaming little faggot.' Then the body that belonged to the voice came into view. All twenty stone of her. She stopped outside the door of their compartment and began to slide it open, shouting over her shoulder, 'There's plenty of room in here.'

'I spoke too soon,' George said, patting Ann's arm before quickly moving to sit next to Maddy on the seat opposite. He guessed they were in for a noisy ride.

As the woman tried to walk forward through the door, George was telling himself she was being very optimistic. Talk abut optical illusion wasn't in it. The only parts of her to make it into the compartment were her enormous bosom and tummy. So she turned sideways and, using the door to hang on to, pushed and squeezed until she was red in the face. When she finally made it she was puffing like mad, and the sweat was running down her face. Taking a deep breath, she turned, and once again using the door for support, popped her head out and bawled, 'Get those kids down here quick, Sammy, move yerself for God's sake! Pass me that bleedin' case, then see to the kids.'

Sammy could be heard muttering but he only came into view when the woman moved away from the door to put a battered case on one of the seats. He was a puny little man, half the size of his wife, with a receding hair line, a flat nose that had at some time been broken, and thin lips. 'They won't come for me, Vera, yer'll have to get them yerself.'

'Not bloody likely!' The woman flopped on to one of the seats. 'If yer think I'm going through this door again, yer've got another think coming. Go and tell them if they don't come now, I'll flatten them.'

His shoulders slumped, the man sighed before disappearing from view. They could hear the children's voices raised in protest, then Sammy reappeared pulling a young girl of about six by the ears. She was yelling in pain as she was thrown into the compartment, but she got no sympathy from her mother. 'Shut yer gob before I start on yer, yer little faggot. Where's yer sister?'

'She said to tell yer she's not coming, she likes it out there.'

'Oh, she does, does she? Well, we'll see about that.' It took three pushes before the woman made it to her feet. She eyed the door opening with misgiving and muttered under her breath, 'Stupid thing, how do they expect anyone to get through that?' Then once again she bent to pop her head out, and screech, 'Sammy, if yer don't get down here pronto with our Monica, so help me I'll bleedin' kill the pair of yer.'

Maddy and Tess were watching the proceedings with interest, and there was little George could do about it, unless they looked for another compartment. But he didn't fancy their chances of finding one that would seat them all. Ann was staring out of the window with a fixed expression on her face that said she was disgusted with the woman for using such language in front of children.

'Let go of me, our dad, or I'll kick yer.' There was the sound of struggling before Sammy came into view, this time dragging a girl by the scruff of her neck. The girl, who looked about ten, was giving him a hard time, and he winced when several of her kicks hit their target.

88

The mother, Vera, was waiting for her and delivered a stinging slap across her face. 'That'll teach yer, yer little flamer. Now sit down and keep yer gob shut.'

But the girl, Monica, was defiant. 'I want to sit by the window.' She dodged her mother's hand and stood in front of Tess. 'I want to sit there, so move.'

George saw his daughter shrink back in her seat, her eyes wide. 'I'm sorry, but that seat is taken,' he said. 'Find one of your own.'

'I want that one, and I've as much right as she has.'

There were gasps of disbelief when the girl was lifted two foot off the floor, held there for a few seconds, then flung on to one of the seats. 'Put yer bleedin' backside down there and stay put. It's the last time I take you anywhere.' The woman dusted her hands together, looked at her husband and jerked her head. 'Put that case on the rack.'

Sammy looked at the height of the rack, then at the heavy suitcase, and shook his head. 'I'll never manage that.'

'God strewth! Ye're worse than the flamin' kids! If yer can't reach, stand on one of the seats! If yer've got any brains, Sammy, which I'm beginning to doubt, I'd like to know where they are, 'cos they ain't in yer ruddy head!'

By this time George was beginning to find the whole situation comical. He knew it wasn't funny to hit young children or swear at them, but it seemed they were used to it and that was the way they lived. It would serve no purpose for his family to worry about something over which they had no control. So he got to his feet. 'I'll put the case up for you.'

'Thanks, mister!' The pat on the back he got from Vera nearly knocked him over. She didn't know her own strength. 'That's real nice of yer.'

'You're welcome.' The case now safely on the rack, George returned to his seat, hoping they could enjoy the rest of the journey in peace. But hopes don't always come true, and they certainly didn't in this case. The Webster family, because that was their name, considered him a friend now he'd done them a favour, and they talked and talked. They even offered to share their sandwiches with them, but were politely refused on the grounds the Richardsons had eaten a very hearty breakfast and weren't hungry.

In the course of the next hour, first impressions were changed somewhat. While the bad language continued, and Vera thought nothing of hitting out if one of her girls gave cheek, it was easy to see there were more hugs and kisses than there were clouts. There was plenty of love there, without doubt, and even Ann found herself warming towards them. The two girls were sitting with Maddy and Tess, sharing the view from the windows, and they were as talkative as their mother. Sammy was the quietest but had a very dry sense of humour compared to his wife's rather bawdy wit.

When the train pulled into the station, George lifted the cases down from the rack. And he laughed when Vera said, 'Your lot had better get out first, I think I'm going to have a bleedin' fight with that door again.' Her round face beamed. 'I know what ye're thinking, that it's me what's too fat, not the door what's too narrow. I won't be able to sleep tonight, thinking about the ruddy thing. That's unless my feller can do something to send me to sleep with a smile on me face.'

That was when Ann steered the girls out of the compartment, after saying goodbye. The language was bad enough, but she drew the line at rude jokes.

George was chuckling as they walked out of the station. 'Well, it certainly wasn't a dull journey, I'll say that! When I first saw and heard them, I had visions of the compartment being wrecked, but they weren't bad. Just a bit rough and ready, that's all.'

'I thought they were very funny,' Tess said, giggling. 'Like a Charlie Chase comedy.'

'There's a tram that would take us to the Vale, Ann. Shall we get it, or would you rather walk to the train station?'

'Let's get the tram, I don't feel like walking.'

'I'll leave you two girls to empty the case while I slip over and see how Mr Critchley is. With Maisie being away as well, they probably haven't had many visitors and they may need a bit of shopping.'

'Shall I put the kettle on, love?' George asked. 'You won't be long, will you?'

'No, I shouldn't be. I suppose I could leave it until tomorrow, but I'd only be thinking about them all night, worrying in case they need help and there's no one to give it.'

'You run along then. I'll help the girls unpack.'

'Anything that needs washing, throw in the dolly tub and I'll put them in to steep overnight. We've nothing in to eat, so I'll have to nip to the corner shop after I've been over the road and had a cuppa.'

'How about chips from the chippy?' George asked. 'Save you bothering.'

'Yes, that's a good idea. But wait until I get back, or they'll be cold.'

It was twenty minutes before Ann came back, and she looked worried. 'Neither of them look well, I didn't like to leave them. Freda looks worse than Arthur, but they insisted they were managing fine. I think the shock affected Freda more than we thought. Anyway, I've told them

I'll be over first thing, but if they need anything in the meantime to give a knock.'

'I'll come over with you in the morning,' George said. 'It might cheer Arthur up having a man to talk to. I've got a full week ahead of me with nothing to do, so it wouldn't hurt to sit and have a chat with him every day. A bit of company will do them both good.'

Chapter Seven

'Back to the grind, eh, Bill?' George greeted his workmate with a nod. 'It doesn't seem like two weeks since we were telling each other to enjoy our holidays, does it?'

'I don't know where the time went.' Bill Jeffrey had worked with George for over ten years now with never a cross word, and he had a lot of respect for him. The only thing they ever argued about was football, and even then they never raised their voices. Although George seldom went to a match, he supported Liverpool Football Club, while Bill was a red-hot Evertonian. 'Mind you, they say that time flies when ye're enjoying yerself.'

'And did you enjoy yourself?'

'Nothing to write home about. Yer know we weren't going away, so it was down to the shore with the kids nearly every day. They enjoyed themselves with their buckets and spades, building sand castles or burying me up to me neck, and we had a good laugh. But that bloody sand gets in everything. I told the wife she'd wasted her money putting cheese in the butties because all we could taste was the flaming sand. And I think me hair is still full of it.'

'You want to start putting a couple of coppers away each week so you can go away next year. That's what we're going to do. It's worth it to get away from it all for a few days.'

'How did your holiday in Wales go?'

'Brilliant. But it's time to start work now, so I'll tell you about it when we're having our break.' After putting on their leather aprons, the pair made their way out of the door and around to the side of the building where four other workmates were standing. One man had his head back and a hand cupping his mouth as he yelled, 'Come on, Charlie, the holidays are over now. Let's be having yer, yer lazy bugger!'

At the very top of the building there were three openings shaped like arched doorways. It was through these that the sacks of grain were lowered by rope to the men below. And it was their job to stack the sacks safely on to trolleys which would be picked up by vans and lorries for the home market, or taken to one of the ships berthed in the nearby Harrington dock. The Port of Liverpool docks were a hive of industry,

93

with ships from all over the world bringing their cargoes of meat, fruit, carpets, cotton, machinery and many other commodities. And when they left they'd be loaded with merchandise for their own country. With many ships anchored in the Mersey waiting for an empty berth, and the tide to be taken into account, the dockers worked flat out for a quick turnaround, and the river tugs, with their shrill hooters blaring, would tow the vessel safely out to sea before guiding another one in to take its place. It was always bustling and noisy, and it was the sound and smell that had captured George's heart all those years ago and which he never tired of.

A man's head appeared, looking down from the middle opening. 'Ye're bloody eager this morning, aren't yer, Joe? It's not like you to be looking for work, ye're usually skiving off somewhere having a sly fag.'

'Suit yerself, Charlie, it's no skin off my nose. But if the boss puts in an appearance, will you explain to him why there's six of us standing here like stuffed dummies?'

They could hear Charlie's loud chuckle. 'So that's where I've seen yer before! Honest to God, I've been racking me brains for years now, wondering who yer reminded me of! Now I know! I've seen yer with the other dummies in Lewis's window.'

A movement caught George's eye. 'I think we'd better move along, I can hear the wheel being cranked. Come on, Bill, duty calls.' They moved to their position below the end opening, and as he looked up a man came to stand so near the edge they could see the soles of his shoes. George's heart stood still. He was glad he was down here and not up there; he couldn't stand heights. 'I wish you'd stand further back, Vin, you've got my heart in my mouth.'

'Don't panic, George, I'm just making sure you're in place, 'cos we're ready to roll. It's back to normal, and in half an hour your holiday will be a distant memory.'

'It's a distant bloody memory now,' Bill said, stepping back with George so they could watch Vin pushing a large iron hook through the ropes tying the top of the sack. The hook was attached to a stout rope which was wound around a grooved wheel and acted as a pulley for lifting or lowering heavy weights.

'I don't know how he does it,' George said, watching with bated breath as Vin manoeuvred a sack to the very edge of the opening. 'I'm blowed if I could, I get dizzy when I look down from the steps of a ladder, never mind from that height.'

'He's being doing it for so long he thinks nothing of it.' Bill saw the sack being slowly lowered and rubbed his hands together. 'Here she comes, first of many.'

'Think of something nice and the time will go quickly.'

'Something nice, eh, George? How about Norma Shearer, is she nice enough?'

George laughed as the two men held on to the sack as it reached the ground. He pulled out the hook and signalled to Vin to take the rope back up. 'It depends on where your mind is. Me, now, my mind is on a farm in Wales and I'm milking a cow.'

'A cow!' Bill's laugh mingled with the sounds of hooters and whistles coming from the ships and tugs. 'Well, there's no accounting for taste, as my old ma used to say. So I'll do some wishful thinking about Norma Shearer, and when the break comes we'll use some of your cow's milk in our tea instead of conny-onny.'

The two men lifted the sack, one at each end, and carried it to the trolley. 'You'd be lucky to get a teaspoonful, Bill, 'cos I was flaming hopeless at it. I was hours just milking one cow.'

'I'll stick to Norma Shearer and me conny-onny, then. At least I know where I stand with them. She's well out of me reach and I can't stand bloody conny-onny! But it doesn't do any harm dreaming about what might have been, does it, George? Yer might as well die off if yer never have a dream. That's as long as the wife never finds out, like, 'cos mine hasn't got much sense of humour. If she thought I was harbouring evil thoughts about a film star I'd be in the dog house for weeks.'

The next few hours passed quickly, and before they realised the time the bell was ringing for their break. It was only a quarter of an hour break, just enough time for a breather and a drink of tea supplied by the boss and served in enamel mugs by the woman who was maid of all work – cleaner and tea lady. Her name was Lizzie Ferguson and she was a real character. With a mop of bright red frizzy hair, vivid green eyes, and a more than generous figure, she was as tough as any man. Dockers were noted for their bad language, but Lizzie could out-swear any of them. And she packed a hefty punch. She'd demonstrated this one day, when one of the men decided to confront her. His workmates had warned him, and tried to talk him out of it, but he'd laughed and said there wasn't a woman born he was frightened of. Five minutes after the words left his mouth, he was lying flat on his back nursing an eye that would be a black-and-blue shiner within the hour. And Lizzie was bending over him, hands on hips and green eyes letting out sparks, telling him if he didn't like her bleedin' tea he could do without. And all the bloke had said was that he liked to know he was drinking tea, and not hot water. But it was the way he'd said it, cocky like, showing off in front of his workmates, that had brought such a hefty punch. He'd have got off with a belt if he hadn't been so cocky. The funny thing about the whole episode was that the man suddenly acquired a liking for weak tea and a healthy respect for Lizzie.

'Here y'are, George.' The cleaner passed over the only enamel mug that didn't have any chips around the rim. She made sure he got this one every day because he was a real gent, never swore or shouted and treated her like a lady. 'How did yer holiday go, lad? Did the kids enjoy it?'

'Lizzie, it was five days of heaven. Lovely place and lovely people. A farmer's wife took some photographs so I'll bring them in to show you when they arrive. We didn't do much last week, though, one day at the park, another on the ferry to Seacombe. We've two elderly neighbours facing us, lovely couple, and they're not too well. Ann went over there every day with our next-door neighbour, Maisie, and I went with them for a chat with the old man. Maisie is convinced the old couple aren't eating enough, that's the problem, and I'm inclined to agree with her.'

'Aren't yer going to ask me if I had a nice holiday?' Bill asked. 'I don't know what George has got that I haven't, but he's certainly a blue eye.'

'I like George because he treats me with respect, which is more than can be said for the rest of yer. Pig bloody ignorant, the lot of yer.'

'Blimey! I treat yer like a lady, too! I treat you better than I treat the wife, if yer must know.' Bill was a man of thirty-five, well built, with black hair, hazel eyes and a smile that invited others to smile too. 'Mind you, I'm more frightened of you than I am of the wife. Ye're a force to be reckoned with, Lizzie.' He leaned closer and looked her straight in the eye. 'We did enjoy our holidays at Seaforth sands, and I'm beholden to yer for asking.'

'Sod off, yer silly bugger!' But a smile was hovering close to the surface. 'Did yer take a bathing cossie with yer?'

'Of course I did! It's not often I get to show off me manly figure. And I have to say, there wasn't a female who didn't glance my way.'

'That's 'cos they couldn't believe what they were seeing. I bet yer looked a right bleeding sight. A big hairy chest and legs like knots in cotton.'

'Nah, I've got muscles like Popeye.'

'Yeah, I can believe that.' Lizzie's laugh was deep and throaty. 'Yer've got a face like his as well.'

'I don't know why yer don't wear yer glasses, Lizzie, 'cos ye're not half missing the best things in life.'

'What! I don't wear no bleeding glasses!'

'That's what I'm telling yer! If yer did wear glasses, yer'd see I don't look like Popeye, more yer Cary Grant, if yer see what I mean.'

Lizzie had fetched the men's mugs on a battered tin tray, and this she now banged against her leg as she doubled up. 'I'm not the only one needing glasses, you're as blind as a bleeding bat! If yer could see proper, yer'd know I'm the spitting image of Maureen O'Sullivan.'

'Who are yer kidding, girl! Maureen O'Sullivan hasn't got no red hair, she's a brunette.'

'Bill, yer can buy glasses in Woolworth's, they're only a tanner a pair. Mug yerself to a pair and see what ye're missing. My hair's not red, yer silly bugger, it's as black as night. And if yer met me and Maureen in an entry one night, yer wouldn't be able to tell the difference between us. Same beautiful face, and slim shapely figure. She'd be better dressed than me, seeing as how film stars are filthy rich, but apart from that we'd be identical.'

Bill thought about this. 'If you're saying that anyone wearing glasses would think you look like a film star, wouldn't it be in yer own interest, like, to buy every man on the job a pair of specs?'

Lizzie heard the bell ringing and held out the tray for their empty mugs. 'You're the only one with bad eyesight. All the others know how beautiful I am.'

While George joined in the laughter, he was thinking of how Ann's face would have looked if she'd been listening to the conversation. The bad grammar would have grated on her nerves, but hearing a woman swearing would have horrified her. Still, speaking nicely didn't automatically make a person any better than others, it was what was in their hearts that really counted. And he knew that Lizzie and Bill were the salt of the earth. Best mates a man could ever have.

As soon as George saw his daughters waiting for him on the corner of the road, huge grins on their faces, he knew what was coming.

'The photographs came by the dinner-time post, Dad,' Maddy told him, slipping an arm through his. 'And they're lovely.'

Tess, linking his other arm, said, 'Yeah, they're great, Dad. You don't half look handsome on them, and so does Goldie.'

George chuckled. 'Well, I suppose I should be flattered to be put in the same category as a horse. At least Goldie wasn't an old nag.'

'I didn't mean that, Dad, you're much more handsome than Goldie.' Tess wondered how to make amends. 'Twenty times handsomer.'

George squeezed her arm. 'Don't worry, love, it's an honour to be mentioned alongside such a beautiful creature. Now, is your mother pleased with the photographs?'

'Delighted,' Maddy said. 'They made us remember what a lot of fun we had.'

Ann came into the hall to greet him and lifted her face for a kiss. 'I wanted them to wait in the house for you, but there was no holding them, they would have their own way.'

'I can't wait to see this handsome man Tess talked about.' George was laughing as he was pulled and pushed towards the living room. 'I think I should have a swill first, because I wouldn't want to dirty them. I won't be two minutes rinsing my hands.'

'Your dinner's ready,' Ann said, 'if you'd like to eat first.'

'What! And die of curiosity? No, dear, the dinner can wait.'

Five minutes later George was sitting at the table with the photographs in his hands. Ann was sitting opposite, and the girls hovering over his shoulders. The first one with his daughters and the piglets, and Grace and Alan, brought forth hoots of laughter. 'I'm sure if those pigs could talk,' George said, 'they'd be telling you to put them down.'

'And I bet they wouldn't,' Tess said. 'Pinky whispered to me on the quiet that he liked being nursed.'

The sight of Goldie, everyone's favourite, raised sounds of pleasure tinged with a hint of sadness that they weren't back in the field with her now. Her head was held high, as though she knew she was having her photograph taken and wanted to look her best. 'What a beautiful creature she is,' George murmured softly as though talking to himself. Then he came to the lambs, with Alan holding one while the girls stroked it. And he remembered the lamb had scampered off as soon as the boy released his hold on it.

Maddy squeezed his shoulder, 'Look, Dad, Alan's got his arm around our Tess. I've told her she's too young to have a boyfriend.'

'Pass them over as you finish with them, love,' Ann said. 'We've nearly worn them out looking at them, but once more won't hurt.'

George passed the four over, then found himself staring down at the Thomas family, with his own, standing outside the farmhouse door. 'My, this is a group of nice-looking people. I wonder who they are?'

Tess giggled as she leaned over him and pointed to herself. 'She's a good-looking girl.'

Ann raised her brows in a haughty expression. 'Yes, she takes after her mother.'

'Ay, I'm not having that, Dad!' Maddy said. 'I take after you and I think we're the two best-looking in the photograph.'

'I won't argue with you over that,' Ann said. 'Seeing as when I met him I thought he was the most handsome man in the whole world.'

George took his eyes from the group of smiling people standing by the tractor and looked across at his wife. Compliments and flattery coming from his wife in front of the girls were rare. He passed the snap over, saying, 'Here's another one of your handsome husband, and I thank you for the compliment.'

Ann leaned across the table. 'We're all waiting for you to look down at the last photo, to see the surprise on your face.'

He chuckled when he found himself staring into the smiling faces of Gwen and Mered. The photograph had been taken in their back garden with the fruit trees behind them. 'Oh, that's nice! I don't remember it being taken.'

'No, it was one taken last summer. Gwen gave it to Brenda and asked her to put it in with the others. She thought we might like it. There's a nice letter, as well, but would you rather have your dinner before you read it?'

'I'll read it while you're putting the dinners out.' When Ann made her way to the kitchen after passing him the letter, George motioned for his daughters to stand beside him. 'We'll read it together, eh?'

'We've read it a dozen times, Dad,' Maddy told him. 'Over and over and over.'

Tess nodded. 'I know it off by heart.'

'Oh, well, if you're tired of it, you help your mother while I sit back and enjoy reading about how our friends are keeping.'

But this was not what the girls wanted. 'We didn't mean we were tired of it, Dad,' Maddy told him, in a tone which said she didn't know how he could even think such a thing. 'We want you to read it out to us, please?'

The letter covered both sides of a single sheet of notepaper, and George read that everyone hoped they'd arrived home safely and the journey wasn't too tiring. The Thomas and Owen families were missing them very much and hoped it wouldn't be too long before they met up again. Both families were well, as were the animals, and they were looking forward to news from Liverpool. Especially Grace and Alan, who asked for the girls to write. They all sent their love, including Goldie, and very best wishes. The letter was signed by Brenda and there was a line of kisses along the bottom.

'Nice letter from nice people, eh?' George looked from one to the other. 'I think we dropped in very lucky with our choice of holiday.'

'We can thank Uncle Ken and Auntie Milly for that,' Maddy said. 'If it hadn't been for them we would never have heard of Rose Cottage, or Hope.'

'Yes, we'll take a walk down there over the weekend and tell them what a wonderful time we had. And we'll take the photographs to show them.'

Ann came in carrying two plates, which she set before the girls. 'I was thinking of that myself. But we won't go overboard on how good

99

everyone was to us, or they'll think we're showing off.'

'We don't need to tell them anything, Mam,' Maddy giggled. 'Just show them the photographs and they'll see for themselves.'

'I wanted to show them to Nita and Letty next door, but Mam wouldn't let me,' Tess said. 'Not until you'd seen them first.'

'You can show them tomorrow.' Ann walked back to the kitchen. 'As long as they don't get dirty, or torn.'

'Would you leave it until the day after?' George asked. 'I'd like to take them into work tomorrow to show Bill, and Lizzie, the woman who makes our tea.'

'You do that, love. The girls can take them next door when you get home. Now put the letter away, please, I'm bringing your dinner through.'

When Lizzie handed out the mugs the next morning she was wearing a pair of glasses. George showed surprise until she winked at him and he realised there was no glass in the steel frames. Bill was busy talking to one of the other men and didn't notice Lizzie until he turned and held out his hand for the mug.

'Who did yer say yer looked like? Cary Grant, was it?' The cleaner's mountainous bosom was shaking with laughter being held back. Cocking her head to one side she said, 'Well, if I was asked my opinion – which I never am, like, 'cos ignorant people think the only thing I've got between me ears is fresh air – but supposing I was asked, like, I'd say yer were more the Boris Karloff type. Ye're a dead ringer for him, especially with that nut and bolt sticking out of yer neck. And yer've got a face like a wet week what would frighten the living daylights out of anyone.' She huffed loudly. 'Cary Grant my bleeding backside.'

Without saying a word, Bill bent to put his mug down on the low wall. Then he whipped around and snatched the glasses from her face before she knew what was happening. 'Lend them to me for a minute.' He put them on and a slow smile crossed his face. 'Well, I'll be blowed! If it isn't Maureen O'Sullivan pretending to be Cinderella's wicked stepmother! It's a smashing make-up job. They couldn't have made yer any uglier, with yer red wig, bad teeth and cross-eyes. Yer really do look wicked, but I'm surprised at yer letting them pad yer body out like that, Maureen, yer look like a bloated whale. In fact yer remind me very much of a woman I work with. Red hair, rotten teeth, and cross-eyed. And she's got a backside as big as the back of a tram. She's got no sense of humour, either, otherwise she'd be laughing right now instead of rolling her sleeves up ready to pulverise me.'

'Nah, I'm not very good at pulverising people. I'm more yer pick-'em-up-and-throw-them-in-the-Mersey type. Or, if that doesn't appeal to yer, I can either kick yer into the middle of next week or belt yer one.'

Bill stroked his chin. 'Can I have a bit of time to consider me options, Lizzie? I mean, there's a lot at stake here. Give me till dinner time, eh?'

'Don't be trying to get out of it, Bill Jeffrey. Yer've wounded me pride now and I can't let yer get away with it 'cos I've got me reputation to consider. If I let you off, the others will all think they can take liberties and I can't be having that.' Then a thought struck Lizzie. 'Besides, I don't make yer tea at dinner time, yer make it yerself. So don't be coming it, soft lad, I wasn't born yesterday.'

When Bill bent to get his mug, he murmured, 'Yer were never born, Lizzie, yer were hatched.'

'What did you say?'

When he turned around his face was that of an innocent baby. 'I never said nothing! I was singing to meself, if yer must know. I would never talk behind yer back, Lizzie, yer know I love the bones of yer.'

George butted in. 'There's the bell now, so will you two call it a day? And by the way, Lizzie, I've brought my holiday snaps for you to see. So can yer spare five minutes at dinner time? I promise to keep the queer lad off your back.'

'Oh, don't yer take any notice of me and Bill, we understand each other. Yer see, George, there's them what I like, and there's them what I don't like. And if I didn't like you and Bill, yer'd have known about it long before now. Anyway, yer'll be sitting out here to have yer sandwiches in the sunshine, I suppose, so I'll come out then, 'cos I'd like to see yer photies. I've never had me picture took in me whole life, but I keep promising meself that one of these days I'll go to Jerome's in London Road, dressed in all me finery, and have me photie took.' She raised her brows and glanced at Bill, who was standing nearby and taking all in. 'Any sarcastic remarks to make about that, me bold laddo? Something like I'll probably break the poor man's camera?'

'I'm not saying a dickie bird, Lizzie, I'm not a glutton for punishment. Already I'm in line for being thrown in the Mersey, kicked into the middle of next week or being belted. The only thing yer haven't threatened me with is tying me to a mast and whipping the skin off me back. And how would I explain to me wife how me back came to be torn to shreds? She'd think I'd been down an entry with another woman, one what had long nails and was very passionate. I mean, she wouldn't believe I'd been tied to a mast, would she? That's something yer only see at the pictures.'

A voice from above yelled to them, and they looked up to see Vin shaking his fist. 'Have you two lazy buggers any intention of working today?'

Lizzie shouted back in a voice that any docker would be proud of, 'If yer want to shout, do it to me, 'cos I'm the one what's kept them talking.'

Vin's face was creased in a grin as he doffed his cap. 'I never argue with a woman, Lizzie, it doesn't pay. I found that out the day I got married. Sweet as honey the wife was while we were courting, but from the minute I slipped that gold band on her finger she changed into a bleeding shrew.'

'Perhaps that's because ye're a tight-fisted sod. How many children have yer got, Vin?'

'It was three at the last count. And I'll have yer know I'm not tight with money. I often buy her a slab of Cadbury's.'

'I bet yer've bought her three slabs of Cadbury's in the twelve years yer've been married. Am I right, or not?'

Vin chuckled. 'Just about, Lizzie, but how did yer know?'

'Three children, three slabs of chocolate. And I'll bet the three times yer went into a sweet shop and put yer hand in yer pocket to buy something for the little wife was nine months before each of the kids were born.' Lizzie's parting shot, as she walked away, was, 'As I said, Vin, ye're a tight-fisted sod.'

'What have you got today, George?' Bill asked, looking down into the small square tin box that had his carry-out in. 'I've got cheese and piccalilli.'

George lifted out a sandwich. 'Brawn with sliced tomato.'

'Do a swap, shall we? One of mine for one of yours?'

'Yes, that suits me. They say variety is the spice of life.'

'I wish my wife knew that. She's so predictable with me carry-out, I know what I'm getting before I open the tin. I'll lay odds on it being fish paste tomorrow, and corned beef the day after. Yer'd think she'd change them around now and again to give me a surprise.'

'I'm not a nosy person,' George said, 'but I can't help seeing that Joe does very well every day for his carry-out. Like now, he's sinking his teeth into a large meat pie which would feed my family of four, with some chips of course. And he always has a cake for afters.'

'That's because there's only the missus and him to feed. But I'd rather be in my shoes than his, and I know you wouldn't swap places with him. Losing two babies before they were two years old must have broken their hearts. It's ten years ago now, but they've never got over it. Joe said he wouldn't put his wife through it again, or himself. So under the circumstances, I'd rather have me fish paste sarnies than his meat pie with a cake to follow.'

George sighed. 'It was thoughtless of me, I should have had more sense. I agree, it must have been terrible for them. Particularly the wife, she must have been devastated.' He bit into his sandwich and was quiet for a while. Then he said, 'I can't imagine life without my two girls, I think I'd go out of my mind if I lost them.'

'Joe never spoke much about it, but living near him I know him and his wife were nearly destroyed. He told me once it was only their love for each other that kept them going.' Bill handed another sandwich over. 'Another swap, George? Yours are far more tasty than mine.'

George passed his box to him. 'Here's Lizzie, I'd better go and get the photographs out of my coat pocket. Help yourself, but make sure you leave enough for me.'

When he came back, the cleaner was sitting next to Bill on the wall. 'I don't know why you don't have your dinner break out here, Lizzie, and take advantage of the lovely weather.'

'I'm afraid red hair and sunshine don't go together, George. I've got enough freckles as it is, but if I sat out sunning meself, yer wouldn't be able to put a pin between the spots.'

He gave her the photos. 'If you'd been there with us, you'd have been as brown as a berry and no one would have known you had freckles.'

'Oh, that's nice! Are these yer two daughters?'

'Yes, the tall one with the dark hair is Maddy, and the other is Tess. They really had a wonderful time. If I'd been able to afford it we would have stayed the whole fortnight.'

'Don't be looking over me bleeding shoulder, Bill, wait yer turn. I can't abide anyone breathing down me flaming neck.'

'Well don't take all day about it, I'd like a dekko before the bell goes.'

But Lizzie took her time, studying each photo with care and wanting to know who was who. 'Yer seem to have enjoyed yerselves all right.' She had another quick look, then passed them to Bill. 'I wouldn't mind a holiday like that meself. Trouble is, my feller won't go anywhere where he can't be back for his pint in the corner pub. I'll swear if he had to choose between the pub and me, I'd be the loser.'

'Ay, these are good,' Bill said. 'Who's this?'

'Gwen and Mered Owen, where we stayed. And the others are Tom the farmer, and his wife and children. And of course the animals are theirs.'

'I'm glad yer had a nice time,' Lizzie said. 'Next year can yer put me in yer case and take me with yer.' She stood up and smoothed down the front of her overall. 'I'll get back now 'cos I'd like another cuppa before the bell goes. Thanks for bringing yer photies in, George, I'll tell my feller about them tonight. Not that it'll make any difference, he's got a one-track mind and it only goes as far as the pub.'

'If you've seen them all, Bill, I'll have them back to put in my coat pocket,' George said when Lizzie had left. 'The wife will go mad if there's a mark on them.'

The bell was going as he made his way back. 'Just in time,' he said, packing his tin box into a canvas bag. 'I'll leave this here for now and put it with my coat later.'

The first sack was lowered and the afternoon started the same as any other. George and Bill chatted as they worked, and up above, Vin kept up a conversation with his mate Greg, who operated the pulley. The four men had worked together for years and enjoyed a good relationship.

'Are yer going for a pint tonight?' Greg asked, as Vin pushed the iron hook through the rope tying a sack. 'I'll meet yer in the pub if yer are.'

'Yeah, okay, but only one pint, mind, I'm not exactly flushed.' Vin pushed the sack to the edge of the opening with his knee and raised his hand to signal it was ready to be lowered. He watched the sack fall away from the building, and in a split second saw the ropes were slipping. He looked down to where George and Bill were facing each other, talking, and yelled at the top of his voice, 'Move! For God's sake, get out of the way!'

Bill was the first to see the sack slipping to one side and he grabbed hold of George's arms and pulled him forward. But the sack had worked loose, and being so heavy it dropped right down like a ton of bricks and fell on the lower part of George's back, felling him, screaming, to the ground. Bill closed his eyes for a second, in horror, then dropped to his knees beside his mate, who had stopped screaming and was lying unconscious with the sack still on his back, spilling its grain over the inert form and on to the ground. 'Oh my God!' Bill was feeling for a pulse when the other men crowded around, and Vin and Greg appeared, ashen-faced.

'Is he breathing?' Vin asked, the whole scene running through his mind over and over. He wasn't to blame because he didn't tie the sacks, but somehow he felt responsible. 'Should we take the sack off him and turn him over?'

'I can feel a pulse, but I don't think we should touch him. For all we know he might have broken his back.'

Lizzie came running and elbowed the men out of her way. She got down on her knees, slipped a hand under George's chest and felt for a heartbeat. 'Go and get the boss! Don't stand there like gormless idiots, as though ye're expecting him to get up and walk, 'cos he ain't! One of yer run to the office, tell Mr Fisher what's happened and say I said it's urgent and he should ring for an ambulance right away.'

'George is going to be all right, isn't he, Lizzie?' Bill felt sick in his tummy. If he'd acted a second sooner he'd have had his mate clear.

'I'm not a doctor, Bill, so I can't say. His heartbeat is strong, so I don't think he's going to die. But yer don't need to be a doctor to know that bleeding sack is a dead weight, and yer don't have one of those fall on yer without doing any damage.' She wiped a tear away before anyone could see it. 'To think it's not half an hour ago he was showing us his holiday photies. Please God things are not as bad as I think they are.'

All work had stopped and the men were milling around, white-faced and silent. They would have done anything to help George, but were helpless.

Mr Fisher came running, took one look at the still figure sprawled on the ground, and told them, 'The ambulance is on its way, it should be here any minute. I'll go to the hospital with George and find out as much as I can about his injuries. If they're keeping him in, which is more than likely, I'll let you know and ask one of you to inform his family. And when we've all got over the shock, and our nerves are settled, I'll be asking questions about how this could happen.'

'I can't go straight back to work, Mr Fisher,' Vin said, mopping his brow. 'I keep seeing the rope slipping and the sack falling to where George and Bill were standing. I couldn't do a thing to stop it 'cos it happened so quick. But I'll tell yer, me nerves are shattered.'

'Mine too!' Bill felt physically sick. 'I was pulling George out of the way, and in another second I'd have had him clear. But that bloody sack came down so fast I didn't have that extra second.'

The boss looked around the faces of the men. 'I'll ask Lizzie to make you a drink and you can sit and calm down for an hour. Anyone who feels they can't carry on after that hour can go home and they will not have their pay docked.'

'I don't think any of us will go home until you come back from the hospital and we find out how George is,' Joe said. 'I wouldn't sleep tonight if I didn't know.'

'The ambulance is here, Mr Fisher.' Lizzie started to push the men back. 'Give the ambulance men room to move.' When George was being carried out on a stretcher, she touched the boss's arm. 'When yer get back, and we know what's what, I'll go and see his wife. Better for a woman to tell her than a man.'

105

Chapter Eight

'Will you clear the table, girls, your father will be home any time.' Ann was drying her hands as she came through from the kitchen. She smiled when she saw the concentration on Tess's face as she was about to flip a tiddlywink into an egg cup. And to prove how hard she was concentrating, her tongue was peeping out of the side of her mouth. 'Put the game away and get the tablecloth and cutlery ready.'

Tess flipped the red tiddlywink and held her breath until she saw it sail straight into the small cup. Then she grinned. 'I'm winning, Mam, by three games to two. And I really did win, didn't I, Maddy? You didn't let me win on purpose, did you?'

'Not likely I didn't!' Maddy began to pick up the small coloured counters. 'You're getting too good to do you any favours. If I could beat you, I would!'

There came a knock on the door and Ann glanced at the clock. 'It's time for your father, but if it was him he'd use his key.'

'I'll go, Mam, shall I?' Maddy offered, placing the lid back on the box. 'It might only be Nita from next door.'

'No, I'll go, you and Theresa see to the table.' Ann threw the towel back on to the drainboard in the kitchen and was smoothing her hair down as she walked along the hall. The woman facing her when she opened the door was a complete stranger and Ann thought someone had the wrong address. 'Yes, can I help you?'

Lizzie's heart was beating fifteen to the dozen. She wasn't looking forward to this, but it had to be done. 'Are you Mrs Richardson?'

'Yes, that's my name. But I don't think I know you.'

'I work with yer husband, George. My name is Lizzie Ferguson.'

Ann looked at the bright red hair and grinned. 'I might have known, George often . . .' Her words petered out as her brain asked what this woman was doing here when George was due any minute. Then she noticed there was no smile, only a look of fear, or was it sadness, in the green eyes. There was something very wrong here. 'What have you come for? Something has happened to George, hasn't it?'

'There was an accident at work, Mrs Richardson, yer husband's in hospital.'

'Oh, dear God!' Ann let out a cry and fell back on to the front door, sending it crashing against the wall. The noise brought her two daughters running.

'What is it, Mam?' Maddy looked at the woman standing on the bottom step, then at the white face of her mother. 'Mam, what's happened?'

Ann was in a state of shock, her mouth was working but no sound would come. The girls had never seen their mother like this, she was always calm and collected. So they knew something dreadful must have happened and clung to her, asking tearfully what was wrong.

Lizzie moved from one foot to the other, not knowing quite what to do. It was no good standing on a doorstep, passing on distressing news to a woman who looked in a state of shock, and two young frightened girls. She couldn't just blurt it out in a matter-of-fact voice and then leave them. 'Don't think I'm being hardfaced, but I do think it would be better if yer let me come in.'

Ann took a deep breath, held it for a while then let it out slowly. She looked at the scared faces of her two daughters and told herself that for their sake she had to pull herself together. Moving away from the door, she said, 'Come in, Mrs Ferguson.'

Tess was shaking inside. 'What's the matter, Mam?'

'Go inside, Theresa, you're blocking Mrs Ferguson's way.'

'But what has the lady come for? And where is my dad?'

'I'm afraid your father has been involved in an accident at work, and the lady has come to tell us. I don't know any more than that, Theresa, and I won't do until you let Mrs Ferguson in. So be a good girl and go into the living room with Madelaine.'

'Come on, Tess.' Maddy put her arm across her sister's shoulders. She was afraid herself, but never would she transfer that fear to her sister. 'I'm sure Dad is going to be all right.'

Ann was clasping and unclasping her hands as she watched the woman take a seat on the couch. 'What happened, Mrs Ferguson, and where is George?'

'The name's Lizzie, queen, and I'm a bundle of nerves meself 'cos I've worked with yer husband for many years and I've got very fond of him. It was a sack that was being lowered, and the ropes tying it up must have worked loose and it fell from the top of the building and caught George on the bottom of his back. It all happened so quick, the man who works on top, Vin, only had time to shout a warning when he saw the ropes working loose. George's mate, Bill, grabbed your husband's arms to pull him out of the way, and in another second he would have been clear. But the sack landed about here,' Lizzie put a hand to the bottom of her spine, 'and it knocked him out.'

'Where is George now?'

'In Walton Hospital. The boss, Mr Fisher, sent for an ambulance right away, and he went with George to the hospital.'

Tess wouldn't be held back by Maddy. She ran to stand beside her mother, tears rolling down her cheeks. 'My dad isn't dead, is he, Mrs Lizzie?'

'No, queen, yer dad isn't dead. And he's not going to die either, yer have me word on that. But he has been injured and they're keeping him in hospital.'

'Did the hospital tell Mr Fisher what injuries he has?' Ann asked. 'Are they serious?'

'They couldn't say at this stage. Mr Fisher waited and saw one of the doctors, but he said it was too early to tell. George is conscious now, and they've given him something to ease the pain, but that's all I can tell yer. Oh, except he asked that you and the girls be told he was going to be all right and ye're not to worry.'

Ann rubbed her forehead. 'I'm going to the hospital now, I've got to see him for myself. Madelaine, the dinner is ready for putting out, so will you and Theresa see to yourselves?'

'I want to come with you!' Tess clung to her mother's arm. 'I want to see my dad and tell him I'm sorry he's been hurt and I love him.'

'Children are not allowed in, queen,' Lizzie said, a large lump in her throat. 'I'll stay with yer till yer mam gets back, if that's all right with you, Mrs Richardson?'

'I can't ask you to do that! You've been very good coming out of your way as it is, and you must have a family to see to.'

'There's only me husband and me now. We've got one daughter but she got married and flew the nest last year. I've asked one of the men from work to give a knock and tell my feller I might be late, save him worrying.'

Ann looked relieved. 'As long as you don't mind, I'll be more than grateful. I'd be worried sick leaving the girls on their own when they're so upset.'

'They'll be fine with me, I'll make sure they have their dinner and a drink. We'll get on like a house on fire, you'll see.'

Tess went to sit on the couch and touched Lizzie's hand. 'You're very kind, Mrs Lizzie, and we'll be good for you. Won't we, Maddy?'

'Of course we will.' Maddy wished she could cry her sadness away, as her sister did. But she was the oldest and it was up to her to be strong at a time like this. 'As soon as Mam leaves we'll make Mrs Ferguson a cup of tea.'

'D'yer know, I rather like being called Mrs Lizzie. So if it's all the same to you, Maddy, can we stick to that?'

Ann came back from the hall pulling her coat on. 'I don't know how long I'll be, but if it gets late, Lizzie, you make your way home. The girls know they can knock next door in case of an emergency.'

'George hadn't been put into a ward when Mr Fisher left, so go straight to the reception desk, queen, and make enquiries there. Otherwise, it's such a ruddy big place yer could get lost wandering around. And they're very strict. They won't let yer stay after visiting time, even if yer've only had ten minutes with him. I'll hang on and wait 'cos I want to know how he is meself so I can tell them all at work tomorrow. And don't forget to tell him all his mates send their best wishes and they want to see him back at his job as soon as possible.'

Ann stepped off the tram outside Walton Hospital and began the walk up the long path. Her nerves were shattered, not knowing what she was going to find. And the old building looked so forbidding it didn't help when she was trying to convince herself that George wouldn't be as bad as she was thinking. One part of her mind was telling her they'd only kept him in hospital for observation and he'd be discharged the next day. While another part was saying they wouldn't have taken him to hospital in the first place unless they'd thought it was serious.

Even though it was a warm summer evening, Ann was shivering as she passed through the main door of the hospital. There were several people there, some standing talking and others coming and going through the double doors facing. Everyone seemed to know where they were going except for her. She looked around and saw an arched window with a glass front which looked like an office. Moving towards it, she could see a handle which would open the lower half of the window from the inside. There was a woman sitting behind a desk which was littered with papers and files, and after a slight hesitation Ann rapped lightly on the glass. The woman looked up for a second, then finished what she was writing before coming to the window. 'Can I help you?'

Ann cleared her throat. 'I don't quite know where to go. My husband was injured at work this afternoon and was brought in here by ambulance. But I don't know which ward he's in or who could tell me. Perhaps you can help me?'

'What time was he brought in?'

'I'm sorry, I don't know. I was told it happened just after their dinner break, so it would be any time after one o'clock.'

Although it wasn't part of the clerk's job, she felt sorry for the poor woman, who looked scared to death. 'I don't deal with admissions, dear, but if you'd like to give me your husband's name I'll see if I can find out anything for you. Please go through those double doors, take a seat in the corridor and I'll come to you as soon as possible.'

As she walked through the doors Ann felt her tummy tightening into knots. It was the strong smell of disinfectant that reminded her she was in a hospital, and hospitals were places they brought people who were sick or dying. But George isn't going to die, he's just been injured, she told herself, so don't be so morbid.

It was ten minutes before the clerk appeared, and she seemed pleased that she'd been able to locate Mr Richardson. 'If you go up that flight of stairs and turn to the left, your husband is in the first ward you come to. But you mustn't go into the ward without first talking to the matron or a sister. Just stand outside the ward and someone will come to you.'

'Thank you, you've been very kind.' Her legs feeling like lead, Ann used the banister to pull herself up the stairs. She was still in a state of shock and couldn't stop herself from shaking. And the smell and the atmosphere were causing her to feel faint. She found the ward and stood outside, as the clerk had said. Visiting time hadn't started, so there weren't many people about. But she could see the nurses moving quietly from bed to bed plumping pillows and straightening sheets, and she wondered which bed George was in.

'Can I help you?' A nurse appeared from nowhere. 'It is not yet visiting time, you really shouldn't be here.'

Ann's mouth was as dry as sawdust and her voice came out husky. 'My husband was injured in an accident at work and was brought to this hospital. I've been told he's in this ward.'

'What's his name, dear?' When Ann told her, the nurse nodded. 'Yes, he's not long been admitted to the ward. But I'll take you along to see Matron, she'll want to have a talk to you before you see your husband.' With brisk steps she led the way down the corridor, their heels the only sound breaking the silence.

The nurse came to a halt outside an open door, rapped lightly and waited to be told to enter. She told Ann to wait, and although her voice was low her words could be heard as she explained that Mrs Richardson was outside and did Matron want a word with her before she saw her husband. Then she stepped outside the room and motioned for Ann to enter. 'I'll take you to your husband when Matron has spoken to you.'

The matron was sitting, but she appeared to be small of stature, with black hair swept neatly under the white pleated cap, a healthy complexion and a no-nonsense attitude. Certainly not a woman to cross swords with. Ann guessed she would be in her late forties.

'Mrs Richardson, I was here when your husband was brought in today. He was in great pain, but the doctor has given him something to ease it. He has injured his back, but it is far too early to say how serious the damage is. Perhaps in a few days we'll know the extent of his

111

injuries, but at present we really can't tell you anything.'

'He hasn't broken his back, has he, Matron?'

Jean Tuffnell had been in nursing since she was seventeen years of age. It was the only work she'd ever wanted to do and it was her whole life. Her dedication and ability had brought her up to the rank of matron, and she was good at her job. Even though the nurses were in awe of her, they had great respect for the woman they said had more knowledge than many of the doctors. 'He has been seen by two specialists, but the damaged area is too bruised and swollen for them to give a true prognosis. However, they're pretty certain your husband's back has not been broken. Badly damaged, yes, but not broken.'

The matron shuffled some papers on the desk, a sign that she had work to do and the interview was terminated. 'That's all I can tell you for now, but come and see me if you have any problems. And although I know it's natural for you to be worried, try not to let it show. A smile works wonders when someone isn't feeling on top of the world, and if Mr Richardson sees you looking cheerful it will do him more good than any medicine we can give him.'

'Thank you, Matron.' Ann left the office feeling a little bit better. At least George wasn't at death's door and that was all that worried her. No matter what was wrong with him, she would take care of him. They could overcome anything, as long as they were together.

There was a group of people waiting outside the closed doors of the ward, shuffling their feet, eager to see their loved ones. The hospital rules were very strict about visiting times and the doors would not be opened until the exact minute. This was to give the nurses time to make the patients comfortable and straighten sheets and covers.

There was a surge forward as the doors were opened and Ann saw the visitors go off in different directions, straight to the bed of the person they were visiting. It was a long ward, with about ten beds either side, some with the screens around, and not knowing where George was, she felt a little apprehensive. But the nurse she'd spoken to earlier spotted her and came over.

'Mr Richardson is in the fourth bed on the right, I'll take you to him. You may find him very drowsy, because he's been sedated to ease the pain.'

Ann stood at the side of the bed and all the love she had for her husband welled up within her. He was lying flat, except for a pillow under his head, his arms were by his sides on the top of the bed cover, and his eyes were closed. Her hand went out to touch him, but she drew back for fear of wakening him.

The nurse saw the movement and smiled. 'It's all right, I'll tell him you're here.' She placed a hand on George's forehead and gently stroked his hair. 'Mr Richardson, you have a visitor. Your wife has come to see you.'

His eyelids flickered as he focused on the nurse, then he turned his head, saw Ann and a faint smile crossed his face. 'Hello, love.' His hand came towards her and she held it between hers, stroking it with her thumbs. 'Bit of an accident, but I'll be up and about in no time.' His voice was a whisper, and he grimaced as a spasm of pain gripped him.

There was a table in the centre of the ward, and the many vases of flowers on top helped relieve the heavy atmosphere. There were a few chairs beside it, and the nurse fetched one and placed it behind Ann. 'You may as well sit down, Mrs Richardson. Visiting is half an hour and the bell will go when the time is up.'

Ann waited until the nurse had left, then pushed the chair as near to the bed as she could. Before sitting down, she bent to kiss her husband on the forehead, then on the lips. 'What am I going to do with you? You're not safe to be let out on your own.' She kept her voice light, but her heart was heavy. 'You certainly frightened the life out of me. I opened the front door thinking you'd forgotten to take your key, and there was this strange woman standing there.' These weren't the sort of things you talked about to someone lying in a hospital bed in agony. But it was the only way she could cope without bursting into tears. 'It was your friend from work, Lizzie, and she kindly offered to stay with the children while I came to see you. She gave me a message for you from herself and all your workmates. They send their best wishes and expect to see you back at work soon. And of course Madelaine and Theresa send you their love and a million kisses.'

'Tell them I'll give two million back, and I'll soon be home to deliver them. I'm glad it was Lizzie who came to see you, she's a good woman is Lizzie. A bit rough and ready, but a heart of gold.'

Ann could see her husband was having difficulty keeping his eyes open. The desire to hold him in her arms and comfort him was like an ache in her heart. But she remembered the words of the matron and tried not to sound unhappy or worried. 'Lizzie told me what happened, love, it must have been terrible for you. I was out of my mind on the way here, not knowing what to expect. But I feel heaps better after seeing Matron.'

George opened his eyes on hearing this. 'What did Matron say? They haven't told me anything yet.'

'They don't know much themselves, love, they haven't had time to do tests on you. And you know what doctors are like, they won't commit themselves. You also know what I'm like, always looking on the black side and expecting the worst. I was afraid you'd broken your back, but

113

Matron set my mind at rest on that score.'

'I thought I had broken my back, love, I was in agony. In fact I passed out with the pain. But although I was half doped, I heard the doctors talking between themselves and they said the sack had landed on the bottom of my spine and the bones were either cracked or broken. They won't know definitely for a few days.' George was slurring his words and kept stopping in the middle of a sentence, his eyelids drooping. Now he said, 'I'm sorry, love, but I can't keep my eyes open. But don't go, please, just hold my hand and I'll know you're here, even if my eyes are closed.'

So for the rest of the visit, Ann sat beside the bed holding her husband's hand. Now and again he grimaced, and she knew he was in pain. If she could, she would have taken some of the pain from him. It was the bell ringing which brought George out of a fitful sleep. And his first thought was for her. 'I'm sorry, love, leaving you sitting there after coming all this way. I'll be better tomorrow, I promise.'

Ann could see the visitors at the nearby beds saying their farewells, and she pushed her chair back before leaning her fists on the side of the bed. 'George, I'd sit here all night if they'd let me, and I wouldn't care if you never opened your mouth. Just being near you would be enough for me. I love you, sweetheart, you know that. And I'm going to miss you like hell. And so will the girls. They're upset that they're too young to come in and see you.'

'I won't be in for long, Ann, perhaps just a week. So tell the girls I love them very much, as I do their mother, and I'll be back home with my family soon.' He raised his hand to stroke her cheek. 'Don't worry your head, everything is going to be all right.'

She bent to kiss him. 'I love you, and I'll see you tomorrow.' Then she left the side of the bed so he couldn't see the tears. This would be the first night since they'd got married that they would be sleeping apart.

Ann was hardly through the front door before the two girls were upon her. 'How's my dad?' Tess asked. 'When's he coming home?'

Maddy's first question was, 'Is Dad going to be all right?'

'Will you let me in first, then I'll tell you all there is to tell.' Ann could see Lizzie standing on the threshold of the living room door and she shrugged her shoulders. 'As soon as these two let me breathe, Lizzie, I'll be able to tell you how George is and then you can get home to your husband. He must be calling me for everything.'

'No, my feller won't mind, he's very easy-going.' This was true; her husband, Norman, *was* easy-going, but only up to a point. And the point was reached when his dinner was so late his mate was a pint up on him when he got to the pub. 'Come on, girls, let yer mam in so she can tell me how yer dad is, and then I'll leave yer in peace.'

'Mrs Lizzie's known my dad for years, and she really likes him,' Tess said, hanging on to her mother's arm when they reached the living room. 'She's been making us laugh, and she can't half play tiddly-winks.'

'All right, Theresa, calm down, love. I know we've all had a shock and our nerves are gone, but if you'll sit down and listen, you might feel better when you've heard what I've got to say. I'll speak to Lizzie because she'll be wanting to get home, but you and Madelaine can listen and that will kill two birds with one stone. Not that it will stop you asking me questions all night, I know that, but at least Lizzie will be home with her family.'

Maddy pulled her sister down to sit next to her on the couch. 'Be quiet, Tess, I want to know how Dad is.'

'Well, he's a bit poorly right now, which is what you can expect with the accident only happening a few hours ago. He was in a lot of pain, but the doctors have given him something to ease it.' Ann was looking at Lizzie as she spoke, and she tried to send a message with her eyes that would tell the woman she was making light of things for the sake of the children. 'He told me to thank you for coming to tell me, Lizzie, and for staying here so I could go to the hospital. And he sends you and his workmates his best wishes. He reckons he'll be home in a week, but I wouldn't be too sure about that.'

'That would be expecting too much, I think,' Lizzie said, her mind flashing back to the screams she could hear coming from George even though she'd been well away from the scene. And with him being in such pain he passed out. He'd still been unconscious when he was put in the ambulance. But she wasn't going to tell his family that. 'I'll love yer and leave yer now, but I'd like to come with yer one night to see George, if yer wouldn't mind?'

'I'd be glad of your company, Lizzie, and I'm sure George would like to see you. But I think it would be advisable to wait for a few days until he's had all the tests done. He was heavily sedated tonight and very drowsy, not really up to visitors.'

'That's understandable. I mean, he's not going to feel good after what happened to him, yer couldn't expect it. But I'll come and keep the girls company tomorrow night while you go to the hospital, if yer like? I could go home first, give my feller his dinner and be here for seven o'clock. That would give you plenty of time to get to the hospital.'

'I couldn't possibly ask that of you, not after you've done a day's work!'

'Don't worry about me, queen, I'm used to being on the go. Anyway, I can ask Mr Fisher to let me go half an hour early, he won't mind.'

'Go on, Mam, say she can, please?' Tess begged. 'It was nice having Mrs Lizzie here, keeping us company and making us laugh, wasn't it, Maddy?'

'Yes it was,' Maddy agreed. 'But we're not babies any more, Tess, and we can look after ourselves. It's too much for Mrs Lizzie, doing a day's work, dashing home to see to her husband and then coming here. It wouldn't be fair, not when we're capable of looking after ourselves.'

'I'd like to come, queen! Don't forget, while I'm keeping you company, you're keeping me company! My feller goes to the pub every night for a pint, so he won't even miss me. I'd only be sitting on me own talking to meself and the flowers on the wallpaper. And they can lock yer up for that, yer know.'

Tess giggled. 'You don't talk to the flowers on the wallpaper, do you?'

'I certainly do!' Lizzie had to keep reminding herself that swear words weren't allowed in this house. 'And I'll tell yer something else, queen, I get more sense out of those flowers than I do out of me husband. There's one rose, it's on the wall just above the sideboard, and I'll swear it went to a high school, 'cos some of the words it comes out with I've never heard in all me born days.'

If someone had told Ann half an hour ago that she would smile before the day was over, she would have told them they were mad. But it was hard not to smile at the red-headed woman, who was, as George had said, rough and ready. He'd also said she had a heart of gold, and that was becoming very obvious. 'If you're sure you don't mind, Lizzie, I would be very grateful. One of these days I might be able to repay your kindness by doing something to help you.'

'Oh, I'm past help, queen.' Lizzie was sitting on one of the wooden dining chairs, and using the table as a lever, she pushed herself up. With a beaming smile she chuckled, 'My feller said I was past redemption years ago. And d'yer know what? I had to buy a dictionary to find out what redemption meant, 'cos I hadn't a clue. Even the flaming rose didn't know, and that's unusual, because it's a clever so-and-so. So it cost me tuppence for a dictionary, just to find out I was a hopeless case.' She reached down for her handbag, which was resting against the leg of the table. 'My feller had a headache for a week, which served him right.'

'Why would your husband have a headache because you bought a dictionary?' Maddy asked. 'Was it because you made him give you the tuppence you'd paid for it?'

116

'No, queen, it was because I hit him over the head with the poker.'
When the two girls clung to each other, laughing, Lizzie added, 'Mind
you, it was a case of cutting me nose off to spite me face, 'cos I bent
the ruddy poker!' She winked at Ann. 'Show me out, queen, I'll be
on me way.' It was as she was putting the handle of her bag in the
crook of her arm that she remembered. 'Oh, ye gods and little fishes!
I'd forget me ruddy head if it was loose! I've got yer photies, queen!
George's coat was taken to the hospital with him, but I whipped these
out in case they got mislaid. He was so proud of them, I wouldn't
like them to get lost.'

'Thank you.' Ann took them from her. 'I'll take them into the hospital
tomorrow, they might cheer him up.'

'The girls are going to write letters to him tonight, for you to take in
tomorrow. I bet George will feel champion when he reads those.
Anyway, I'll see you two tomorrow.' Lizzie shook her head when Maddy
and Tess went to follow her to the door. 'No, you be good girls and
make yer mam a cup of tea, I want to have a word with her in private.
Woman to woman, like, if yer see what I mean.'

Ann had her hand on the door knob when Lizzie stepped down on to
the path. 'I hope it's not bad news, Lizzie, I couldn't take any more.'

'No, queen, it's about George's wages. Yer don't need to worry about
them, I'll ask the boss to let me have them and I'll bring them straight
from work on Saturday. So that's one worry less for yer. Yer'll have
money to get yer shopping in and pay yer ways.'

'I wish I could say money was the last thing on my mind, but I'm not
in a position to do so. Our rent man is very nice, and he'll probably
have every sympathy for George. But he'll still hold his hand out for
the rent money. Oh, he'd no doubt let me go a week or two without
paying because we've been good tenants over the years, never missed
a week. But if I couldn't pay one week, there's no way I could pay two
the next.' Ann sighed as she looked down at the homely face framed
by red hair which had been allowed to grow wild. 'Until three hours
ago I didn't know you. You were just a name that George has mentioned
over the years. Yet in those three hours you've done more to help me
than anyone ever has. I don't know what I'd have done without you, I
really don't. Our neighbours are very kind, but I've never been one for
popping in and out of each other's houses. So you've been a godsend.
My husband said you had a heart of gold, and he never spoke a truer
word.'

'Yer'll find most people are good at heart when help is needed. But
I'm glad yer don't think I was being pushy and sticking me nose in
where it wasn't wanted.'

'Anything but, I think you've been a brick! And as long as it isn't putting you or your husband out I'll be glad to see you tomorrow night. Goodnight, Lizzie.'

'Ta-ra, queen, and don't yer be worrying yerself sick. Everything will turn out fine, you'll see.'

There wasn't much change in George when Ann went to visit him in hospital the following evening. He was still lying flat, his arms by his sides, but he wasn't quite as drowsy. 'It's good to see you, love, I've been waiting all day for this. The time drags, not being able to move. If I could sit up, at least I'd be able to talk to the other patients and see what's going on.'

'I know it must be rotten for you, George, and I wouldn't like to change places with you. But you must try to have a little patience. You only came in yesterday, you can't expect miracles.' Ann kissed him over and over, saying, 'One from Madelaine, one from Theresa and three from me. You'll get more from me before I leave of course, but that's to be going on with. Now, I'm going to get myself a chair and sit and hold your hand while you tell me how you feel.'

George waited until she was settled. 'I had a surprise visitor this morning, the boss, Mr Fisher, came to see me.'

'Oh, that was nice of him! He must be a caring man.'

'He's also a businessman, love. He was wondering how long I'm likely to be off, because if it's any length of time he'll have to take another man on.'

'Here's me thinking he came to visit you out of the goodness of his heart, when all the time he was worried about his business! That's a bit thoughtless, considering you were carrying out his business when you got hurt.'

'He wasn't being thoughtless, love, he was being realistic. Bill can't work on his own, the job requires two men. Mr Fisher has put a bloke from the office with him for the time being, but whichever way it goes, he's a man short.'

'And what happened? What was the outcome of his visit?'

'He had a word with the matron, but she said she couldn't tell him anything yet. And it was no use asking to see a doctor because he'd only get the same response. It will be a few days before they can say with certainty what my injuries are.'

'How come he was allowed in this morning? If I came to visit, they'd chase me.'

'His air of authority must have done the trick. He carries himself well and can hold his own with the best. You'd know what I mean if you saw him, he's certainly not one you would talk down to.' George closed his eyes briefly as pain shot from the bottom of his back to the top of his head. He breathed in and out several times before carrying on. 'Anyway, he's going to take another man on temporarily until I get back on my feet.'

'Your friend Lizzie has been kind, an absolute gem. She's going to ask the boss if she can have your wages, and she's bringing them Saturday straight from work.'

'Oh, that was another thing Mr Fisher told me. He'll keep on paying my full wages until such time as we know what's what. So that's one of the worries I can cross off my list.'

Ann gripped his hand. 'The only thing you need to worry about is getting better. Are you still in as much pain?'

George nodded. 'I'd hate to think what it would be like if they weren't giving me something for it, I'd probably be screaming my head off. One of the sisters is very nice, the type you can talk to. She said the bruising is causing a lot of the pain, and that will ease off as the days go by.' He wasn't going to tell her he was worried sick in case his injuries were such he would be confined to a wheelchair. He couldn't get that nightmare out of his mind, no matter how reassuring the sister had been. 'Enough about me, how are you and the girls?'

'The house is not the same without you. The girls miss you very much, and they've told you in letters they've written. I'll leave them on the bed and you can read them when I've gone. They go back to school in a fortnight, and I'm going to have to see someone about Theresa. If they say she's not ready for the senior school, she'll be so disappointed. But I won't let that happen without putting up a fight. She's come on a lot over the past few months, thanks to Madelaine, and she's not so far behind she couldn't catch up if they'll only give her the chance.'

'Be firm about that, love, because every child deserves the best education they can get. It is their right, you're not asking for anything they're not entitled to. It's nineteen thirty-two, and every child should be encouraged to learn, not left behind because someone sitting at a desk says so.' A faint smile crossed George's face. 'Take Lizzie with you, she wouldn't stand any nonsense. And it would be a brave person who argued with her.'

'The girls have really taken to her. You should hear the things she tells them about talking to the flowers on the wallpaper, and hitting her husband over the head with the poker. She really cheered them up last night, they were in pleats laughing. And she was just what I needed, a shoulder to lean on.' Ann was pleased her husband was talking more and taking an interest. She'd lain awake nearly all night, lonely in the big double bed they'd shared for so long. And all she could see was his face creased in pain. 'By the way, love, you know Madelaine is thirteen tomorrow. I've bought a birthday card and put both our names on it. But could you manage to do a few crosses on the bottom and I'll tell her they're kisses from you? She'd be thrilled if she knew you'd put them on yourself. I've got a pencil here and I could guide your hand.'

George let his head drop back. Even that small task seemed like climbing a mountain. 'Tell her I hope she has a lovely day and I'll get her a present when I'm back home. I don't half miss them, Ann, and you.' There was a catch in his voice. 'I love you all so much.'

'Oh come on now, George, don't be getting depressed. Another couple of days and you'll feel a lot different. Think on the bright side and tell yourself that this time next week you'll be back home.'

'You can't help being depressed, love, just lying on your back staring at the ceiling all the time. Nothing to do but feel sorry for yourself. And I know I shouldn't because I've got a lot to be thankful for. At least what ails me isn't life-threatening. Not like some poor beggars in this ward. A man in the bed opposite died last night, and he leaves a wife and three kids. I keep telling myself to think of how lucky I am and not to be so pessimistic.'

Ann tutted when the bell rang. 'That half-hour just flies over.' She bent to kiss him. 'I'll slip down to your Ken's tomorrow and let him and Milly know.'

'Ask him to leave it a day or two before coming in, I might be up and about by then.'

Ann didn't think there was any possibility of that but wisely didn't voice her feelings. 'I won't see you in person until tomorrow, love, but not a second will go by that you aren't in my thoughts.' She kissed the tips of her fingers then pressed them against his lips. 'I love you.'

Chapter Nine

Maisie Wilkins leaned over her clean step to put the bucket down in the hall. Then she wiped her hands down the sides of her pinny and stepped over the low wall which separated their house from the Richardsons'. 'How was George last night?' she asked when Ann opened the door. 'Any improvement?'

'Just about the same really, Maisie. He's still flat on his back and still in pain. He reckons it'll be next Monday before he knows anything definite. He'll have been in hospital two weeks then.'

'Aye, well, I hope all goes well with him. Give him my regards when yer go in tonight.' Maisie turned her head to look up and down the road. 'Can I come in a minute, Ann, I want to talk to yer about something?'

'Of course you can.' Ann held the door wide. 'The girls are upstairs playing school. They go back on Monday, and Madelaine said they're rehearsing.'

'I'll be glad to see the back of mine, they've been a menace,' Maisie said, wiping her feet on the cord mat. 'Seven ruddy weeks is far too long for a holiday, the kids don't know what to do with themselves.'

'Would you like a cuppa?'

'No thanks, Ann, I've left me front door open. The truth is, apart from asking after George, I wanted to talk to yer about the Critchleys. I don't know whether it's me imagination, but they seem to be fading away before me eyes.'

Ann nodded. 'I know, I can see the difference in them. But if you ask, they say they're fine.'

'Well, I'm convinced they're not. And if anything should happen to them, how would we feel? It wouldn't be very neighbourly of us to let two old people die without trying to do something about it.'

'Maisie, I've asked and asked, but each time they tell me there's nothing to worry about. I'm going over in a minute, so I'll have another go, but they'll still tell me the same.'

'Bloody pride, that's what it is. I've got a bee in me bonnet, and I'm sure I'm right. So I'll go over with yer. And don't think I've lost me marbles if yer see me doing something I shouldn't, just go along with

121

me, I'll only be doing it for their good.' Maisie made for the door. 'I'll just take me bucket in, take me pinny off and comb me hair. I'll be with yer in five minutes.'

'Ooh, two visitors this morning, me and Arthur are very lucky.' Freda Critchley was a shadow of the woman she'd been a month ago. Her face was thin and lined, and there wasn't a pick on her body. 'Come on in.'

'Good morning, ladies!' Arthur tried to put some life into his voice but it didn't come off. Like his wife, he didn't look as though he had the strength to even blink.

The women sat down and they talked for a while about this and that. Then, out of the blue, Maisie asked, 'Did yer have a good fried breakfast?'

The old couple were taken by surprise, and after exchanging glances Freda said, 'No, we don't have a fried breakfast, we don't feel like it in the mornings. We just have a round of toast. When yer get to our age, yer don't need to eat as much.'

'Yer need to eat, Freda, yer can't live off fresh air. If yer haven't had a decent breakfast, I hope yer've got the making of a pan of stew in the house, or a sheet of ribs.'

'We'll be having a hot dinner, so you don't have to worry about us.'

'Have yer got the makings of yer dinner in? If yer have, I'll get it started for yer, save you bothering. I've done all me own housework so it's no trouble to get a pan of stew on the go for yer.'

Maisie's direct approach was causing Ann to feel uncomfortable. But drastic action was required and she herself didn't have the guts to be so outspoken. And she knew Maisie was doing it out of concern, not curiosity.

Freda looked flustered. 'No, I can manage meself. I'm not in me dotage yet.'

'Nobody said yer were, Freda,' Maisie said, her voice gentle. 'It's just that me and Ann are concerned for yer. And it's no good yer telling us there's nowt wrong, because our eyes tell us different. Yer can throw me out if yer want, but I've got to speak what's in me mind. You and Arthur have lost so much weight in the last month, since Arthur wasn't well, really, and I'm afraid that for some reason ye're starving yerselves.'

It was Arthur who answered. 'We're not exactly starving ourselves, lass, but we have cut down a lot on everything. Yer see, it was me having that turn what started it. Freda was worried sick that if I died, she wouldn't have enough money to bury me.'

'Blimey, that's being cheerful! You were getting better, so there was no point in her worrying.'

'Yer don't think like that when yer get to our age, Maisie,' Freda said. 'We do have a small insurance policy each, but it wouldn't pay for a decent burial. And I don't want either of us to have to go in a pauper's grave.'

Ann shook her head. 'And you've cut down on your food so you can save for a decent funeral? But don't you see, you're both starving yourselves to death?'

Maisie was tutting loudly. 'I've never heard anything like it! Are the pair of yer just sitting here waiting to pop yer clogs? My grandmother lived until she was ninety-two, Freda, and she was doing her own shopping until the week before she died. She used to wear a man's cap, smoked a clay pipe and enjoyed a milk stout every night. Now while I'm not suggesting yer should wear a man's cap or smoke a clay pipe, I am saying she was over fifteen years older than you and Arthur are, and there's no reason on God's earth why you shouldn't live to that age. Unless yer starve yerself to death before then, of course.'

Arthur was grinning. 'I've been telling the wife, but she wouldn't listen. Too worried about what the neighbours would think if there was only one funeral car. I told her, I don't care what happens to me when I'm dead, 'cos I won't be here.'

'Yer've got ten good years ahead of yer if yer look after yerselves,' Maisie said. 'So can we stop this starving lark, so me and Ann can sleep at night?'

'Ann's got enough to worry about without bothering her head about us. You worry about yer husband, love, we'll be all right.'

'I will if you promise to look after yourselves.'

'I told her it was a daft idea,' Arthur said. 'I was beginning to feel fine until she told me how worried she'd been. Now we're both as weak as kittens. But seeing as Maisie has predicted we've got a good ten years to look forward to, I'll make sure she's in that kitchen every day cooking and baking me favourite dishes.'

'Thank God for that!' Maisie said. 'Now I can go home and do me work with a peaceful mind. Well, perhaps not peaceful, not with my two shouting and fighting with each other. But I'll be more settled. And me and Ann will still take it in turns to nip over and make sure ye're all right.' Maisie struck up the pose of a panto dame. Her arms folded, she hitched up her bust and said, 'Eh, she can't half talk, can't she? I don't think her mouth's stopped for a single second since we got here. I haven't been able to get a word in edgeways.'

'That'll be the day when I can out-talk you, Maisie,' Ann said. 'But I'm learning and I'll catch up with yer one of these days. For now, though, can we go and see to our children?'

Ann stood with her daughters outside the school gates. It was the first day back after the summer holidays and there was a lot of noisy chatter as classmates met up for the first time in seven weeks. Maddy saw one of her friends and waved. 'There's Dorothy, Mam, I'll go in with her.' She took hold of her sister's arm and grinned. 'Good luck, Tess, I'll look out for you at playtime to see how you got on.'

'We'll wait until all the children have gone in, Theresa.' Ann could practically feel how taut her daughter's nerves were and knew that nothing she could say would help to release the tension. But she tried. 'Don't look so scared, there's nothing to worry about no matter what happens. You can only do your best, no one can do more than that. If you're asked any questions try and answer them clearly and politely and you won't go far wrong.' Ann took her arm. 'Come on, perhaps we can catch Miss Bond before she goes into assembly.'

Tess hung back. 'I don't want to go into the junior school, Mam, they'll all make fun of me.'

'Let's cross that hurdle when we come to it, love. I have no intention of standing back and letting that happen.' She smiled to try and lighten the mood. 'So the headmistress has got two of us to contend with. Two against one, we can't lose, can we?'

There were a few stragglers in the corridor, hastily making their way to the assembly hall. Lateness was frowned upon, and unless the hapless victim had a good excuse then there would be a punishment. 'This is Miss Bond's office, let's see if she's still here.' The door was open and the headmistress could be seen rifling through one of the drawers. Taking a deep breath, Ann crooked a finger and rapped with her knuckle.

The headmistress looked up and gave a slight jerk of her head as though impatient that someone would delay her when she was already late for assembly. Her very appearance was intimidating, with her ramrod-straight back, pince-nez spectacles resting on a long thin nose and iron-grey hair combed back severely from her face and tied in a chignon at the back of her head. 'Yes, Mrs Richardson?'

'I wanted to speak to you about Theresa coming back to school.'

Miss Bond waved a hand as though in dismissal and went back to searching the drawer. 'You should know this is not the time. Make an appointment and come and see me this afternoon or tomorrow.'

'I'm prepared to wait until after assembly, Miss Bond. This is the first day of term, and as my daughter's education is a priority to me and my husband, I would like it sorted today.' Ann stretched to her full height, her face set in determination. 'I know she has missed a lot of schooling, but she hasn't missed lessons because I have been taking her for them. Her whole future is at stake, and I'm sure you will understand my concern.'

'One of the teachers informed me that your husband met with an accident and is in hospital, Mrs Richardson. I was sorry to hear it and hope he is on the road to recovery.'

'That I can't tell you. I am hoping for some definite news when I visit him tonight. I also hope to be able to tell him that Theresa is back at school and in the seniors where she belongs.'

Miss Bond pushed the drawer closed with a look of annoyance on her face. It would appear she couldn't find what she was looking for. 'If you wish to stay until after assembly I will talk to you then. Please take a seat in the corridor.'

'Would you kindly allow Theresa to sit in the hall with the rest of the pupils, please? At least she could join in the prayers.'

For a second it looked as though the headmistress would refuse, then her stern expression relaxed and she nodded. 'Very well, come with me, Theresa.'

While Ann sat in the corridor her thoughts were with her husband. He still wasn't sitting up, and he was still in pain. But yesterday he'd seemed brighter in himself, and this was due to the doctor informing him that today they would be able to tell him exactly what damage had been caused to his back. And as the voices of the children praying came to her, she said some prayers of her own. That today there would be good news when she got to the hospital, and that Theresa would be allowed to take her place in the senior school.

The doors of the hall burst open and the children poured out. They would all go to their old classrooms first, and from there they would be directed to their new classrooms and new teachers. Ann stood up and scanned the faces for Theresa, and when she saw her, she pulled her to one side. 'Stand here, love, until the corridor is clear.'

'I enjoyed that, Mam. It was nice sitting with all the girls, saying our prayers. I hope Miss Bond lets me stay.' Tess leaned closer and whispered, 'Don't tell her, but that was one of my prayers.'

'Come, Mrs Richardson.' The headmistress strode towards her office like a soldier on parade. Back straight, arms swinging and steps uniform. When she entered the room, she picked up a chair near the door and placed it next to the one facing her across the desk. 'Be seated, please.'

'Sit down, love,' Ann said to her daughter, who was looking decidedly nervous. 'Miss Bond isn't going to eat you.'

A rare smile crossed the stern face. 'Not now, anyway, dear, it's too soon after breakfast.' The headmistress looked for something on the desk to busy her hands with, but it was clear except for a few papers. So she opened the narrow drawer in the middle of the desk and took out a pencil. This she rapped on the desk as she looked from daughter to mother. She was aware that Ann had once been a teacher herself, and so treated her a little less brusquely than she would perhaps have treated any other parent. 'Right, Mrs Richardson, tell me why you think Theresa is ready to move up to a senior class when she's missed so many months away from school?'

'I'm sure you expect honesty, Miss Bond, so I'll be straight with you. Theresa has missed school through ill health, no other reason. And I don't want her to suffer because of this. She is exceptionally good at English and arithmetic, and I'm sure she could hold her own in those two subjects. To my mind they are the most important subjects when it comes to her seeking employment when she leaves school. She is not good at history or geography, but with a little patience and understanding I'm sure she could reach an acceptable standard. She will certainly be given extra tuition at home.'

Miss Bond turned her attention to Tess. 'Does Madelaine help you, Theresa?'

Mention of her sister's name brought a smile to the pale face. 'Oh yes, me and Maddy write letters to each other. And we give each other sums to do.' Forever thoughtful of others, Tess added, 'And my mam helps me a lot.'

'Your sister is one of our best pupils. She is never far from the top of the class in every subject, she is willing, pleasant and polite. A sister and daughter to be proud of.'

'My husband and myself are very proud of both our children,' Ann said. 'Madelaine is two years older, so Theresa has time to catch up. She has surprised me over the last month or two, far exceeding my hopes. I'm sure you too will be agreeably surprised if you give her the chance to prove herself.'

Miss Bond had doubts about that. The few times the girl had attended school she was way behind the other pupils. And with an average of twenty-five to thirty children in each class, the teachers didn't have time to concentrate on one pupil. 'Perhaps it would be better if Theresa stayed in the juniors for a while, say a month, to see how far she has progressed?'

Ann shook her head. 'Miss Bond, I really am prepared to do battle for my daughter. She's suffered ill health through no fault of her own, missed the companionship of school friends, missed playing out with other children, and all without complaint. Now she deserves something good for a change, and I'm begging you to help her.

Instead of putting her in the juniors for a month's trial, why not put her in the seniors for the same length of time? In fact, if you are harbouring thoughts that I'm just another mother who thinks her child is better than she really is, why not try her out for today? Set her an essay to write on any subject at all, and test her arithmetic by giving her sums that a girl of her age would be expected to answer correctly. But don't disappoint her by turning her down without even giving her a chance.'

The headmistress raised her brows. 'By Jove, you really are prepared to do battle, aren't you, Mrs Richardson? And you argue your case well. So, well, I wouldn't sleep tonight if I didn't agree to do as you ask.' She tilted her head to look at Tess. 'Are you afraid of me, Theresa?'

The girl considered this for a while, a frown on her face. 'I don't think so, Miss Bond. I'm only afraid of people who have loud voices and I think they're telling me off.' Her humour came to the fore. 'I'm glad you've had your breakfast, though.'

A smile on the stern face was rare, a chuckle even more so. 'I have something in mind, but it's only if you agree, Theresa. How would you like to spend the morning in this room with me? At least I wouldn't be here all the time, I have classes to attend to. But I could set you some lessons and pop in now and again to see how you're getting on. Would you like that?'

The girl's eyes rolled. 'You mean I could sit at your desk? Oh yes, I would like that very much.' She glanced at her mother. 'Aren't I lucky, Mam?'

'You are very lucky, Theresa, and you must do your best to show Miss Bond that her kindness and trust in you is appreciated.'

'Now that is settled, I'm going to have to ask you to leave, Mrs Richardson. The first day of term is always hectic, with most girls moving to higher classes with different teachers, while others who haven't made the grade stay where they are for another term. So there is much to be done. However, I will not neglect Theresa, I promise, and I'll give her enough work to keep her going until twelve o'clock. I suggest you come back then and we can discuss the situation in more detail.'

Ann got to her feet. 'I really can't thank you enough, I wasn't expecting such co-operation.' She bent to kiss Tess and gave her a hug of encouragement. 'You'll be fine, love, don't worry. I'll see you at twelve o'clock.'

When Ann turned the corner of the road, the first thing she noticed was her neighbour's legs sticking out on to the pavement, and every few seconds Maisie's bottom would appear briefly as her body moved with the scrubbing brush. The paths in front of the houses in Hanford Avenue were very short, barely a yard or so of square tiles up to the step. But her neighbour spent half an hour on path, two steps and windowsill every morning without fail. The only time she missed was when the snow was inches deep, and even then she was out first thing in the morning with a shovel and stiff brush to clear it away so it wouldn't be trodden into the house. 'This has become an obsession with you, Maisie, you're addicted to it. Your path is cleaner than most living rooms. You put the rest of the road to shame.'

Maisie sat back on her heels. 'It's a habit, I admit. But me mam used to do her front every morning and I must take after her.' She threw the floor cloth into the bucket and rubbed her hands on her pinny. 'Tess gone to school, then?'

Ann explained briefly what had happened. 'I'm going back at twelve, so keep your fingers crossed for us. If all goes as I hope, and as I think it should, I'll have some good news to take in to George tonight that will cheer him up.'

'How is George? Anything definite yet?'

'Not as yet. But he's having more tests today, and the doctors are hoping to find out exactly what the problem is. All the way from the school I've been praying for two lots of good news today. Theresa moving into the seniors, and George with a date for coming home. If I get both my wishes, I'll be the happiest woman in the world.'

'Yer know, Ann, if there's anything I can do, all yer have to do is ask. Washing, shopping, or minding the girls while yer go to the hospital, anything at all.'

'I know, and it's very kind of you. But I'm all right during the day, I just carry on as normal.' Ann grinned. 'And it's normal for me to only wash my step once a week.'

'That's something I could do for yer! Blimey, I'd only have to move me bucket a couple of yards. Mind you, I'd be daft to put as much elbow grease into cleaning yours and having you vie with me for the cleanest step.'

'Thanks for offering, but there's no way I'd let you get on your knees and clean my step while I'm inside watching you through the window. But there may come a time when I'll be glad of your help, Maisie, and I won't let my pride get in the way of asking you. It depends on whether George is confined to bed when they discharge him from hospital. Oh, I don't mean confined to bed for good, I just mean until he's able to sit up and walk.'

'All you have to do, Ann, is knock on the door and ask. And in an emergency, just hammer on the wall and I'll come running.'

Maisie laughed loudly. 'In fact, girl, if yer hammered hard enough to make a hole in the wall I could just step through. Home from home, like.'

'Are you going to the pictures this afternoon?'

'It's Monday, so do yer need to ask? Yer'll see me sneaking down the entry at two o'clock on me way to the Carlton to sit and drool over Robert Donat. And just after four I'll sneak back to get the dinner on. And while my feller's eating his dinner, I'll be wondering why he hasn't got what it takes to make me drool.'

'Away with you, Maisie, your Will is a fine-looking man!'

'So he keeps telling me, but I still ain't drooling! Perhaps I'm just hard to please.' Maisie got to her feet and picked up the bucket. 'It's time to get cracking on me spuds. But I'll give yer a knock later to see how Tess got on. Ta-ra for now.'

'Ta-ra, Maisie. But when you're watching Robert Donat, remember what I said. Your Will knocks spots off him for looks.'

Ann was standing inside the hall taking the key out of the lock when she head her neighbour mutter, 'Either she needs glasses, or I do.' Then Maisie raised her voice to make sure she was heard. 'And I hope she doesn't tell Will, 'cos he spends enough time looking in the flaming mirror as it is. The next thing yer know, he'll be getting his hair permed.'

Ann was smiling as she walked into the living room. But the silence and emptiness made her shiver, as though someone had walked over her grave. The best way to take her mind off things was to keep busy. It was a quarter past ten now, only an hour and a half before she went back to the school. She'd change the girls' bed and put the bedding in to steep. By the time she'd done that and dusted around, it would be time to leave.

The office door was open when Ann arrived, ten minutes early, but the room was empty and her heart dropped. Surely Miss Bond wouldn't have taken Theresa through to the juniors without discussing it with her first. She heard footsteps echoing on the wooden floor of the corridor and knew immediately who those footsteps belonged to. She turned, ready to do battle on behalf of her daughter, but the smile on Miss Bond's face threw her mind into a state of confusion. 'Where's Theresa?'

'Come into the office, Mrs Richardson, I have much to say to you.'

But while Ann followed, she told herself she wasn't going to be sweet-talked out of what she believed to be right. 'Where's Theresa?'

Miss Bond sat down and indicated Ann should take a seat. 'At this very minute, your daughter is in Miss Harrison's class, and her essay is being read out to the class.'

Ann's mouth gaped. 'I beg your pardon?'

'You might well show surprise, Mrs Richardson, I certainly did. I asked Theresa what she would like to write about, and she said her holiday in Wales. I gave her a notepad, on the first page of which I had jotted down some sums for her, then I left her to get on with it. I popped my head around the door on a number of occasions and each time she was busy writing.' The headmistress put a hand to her mouth and gave a slight cough, a movement to hide a smile she couldn't keep back. 'Does your daughter always have her tongue hanging out of the side of her mouth when she's writing?'

'When she's concentrating hard on anything, yes, it's a habit. But I don't understand what you're saying to me, Miss Bond. Will you tell me again what Theresa is doing and where she is doing it?'

The headmistress was looking decidedly pleased with herself. 'I'll start from the beginning, Mrs Richardson, so you have an honest and exact account of what has happened. I only agreed to give Theresa a test because you were so forceful, and I wanted to humour you. I was quite convinced you were inclined to think your daughter was brighter than she really is. My expectations were not high, but I went along with you so that when you came back this afternoon I could say I had tried but that, unfortunately, Theresa must stay in the juniors for another year. Anyhow, the last time I came in, it was to find she had completed the arithmetic exercise and the essay, and was sitting quite still just chewing on the end of the pencil. I had no intention of reading the essay at that particular moment as I was needed in one of the classrooms. However, curiosity got the better of me and I glanced at the first two lines. To say I was surprised would be an understatement, and I became so absorbed I read the whole essay. Your daughter is a natural story-teller, Mrs Richardson, a gifted child. The tale she told was interesting and the words flowed freely. The essay would have been a credit to a child many years her senior. I was so impressed I took it along to a teacher and asked her opinion. She agreed with my view, and suggested that it should be read out to the class as an example of how a story should be told.' Miss Bond shook her head. 'I'm finding it hard to believe this is the same girl who seldom attended school, and was far behind the rest of the class when she did.'

Ann sat back in her chair and breathed out a sigh of relief. 'Me and my husband have always known she was special, but her health kept her back. I am so happy for her, and so proud.'

'You have every right to be, because from what I've seen of her today, I'd say she has a good future ahead of her. And Miss Harrison is looking forward to having her as a pupil. She has assured me she will give Theresa all the help and encouragement she needs in the subjects you say she falls behind in.'

'I remember Miss Harrison from when she taught Madelaine. And I can't thank you enough, Miss Bond, for giving my daughter the chance to prove herself. My husband will be delighted when I tell him.' Ann glanced at the large round clock on the wall behind the desk. 'I'll go now, because I don't want Madelaine to get home before I do as she hasn't got a key. When they've had their lunch, shall I bring Theresa back to Miss Harrison's class?'

The headmistress tilted her head. 'I think you should allow Madelaine to bring Theresa back, don't you? The child might be embarrassed being the only girl whose mother brings her to school. She's an eleven-year-old now; we should all treat her as one.'

Ann had her coat on when Lizzie came that night. 'You won't be able to get a word in edgeways, Lizzie, I'm afraid. Our Theresa has a lot to tell you.'

'She's given me an earache already,' Madelaine said, jokingly. 'If I've got to listen to it all again, I'll go gaga.'

Tess's cup of happiness was full to overflowing. Her memories of school hadn't been pleasant ones, always behind her classmates and constantly feeling sickly and weak. In her own young mind she knew she was capable of more, but didn't have the energy. But today she was on top of the world because at last her parents, and Madelaine, could be proud of her. And that was all she'd ever craved. 'I'll tell you what, Maddy. You tell Mrs Lizzie and I'll sit back and listen to how clever I've been.'

Ann grinned as she kissed each of her daughters. 'Just don't talk the poor woman to death, that's all. Otherwise she might decide she'd rather stay home and talk to the rose on her wallpaper than come here.'

'Nah,' Lizzie said. 'Yer know they say familiarity breeds contempt, well, it's true. Me and the rose know that much about each other, there's nowt left to talk about. I do miss me little chats with it, though, 'cos our house is as quiet as a bleeding graveyard.' The swear word was out before she could stop it. Wagging her head, she slapped herself soundly on the cheek. 'That's for swearing in front of the children. Do it again and I'll cut yer ruddy tongue out.'

'But it's your own tongue, Mrs Lizzie!' Tess said. 'You wouldn't want to cut your own tongue out, would you?'

'I'll have no favouritism, queen, not in my mouth I won't. Me teeth started to get funny with me a few years ago, started playing me up something rotten. So I taught them a lesson they'll never forget, I can tell yer.'

Maddy was giggling as she asked, 'What did you do to them, Mrs Lizzie?'

'I had them all pulled out, didn't I, queen? They've never bothered me since.'

Ann was laughing as she pulled the front door shut behind her. What a colourful character Lizzie was. Always a smile on her face and a joke on her lips. In the short time they'd known her, the girls had really taken her to their hearts. They'd miss her when she stopped coming, as Ann herself would. But there was no reason for her to stop coming, she'd always be welcome as a very special friend.

It was as Ann was pulling herself up on to the tram platform that a frown furrowed her forehead. Did Lizzie have false teeth? She'd never noticed.

It was only a few stops on the tram from Orrell Park to Walton Hospital and Ann could see by the huge clock that towered over the hospital that visiting started in fifteen minutes. By the time she'd walked up the very long driveway to the main entrance, then up to the ward, she'd just about make it on time. Some of the pleasure she'd felt during the day over Teresa was starting to fade as she neared the entrance. George would know by now how serious his injuries were and she knew he was dreading what was to come.

The ward doors hadn't been opened yet, and there was a group of people waiting. Some were holding bunches of flowers, others had paper bags containing fruit. George was fond of oranges and pears, so Ann had brought him one of each, and a small bunch of grapes. She was deep in thought and jumped with fright when a hand gripped her arm with some force. Startled, she turned her head to see Ken smiling at her. He was so like his brother, her heart turned over. 'I was miles away then, I nearly jumped out of my skin with the fright you gave me.'

Ken grinned. 'Guilty conscience, eh? Did yer think I was yer club woman, or a moneylender yer've been dodging?'

'Thank goodness I don't have either. Have you been here long?'

'About five minutes, that's all. They're late opening the doors.'

'I'm not looking forward to this visit,' Ann told him. 'If George has had bad news, and is upset, I'll probably make a show of myself and start crying.'

'Yer better hadn't, girl, 'cos that's the last thing he'll need. No matter what happens, you keep yer pecker up for his sake. You've got to be the strong one now.'

132

Ann nodded. 'I keep telling myself that, Ken, and I will try. I'm glad you're here and I'm not on my own. It's all very well saying I'll be strong and brave, but I can't make myself be those things, not when it's my husband lying in that bed and I love him so much.'

They were both pushed along in the surge when the doors were opened, and George, whose head was raised on two pillows tonight, was eagerly looking out for his wife. He lifted his hand in greeting to his brother, who towered above most of the other visitors, but it was Ann his eyes were hungry for the sight of. 'Hello, love.' He raised his head further to meet her lips. 'It's good to see you.'

'Don't mind me,' Ken laughed. 'I don't mind playing gooseberry. Just don't get too loving or yer'll have me blushing.'

Ann put the bag of fruit down on the locker at the side of the bed. She didn't want to get her hopes up, but surely the fact that George was no longer lying flat was a good sign. 'Well, things must be improving seeing as they're now letting you see what's going on around you.' She tried not to sound too concerned. 'Did you have all the tests today?'

Her husband nodded. 'Yes, they really gave me a going-over. They couldn't give me anything for the pain, 'cos as the head doctor said, they needed me wide awake. So I had to grit my teeth and let them get on with it. But it's not something I would recommend, I was in absolute agony.'

'And did the tests tell them what they wanted to know?' Ken asked. 'Have they told yer what's wrong with yer?'

George gripped Ann's hand as he nodded. 'I've got two fractured bones at the bottom of my spine, and a couple have been splintered. The doctor said they'll mend in time if I'm patient and do as I'm told. They've bound me up and I've to keep the binding on until my own doctor tells me otherwise.' He managed a grin. 'I know now how women who wear corsets feel, and I think they must be crazy. I'm blowed if I'd get trussed up like this for vanity, to make out I've got a slim figure.'

'So they'll be letting you home soon, then?' Ann asked, eagerly. 'I can do any binding that needs doing, and I'll make sure you get plenty of rest.'

'I can't walk yet, love. The nurses tried me with a few steps this morning, after I'd had the tests, and I couldn't do it, the pain was unbearable. But the sister said it'll get a bit better every day, and by the end of the week the doctor might consider discharging me.'

'That's good news, George,' Ken said. 'Things could have been a lot worse.'

'Don't I know it! My biggest fear was being confined to bed, or a wheelchair, for the rest of my life, so I've got a lot to be thankful for. I'll be able to live a normal life, except there'll always be a weakness at the bottom of my spine and I've been told I shouldn't do any work which required heavy lifting.'

'But the job you do does require heavy lifting!' Ann said. 'Did you tell the doctor that?'

'Yes, I did, love.' George averted his eyes. 'We'll worry about that when the time comes, eh? My main concern is getting home, so let's just concentrate on that. I'll persevere with walking a few steps every day, even if it's torture, so by the weekend they may think I'm fit to be discharged.'

'Walking a few steps isn't climbing a flight of stairs,' Ken reminded him. 'Don't go rushing things, our kid, because yer might end up a damn sight worse than yer are now. Once ye're out of hospital, yer won't want to be carried back in again just 'cos yer didn't have the patience to do as yer were flamin' well told.'

George grinned. 'That's my big brother giving orders. But you're right, Ken, I certainly wouldn't want to be brought back here again. I can't wait to see the back of the place, even though everyone is so kind and they're helping to make me better. I mean, where would I have been without them? But still, there's no place like home.'

'Neither of you need have any fear of you not doing as you're told, George, because me and the girls will make sure you do.' Ann nodded to show how determined she was. 'And you don't have to let the stairs put them off sending you home, 'cos I'll bring the bed down and put it in the front parlour.'

'See, she's got everything figured out,' Ken said. 'She's dying to get yer home so she can wait on yer hand and foot.'

'Just like Milly would do for you, if it was you in this bed and not your brother. And she'd not be sleeping at night for worrying about you.'

'You're not losing your sleep, are you, love?' George asked. 'There's no need for that.'

'I won't tonight! I'll sleep like a top, knowing you'll soon be home.' Ann groaned when the bell rang. 'I hate that ruddy bell, it's got no sympathy, no feelings.' She slipped a hand under her husband's head and raised it to meet her lips. 'I had such a lot to tell you, all good news, but we haven't had enough time for anything. But just quickly, so you've got something to smile about, Theresa started in the senior school today. And tomorrow night, when I've more time, I'll tell you what a surprise she was to Miss Bond.'

'Roll on tomorrow night, it'll give me something to look forward to.' George kissed her soundly before stretching an arm to shake hands with his brother. 'Thanks for coming, Ken, it's always good to see you. Give my love to Milly and the kids.' His eyes followed his wife and brother to the ward door, and he waited until they were out of sight before allowing his thoughts to go back to his and his family's future. If he couldn't keep on with the job he'd had since he left school, what other work could he do? He was only a labourer, had no trade or skill. And there were so many men out of work, jobs were hard to come by. But he'd have to be honest with Mr Fisher when he came in to see him again. He'd been a good boss, and it wouldn't be fair not to tell him the truth. Perhaps there was a lighter job he could do, anything to stay with the same firm and same workmates. It would be a bitter blow if it turned out that wasn't possible.

Chapter Ten

When Ann and Ken walked towards George's bed on the Friday night, it was to see him smiling broadly at them. He was raised from the shoulders now, and could see everything that was going on in the ward. Ann felt this was a great stride forward. 'Well, things are really looking up,' she said, giving him a kiss. 'You must be on the mend.'

After greeting his brother, George said, 'I'm not only on the mend, I'm on my way home tomorrow, all being well.'

'Good for you!' Ken had brought the *Liverpool Echo* in, and he laid it on the bedside locker. 'I didn't expect yer to be discharged until next week, at the earliest.'

'What did you mean, you'll be on your way home all being well?' Ann asked. 'Isn't it definite they're discharging you?'

'I asked the doctor this morning, when he was examining me, if I could go home. He wasn't agreeable at first, said I shouldn't try to rush things. But I told him there was nothing I was doing in here that I couldn't do at home. I also said I'd come on better because I'd have my family around me. So he promised to discuss it with the matron when he'd finished his rounds. He must have done, because Sister said she wanted to see you tonight, Ann, and there's no other reason why Matron would do that. I've been on pins all day, building my hopes up, and I'll be really disappointed if she turns me down.'

'I'll go along to her office now and get it over with,' Ann said. 'Save you being in suspense any longer. I'll do my best, love, even get down on my knees to her if that's what it takes.'

'Pretend she's Miss Bond, you did all right with her.'

As she walked away, Ann heard Ken asking, 'Who's Miss Bond when she's out?' And she knew her husband would be telling the tale of how Theresa came to be in the senior school now. And he'd tell it with pride in his voice.

The matron was standing outside her office talking to a nurse when she saw Ann approaching. 'Go in, Mrs Richardson, I'll be with you in a minute.'

Ann couldn't hear all that was being said, but she could tell by the tone, and the odd words like 'slipshod' and 'careless', that the matron wasn't in the best of moods. That doesn't augur well for me, she thought. It might take more than getting down on my knees to win this request.

She took a deep breath and squared her shoulders when she heard Matron dismiss the nurse. Oh dear, now for it. But she had to win, because George desperately wanted to be home, and she and the children needed him there. So she decided to take the bull by the horns and go on the offensive. 'Good evening, Matron, I believe you wish to talk to me about my husband being discharged tomorrow? He is so looking forward to seeing the children again and they'll be over the moon when I tell them.'

'On the instructions of the doctor, Mrs Richardson, I have to make sure that going home is the best thing for him. While he's here, we can control the pain to a certain extent, whereas at home that wouldn't be possible. Also, he needs the binding attended to each day, and that is not easy for someone like yourself who hasn't the experience. Then there's the walking exercises, which are very important. He's a big man, Mrs Richardson, I don't think you could manage him. I'm inclined to think it would perhaps be better if he stayed here for another few days.'

'Oh, no, Matron, please reconsider. I'm having the bed brought down to the parlour and I know I can manage. I won't be entirely on my own, I have a very good neighbour who will give me all the help I need. And I'm sure our doctor, Dr Greenshields, will call in and see he's being well looked after. If I didn't think it was right for George, I wouldn't be asking you, because I only ever want what's best for him. So I'm asking you to please let my husband come home tomorrow.'

The matron rested her chin on a curled fist, her eyes thoughtful. Then she said, 'I know Dr Greenshields very well, which is a point in your favour. I could ask him to arrange for a nurse to call in each day, just for the first week, to see to the binding and help with walking exercises. I would be satisfied with those arrangements, Mrs Richardson, would you?'

'More than satisfied, Matron.' Ann's eyes were shining with unshed tears of joy. 'Thank you, I am very grateful and I can't wait to see his face when I tell him. He's told me how kind everyone here has been, and I want you to know he appreciates very much all that you've done for him. It's just that he misses our two daughters and he's pining for them.'

'Right, that's settled then. I'll contact Dr Greenshields and ask him to organise a nurse to call each day and check your husband's progress. He'll be going home by ambulance as he's not fit to travel any other way. But I can't give you a time, it depends upon when a vehicle is available.'

Ann pushed her chair back and stood up. 'I'll have everything ready for him.' She got to the door and turned. 'Thank you for taking such care of my husband, Matron, and putting him on the road to recovery. We would be in a sorry state without doctors and nurses.'

Running in a hospital corridor was frowned upon, so Ann kept to a brisk walk. She couldn't keep the smile off her face, though, and as soon as she entered the ward Ken said to his brother, 'It looks as though ye're on yer way tomorrow.'

George tried to sit up but a shaft of pain caused him to sink back against the pillows. But he refused to let it show, and he was smiling when Ann reached the bed. 'Well, love?'

'You're coming home in style tomorrow, by ambulance. Matron couldn't give me a time so you'll have to be patient. I'll see if me and the girls can manage to get the bed dismantled and brought downstairs. It's got to be ready for when you arrive.'

'You'll never manage that, love, it weighs a ton!'

'I'll do it,' Ken said. 'I'll go back with Ann and get cracking.'

'Isn't Friday night pub night?' George asked, raising his brows. 'I thought you never missed a few pints on a Friday?'

'I'll be home before closing time. It shouldn't take long to do the bed.'

Ann didn't argue, having doubts about her own ability to do the job. It took her all her time to push the big iron bed a few inches to brush underneath. She'd never be able to dismantle it and carry it downstairs, even with the help of the girls. It definitely required the strength of a man. 'Would you mind if we left now, love? It'll give Ken a bit more time, and visiting must be nearly over anyhow.'

'Yes, you go! I'm quite happy to be left with my thoughts. This time tomorrow I'll be back home with my family, and it's a wonderful feeling.'

They were halfway down the hospital path when Ann tugged on Ken's arm to slow him down. 'Don't walk so fast, I can't keep up with you. I've got a pain in my side and I'm puffing like a steam engine.'

'Yer must be out of condition, girl, that's all I can say. I'm not walking any quicker than I normally do.' Ken was grinning as he rubbed his hands together. 'My brother has got me well taped. I won't miss me Friday-night pints with me mates if I can help it. I wouldn't leave yer swinging with the bed, though, Ann, I'm not that bad. It shouldn't take me more than an hour, so I'll have plenty of time.'

They were sitting on the tram when Ann said, 'Lizzie will get a surprise, me getting home so early. Still, it means she'll be able to get away handy.'

'Who's Lizzie?'

'I told you about her, she works with George. She's been smashing, sitting with the girls every night.'

'What will George do if he can't go back to his old job?' Ken asked. 'He said the doctor told him the bones will take months to mend, and even then he'd be daft to start lifting anything heavy. He'd be asking for trouble.'

'I'm trying not to think about that. Mr Fisher said he'll keep paying his wages, but that's because he expects George to go back to his job.' Ann sighed as they stood up when the tram was nearing their stop. 'I'm not going to worry about it until I've got to. The main thing is getting George back on his feet, fit and healthy.'

'It's nice around here,' Ken said, as they walked up tree-lined Moss Lane. 'It's a change to see a bit of greenery.'

When Lizzie opened the door her face showed surprise. 'Ye're early, queen.'

'George is being discharged tomorrow, and Ken here has come to bring the bed down. This is Lizzie, Ken, the woman I've told you about, who has been an angel. And this, Lizzie, is George's big brother.'

'Yer've no need to tell me that, queen, he's the spitting image of him.'

The girls came dashing out of the living room. 'Is Dad coming home, Mam?' Maddy didn't wait for an answer as she linked her arm through her uncle's and grinned up at him. 'He must be if you're bringing the bed down.'

Tess linked his other arm. 'Oh, isn't that the gear, Uncle Ken? I haven't half missed my dad, and I've got loads and loads to tell him.'

'Leave your uncle alone, girls, he hasn't got a lot of time. I think it might be as well if I ask the man next door to give you a hand, Ken, you couldn't manage it on your own and I'm absolutely hopeless. It's a great big heavy thing and I don't want you ending up in hospital.'

'There's no need to get the man next door, queen, not while I'm around.' Lizzie bent her arm and patted a muscle that any man would be proud of. 'I didn't get that peeling bleedin' grapes.'

Tess gasped. 'Mrs Lizzie, you said a bad word again! But don't cut your tongue out, 'cos I don't think it meant it. Give it another chance.'

Ken chuckled. That was the first time he'd heard a swear word in this house, and Ann hadn't batted an eye. He usually watched what he was saying, even though he swore like a trooper at work, and at home. His brother's wife had that effect on you. She was so prim and proper you were on your toes all the time. Perhaps Lizzie coming into their lives was the best thing that could happen for the two girls, to teach them what life was really like. 'Ann, have yer stripped the bed? And have yer got the right spanner for the bolts?'

'Oh, ye gods! I'm standing here like a spare part, instead of getting on with it. I'll have a look for the spanner, I've got an idea where it might be. And you two girls can see to the bedclothes. Just put the pillows in the middle, fold the clothes over them and carry the lot down as they are. Hold one each end and carry them between you, but mind you don't trip on the stairs.'

Maddy took the stairs two at a time, with Tess close behind. And Ann was going through to the pantry, where she knew George kept a box of tools, when she heard Ken say, 'We'll manage it between us, Lizzie, no problem. You can be my labourer.'

'Your labourer indeed! Yer can sod off, Ken Richardson, I ain't going to be no one's bleedin' labourer! I'll be the gaffer, you can do as ye're told.'

'I heard that, Mrs Lizzie,' Tess called down from the landing. 'That's two swear words you've used.'

'It's all right, queen, I'm keeping count. I'll give meself a damn good hiding when I get home for not being able to control me tongue.'

Ann fetched the biggest spanner she could find in the tool box. 'Is that about right?'

Tongue in cheek, Ken said, 'Yer'd better ask the gaffer, I'm only the labourer.'

'Any more sarcasm out of you,' Lizzie told him, 'and I'll dock yer ruddy pay. Now move out of the way while the girls carry the bedding into the parlour, and then perhaps we can start.'

Thinking of her brother-in-law, Ann said, 'Ken likes to go for a pint on a Friday, Lizzie, so he wants to be away handy.'

Lizzie fixed her green eyes on Ken. 'Oh, ye're one of them, are yer, a flippin' boozer?'

'I wouldn't call meself a boozer, Lizzie.' Ken had taken a liking to the woman, whose hair was so red you could warm your hands in front of it on a winter's night. 'I just like me pint.'

Lizzie put a cupped hand to her ear. 'Me hearing's not what it used to be. Did yer say pint, or was it pints, as in two or three?'

He chuckled. 'One most nights, but three every Friday. It's a ritual with me mates.'

'I've got a man at home like you, he doesn't think he's a boozer either. But anyone who has to have a beer every night is a boozer in my eyes. Saturday is Norman's night for getting together with his mates, 'cos like all the workers, that's the day he gets paid. How come you're in the money on a Friday when everyone else is skint?'

'An understanding landlord, he puts it on the slate for us. He wouldn't do it for just anyone, mind, it's because we're such good customers and he'd be out of pocket if we took our custom elsewhere.'

'Blimey, I've heard everything now! Pints of beer on tick! Have you ever in yer nellie heard the likes of it?'

'Haven't you ever had a loaf of bread put on the slate at the corner shop?' Ken asked. 'I bet a pound to a pinch of snuff that yer have.'

'A bit of difference between a loaf of bread and a pint of beer, lad. One is a necessity, the other's a bleedin' luxury.'

Tess's head appeared around the parlour door. 'Watch it, Mrs Lizzie, your tongue is really getting out of hand.'

'I'm keeping me eye on it, queen, and as I said, I'll give it the hiding of its life when I get home. I'll teach it who's boss. And talking of boss, would you pass that spanner over to me labourer, Ann, please, and we can make a start?' There was devilment in the green eyes as she jerked her head at Ken. 'Come on, lad, let's see what stuff ye're made of.'

Ann watched as Lizzie took the lead in climbing the stairs, and she could hear Ken's hearty chuckle. They'll get on like a house on fire, she thought as she went into the front parlour to see what the girls had done with the bedding. The room, which was seldom used, contained very little in the way of furniture. A few straight-back wooden chairs, a small table under the window with a plant on, a couple of ornaments on the mantelpiece under a gilt-framed mirror and two pictures on the walls. Ann had always been going to furnish it properly when they had the money, but that time had never arrived. And tonight she was glad, because there was no furniture to move out.

'I'm glad Dad's coming home, Mam,' Maddy said. 'Me and Tess have missed him, but it must have been worse for you going into the hospital every night and seeing him in pain.'

'Well, the worst is over, thank God. What we've got to do now is make sure he does what he's been told to do, so he's soon up and about again.'

'Me and Maddy are going to be very good and help you all we can,' Tess told her. 'We can go for your shopping when we come home from school, and I can peel the potatoes while Maddy does the ironing.'

They heard roars of laughter coming from above and hurried into the hall to hear Lizzie shouting, 'Ye're bloody useless, Ken Richardson! Just like a ruddy man, not a ha'p'orth of good. I could have done this job on me own, standing on me flaming head and singing "Nellie Dean".'

Then Ken said, 'Go on, show me!'

'Yer what!'

'I said show me! Go on, prove it! Let's see yer standing on yer head and singing "Nellie Dean" while ye're loosening those bolts.'

'Listen, lad, any more lip out of you and I'll loosen your ruddy bolts.

And if I do that yer'll have to stand at the bar drinking yer pints, 'cos yer won't be able to sit down. Now hold that headboard while I lift this end of the iron bar.'

'Do you want me to come up?' Ann called. 'To give you a hand?'

'Not on yer life!' Ken shouted. 'I've got enough trouble with this woman, I couldn't cope with another.' His voice cracking with laughter, he added, 'Mind you, Lizzie is a woman and a half. She's got bigger muscles than me.'

'Yer'll be feeling me muscles if yer don't hold that ruddy headboard.'

At the bottom of the stairs Tess asked, 'Mam, is "ruddy" a swear word?'

'Not really, but it's not a word for young girls to use, so don't let me hear you using it.'

From above they heard a crash, followed by a howl. 'Yer've just dropped the flaming iron bedstead on me foot! Lift it up so I can see if me toes are broken.'

They could hear the springs of the bed make a twanging sound, and then Lizzie's voice. 'Holy suffering ducks! Yer've done nothing but fiddle-arse about since we started. Now stop crying, wipe yer eyes and let's get this bedstead downstairs.'

'I'm not going down first, I don't trust yer,' Ken said. 'You go first.'

'Oh, ay, soft lad, let the woman do the heavy work, eh? I bet yer'll stand at the bar tonight and tell yer mates how hard yer've worked and they'll all think ye're a knight in shining armour. When all yer've managed to do so far is put yer bleedin' foot in it! And I'll swear yer did that deliberate, to get a bit of sympathy, thinking I'd kiss it better.'

'Have yer got no heart, woman?' Ken was chuckling to himself as he rubbed his foot. This was one funny lady. 'Yer could at least ask me if I've broken any toes.'

'Not until we've got this bed downstairs and put together. After that, lad, I'll be all sweetness and light.'

'Oh, this I have to see.' Ken took the end of the bed nearest the door. 'I'll go down first, but keep hold of the ruddy thing, I don't want it landing on me back. I know there'll be an empty bed in Walton Hospital when our George comes out tomorrow, but I don't want to be the next patient in it.'

Ann and the girls moved down the hall to allow the heavy iron spring base to be carried into the parlour. Then Ken ran upstairs to fetch one of the headboards down. 'I'll get the big one, Lizzie, I'll leave the little one for you. And don't ever say I'm not a gentleman.'

It took twenty minutes to put the bed up, Lizzie working as hard as Ken. Sweat was running down their faces when they stood back to admire their handiwork. 'Is it all right for yer there, Ann, or do yer want us to move it?'

'No, Ken, that's fine where it is. Me and the girls will make it up when you've gone. You and Lizzie have been marvellous, I'm very grateful.'

'Think nothing of it, queen, it was an eye-opener working with his nibs here. He was better than my feller would have been, and almost as good as me.'

'And I bet he's on pins to get away, aren't you, Ken? I don't want you to miss your friends, so poppy off, I can manage the rest now the bed is down. I was worried about how I was going to manage.'

'I'll go with him, queen, and let you get on with fixing things ready for George coming home. I'll call in and see him on Monday night, if that's all right with you?'

'He'd be very pleased to see you, Lizzie, and so would me and the girls. You'll always be welcome here.'

'Don't stand here talking all night, missus, I'm losing valuable drinking time. If ye're coming out with me, get moving.' Ken held his arms out and gave the girls a hug and a kiss. 'I'll see yer soon.' He turned towards the door. 'Which way d'yer go, Lizzie?'

'Down Northfield Road to Hawthorne Road. I live in Willard Street, just off Hawthorne.'

'Go 'way!' Ken came back to stand in front of her. 'We're practically neighbours! I live in Elizabeth Road, off Monfa.'

'Yer don't say! Well I never! Fancy living so near and never seeing each other before! Now that's what I call a coincidence.'

'You've probably passed each other dozens of times but never taken any notice,' Ann said. 'It's easily done.'

'What!' Ken laughed. 'With hair her colour, yer couldn't miss her!' He stroked his chin, looking thoughtful. 'Which pub does your feller drink in?'

'The Linacre.'

'That's where I drink! This is unbelievable!'

Lizzie grinned. 'Ye're not going to tell me I'm yer long-lost sister, are yer?'

'What's yer second name, Lizzie?'

She squared her shoulders and rose to her full height. Even the hairs on her head seemed to stand to attention. 'Ferguson, and proud of it.'

Ken slapped his thighs and chuckled. 'Ye're Ginger's wife! Well I'll be blowed! Just wait until I tell him I've spent an hour in a bedroom with his missus. Holy suffering ducks, I can't wait to see his face.'

'I don't think yer'll have time to see his face, lad, 'cos yer'll be flat out on the floor. He's a mild man most of the time is my Norman, but if he ever loses his temper then yer'd better look out. If he thinks ye're blackening my name, he'll belt yer one before yer've got time to tell him it was a joke. So if I were in your shoes, I'd choose me words carefully, otherwise yer might not be in a fit state to drink one pint, never mind three.'

'Nah, he's got a sense of humour has Ginger! I've known him for donkey's years and he's a real nice bloke.'

The girls had been quietly listening with interest, but now Tess asked, 'If his name's Norman, why do you call him Ginger?'

'Because of the colour of his hair, pet. It's not as red as Lizzie's, more ginger, like.' Ken was looking pleased with himself. 'This is a turn-up for the books, I can't get over it! Why d'yer never come to the pub with him, Lizzie?'

'Better things to spend me money on, lad. And I don't think a pub is the place for a lady, anyhow.' She pointed a stiffened finger at him. 'Don't yer dare say anything about me not being a lady, or yer won't even make it to the flaming pub.'

'Come on.' Ken took her arm. 'We can talk about it as we walk. I'm wasting drinking time standing here nattering.'

Ann followed them to the door. 'I hope you two don't come to blows.'

Lizzie winked. 'No, I only pick on someone me own size, not a skinny weakling like yer brother-in-law. We'll get along fine as long as he behaves himself.' She linked her arm through Ken's. 'Seeing as ye're going to tell everyone we've spent time together in the bedroom, we might as well give them something to talk about.' She raised her voice. 'Come along, darling, I thought yer were eager for an early night in bed.'

Ann didn't know whether to laugh or cry or watch for the neighbours' curtains moving. She could see the funny side, though, when Ken's feet nearly left the ground as Lizzie tugged hard on his arm, saying in her loud voice, 'My, my, we are eager.'

When they'd turned the corner and were out of sight, Ann returned to the parlour to find the girls making the bed up. She didn't realise she had a smile on her face until Maddy asked, 'What are yer smiling at, Mam? Did Mrs Lizzie say something funny?'

'No, love, I'm smiling because your dad's coming home tomorrow. Just think, this time tomorrow he'll be in this bed and we'll be sitting talking to him.'

'I'll be holding his hand and kissing him,' Tess said. 'I'm going to give him a kiss for every day he's been away.'

'Me too,' Maddy said, plumping a pillow. 'I can't wait to hug him.'

'Seeing as I'm his wife, and the eldest, I get first turn,' Ann told them, starting to feel the excitement rise. 'That's only fair, I think. But

145

you'll have plenty of time for hugs and kisses, as long as you remember you can't be too rough with him because he's still in pain.'

Tess took her words to heart. 'We'll be very gentle with him, Mam, honest.'

Ann was out by nine o'clock the next morning to get her shopping in, and she wasted no time. The shops were only around the corner and she kept her eyes peeled for sight of an ambulance. At twelve o'clock she was still keeping watch, with the girls, from the parlour window. 'I thought he would have been here by now.'

'They won't have changed their minds about letting him out, will they?' Tess had been going to the front door almost every five minutes, which made the waiting time seem longer. 'I'll cry if they have.'

'Of course they won't have changed their minds. Matron told me they would have to wait until an ambulance was available, and that could be any time because a lot of people take sick and need an ambulance urgently. We'll just have to be patient, that's all.' Ann was a bundle of nerves herself, but she tried not to let it show. 'I'll make us a pot of tea and some sandwiches to keep us going.'

'Can we have them in here, Mam?' Maddy asked. 'So we can keep watch out of the window.'

At that moment an ambulance pulled up outside and the girls flew past their mother and out of the front door. She hurried after them and held them back as the driver and another man came around to open the back doors of the vehicle. They were pleasant men and smiled at the group waiting eagerly to welcome home the patient. 'Is he going upstairs, missus?'

'No, I've had the bed brought down to the front parlour.'

'God bless yer for that, missus. Stairs can be a killer when ye're climbing them about ten times a day with a stretcher. It does yer back in.' They stepped inside the ambulance and Ann heard one of them saying, 'Not long now, Mr Richardson, before ye're back in yer own bed.' Then his colleague said, 'Yer family are here waiting for yer.'

It was then the thought passed through Ann's mind that perhaps George might not want his children to see him being carried on a stretcher. Particularly with Theresa's delicate disposition. 'Look, girls, we're going to have to move because we'll only be in the way. Why don't you two go inside and make your dad a welcome-home cup of tea? I'm sure he hasn't had a decent cup of tea since he went into hospital. Will you do that for him?'

With anxious eyes trying to see what was going on in the ambulance, and eager to have first sight of their father, the sisters weren't very enthusiastic about going inside now. But a gentle prod from their mother sent them up the steps and through to the kitchen. While outside, Ann watched the stretcher being lifted and could feel her heart pounding. If she stayed there, she knew she'd burst out crying when she saw George and it was the last thing she wanted. 'I'll go and see everything is clear for you. It's the first door on the right.' With that she fled inside and gave herself a good talking-to. She was behaving like a child, and if the girls saw her crying it would set them off. Pull yourself together, you silly woman, you don't want your husband to come home to a crying match.

'In here, missus?' The men took a few seconds to manoeuvre the stretcher through the parlour door, but after that it was plain sailing and George was soon in his own bed, with Ann fussing over the pillows. 'Ye're a lucky man, Mr Richardson.' It was the driver who spoke over his shoulder as he was leaving the room. 'Not everyone gets this kind of welcome.'

'Thank you, you've been very kind.' George gestured to his wife. 'See them out, will you please, love?'

Maddy and Tess had been listening with their ears to the door, and when Ann returned it was to find them smothering their father's face with kisses. And the look on his face was absolute bliss. The three of them were laughing and crying, but, thank God, the tears were of joy. 'Ay, I thought we'd decided that I was to be the first to greet your father?'

Tess looked across the bed at her sister. 'You tell her, Maddy.'

'Yes, you decided, Mam, but we didn't say we agreed, did we?'

'You cheeky beggars! Now, have you made that pot of tea?'

'Yes, and we've set the tray all posh,' Tess said. 'Dad's going to be treated very special today.'

Maddy nodded. 'Waited on hand and foot. We'll be at his beck and call until we go back to school on Monday morning.'

'There's no time like the present to start, so off you go and bring the tea in.' Ann waited until they'd left the room before making her way to the bed. She had just pressed her lips on to her husband's when there was a knock on the front door. She closed her eyes and moaned. 'Oh dear, who can this be? Probably a hawker trying to sell something. I won't be a minute.'

It wasn't a hawker, it was Maisie from next door, and she was holding out a bunch of flowers. 'These are from me and the Critchleys, just to tell George we're glad he's back home again.'

'Oh, Maisie, they're lovely!' Ann pressed her nose to the red roses, pink carnations and white marguerites. 'What a nice thought! George will be over the moon! Thank you!'

'I won't keep yer 'cos I know he's just got home.' She grinned and

147

said, 'I just happened to glance through my window and saw the ambulance. And if yer believe that, yer'll believe anything. Me and the kids have been watching all morning.'

'What about us? We've been on pins since nine o'clock. But he's home at last, and I can't express how happy I feel.'

'Go and tell him, and when ye're doling out yer kisses, slip one in for me. Ta-ra now, I'll see yer tomorrow.'

'Thanks, Maisie.' Ann turned to find her daughters wide-eyed at the huge bunch of flowers.

'Can we put them in a vase, Mam, and they can go in the parlour so me Dad can see them?' Tess was holding out her arms. 'Please?'

'I'll help her, Mam,' Maddy said. 'I'll look for the vases.'

Ann handed over the flowers. 'Give me and your father five minutes together, please. I haven't even had a kiss yet.'

'We'll let you have ten minutes,' Maddy said, with mock seriousness. 'I'll put the cosy over the teapot to keep it warm, but don't be too long.'

Ann closed the parlour door behind her and crossed to the bed where George was watching her with hunger in his eyes. 'We've got ten minutes, love, before our daughters come knocking with the tea. So can we get our kissing over before I ask you how you are, and is it all right if I sit on the side of the bed?'

George reached for her hand. 'I'm still in pain, love, but it's bearable, now I'm home. And yes, you can sit on the side of the bed. And yes, you can sleep in this bed with me, tonight and every night.' He reached up, put a hand behind her head and brought it down so their lips were touching. 'I have a few things to tell you, but they'll wait. This is far more important, seeing as our daughters have only given us ten minutes.'

Chapter Eleven

'You're making excellent progress, Mr Richardson.' Dr Greenshields snapped his bag shut and transferred it from the bed to the floor. 'And it is in no small way due to yourself and your determination to get better.'

George was sitting on the side of the bed, pulling on his trousers. 'How long before I can go back to work, Doctor? It's been eight weeks now.'

'Ask me in another two weeks and we'll discuss it then. The bones seem to be mending nicely, but we don't want to overdo it.' The doctor had been calling once every week to examine George, and he had come to admire him for his fortitude. 'You have done very well, keeping to the exercises, but it would be silly to rush things. I can understand you wanting to get back to work as soon as possible, but it would be foolhardy not to recognise the risks in attempting something you are not yet fit for.'

George stood up and pulled his braces over his shoulders. 'It's my job I'm worried about, I can't afford to lose it.'

'Under the circumstances, I'm sure your employer is sympathetic.' Dr Greenshields placed his tall hard hat on his head, using both hands to set it straight. 'As the accident was caused by the negligence of one of his workers, I don't think he can sack you even if he wanted to.'

'Oh, he could if he wanted to, there's nothing to stop him. You see, workers don't have any rights. But he's a good man and wouldn't do that. He has assured me there will be a job waiting for me as soon as I'm fit. It won't be my old job, because of the heavy lifting, more like office work, really. Lighter work, with less hours, but a big drop in pay.'

'No matter how light the work, I can't sign you off as being fit if I don't think you are. I won't call next week because you don't really need me. But I'll call the week after, and if you have continued to improve I will no doubt say you may start work the following Monday. Until then, keep up the exercises.' The doctor nodded a goodbye before opening the parlour door to find Ann hovering outside. 'Your husband is doing very well, Mrs Richardson, very well indeed.'

Ann saw him out, then hastened to the parlour. 'Well, love, what did he say?'

George was sitting on the bed looking a picture of dejection. On a big sigh, he said, 'I'm doing fine, but he won't sign me off for at least another two weeks.'

Ann dropped down beside him and put an arm across his shoulders. 'He's the doctor, love, so he knows what he's talking about. Two weeks isn't so bad, it'll soon pass.'

Her husband didn't answer right away. Mr Fisher was still paying him the same wages, which Lizzie brought every Saturday, but George hadn't told his wife that the last time his boss came to see him, it was to tell him about the job he would be going back to. One which would make his wage packet nearly six shillings a week lighter. He hadn't mentioned it to his wife because he saw no point in worrying her until he had to. They barely made ends meet now, so how would they manage with six shillings a week less? But he had to tell her, it was only fair to warn her.

George took his wife's arm from around his shoulder and held her hand. Looking into her eyes, he said, 'I haven't been honest with you, love, because I didn't want to worry you. I told you when Mr Fisher came to see me that he had offered me a lighter job, one with no lifting. But what I didn't tell you was that the new job pays less money and I'll be dropping nearly six shillings a week.'

Ann's heart sank. Six shillings a week was a lot of money, they'd never be able to manage. But her gaze stayed fixed on his face. Not for any money would she upset him, not after all he'd been through. 'We'll just have to make the best of it, love. The main thing is you're on the mend, and that's more important to me than money.'

'You can't live without money, Ann, and we've had a struggle to manage on what I've been earning. With so much less coming in, we'll have to starve ourselves to get by.'

'We can't alter things, love, so we'll just have to grin and bear it. It won't be for that long, because Madelaine leaves school in nine months' time and we'll have her wage coming in.'

George managed a crooked grin. 'Ann, love, Maddy will be lucky if she starts work on four shillings a week. By the time her fares and pocket money are taken out, plus her carry-out, there'll be little left. And while I know she would pass all her money over if she thought we needed it, I don't want that to happen. I couldn't live with myself if I thought she couldn't have what the other girls she'll be working with have. She'll be making friends and I don't want her tied down to helping the family. New clothes and a few coppers in her pocket so she can go out and enjoy herself, that's what I want for her. She'll be starting on the road to becoming a young woman, and I want her to know the fun and sense of freedom that I knew when I was her age. Out with her mates, not tied down to helping support the family.'

'Then I'll look for a part-time job to make up the difference,' Ann said, hoping to take the look of failure from his face. 'A couple of hours each morning when the girls are at school. We'll manage, love, I know we will.'

George patted her hand, thinking how little his wife knew of what went on outside her home. She didn't know that there were so many men out of work their wives had taken any kind of jobs to bring a few bob into the house. But the only work they could get was menial work, like scrubbing floors or taking in washing. He couldn't see Ann doing either. She was an intelligent woman who would be good at any type of office work, if she could get it. But from what he knew, most firms were employing young girls because they were cheap labour. 'We'll worry about it when the time comes, eh, love? My mother always used to say, "Don't go looking for trouble because it'll find you soon enough." So let's take her advice, shall we?'

'Yes, we'll do that.' Ann got to her feet. 'I'll make us a nice pot of tea. I bet you could do with one after being put through your paces.'

'Oh, it's not so bad, only a case of lying on the bed and the doctor pressing lightly on the bottom of my back. There's no real pain now, it's just tender in parts.'

'Come on through to the living room and we'll have a quiet cuppa before the girls come home for their lunch. And when they go back to school you can walk to the shops with me for a bit of exercise. I need to get something in for our dinner tonight.'

Following on his wife's heels, George said, 'D'you know what I fancy? A sheet of bacon ribs with cabbage cooked in the water. My mouth's watering at the thought.'

'Then you shall have it, my love. It's the girls' favourite, so they'll be delighted. But let's not tell them, eh? Let it be a nice surprise.'

Tess came through the living room door, sniffed up and rolled her eyes. 'Ooh, yummy, yummy! Spare ribs and cabbage!'

George grinned. His younger daughter was eating better these days and even had some colour in her cheeks. 'It's next door you can smell, sweetheart, we're having corned beef and mashed potato.'

She put her arms around his neck and kissed him noisily. 'You're telling fibs, Dad, aren't you? I can feel the smell coming from our stove, and it's going up my nose and making me feel very hungry.'

Maddy elbowed her aside. 'Move over and let me have my kiss.' Her deep brown eyes smiling, she said to her father, 'If you're not telling fibs, I'm going next door to ask Mrs Wilkins if I can have my dinner with them. I'm sure she could manage an extra one at the table.'

'Dinner will be half an hour yet, and it *is* your favourite,' Ann said, hanging a towel on the hook behind the kitchen door. 'But the tea in the pot is still fresh if you feel like a cup?'

'I'll have one, what about you, Tess?'

'Yes please! It felt a bit cold coming home, Mam, so can I put my singlet on tomorrow?'

'The weather has gone chilly, so I think you should wear it all the time now. We're into October so we can expect it to get colder.'

Ann was getting up from her chair when Maddy put a hand on her shoulder. 'I'll pour our tea out, Mam, you stay where you are.' She was back a minute later, carrying two cups, one of which she handed to her sister before sitting down. 'How are Mr and Mrs Critchley these days, Mam? I haven't seen anything of them for weeks.'

'They seem fine now, and they're eating better. Maisie and I take turns in going over each day to check on them. They walk to the shops every morning to get some exercise and fresh air, but that's the only time they go out. And, of course, with you being at school then you wouldn't see them.'

'You don't know when their birthdays are, do you? You see, our teacher is showing us how to make cards for Christmas, and I could easily make one for birthdays. I'd like to make one for them, they're so nice and don't have any family to send them cards.'

'I couldn't tell you, Madelaine, but I suppose I could find out by asking in a roundabout way. I'll do a bit of digging tomorrow and see if I can wheedle it out of them.'

'You can show me how to make cards, Maddy,' Tess said. 'I'd like to send one to Mrs Gwen and Uncle Mered, and to the Thomases. They'd like that, wouldn't they, Dad? Especially if I've made them myself.'

'I'm sure they'd be over the moon, pet! I know I would be if someone went to the trouble of making a card for me. It shows there's a lot of thought gone into it.'

'You need stiff paper for it,' Maddy said. 'Ordinary paper is no good. But my teacher said you can buy a sheet of it for a penny and it will make about six cards. Then you need green and red colouring pencils for trees and Father Christmas. We've already got black and brown crayons, they'll do for the reindeers and chimney pots.'

Tess was clapping her hands in delight. 'Oh, it sounds lovely, Maddy, you'll have to teach me. Will you show me tonight, after dinner?'

'Patience, Theresa, you haven't got the necessary paper and crayons,' Ann said. 'When you get your penny pocket money on Saturday you can buy the paper, and unless Madelaine has something else to spend her penny on, perhaps she'll buy the crayons.'

Maddy nodded. 'I'll go to Woolworth's in the Vale on Saturday afternoon and get what we need from there. I'm quite looking forward to it now.'

'Will you take me with you to Woolworth's?' Tess asked. 'Please, pretty please?'

George could tell by his wife's face that the request didn't find favour with her, so he got in before she had a chance to speak. His younger daughter needed some room to grow up, to have confidence in herself. The day would come when she'd have to go out into the world on her own, and she had to be prepared for it. 'Of course Maddy will take you. If you promise not to leave her side for a second. The Vale is a very busy place on a Saturday.'

Looking as though butter wouldn't melt in her mouth, Tess shook her head. 'Cross my heart and hope to die, Dad, I'll stick to her like glue.'

Maddy groaned and squeezed her eyes tight. 'You've just reminded me, we need glue! We can't finish the cards off without it! Not the Christmas cards, anyway! We need to stick bits of cotton wool on to make it look like snow, and Father Christmas has to have a white fluffy beard! The cards won't look nice without all the trimmings.'

Ann saw the disappointment on the faces of both her daughters and thought quickly. 'You won't need to buy glue, I'll make you some with flour and water.'

'Will that be any good, Mam?' Maddy asked.

Her mother waved her hand around the room. 'This wallpaper was stuck on with flour and water, and it's lasted five years.'

George chuckled. 'There you are, girls, saved by the bell.'

Ann put a finger to her lips. 'Shush! Listen! Isn't that Maisie shouting? It sounds as though there's something wrong, I'd better go and see.' She ran down the hall with the girls close behind and George following more slowly.

The shouting got louder as Ann neared the front door and she feared there'd been an accident of some kind. She pulled the door wide, to see Maisie standing on her path shouting and pointing a finger at her two daughters, who were crying.

'You stupid pair of nits,' Maisie yelled. 'Have yer not got the sense yer were born with? At your age yer should be able to stick up for yerselves without coming crying to me.'

'What is it, Maisie?' Ann asked, stepping down to the low wall which separated the two paths. 'What on earth has happened?'

'It's these two stupid beggars, honestly, I could strangle them. Yer know we bought them a rubber ball each and a bat, when we were on holiday? Well they went out half an hour ago to have a game of rounders, and two lads came and pinched the balls off them. And these two stood like lemons and let them!'

'We didn't just let them, Mam, we tried to stop them!' At thirteen, Nita was a year older than her sister, Letty. 'We ran after them and tried to get the balls back, but they punched us, and one of them pushed our Letty over.' Tears were flowing freely at the injustice. It was bad enough having their balls stolen and being punched, but to be told off for it was unfair. 'Look, all her leg is scraped and it's bleeding.'

Letty lifted her leg as proof. 'It's not half sore, Mam.'

Maisie looked down at the grazed knee and her temper against her daughters evaporated. 'Yer mean they did that to yer?'

The girl sniffed up. 'Yeah, and they ran away laughing.'

'You can't blame the girls,' Ann said. 'It wasn't their fault. The boys must be real bullies as well as thieves.'

'Young ruffians would be a better description,' George said. 'Do you know the boys?'

Nita wiped a hand across her eyes. 'They both go to our school and they live in Chatsworth Avenue. They're horrible, and always in trouble with the teachers for hitting boys from the juniors.'

'They'll be in trouble when I get hold of them,' Maisie said, through gritted teeth. 'I'll strangle the pair of them.'

'One of them wouldn't be Greg Saunders, would it?' Maddy asked. 'Tall, with black curly hair and walks with a swagger as though he owns the world?'

'Yeah, and Billy White was with him,' Nita said. 'But it was Greg what did it, Billy only stood and watched.'

'D'yer know what number Chatsworth this Greg lives at?' Maisie asked. 'I think I'll pay his mother a visit.'

When Nita shook her head, Maddy said, 'I don't know the number, but I can point the house out to you.'

'Right, I'll just get me coat.'

'Maisie, don't you think it would be better to wait until Will gets home?' George was thinking that if the parents were anything like their son, Maisie might find herself in trouble. 'I'd come myself, but I don't think I'm up to fisticuffs yet.'

'I wouldn't dream of letting yer come, George. I'll be all right, I'm quite able to look after meself. If Maddy will just point the house out to me, then I'll send her back.'

'I'll come with you,' Ann said, surprising herself, because she thought it was really common for women to have a slanging match in the street. But Maisie was a friend, and if the positions were reversed she knew her neighbour would be the first to stand beside her. 'Will you keep an eye on the pans, George, till I get back? We shouldn't be long.'

'I'm coming with you,' Tess said, linking her arm through her mother's. 'I know that Greg Saunders and he's always swearing and hitting people. I'll make sure he doesn't hit you.'

'No, love, you stay and help your father with the dinner, there's a good girl.'

'But Maddy's going with you, that's not fair!'

'Madelaine is not coming with us. She's going to point the house out and then she'll be sent straight home. Now get my coat off the hall stand, please, and then help set the table.'

'You don't need to come, yer know, Ann,' Maisie said. 'I don't mind going on my own.'

'I wish you'd both wait until Will gets home.' George wasn't very happy about this. Maisie might be able to stand up for herself, but his wife certainly wasn't. 'He'll be home in about half an hour.'

Maisie shook her head. 'No, George, the way I look at it is, if I take a man with me it looks as though I'm expecting trouble. And I'm not, unless the mother is as bad as her son, and I can't see that. I'm confident of coming home with two rubber balls, not two black eyes.'

Maddy pointed to a corner house. 'That's where Greg Saunders lives, but I don't know which house Billy White lives in.'

'That's all right, love, now you run off home. Make sure the pan with the ribs in doesn't boil dry, there's a good girl.' Ann watched her daughter walk away, then turned to her neighbour. 'D'you know what you're going to say, Maisie?'

'I haven't got a clue, girl, but I'll think of something. The woman can't be that unreasonable she doesn't know it's wrong for her son to steal and push young girls over. But even if she is that unreasonable, even if she's a dragon what breathes fire, it's not going to stop me from getting the two balls back for my daughters. And I'll tell yer this much, Ann, I ain't going home without them.' With those words of determination, Maisie walked up the short path and rapped on the door with the brass knocker.

'Yeah, what d'yer want?'

The woman was as big as a house, and the lack of friendliness or politeness in her voice sent shivers down Ann's spine. She wouldn't want to get on the wrong side of this one.

'Are you Mrs Saunders?' Maisie asked.

'What if I am? What's it got to do with you?' The woman went to close the door, saying, 'I've got no bleedin' time to waste on you, go and get lost.'

155

But Maisie was quick and her foot shot out to stop the door from closing. As soon as she'd set eyes on the woman, who must weigh at least twenty stone, she had her taped as a bully who got away with murder because people were frightened of her. Well, she'd play her at her own game. 'You've got no bleedin' time! Well, I like that! I've got no bleedin' time to waste either! If your son wasn't such a bleedin' thief, I'd be at the stove now getting my feller's dinner ready.'

The door was opened wide and the woman came to stand at the edge of the step and folded her enormous arms. 'What did yer say? Did I hear yer call my son a thief?'

'There's nothing wrong with yer bleedin' hearing, is there? Yeah, I called yer son a thief, and he's a bully as well. Him and his mate, Billy White, stole two balls off my daughters and pushed one of them over, cutting her knee open.'

'Sod off, the pair of yer, before I belt yer one.' The woman straightened her arms and flexed her muscles. 'You call my son a thief again and ye're asking for trouble. Now get out of me sight before I lose my temper. Yer cheeky pair of bleeders.'

Maisie was shaking inside, but her determination never wavered. Pushing her face so close to the woman she could feel her breath, she said, 'Go on, belt me one, I dare yer.'

Greg Saunders' mother was taken aback, but not for long. 'I'm warning yer, yer stupid cow, get away from here or yer won't know what's hit yer.'

'Oh, I will know what's hit me. And when I fetch the police, both you and yer thieving son will be in trouble.'

'Police! What police? I haven't done nothing wrong, so yer needn't bring the bleedin' police to this house.'

'I'll have to bring them to this house for yer son. That's after they've seen the injuries he's caused to me daughter's leg when he stole the two balls. So, you belt me one and I can kill two birds with one stone.'

Ann decided it was time she said something. 'Come along, Maisie, don't lower yourself by arguing with her. She won't listen to reason, and there's no way she's going to get the balls back for you. So let's go to the police station and get it over with.' She glanced at the woman and said, softly, 'They should be here within the hour to see your son. Robbery with violence is a serious offence.'

The two women had stepped from the path on to the pavement when a very subdued voice brought them to a halt. 'Yer didn't ask me to get the balls for yer.'

'Oh, yer knew what I wanted, why else would I be here?' Maisie could sense victory but wasn't going to let the woman get away with it so easily. 'Not to worry, though, the police will get them back for me.'

'If our Greg's got them, I'll get them off him. And break his bleedin' neck into the bargain. Just hang on a minute.'

'No!' Maisie stopped her in her tracks. 'I want your son to bring the balls out himself. Let's see if he's so brave when he's facing grown-ups. And I want him to know that if he as much as looks sideways at either of my girls again I will personally give him a good hiding before taking him along, by the scruff of the neck, to the police station.'

The woman used the frame of the door to pull herself up the steps, and her massive bulk filled the doorway. 'Our Greg, get yer bleedin' arse down here, right now.'

The voice that called back sounded as though it came from upstairs. 'I'm doin' something, yer'll have to wait.'

'I don't care what ye're doing, get yerself down here quick.' The woman had waddled along the hallway to stand at the bottom of the stairs. And when she bawled, the whole of the street must have heard her. 'If I have to come up there yer'll be sorry, 'cos I'll break every bleedin' bone in yer body.'

Ann winced and shook her head in disgust. Fancy talking to your child like that. No wonder the lad was out of hand, you couldn't expect anything else. This woman, with her common-as-muck voice and bullying ways, wasn't going to set anyone a good example.

Footsteps running down the stairs could be heard, and then, 'What d'yer want? I was in the middle of doin' something and yer've gone and spoilt it now.'

'Any more lip out of yer and I'll spoil yer bleedin' face for yer. Now, where's the two balls yer nicked off some girls, their mothers are here asking for them back.'

'I didn't nick no balls, it must have been someone else. Tell them to get lost.'

Maisie and Ann saw the lad turn on his heels, ready to go back up the stairs, but he never made it. A hand as big as a shovel shot out and grabbed him by the scruff of the neck, shaking him like a rag doll. 'Don't give me that, smart-arse, I want you in front of me with the balls in yer hand inside two minutes.' The woman flung him into the living room. 'You heard what I said, two flaming minutes.'

'Blimey,' Maisie said softly, 'fancy having to live with that. I almost feel sorry for the lad, but he needs to be taught a lesson. He's not going to learn the difference between right and wrong from his mother, that's a dead cert.'

The lad, who was pushed to the door by hands from which there was no escape, wore a scowl on his face, plus a look of defiance and cockiness. 'There's the ruddy balls, missus, and I didn't nick 'em, the girls gave them to me.'

157

Maisie was taken aback by the hardness of a lad so young. The look of insolence on his face was frightening. God help him when he grew older, he'd be like a gangster. And the woman standing behind him, looking as hard as nails, would be responsible. 'So, ye're a liar as well as a thief and bully who knocks young girls over, eh?'

The boy's top lip curled in a sneer, as though he found the whole thing funny. 'I didn't knock her over, she tripped up.'

Maisie took the balls and passed them to Ann, and waited, both hands ready, for the boy to turn to go back inside the house. Then she moved as quick as lightning. With one hand on his back she pushed him hard, and with the other she grabbed his arm to save him before he hit the ground. But her action had the desired effect, because his face drained of colour. He'd got a fright when he'd seen the ground coming towards him, and it showed. He turned to his mother, expecting her to come to his aid as she always did, but she stood there with her arms folded under the mountain of flesh that was her bosom. The word 'police' had caused her to become very docile, because if a copper came to the house, her feller would blow his top, and he was the only person in the world she feared.

Seeing no help was coming from that quarter, Greg Saunders decided to bluff it out. He was the leader of a gang of local youths who all did as they were told because they were frightened of him. It wouldn't do his reputation any good if it got out that he'd been pushed over by a woman. 'What the hell did yer do that for, yer silly cow?'

'Gave yer a fright, did it? Well that's how my daughter felt when you pushed her. Only you got off lucky. I stopped yer from hitting the ground, so yer haven't got yer knee split open like she has.'

'I told yer,' the boy snarled, 'she tripped up.'

'Yer deserve to be punished to put a stop to yer bullying, but it's not up to me to punish yer. And from what I've seen, yer don't get any discipline at home. So my best bet is to take my girl along to see your headmaster tomorrow and let him punish yer.' Maisie took Ann's arm. 'Come on, let's go.' They'd only gone a few steps when they heard a loud howl. And they turned to see the boy with his head bent and a hand cupping his ear. He was crying out in pain and this brought about Ann's temper.

'Excuse me a minute.' She took her arm from Maisie's and walked back. 'If you had brought your son up properly, shown him love instead of clouts, he wouldn't be the young ruffian he is. Everything he does is down to you, because you haven't brought him up the right way. I feel sorry for him having a mother like you, and you're to be pitied.'

With the roar of a lion the woman moved forward, her fists curled ready for action. But Maisie acted quickly to stand between them. 'Fancy a night in the police cells, do yer, Mrs Saunders? It can easily be arranged, all yer have to do is lay a hand on me or me friend. As I'm the nearest, yer may as well make it me.' She tilted her head and pointed to her chin. 'I dare yer.'

'Don't do it, Mam,' the boy cried. 'Me dad will kill me if the police come round.' His words didn't seem to be having any effect, and seeing his mother with nostrils flared and growling like an animal ready to attack, he said the only thing he knew that would stop her. 'And he'll belt you, as well. He told yer last time yer had a fight with one of the neighbours that if yer did it again he'd slaughter yer.'

This gave the woman food for thought, and as she hesitated, Maisie grabbed Ann's arm. 'Come on, we've got what we came for. We'll have a word with our husbands and see if they want to take the matter further.'

As they walked away, the two women could hear muttering, peppered with swear words. Then the boy ran past to stand in front of them, causing them to stop. 'I'm sorry, missus, I won't do it no more.'

'Yer better hadn't, son, or next time I'll have yer guts for garters. Now move out of our way, we've wasted enough time.'

'Oh dear,' Ann said when they were out of earshot. 'I really thought she was going to let fly there. And one punch from her would have knocked me out.'

'Yeah, she's some woman, I'll give yer that.' Maisie squeezed her arm. 'It was exciting, though, wasn't it, girl? Wait until I tell my feller, he'll be sorry he missed it.'

'I'm afraid it's not the sort of excitement I enjoy. I'm not cut out for dealing with people like Mrs Saunders, they terrify me.'

When they turned the corner into Hanford Avenue they could see a group outside their houses. 'Looks like a welcoming committee,' Maisie laughed. 'That's Will talking to George, he's probably getting the low-down on what's gone on. I hope his ruddy dinner hasn't boiled dry or he won't be a happy man.'

'George will have been keeping an eye on mine. Mind you, I didn't think we'd be away so long, not over two rubber balls.'

'They only cost tuppence each, Ann, but it wasn't the money, it was the principle. I'll not have my girls bullied by anyone. And talking of my girls, here they come to see how I got on. Our Letty's knee doesn't seem to be bothering her, she can run all right.' Maisie took the balls out of her pocket and lobbed them high. 'Here yer are, catch!'

The girls were delighted and wanted to know what had happened and why they'd been away so long. But Maisie silenced them and said she'd tell all after they'd had their dinner. That was if there was any dinner left, like.

George was a very relieved man. 'I thought you'd walked into trouble, love, the time you've been away.'

'It could have turned out very nasty, and I've got to admit I was shaking in my shoes most of the time.' Ann smiled when she saw the table nicely set. And thinking of the Saunders family, she told herself she was very lucky to have a good husband and two lovely daughters. 'But Maisie found the one word Mrs Saunders didn't like, and that was "police". She was going to tear us apart until she heard that.' Maddy and Tess were listening, wide-eyed and ready to hang on to every word. Well they weren't going to hear every word, because most of them were not for the ears of children. Not in this house, anyway. 'Do you remember the woman we met on the train, Vera Webster?'

'You didn't see her, did you, Mam?' Maddy looked surprised. 'I didn't know she lived around here.'

'No, I haven't seen her, I just wanted to give you an idea of what Greg Saunders' mother is like. You know how big Vera was, well, Mrs Saunders is twice the size of her. And her language is twice as bad.'

'I believe you're exaggerating a little,' George said. 'No one could be twice the size of Mrs Webster, it's impossible.'

'Well, let's say she's half as big again. And where I found myself liking Vera, I couldn't like this woman if I was paid to.' Ann bustled out to the kitchen. 'Anyway, the girls got their balls back and that's what it was all about. Any more questions will have to wait until after I've put the dinner out, because I'm famished.'

It was two o'clock on Saturday when Lizzie called with George's wages. And as usual she brought the living room to life with her loud voice and laughter. 'That feller what took your place, George, is a real head case. He's as thick as two short planks and can't add up for nuts.' She allowed Maddy to relieve her of her coat before sitting down and holding her hands out towards the fire. 'There's a cold wind coming in from the Mersey and yer can't half feel it down by the docks. I'm frozen through to me marrow. And we're only into October, so God help us when winter sets in.'

'Move closer to the fire, Lizzie,' George said to the woman who had been more of a friend than anyone. She called at least one night through the week, and every Saturday. 'You'll soon thaw out.'

She gave her cheeky grin. 'It's the poor brass monkeys what I feel sorry for, George. Yer know what happens to them when it's freezing.'

Tess was all ears. 'What happens to the poor monkeys, Mrs Lizzie?'

'Nothing bad happens to them,' George said quickly, before the woman could say something that would horrify his wife. He could feel a chuckle deep inside him, but Ann wouldn't think it a bit funny. 'It's

160

just that they don't have very thick fur to protect them from the cold.'

'That's just what I was going to say.' Lizzie was thinking she'd nearly come a cropper there. 'But yer dad beat me to it.'

Maddy had heard the expression about brass monkeys, because the girls in school used it and you couldn't go around with your ears closed. But her parents wouldn't appreciate that school was a place where you learned many things that weren't taught by the teacher. 'I didn't know that, Mrs Lizzie. The poor things must hate the winter coming.'

'Why can't someone give them coats to wear?' Tess asked. 'And gloves and scarves, then they'd be nice and warm.'

'Never mind worrying about monkeys,' Ann said. 'You want to go to Woolworth's and I have my shopping to get in. So hurry and put your coats on, and scarves.'

'Going to the Vale, are yer, Ann?'

'Yes, there's more selection there than the shops around here. But you stay by the fire and keep warm, we won't be very long.'

'I'll stay for half an hour and have a natter to George,' Lizzie told her. 'But I'll be gone before you get back 'cos I need some shopping meself. I'll see yer through the week, though, as usual.'

When they were alone, Lizzie asked, 'What did the doctor have to say this week, George?'

'Same as last week, I'm doing fine but he won't sign me off until the week after next. And that's only if he feels sure I'm fit.'

'How d'yer feel in yerself? Do you feel up to it?'

'Some days I feel on top of the world, but I have the odd days when I don't seem to have any energy. Still, in another two weeks I'll be as right as rain.'

'Ye're going back to a light job, that's a blessing. No heavy lifting, just walking and making an inventory of what comes in, what's in stock and what goes out. And it's less hours so yer can have an extra half-hour in bed every morning.'

George leaned his elbows on his knees and sighed. 'It's also less money, Lizzie, and we'll have a struggle to manage.'

'Yeah, I think that's bleeding lousy, I really do. Through no fault of yer own, yer spend weeks in agony and then go back to work on less pay. It just don't seem right to me.'

'It could have been worse, Lizzie, I could have ended up in a wheelchair for life.'

'Yeah, there's that way of looking at it. And yer'll get by, it's just a case of cutting down on everything. After a while it becomes a way of life.'

'I suppose so. Anyway, Lizzie, tell me about the bloke who's got my job.'

161

'His name's Phil Easton, in his thirties, married with three kids. He's as thin as a beanpole, with sandy hair and a pale face. He's a nice enough bloke, but as I said, he's as thick as two short planks. Definitely tuppence short of a shilling. Take yesterday, for instance, I was going to the chippy for the men. With the weather being colder most of them don't bring sandwiches, they'd rather have something hot. He'd heard me asking all the men what they wanted, and it was the same as usual for all of them. A pennyworth of chips and a pennyworth of scallops. When I got to Bill, he said chips and scallops and the queer feller said he'd have the same. And he gave me a thrupenny joey. When I got back, I gave him his bag wrapped in newspaper and a penny change. Then he said I'd made a mistake, he should have tuppence change. I tried to keep me patience, and explained that two one pennies made tuppence and he was only entitled to one penny change. But would he have it? Would he buggery! He said he'd heard, with his own ears, Bill saying a penn'orth of chips and scallops and he'd said he'd have the same. I talked till I was blue in the face, and me own chips were getting cold. The men were standing around laughing their heads off, they thought it was hilarious. At least they thought it was until I blew my top and then they moved away. I was just about to clock this Phil one, when Bill came along and he tried to explain to the stupid nit that I wasn't diddling him. What a bloody performance it was, all over a penny.'

George could see the scene in his mind's eye, with Lizzie shaking a fist and getting more angry and red-faced by the minute. And he knew he would have found it funny, but he kept his face straight. 'How did it end up, did Bill convince him?'

'Did he hell! Nothing would convince the silly bugger that I wasn't trying to do him out of a penny. So it ended up, George, with me opening his parcel and counting the bleeding chips and scallops into two piles on the newspaper. And he actually stood there and counted with me! That's when I really lost me rag, and I did no more than pick the lot up and emptied it over his head. He'll not ask me again to get anything from the chippy, I can tell yer.'

George chuckled. Oh, he'd be glad to get back to work to have a laugh with his mates.

Chapter Twelve

'You don't have to leave yet,' Ann said as she watched her husband pulling on his coat. 'Eight o'clock would give you plenty of time to get there.'

'I don't want to take a chance on being late on my first day back, love, it wouldn't look too good.' George suddenly remembered how he'd felt when he was fourteen and his mother was standing on the front step seeing him off to work on his first day. He'd been sick with excitement and apprehension. And that was the feeling he had now. The only difference being he was a forty-two-year-old man now, not a young boy. 'I can't walk as fast as I used to, so I'd rather give myself that bit of extra time.'

Maddy came running down the stairs, followed by Tess. When she saw her father ready to go out, she said, 'We're just in time for a kiss, Dad.' And as she moved back to make way for her sister, she added, 'I hope you get on all right at work.'

'Yes,' Tess told him, her face serious. 'Remember what the doctor told you and don't go lifting anything heavy.'

'I'll remember.' George stroked their hair, which was ruffled after a night's sleep. 'Don't forget, I'll be home half an hour earlier. That's one of the perks of the job.'

'Let your dad be on his way now, girls, so he doesn't have to rush. You get washed while I'm seeing him out and I'll start your breakfast in a few minutes.'

George kissed his wife before stepping down on to the path. 'I feel like a new boy, instead of someone who's worked there for the last twenty-six years, except for the war years. I'm looking forward to seeing all my mates again and having a laugh, but I'll be glad to get this first day over.'

'Get the first half-hour over, love, and you'll be fine. Just don't try to do too much on your first day.'

George pulled the collar of his coat up to protect his ears against the cold wind. 'I'll see you tonight.' With a wave of his hand he was off, and Ann watched until he'd turned the corner of the street before going back into the house. She knew he'd be all right because Lizzie had assured her she'd be keeping an eye on him and making sure he didn't overdo things. And Ann had great faith in Lizzie.

George reported to the office as he'd been told to do, and was greeted warmly by the clerk and young typist. The clerk, Joe Brogan, had been with the firm as long as George and acted as book-keeper and wages clerk, while the young girl, Irene, did the typing and filing. 'Glad to be back, are yer, George?' Joe asked, his dark hair showing more white than George remembered, and he was getting quite a paunch. 'I bet yer missed the old place, eh?'

'I didn't for the first few weeks, Joe, I was too busy feeling sorry for myself. But once I was on my feet I did. I missed all my mates, the smell of the Mersey and being busy. Right now, though, I feel like a loose end not knowing what I'm supposed to do.'

'The man who's doing the job now will show yer the ropes. He's a friend of Mr Fisher and only came to help out until you were fit again. Proper gent he is, yer'll like him.' Joe grinned as he pointed to the man just coming through the door. 'Speaking of the devil, here he comes, the man himself.'

George tried to hide his surprise as he shook hands with the man, who was introduced as Mr Hancock. He was much older than George, probably in his late sixties, slight of figure with sparse white hair. 'I'm pleased to meet you, Mr Hancock.'

'Call me Albert, and I'll call you George, it sounds much more friendly.' The man's smile was kindly. 'I can see you're wondering what on earth an old codger like me is doing here. Well, my friend Mr Fisher asked me to fill in as a favour. I used to work in a solicitor's office but have been retired now for some five years.' It was obvious he was an educated man, well spoken and wearing a suit that, although showing wear, was made of the finest cloth. 'I have enjoyed my stint here, but won't be sorry to go back into retirement when you have settled into the job. And my wife will be very happy, she misses having me around to boss.'

'I hope I won't be a disappointment to you, Albert,' George said. 'I'm usually quite quick at picking things up, but this job is completely new to me.'

'It was new to me, but it only took me a week to find my feet, it's really very easy. I've found myself an old desk just outside this office, and I think it would be helpful if you and I sit down and I'll go through this with you.' Albert patted a thick hardback book he had under his arm. 'Shall we get started? We'll work until the bell goes, then we'll have a break and a cup of tea.'

When the book was opened, and George saw all the figures, he wished he was back lifting the heavy sacks. He'd never get his head around this in a month of Sundays. But he was soon to find Albert had a way of explaining things that made them easy to understand. And he possessed the patience of a saint. 'If there's anything you don't understand, George, tell me and I'll go over it with you again. Don't be afraid to speak out.'

George quickly decided there was no point in nodding and trying to look intelligent when he hadn't a clue, there would be nothing to gain by that and he'd soon find himself in hot water. So anything he wasn't sure of, he would query. And he was so wrapped up in what his brain was taking in, he was amazed when the bell rang. 'Good grief, is that the time? That hour has just flown over.'

Albert grinned. 'Are you any the wiser?'

'Let's say I'm beginning to see the light.' George returned his grin. 'You're a very good teacher, Albert.'

'A teacher is only as good as his pupil. Now, when we've had a drink, I'll take you around and show you where I've gathered all these figures from.'

George leaned back in his chair. 'I'm a little confused, so perhaps you can help me. I was told the bloke who had this job for years, Dave Pilkington, had been put on my old job as a temporary measure. Then last week I was told another man, Phil Easton, was doing my job. So what has happened to Dave? He hasn't been sacked to make way for me, has he?'

'No, he's upstairs in the weighing department. And he's quite happy because the pay is better. This job doesn't pay very well, I'm afraid.'

'I know, I'm going to feel the pinch. But it's a job, and there's many a man would be glad of it.'

'Ah, I see we're being done proud today, the lovely Lizzie is bringing our tea.'

Lizzie's smile stretched from ear to ear. 'It's good to see yer back, George.' She plonked two mugs on the desk before standing back and folding her arms. 'George is me best mate, Mr Hancock. Me very own heart-throb.'

'Watch it, Lizzie, you'll be getting me a bad name. Don't think I'm not flattered, though, because what man wouldn't be?'

'See, I told yer he was a real gent, didn't I? He wouldn't hurt no one's feelings would George.' Lizzie nodded to emphasise her point. 'He's a gentleman, just like yerself, Mr Hancock. Not like the rest of them, I can tell yer. One of them once said I had a backside as big as a hippopotamus, and before I had time to clout him one, his mate, the cheeky bugger, said I had a face to match! Now, that's no way to talk to a lady, is it?'

'I'm sure it was said in jest, Lizzie,' Albert told her. 'All the men seem to think very highly of you.'

'Yeah, they're not a bad lot. It's a good job I've got a sense of humour, though, which is more than can be said for those two buggers when I belted them.'

George chuckled. She was a real pick-me-up was Lizzie. 'They'll be cursing you now if they're waiting for their tea. It's bitterly cold out there, they need something to warm them up.'

'I took theirs out to them before I brought yours.' Lizzie's bosom moved up and down as the laughter came. 'I told yer about Phil Easton, didn't I? He's the feller what works with Bill now, and what a long string of misery he is. I don't think a day goes by that he doesn't have something to moan about. Either the tea's too hot, too strong, or I haven't put enough milk in. His moan today was not enough sugar. I'd put two spoonfuls in, but he had the cheek to say he was used to getting three at home. I told him it wasn't the bleedin' Adelphi Hotel, and he should count himself lucky to be getting three free cups of tea a day. I mean, Mr Fisher is good enough to supply the tea, sugar and milk, and I'm not going to be dishing it out willy-nilly to some silly sod what's got a sweet tooth. Yer should have seen the gob on him, honest, it was enough to stop the clock on the Liver Buildings.'

'Is he a good worker?' George asked.

'Oh yeah, he keeps up, but he never stops moaning. Bill doesn't take any notice now, he just lets it go in one ear and out the other. He'll tell yer himself when he sees yer. If he gets down on his knees, yer'll know he's begging yer to come back to being his mate.'

'I'm looking forward to seeing Bill again, and all the others. I've brought my carry-out, so I'll sit with Bill and we can have a good natter.'

'Are yer not having chips, then?' Lizzie asked. 'Yer need something warm in yer tummy this weather.'

'I wasn't quite sure what was happening, so I brought some sandwiches to be on the safe side. Perhaps I'll have chips tomorrow.'

Lizzie moved away when the bell rang. 'I'd better go and collect the mugs. But I'll get yer a pennyworth of chips, George, and you can put them in yer butties.'

Albert called after her, 'If it wouldn't inconvenience you, Lizzie, I'd like some chips too.'

'No trouble at all, Mr Hancock.' She came back and held out both hands. 'I'll take a penny off each of yer. If I don't get the money first, then I charge a farthing interest.'

'You strike a hard bargain, Lizzie,' Albert said, handing over a threepenny bit. 'You can take George's out of that, I'll treat him seeing as it's his first day back.'

George shook his head. 'It's very kind of you, but there's no need to do that!'

Lizzie bent to look in his face. 'Never look a gift horse in the mouth, soft lad, 'cos if yer refuse once, you might never be asked again. Besides, it's bad manners to refuse a kind offer.' With that she walked away, slipping the threepenny bit into her overall pocket and muttering, 'Pride has got a lot to answer for, and I'm glad I haven't got none.'

'George, me old mate, it's good to see yer!' Bill's handshake was strong, his smile warm and welcoming. 'Are yer feeling all right now? No pain or anything?'

'No pain now, thank goodness, but the first few weeks I was in agony. The doctor says as long as I don't push myself, I should be all right.'

'I haven't half missed yer, it's not been the same here since yer left.' Bill pulled a face and jerked his head. 'I've got a right one working with me now. Miserable as bloody sin he is, and never stops complaining. The whole day long he's at it, and when I lose me temper and tell him to put a sock in it, he sulks! A grown man, sulking! It's enough to give yer the willies.'

All the gang came around then, and George realised how much he'd missed them. Vin, Greg, Charlie and Joe, all the men he'd worked with for years. And they looked as happy to see him as he was to see them as they shook his hand and slapped him on the back. 'I still have nightmares about that day, George,' Vin told him. 'I see it in slow motion, the rope beginning to slip and you and Bill standing right underneath it. There wasn't a thing I could do about it, only shout me flaming head off. I really thought yer were a goner, and I was sick with fright.'

'We all were,' Joe said. 'Seeing yer lying on the ground, not moving or speaking, I didn't think much of yer chances.'

'From what I've heard, I could have been killed if Bill hadn't had the presence of mind to pull me that fraction forward. The weight of one of those sacks on me head, I would never have survived it. But,' George rubbed his hands and grinned, 'I'm here to tell the tale, thank God.'

'How d'yer think yer'll like yer new job?' Joe asked.

'Beggars can't be choosers, Joe, I'm stuck with it whether I like it or not.' George wasn't going to mention the drop in wages, it was his worry, not theirs. 'It'll take some getting used to, 'cos it's many a long year since I did adding, subtraction and multiplication. But according to Mr Hancock, I'll get there in the end.'

'If yer get stuck, George, yer can always come and ask me,' Bill said jokingly. 'I was good at arithmetic in school.'

'He'd be better off asking yer mate Phil Easton.' Vin's words brought forth loud guffaws. 'He's got counting chips off to a fine art.'

'Ay, George, he's caused Lizzie some grief.' Bill started to laugh and almost choked when a chip he was eating went down the wrong way. 'Did she ever tell yer about emptying a bag of chips and scallops on his head?'

'Yes, she did tell me. It must have been very funny.'

'Funny! It was like something out of Laurel and Hardy.' Vin conjured up the scene in his mind and doubled up. 'She did no more than plonk the open paper on his head and walk away. Chips were hanging from his head and shoulders, he looked a scream. And d'yer know what he shouted after her? "I'm going to count these chips, Lizzie, and if I'm any short, I want me money back."'

'Where is he now?' George asked. 'Doesn't he eat with you?'

'Not on yer life,' Bill said. 'I have enough of him in working hours, that's all I can take. Me dinner break is for nourishment, not punishment. He goes for his own chips now, and God only knows where he eats them. But I don't care, as long as it's not sitting by me and moaning.'

George was enjoying the company of his mates and he grimaced when the bell rang. 'It's great to see you all again and be back in the fold. I'll probably see you on my rounds, but I'll definitely be here every day for my lunch.'

'Don't worry, George,' Bill called as he walked away. 'Yer'll soon get the hang of it.'

George waved over his shoulder. He'd get the hang of it all right, it was a case of having to, there was no choice.

Ann lifted her face for a kiss, then helped George off with his coat and hung it on the hall stand. 'How did it go, love?'

He shrugged his shoulders and spread out his hands. 'Well, I didn't break eggs with a big stick, but I didn't make a fool of myself either.' He walked through to the living room to find Maddy and Tess with their heads bent over exercise books, busy with their homework. 'Are you too busy to give me a kiss?'

Two chairs scraped back and four arms reached out to him. 'Never too busy for that, Dad,' Maddy said. 'We just started doing homework to pass the time until you came in.'

'I've nearly finished my sums, Dad,' Tess said. 'Then I've got to study a map of the world that Miss Harrison lent me. Maddy's going to help me with it after we've had our dinner.'

He held his daughters close. 'Wouldn't it be nice if we were rich enough to sail around the world, instead of looking at a map?'

Tess, her head always full of fanciful dreams, said, 'If we could find a magic lamp, Dad, with a genie who told us we could have three wishes, we could ask for a magic carpet to take us way up in the sky and fly us around the world. Wouldn't that be wonderful?'

'It would indeed be wonderful, pet, but where do we find a magic lamp?'

'In a pawn shop! There's one on Stanley Road and it's full to the brim of everything you can imagine. They're all old things, and I wouldn't be a bit surprised if somewhere under all the old chairs, pictures and furniture there was a lamp just waiting for someone to find it.'

Ann tutted. 'Come along, Theresa, clear your things off the table so I can serve the dinner. And if you ever do come across this genie in a lamp, you and Madelaine can wish for the magic carpet. Then your father and I would like the other two wishes.'

Maddy turned after placing the books and pencils on the sideboard. 'What would your wish be, Mam?'

'A cottage in Wales and enough money to keep the wolf from the door.' If only this wasn't just make-believe, Ann thought, then life really would be wonderful. 'What would you wish for, George?'

'The one thing I'd ask for would be for your wish to come true, love, then we'd all be happy.'

Maddy came to put her arms around his shoulders. 'We'll never be able to afford our own cottage in Wales, Dad, but we've got the next best thing. Mam hasn't told you yet, but we've had letters from Wales today.'

'I haven't had a chance to tell him! I was going to leave it until we were all seated and having our meal.'

'Then leave it, love, and you see to the dinner while I have a swill.'

For the first time Ann noticed her husband's pallor. 'You look worn out, love, has today been tiring for you?'

'I do feel tired, yes, but it's more to do with my body being out of the routine than anything else. It's certainly not due to hard work, because the job involves using your mind rather than your body. A couple more days and I'll forget I've even been away from the place.'

'Well, after dinner you can stretch out on the couch and relax for a few hours. You can't expect to get over what you've been through so soon, it's asking too much.' Ann bustled out to the kitchen where a pan of stew made with shin beef was simmering and smelling delicious. 'Knives and forks out, please, girls.'

They had started their meal when George said, 'Tell me what our friends in Wales had to say, save me waiting. I'll read the letters later.'

'Gwen and Mered send their best wishes and hope you are well on the way to recovery. They said if you need to convalesce then we are

169

very welcome to stay with them as friends, not paying guests. Gwen said she'd look after you and build you up. And her and Mered would love to see us again.'

'That's very nice of them, what lovely people they are. I only wish we could take them up on their offer, I rather fancy a week in the country.'

'Ooh, don't we all!' Tess was swivelling her bottom on the chair, her eyes bright with the knowledge she was carrying in her brain and couldn't wait to impart. 'And Mrs Thomas said the same in her letter, Dad. That we would be welcome any time, they would be delighted to have us.'

George smiled at her. 'We are very popular, aren't we, pet? I suppose Alan and Grace wrote as well?'

'Of course!' Maddy said. 'They put their letter in with their mother's. And Grace said she wished we could go down for a few days. They can't come here because they can't leave the farm and the animals.'

'Alan said we wouldn't know Pinky and Curly now because they've grown so much.' Tess went from swivelling her bottom to swinging her legs. 'I bet when we go next year they won't know us 'cos we'll have grown too! I'll be as tall as Alan.'

When Maddy glanced at her sister there was tenderness in her eyes. 'Oh, so Alan's not going to grow any more, eh? He's going to wait for you to catch up?'

Tess giggled. 'Aren't I a silly girl, I never thought of that.'

Maddy hadn't missed the look exchanged between her parents when next year's holiday was mentioned, and she was thoughtful as she chewed on a piece of meat. Her parents didn't know, but she'd overheard them talking one night about the difficulty they'd have trying to manage with less money coming into the house. She was old enough to understand that if they were having a struggle to make ends meet, a holiday would be out of the question. So it would be better if Tess didn't keep on about it, making them feel guilty. 'Anyway, something might turn up to stop us going next year.'

'No it won't!' Tess was adamant. 'Dad promised us, didn't you, Dad?'

'Yes, I did, pet, and I promise that I'll do all in my power to bring it about. But, as Maddy rightly said, you never know what's going to crop up.'

'Nothing is going to stop us, I know in my heart it isn't, so there!'

'Theresa, don't tempt fate, love,' Ann said. 'No one knows from day to day what's going to happen, or what's in store for us. And it is not in our power to change things. So put it out of your mind until nearer the time.' When she noticed her younger daughter's mouth open

170

in protest, she lifted a hand. 'Get on with your dinner and let's hear no more about it.'

The meal continued in silence, but George had lost his appetite. He couldn't bear the thought of letting his children down, but there would be bigger hardships ahead than the loss of holidays, and there was little he could do about it. Unless he found himself a job that paid better wages. He could ask around, but he was only a labourer and most jobs would require lifting of some kind. He sighed. It would be best to do as Ann said, put it out of his mind and see how things went.

When George put the key in the lock on Saturday afternoon, it was with a heavy heart. The wage packet in his pocket was six shillings lighter, and although he'd known it was coming, he felt saddened. But when his wife came into the hall to meet him, he kissed her with a forced smile on his face. 'Always a nice welcome, love.'

'That's because I'm always glad to see you.' She reached up to take her coat from the hall stand. 'I had nothing in the house to make dinner with, so I made you sandwiches to be going on with until I come back from the shops. The girls want to come with me, so you'll have the house to yourself for an hour.'

George put a hand on her arm while he reached into his pocket for the wage packet. 'Bad news, love, I started on the lower wage this week.'

'It can't be helped.' Ann had been bracing herself for this and was determined not to upset him. 'We knew it was going to come and we'll just have to get on with it.' She stroked his cheek with the back of a finger. 'Don't look so worried, love, we'll scrape along. At least we've got each other and the girls.'

'What about the girls?' Tess asked as she popped her head around the living room door. 'What have we been up to now?'

'I was just telling your father that you're coming to the shops with me. So go and tell Madelaine to get her coat on, and we'll be off.'

'I'll stay in with you, Dad, if you want me to.'

'No, pet, you go out and get some fresh air.'

'Is Mrs Lizzie coming today, she usually does on a Saturday?'

'You know, I never thought to ask her. I was pretty busy this morning as Mr Hancock was going through things with me for the last time. And when Lizzie brought our tea I was up to my neck and it never crossed my mind to ask her.'

'She'll come,' Ann said. 'She's never missed a Saturday yet. Lizzie's visits are the highlight of the day, we'd be lost without her.'

'Yes, but that was to bring my wages and she had a reason to call. So I wouldn't be too sure about today.'

'She'll come,' Ann said, ushering the girls through the door. 'I know she will.'

But when Lizzie hadn't put in an appearance by seven o'clock, even Ann gave up on her. 'She won't come now.'

'Oh, I hope she hasn't stopped coming altogether now you're better, Dad,' Tess said. 'We really love Mrs Lizzie, and me and Maddy will be very sad if we don't see her again.'

'Of course you'll see her again, she's our friend now,' Ann told her. 'But while your dad was off, she put us before herself. Now she's able to get back into her own routine.'

Disappointed, Maddy asked, 'Well, can we go upstairs to do our homework, then? It's more comfortable sitting in bed and we'll be out of your way.'

'You're not in our way, Madelaine, what a thing to say! And you'll freeze up there, it's a cold night.'

'We can snuggle up together,' Tess said, 'and we'll be as warm as toast.'

'Let them go,' George said. 'They'll soon come down if they get too cold.' He wanted to talk to his wife and didn't want the children to hear his worries. 'When the tips of your fingers go blue, that's when you'll know it's as cold in your bedroom as it is in Iceland.'

The girls ran up the stairs giggling. 'We'll wrap the eiderdown around us and the feathers will keep us as snug as a bug in a rug,' Maddy said. 'Last one in bed is a dunce.'

George heard the bedroom door closing and moved to sit on the couch. 'Come and sit next to me, love.' He waited until she was comfortable, her arm linked in his, then said, 'We have to talk about it, Ann, it's not going to go away. It's no good pretending everything is fine, and saying we'll manage somehow, because the drop in money is too much not to make a big difference to the way we live. It isn't only the six shillings, it's the odd hour's overtime I used to get that helped with what few luxuries we did have, like the girls going to a Saturday matinée, or me going for a pint with our Ken now and again. All those things, and many more, will have to go by the board now.'

'I know,' Ann sighed. 'I've been doing some mental arithmetic and can't see any way we'll manage. You know I put everything away on a Saturday that I have to pay out through the week, like rent, gas, coal and three shillings towards clothing. By the time I've done that, there'll be very little left for food. And I'm careful with money, I don't buy anything we don't really need.'

'You don't have to tell me that, love, I know you're a very good housekeeper. One solution would be for me to look for another job, but not being skilled, I'd never find a labourer's job that doesn't involve heavy lifting. And that would be asking for trouble.'

'Don't even think about that, it's out of the question. The obvious answer is for me to find part-time work. A couple of hours in the morning or afternoon, when the girls are at school. I'll ask around on Monday and see what the possibilities are.'

A knock on the front door had Ann jumping to her feet. 'I'll go, it'll be Lizzie.'

'Hello, queen, I'll bet yer'd given up on me by now.' Lizzie bustled in, unbuttoning her coat. 'I'll take this off, otherwise I won't feel the benefit of it when I leave.'

There was a mad scramble down the stairs and Lizzie found herself being hugged and kissed. 'I knew you'd come, Mrs Lizzie,' Tess said, her face alight. 'I know why you're late, you've been talking to the rose on your wallpaper again.'

There came a deep chuckle. 'Fancy that now, queen! Ye're dead right! Honest to God, she'd talk the hind legs off a donkey. Would she let me out, would she hell! Every time I got to the door she started again. I think she gets lonely, yer see, and she wanted me to stay in to keep her company.'

'What was she talking about, Mrs Lizzie?' Maddy asked. 'Was it anything funny?'

'Let me get in by the fire and I'll tell yer.' She entered the living room with a girl on each arm and grinning broadly. 'I know yer see enough of me at work, George, so just ignore me and forget I'm here.'

'That would really take some doing, Lizzie, taking all things into consideration.'

'Are yer insulting me size, George, or the fact that I talk too much?'

He lifted both hands in mock surrender. 'Heaven forbid! You're as slender as a reed, Lizzie, and as meek as a lamb. I stand in awe of your beauty.'

'Blimey days, George, me head will be so big I won't get through the bleedin' door! But it was well said, and until I look in the mirror I'll believe yer, 'cos it's bucked me up no end. I'll have to remember what yer said so I can tell my feller. Yer see, when he looks at me, he doesn't see me as slender and meek. And I'm bloody sure that in all the years we've been married, he's never once stood in awe of me beauty. In fact, I'll bet a pound to a pinch of snuff that he wouldn't know what it means. Dead ignorant is my feller.'

'Well *I* think you're beautiful, Mrs Lizzie,' Tess said. 'And if your husband doesn't think so, then he needs a pair of glasses.'

'Theresa, that's a naughty thing to say,' Ann told her, fighting back a desire to laugh. 'I'm sure Mr Ferguson thinks his wife is very beautiful.'

'You'd like him if yer met him, queen, it's me what makes out I'm hard done by, but I'm not really.' The cheeks moved upwards to cover her eyes, and Lizzie shook with laughter. 'My feller's not a bad old stick – but who the hell wants an old stick!'

George chuckled. 'Lizzie, you're incorrigible.'

With a hand on each cheek, she said, 'My God, this is my day all right! I'm slender, meek, beautiful and incoggital!'

When the laughter rang out, George looked across to see Ann doubled up. How easy it was to put your worries aside when laughter was in the air. It didn't solve your problems, but it helped you forget them for a while. 'I didn't say you were incoggital, Lizzie.'

'Yes yer did! Don't yer be trying to get out of it now, George Richardson, I'm keeping me eyes on yer.'

With a laugh in her voice Ann said, 'George said you were incorrigible, Lizzie.'

'That as well! By God, I'm having a field day! Will one of yer write them out for me so I don't forget? I'll baffle my feller with science tonight – that's if I can sober him up, like.'

'I'll write them down for you, Mrs Lizzie, if you'll tell us what the rose was talking about,' Maddy said. 'It's nearly time for me and Tess to go to bed, and we'd love to hear what you had to say to each other.'

'Well it's like this, queen. I forgot about her listening in to everything we say, and I was having a go at my feller when he was getting ready to go out. He's bloody hopeless around the house, and if I want anything doing, I have to do it meself. Anyway, here I was telling him he'd be better off decorating the living room for me than going to the pub, forgetting there were ears listening to every word what came out of me mouth. And after my feller went out in a huff, didn't I get the height of abuse off her! She didn't pull any punches, I can tell yer, called me for everything under the sun.'

Lizzie looked around the faces, all smiling except Tess. The girl was wide-eyed with wonder, her imagination taking her into Lizzie's sitting room, and she felt she was seeing and hearing every word. It was then she made up her mind that the next time the class were told to write a composition she would write about the talking rose on Mrs Lizzie's wallpaper. She knew it was all made up, that there was no such thing as a talking rose, but it appealed to her because it was like a fairy story.

Maddy was leaning forward, all ears. 'Go on, Mrs Lizzie, tell us the rest.'

'Well, muggins here started to feel sorry for her. I mean, she did

174

have a point, didn't she? And I asked meself how I'd like to be scraped off the wall what had been my home for four years and chucked in the midden. Just put yerself in her position for a minute and yer'll see how bad she must have felt. Queen of the roses one day, then being thrown on a dust-cart the next. So I started to weaken, and in the end she had me feeling so sorry for her I promised I'd kill my feller if he went near her with a scraper. She was ever so grateful, and when I left she was a very happy rose indeed.'

'But you'll have to have your room decorated sometime, Mrs Lizzie.' Maddy's face was deadly serious. 'I mean, you can't never have it done.'

'Oh, I can if my feller has his way. He'd have been in his element if he'd heard what I said to the rose.' The red hair unruly as ever, and her freckles more noticeable now on the pale face, she hitched up her bosom. 'She'll be his friend for life. I'll have to keep me eye on him or he'll be watering the ruddy thing.'

It was with great difficulty that George managed to compose himself. 'D'you know, Lizzie, I really don't know who's the daftest, you or us! Anyone listening would think we were all mental and have us certified.'

'Nah, it's only me they'd think was barmy. But I want yer to promise me that if they ever do take me away in a straitjacket, yer'll visit me in the loony bin and bring the rose with yer so I'll have someone to talk to.'

'I'll promise you, Mrs Lizzie,' Tess said. 'And I'll bring you some jelly babies, 'cos I know they're your favourites.'

'Thank you, queen, it's nice to know I'm not without friends.'

'Your friends should be thanking you for keeping them amused until their bedtime.' Ann's words brought groans of protest from the girls but she didn't let it sway her. 'You've done very well, so be thankful for what you've had. Now say goodnight and poppy off. I'll bring you a hot drink up when you're in bed.' With that the girls had to be satisfied. They were reluctant to leave while Lizzie was there, but they never argued with their mother and never sulked. After noisy kisses and hugs, they left the room and could be heard laughing as they elbowed each other out of the way to be first up the stairs.

'They're good girls,' Lizzie said. 'Always polite and never give yer any lip. Not like my Vera when she was young. She could be a real little faggot at times.'

Ann came through carrying a cup in each hand. 'You never talk much about your daughter, don't you see her often?'

'She comes with her husband every Sunday. They're living with his mother until they can afford a place of their own, and that's in the Dingle so it's quite a journey. They should have waited another year before they got wed, but yer can't tell youngsters anything these days, they know it all. Nineteen they were, both of them, and not two ha'pennies to rub together. And now Vera's in the family way it's going to be more of a struggle for them.'

'Is he a good husband to her?'

'Oh yeah, he thinks the sun shines out of her backside.' Lizzie pushed herself up from the chair. 'Let me open the door for yer, otherwise those drinks will get cold.'

When she was seated again, Lizzie tilted her head at George. 'Well, me old mate, how did yer first week go?'

'All right, I think. I know what's what, but I'm going to be slow until I really get the hang of it. There's so many figures, they swim before your eyes. But as Mr Hancock said, in a couple of weeks I'll have it off pat.'

Ann came in rubbing her hands. 'It's cold up there, but the girls don't seem to feel it.'

'Young blood, queen, that's what it is. If yer think back to when yer were their age, I bet you didn't feel the cold as much either.'

'You're right, Lizzie, I didn't.' Ann held her hands out to the fire. It wasn't very bright because she was saving coal and hadn't built it up, but it was still giving out a bit of warmth. Then she asked casually, 'I don't suppose you know where there's any part-time jobs going, do you? A couple of hours a day.'

'Who for, queen?'

'Me, of course.' Ann kept her eyes on the fire. 'We could do with a few extra shillings a week coming in.'

'Can't yer go back to teaching?'

'No, I've been out of it too long. I'd have to take a course again, and I don't fancy that. Besides, the hours would have to fit in with the girls being at school. I don't want them coming home to an empty house.'

'Yer'll not find a job that easy, queen, 'cos there's so many men out of work, the wives are taking anything they can get for a few bob a week. It's slave labour, really, what they have to do to earn a tanner. If they got a shilling for a morning's work they'd think they were quids in.'

'Is it so bad?'

'It might not be for you, with your education, but the women I know are nothing but skivvies for rich bosses who know people are so desperate they'll put up with anything. Your best bet, queen, is to try the shops on the Vale, or look for an office job. They'd be more in your line.'

'You're not going to be a skivvy for any man, that's definite,' George said, anger in his voice. 'I'd go begging before I'd let you do that.'

'I'm not that soft, George, and you know it. I'll look for a job that suits me.' Ann jumped to her feet, embarrassed that she seemed to have belittled her husband in front of Lizzie. 'I'll make a cup of tea and put another lump of coal on the fire. Both should cheer us up.'

Lizzie smiled, but wisely kept her thoughts to herself.

Chapter Thirteen

'I'm sorry, Mrs Richardson, but we're not looking for staff at the moment.' Norman Hawkins was the manager of Irwin's grocery store, and as he was speaking he was wishing he had a penny for everyone who'd come looking for work that he'd had to turn down. 'I'd like to help, but unfortunately I can't.' And the man meant it. He felt heartily sorry for anyone who was desperate for work and couldn't get a job for love nor money. And he had strong views about the vast number of people who were unemployed through no fault of their own. They shouldn't have to beg, it should be a person's right to have a job and a decent standard of living. 'Perhaps if you tried one of the other shops?'

'Yes, I'll do that. And thank you for your time.' Ann fought back the tears until she was out of the shop. This was the tenth time she'd enquired about work in the last three weeks, and ten times the answer had been the same. The experience was depressing and left her feeling humiliated, and worthless. She'd been told it wouldn't be easy finding work, but never had she thought it would be impossible.

With her basket in the crook of her arm, her fingers laced across her tummy and her head held high, Ann turned in the direction of home. She'd started out three weeks ago determined to find work no matter what it took, but she couldn't face another rejection today, her heart wouldn't take it. And although she would never admit it to George, her pride had been badly dented. Nor would she worry him by letting him know she wasn't able to manage on his wages, even though she'd cut everything down to the bone. She was four shillings behind with the rent, for the first time in her married life. And there was no way she could make that money up, she could only see herself getting deeper into debt. But only a fool would blindly carry on until it was too late. There had to be a way out, and she had to find it soon.

'No luck today then, love?' George didn't really need to ask, he could tell by his wife's face that she was downhearted. But she'd think he wasn't interested if he failed to mention it.

She shook her head. 'No, I was out of luck. But I'll try again tomorrow.'

'You will get a job, Mam,' Maddy said. 'I'm surprised you haven't been snaffled up, 'cos there's nothing you can't do.'

Tess nodded in agreement. Both girls knew their circumstances had changed by the cuts that had been made. No pocket money, the fire only lit at tea time, and food that was filling but not really appetising. Their mother had explained everything to them, and they wanted to do everything they could to help. 'Yes, you're very clever, Mam.' Then the girl let out a low cry and held her hand to her mouth. 'Oh, I forgot, Mam, Miss Bond told me to ask you if you'd call in and see her tomorrow.'

'Oh dear, is there something wrong?'

'I don't think so, but she didn't say.'

'You're getting on well with your lessons, aren't you, Theresa? Still making progress in history and geography?'

'Yes, Miss Harrison is very pleased with me. It can't be anything to do with that, Mam, or I'd tell you.'

'Then have you been naughty, or giving cheek? There must be something, Theresa, for her to want to see me.'

'Well, I haven't been naughty and I would never give cheek. So whatever it is has nothing to do with me.'

'Of course Tess wouldn't give cheek,' George said. 'She never has and never would. I'm sure whatever it is doesn't concern Tess's behaviour. The only way to find out is to call to the school tomorrow and see Miss Bond.'

Ann nodded. 'I'll go about ten o'clock when assembly is over and the girls are all in class. I just hope it isn't another worry to add to the ones I already have.'

There was a reprimand in the look George gave his wife. Whatever troubles they were experiencing had nothing to do with the children, and they shouldn't be burdened with them. Both girls were of a sensitive nature and the less they knew the better. 'Now let's get on with our meal, because Lizzie is coming tonight, don't forget.'

This brought smiles. 'Oh, we haven't forgotten, Dad,' Maddy said. 'We look forward to Mrs Lizzie coming. I hope she's got a new tale to tell us.'

He grinned. 'Lizzie always has a tale to tell, pet, she can just reel them off out of the top of her head. And she never tells the same one twice.'

Lizzie brushed past Ann then turned to put a hand on her cheek. 'That's how cold it is out, queen, the wind's bitter.'

'Go in and warm yourself by the fire, such as it is.' Ann closed the door and followed her friend to the living room. 'It doesn't run to a fire

180

up the chimney these days, but seeing as it's you I might go mad and put another lump of coal on.'

Lizzie took one look at the miserable fire and jerked her head. 'If I'd known that, I'd have brought a few cobs with me.'

'Stop your moaning,' Ann told her, bending to take the prongs from the companion set and using them to pick out two large pieces of coal from the brass scuttle. 'We'll have you warmed up in no time.'

After giving Lizzie a kiss, the two girls stood either side of her chair. 'You won't stop coming when the snow's on the ground, will you, Mrs Lizzie?' Maddy asked. 'If you really loved us, you wouldn't care if you were knee-deep and kept falling flat on your face. People do that when they love someone.'

'Oh, I don't mind the snow, queen, I quite enjoy it. Yer see, I've got me very own sleigh so me feet don't even touch the ground.'

Tess giggled. 'How can you have a sleigh, Mrs Lizzie? They don't sell them around here.'

'This is a very big secret, queen, and yer'll have to promise not to breathe a word to a living soul if I tell yer how I came to have a sleigh.'

The girls made a cross over their hearts and said in unison, 'Cross my heart and hope to die, if this day I tell a lie.'

'There's no need to go that far, I don't want no one dropping dead because of me. So yer'll have to promise not to tell me secret, and also that yer won't do anything silly like dying on me. I mean, like, what I've got to tell yer is worth listening to, but it certainly isn't worth laying yer life down for. And just think what it would do to me conscience! I'd never be able to live with meself.'

The girls squatted down on the floor in front of her. 'Go on, Mrs Lizzie, before our mam says it's time for bed.'

'Well, it happened a long time ago, when our Vera was only three. It was Christmas Eve and the snow was thick on the ground. I'd put Vera to bed, my feller had gone out for a pint with his workmates, and I had to go to the corner shop for some stuffing 'cos I'd forgot to get it when I was out shopping. I put me coat and muffler on and opened the door. But when I saw how deep the snow was, I nearly died. I looked down at the wafer-thin soles on me shoes and thought, bugger it, I'm not going out in that, they'll have to do without stuffing.'

Lizzie's eyes went around the group and she was well satisfied with the interest she saw on each face. After all, she thought, there's no point in stretching me imagination if it isn't appreciated. 'Anyway, I was just going to close the front door when I heard the sound of bells jingling. At first I thought it might be the Salvation Army singing Christmas carols, but I couldn't hear no singing, only the bells. And I knew it wasn't the church bells ringing 'cos it was too early for them.

So I stood on the step and looked up and down the street, but there wasn't a soul in sight.'

There now came a pause for dramatic effect, before Lizzie carried on in a hushed tone. 'Then suddenly, out of the darkness, came this sleigh being pulled by a reindeer. Yer can imagine me surprise, and I rubbed me eyes thinking I was seeing things. But I wasn't, 'cos when the sleigh went past the street lamp I could clearly see Father Christmas sitting there, surrounded by sacks and parcels. I saw him as clear as day, with his red coat and hat, his round face and pure white moustache and beard. It was a wonderful sight to behold, and I was the only one in the deserted street to see it.' Once again there was a dramatic pause, as she placed the back of her hand on her forehead and assumed a pose she'd seen Lillian Gish do in a film. Her bosom was six times that of the film star, but she heaved it none the less for good measure and said softly, 'I was definitely the chosen one that night.'

Lizzie then sat back in her chair and lapsed into silence as she stared into the flames licking around the pieces of coal. She was having a good laugh to herself, knowing the girls would be all keyed up waiting for her to carry on with her make-believe story. But the waiting made it all the more exciting.

'Mrs Lizzie.' Tess pulled on her skirt. 'That can't be the end of it, 'cos you said you had a sleigh in your back yard.'

'I did have, queen, but I haven't got it now. It was out in all weathers for years and it just rotted away.'

But this didn't satisfy Tess, and she wanted to know, 'But where did you get the sleigh from, Mrs Lizzie?'

'Well, where was I up to?' Lizzie leaned forward to ruffle the girls' hair, one very dark the other mousy. 'Oh, I remember now. I was standing there with me eyes popping out of me head, thinking I was going round the twist, when the sleigh stopped right outside a house opposite. And who should step down but Father Christmas himself, with a big sack over his shoulder. He patted the reindeer and whispered something in his ear, then, believe it or not, he started shinning up the drainpipe to the roof. The next thing I know, he'd disappeared down one of the chimneys and I lost sight of him.'

'I hope the woman opposite didn't have a fire in the grate, Mrs Lizzie.' Maddy was enjoying the tale, but she wasn't living it like her sister, who was listening with mouth wide open. 'Because Father Christmas would have got a very warm reception.'

'Oh, I don't know about that, queen, 'cos I was too busy thinking how to make the best of the situation. I mean, there was me with no bleedin' stuffing in the house, a pair of flimsy shoes on me feet and twelve inches of snow on the ground. And facing me was transport which would get me to the shop and back without getting me feet sopping wet. The trouble was, how d'yer say gee-up to a reindeer? Still, I wasn't going to let a little thing like that stop me. And I was worried about time, 'cos I didn't know how long Father Christmas was going to be and I didn't want him to catch me at it in case he took all our Vera's presents back from under the tree. So I dashed into the house, grabbed one of me home-made mince pies and hot-footed it across the street. And the reindeer must have been hungry, 'cos he wolfed it down. Mind you, even though I say it meself, I do make very good mince pies. And if yer like, Ann, I'll make yer a batch for Christmas.'

Maddy was watching the minutes tick by. 'Come on, Mrs Lizzie, you can tell our mam about the mince pies when we're in bed. Finish the story for us, please?'

'I'm sorry, queen, I do ramble on a bit, don't I? My feller's always telling me to put a sock in it. Anyway, the reindeer was very obliging. It let me get in the sleigh and it took me up to the shop. My chest was sticking out a mile with pride, and I told everyone in the shop to look through the window and they would see a wondrous sight. But not one woman said they could see it. The miserable buggers laughed their heads off and said I was going doolally. I was that mad, I walked out of the blinkin' shop without getting what I'd gone for. And to make matters worse, when I got outside, the flaming reindeer had done a bunk with the sleigh and I was left to trudge home with the snow coming over me ankles.'

'Ah, you poor thing,' Tess said. 'All that and no one believing you.'

'It's not the end of the story, though, queen. Yer see, me feet were like ice, so as soon as I got in I boiled some water, poured it into the bucket, and sat with me poor feet in soak. I was sitting there nice and comfortable, with a look of bliss on me face, when there came a hammering at the door. I wasn't going to answer it at first, but I've got nose fever and I couldn't resist. So I took me feet out of the water and dripped all the way to the front door. And the surprise I got when I opened it, well, it nearly made me swallow me false teeth. For standing in front of me was Santa Claus himself, and I could smell the drink on him before he opened his mouth. He asked if he could leave his sleigh in our back yard as he was feeling tipsy with all the glasses of sherry that had been left out for him. He said he'd never be able to steer, so he'd ride the reindeer and come back for the sleigh later, when he sobered up. But he never did, and as I said, it rotted away over the years.'

'That's a lovely story, Mrs Lizzie.' Tess sighed in appreciation. 'It was the best yet, and I did enjoy it.'

Maddy was giggling at her thoughts. 'Are you sure it wasn't you who was tipsy, Mrs Lizzie, and not Father Christmas?'

'Ah, now, queen, that's for me to know and you to find out. I made that story up in bed last night, and I thought it was pretty good.'

'I think you surpassed yourself,' George said. 'Don't you agree, Ann?'

'It was so good it gave the girls an extra half-hour reprieve,' his wife answered. 'But it's time for bed now, and I want you to go up like good girls and don't make a fuss. You can discuss the story in bed when you're snuggling up to keep warm. Your dad will bring you a hot drink up when you're settled. Say goodnight to Mrs Lizzie and poppy off.'

Ann was waiting for an opportunity to talk to Lizzie alone, and the time came when George took the girls' drinks up. She knew he would sit on the bed and talk to them for a while so it was safe to unburden herself to the woman she regarded as a very close, dear friend. 'I've tried everywhere for a job, Lizzie, but without luck. There's too many people chasing too few jobs. And I'm getting desperate now with Christmas not far off. I don't suppose you've any suggestions, have you? I'll take anything that's going, and I mean that. I'm four shillings behind with the rent and I'm worried sick over it. There's no way I can make it up, it's just hopeless. George doesn't know, so please don't tell him.'

Lizzie kept her voice casual. 'How much is the rent on this house?'

'Eleven and six a week.'

'Bloody hell, queen! No wonder yer can't manage, that's nearly half of what George earns!' Lizzie pursed her mouth and let her breath out slowly. 'That's a lot of money just for rent, I'm buggered if I'd pay that out every week.'

'We were getting by before, even though we didn't have money to throw around.' Ann's eyes slid sideways. 'How much rent do you pay, if you don't mind me asking?'

'Six and thruppence a week. It's only two bedrooms and there's no bathroom, only an outside lavvy, but it suits me.' Lizzie decided to say what she'd been thinking for the last few weeks. 'I'm blowed if I'd skint meself every week just because I can't be bothered going down the yard to spend a penny. And you don't use the extra bedroom, queen, so it's a waste of money. Money that yer haven't got.'

They heard footsteps coming down the stairs and Ann put a finger to her lips. 'Not a word, Lizzie, please. I'll talk to you on Saturday.'

There was a smile on George's face when he came into the room. 'You've certainly entertained the girls tonight, Lizzie, they can't stop talking about it. And with Christmas looming up they'll be very disappointed if Father Christmas doesn't pay them a visit in person.'

'Well, we'll have to see what we can do, won't we? I know where I can borrow a Santa outfit, but the moustache and beard would be more difficult.'

'No it wouldn't,' Ann said. 'We could use cotton wool for the beard and the moustache, and put some on the front of your hair to hide the colour. I could help you with that because I did it when I was teaching. All you need to do is teasel the cotton wool to make it fluffy.'

'That sounds good, queen!' Lizzie put her hands on her tummy and grinned. 'I've got the tummy for it, all I need to do is learn how to say "ho, ho, ho" in a deep voice.'

'And the sack would be no problem,' George said. 'We could get one from work.'

'Producing a sleigh would be more difficult.' As she spoke the words, Ann was thinking it would be easier to find a sleigh than it would be to find the money for toys to fill the sack. But she didn't want to put a damper on the evening. So she made a pot of tea and sat listening to George telling Lizzie how he was beginning to see the light on his new job. He was certainly looking better, much more fit. The extra half-hour lie-in every morning was doing him good, and he was home half an hour earlier every night. There'd be no dark clouds in their sky if it weren't for that old enemy called money.

Ann stood on the step the next morning waving the girls off. 'If Miss Bond asks you, Theresa, tell her I'll be there at ten o'clock.'

When they turned the corner and were out of sight, she closed the door and leaned back against it. She couldn't imagine what the headmistress would want to see her for, it had never happened before and she couldn't help feeling apprehensive. But standing there guessing wasn't going to get her anywhere, so she might as well get on with her work and try to put it out of her mind for the next hour. She wasn't feeling very energetic this morning because she hadn't slept well. Lizzie's words kept running through her head: 'I'm blowed if I'd skint meself every week just because I can't be bothered going down the yard to spend a penny.' And the difference in their rents was five shillings and threepence a week, which was a lot of money.

Ann sighed as she climbed the stairs to make the girls' bed. She loved this house and the area, and would hate to move away. But she might not have any choice because they couldn't afford it. The rent man was due this afternoon and she was a shilling short. That would make her five shillings in arrears. And there was no prospect of her making it up. Something had to give, somewhere, and soon.

'Come in!' Miss Bond smiled when Ann popped her head around the

185

door. 'Thank you for coming, Mrs Richardson, please sit down.'

'I hope it's not trouble, Miss Bond.' Ann sounded weary. 'I seem to be getting more than my share of it lately.'

'Far from it, dear.' The headmistress was looking very pleased with herself. 'In fact it's just the opposite. I have some wonderful news for you. We had one of the school inspectors visit us a few weeks ago, and I showed him Theresa's composition. He was very impressed and asked if he could have a copy. I believed he wanted it for himself and thought no more of it. But he called yesterday and informed me he had shown it to a friend who is editor of several magazines. His friend found it delightful and is prepared, with your permission of course, to publish it in two of their weekly magazines. If you agree, they will pay Theresa the sum of five shillings. The money will be paid to you, of course, as Theresa is under age, and you can advise her on what to spend it on.'

'Oh, that's marvellous! Oh, I'm so proud of her! And when I asked her why you wanted to see me, she said she didn't know! She didn't even mention it!'

'Theresa *doesn't* know yet, Mrs Richardson. I thought it wise not to tell her until I'd spoken to you. It was possible you might object, and that would perhaps have meant a disappointment for the child.'

'I certainly have no objection, I'm delighted for her. It is something that could stand her in good stead for the future. Oh, I can't get over it! My husband will be so pleased. And Madelaine, does she know?'

Miss Bond shook her head. 'You and I are the only people who know. Apart from the school inspector, but then he's not likely to tell anyone. I'll leave it to you as to how Theresa is told. Perhaps, now, in this office? Or would you rather wait and tell her tonight, when your husband is there?'

'I think the honour of telling her should go to you, Miss Bond. After all, it was you who had faith in my daughter's work and did something about it. I'd be more than happy for you to tell her. That's if you want to, of course?'

'It's very kind of you, and I'd be delighted. I can't wait to see her face. Being her mother, you will know what I mean when I say Theresa has a face that mirrors her thoughts. Open and honest. She would make a very bad poker player.'

'Yes, my daughter is very innocent in many ways. She doesn't tell untruths and unfortunately believes others are as honest as herself. I fear she will get many knocks in life unless she becomes a little harder and learns to stick up for herself. Madelaine is a good example. She is neither forward nor cheeky, but well able to fight her corner when necessary.'

'Give Theresa time, Mrs Richardson, she has another three years at school yet, plenty of time to blossom. Frankly, though, I wouldn't wish her to change too much. She has a lovely nature and that will bring her many friends.' Miss Bond pushed her chair back and got to her feet. 'I'll go and fetch her. And if you have no objection I will bring Miss Harrison. She has worked hard with Theresa and I'm sure she'll be very pleased that one of her pupils is going to have a composition printed in a magazine. Who knows, one day your daughter might be famous, Mrs Richardson.'

When she was left alone, Ann allowed a tear to escape and trickle down her cheek. After months of worry, first with George's accident, then concern over money, this bolt from the blue was like a ray of sunshine. And it came from a girl who had caused her and her husband so much heartache because they feared she would never have a decent future. And now she had achieved more than any of them had. This was better than one of Lizzie's stories because this was a fairy tale come true.

Ann shook herself when she heard voices outside. She must pull herself together and show her daughter how happy and proud she was on this special day. She could make out Theresa's voice asking the headmistress if her mother was here yet, and saying she hoped she hadn't done anything wrong because her mam and dad would be very upset.

'You have nothing to fear, Theresa,' Miss Bond said, her hand on the girl's shoulder as they walked through the door, followed by Miss Harrison, whose face was wearing a puzzled expression. 'There now, does your mother look upset?'

'Hello, Mam.' Tess looked relieved when she was greeted with a smile.

'Hello, love. Miss Bond has something important to tell you.'

'As there are no chairs, I'm afraid you'll have to remain standing, Miss Harrison, but this won't take long.' The headmistress spread her arms and laid her hands, palms down, on the desk. And Miss Harrison, who had taught at the school for many years, thought she had never seen such a look on Miss Bond's face before. I know I'm being stupid, she told herself, but she has the look of someone who has won a great battle.

'Theresa, do you remember when you were asked to write an essay, and you chose to write about your holiday in Wales? Well . . .'

Ann was watching her daughter's face as the story unfolded, and saw her expression change from interest to pleasure, and then disbelief. She stood like a statue, with her eyes and mouth growing wider as the words she was hearing penetrated her mind. And when the headmistress had finished, the girl didn't move or speak, she just stared as though in a trance.

'Well, Theresa, isn't that wonderful news?' Miss Bond asked. 'Have you nothing to say, or has the cat got your tongue?'

Tess licked her lips and turned to her mother. 'Mam, is it true?'

'Of course it is, love, Miss Bond wouldn't make up a story like that. She brought this about because she had faith in you, and you have every reason to be grateful to her.'

Miss Harrison couldn't contain herself. She put her arms around Tess and hugged her. 'It's the best news I've ever heard. I am so proud that one of my pupils is to have an article published in a magazine. It's something you only dream about.'

Tess looked across the desk to where Miss Bond sat, and in a quiet voice said, 'Thank you.' Knowing those two words were inadequate, she swallowed the lump in her throat and rounded the desk. Before the bewildered headmistress knew what was happening, she was being hugged and kissed. It was the first time this had happened in her thirty years of teaching, and she found she liked it. 'You're very good and kind, and I'll never forget you.' Tess suddenly realised that kissing your headmistress wasn't the done thing, and she sniffed up before grinning. 'I shouldn't have done that, but it's your own fault for being so good to me.'

'I think your mother is waiting to congratulate you, so do that before I tell you the rest of the good news.'

'You mean there's more?' The words came out in a squeak. 'Oh, this is going to be the best day of my life.' The girl hastened to where Ann sat, and she knelt down and held her arms out. 'Mam, I won't half be able to swank now.'

'That is something you should never do, love, you should just thank God for your own good luck.'

'Not even a teeny-weeny bit, to Nita and Letty next door?'

'Only if I'm there to make sure you don't go overboard. Knowing what a vivid imagination you've got, I'd hate you to get carried away.'

'Are you ready to hear the rest, Theresa?' This was a day that would go down in Miss Bond's diary. Many of the pupils in the Corporation school came from poor backgrounds, but every one had found employment when they'd left at fourteen. The majority in shops or factories, and some in good positions in offices. But this was the first time any girl from the school had achieved what this young girl had, and she was proud of her own part in bringing it about. 'The publisher was quite keen and has agreed to pay the sum of five shillings for the article.'

188

Tess drew in her breath. 'Five shillings! Ooh, er, that's a lot of money!'

'It will come in the form of a postal order, and made out to your mother as you are under age.' The headmistress smiled kindly. 'Your holiday has brought you good fortune, Theresa, and I am very pleased for you.'

'I'll have to get back to my class, Miss Bond,' Miss Harrison said. 'Am I to tell them the news or would you rather I didn't?'

Overexcitement gave Tess a fit of the giggles. 'I'll be telling them, Miss Harrison, so it won't be a secret. I'm so happy I couldn't keep it to myself or I'd burst.'

The headmistress raised a brow. 'There is your answer, Miss Harrison.'

Eight o'clock that night found Ann and George alone in the living room. They'd both been so concerned about Tess, whose eyes were unnaturally bright and her pale face flushed, Ann had suggested an early night in bed for her. And Maddy had immediately offered to go as well, making the excuse she was tired out herself by all the excitement. But the truth was, she could see her sister would make herself ill if she didn't calm down. And the best place for that to happen was in bed, cuddling under the eiderdown.

'This has certainly been a day and a half, love,' Ann said as she swivelled her bottom around so she could stretch her legs out on the couch. 'I haven't got over the shock yet.'

'I'm still trying to take it in myself, coming like that, right out of the blue. It's wonderful for Tess, it will boost her confidence no end.' George twirled the ends of his moustache until they were sharp points. 'It was a bit too much for her, though, and I wouldn't be surprised if she was sick before the night is over.'

'Madelaine will keep an eye on her, but if she can get a good night's sleep she should be all right in the morning.'

'We have two lovely daughters, Ann, we've got a lot to be thankful for. Both girls are kind and considerate. Take Maddy now, many a girl would be jealous of their sister getting so much attention, but not her. She was overjoyed and so proud. And Tess, saying she didn't want any of the money, she wanted you to have it to help out. I didn't realise they knew of the change in our circumstances. Have you discussed it with them?'

'Yes, but I didn't need to, they could see for themselves. Their penny pocket money was stopped, and the food they get is hardly what they're used to.' Ann made a quick decision and slipped her legs back over the edge of the couch. 'I want to tell you something, George, and I want you to hear me through before saying anything.' She wiped a hand across her forehead and took a deep breath. She wasn't looking forward to this because he would be so hurt. But it had to be done, she'd put it off long enough. 'If I'd been able to get a job, as I'd hoped, it would never have come to this. But it wasn't to be, and I'm really sorry. You know I've had a struggle the last few weeks, but I didn't tell you how hard a struggle. I haven't been honest with you, love, and I think the time has come to bring everything out in the open.'

Ann saw a frown of worry come to his face and she forced a smile. 'It's not the end of the world, love, but it's something that has to be talked about before it gets out of hand. You see, no matter how many corners I cut, I can't stretch the money to cover everything. And I'm now five shillings in arrears with the rent and no way of making it up.'

George left his chair to sit next to her on the couch, and he reached for her hand. 'Why didn't you tell me before, love?'

'That wouldn't have solved anything, it would only have put the burden on to your shoulders and I didn't want that, not after all you've been through.'

'Then take Tess's five shillings when it comes, and clear the rent arrears. That will save you worrying, and we can make it up to her when we can.'

'That's not the answer, George, because by the time the money comes through I'll be ten shillings in arrears. It's the rent that's crippling me, it's so high. I was talking to Lizzie last night and I asked how much her rent is. She pays six shillings and threepence a week, compared to the eleven and six I pay. The difference is over five shillings a week, and that is a lot of money.'

'Why are you telling me this, Ann?'

'Because if we moved to a cheaper house, our troubles would be over.'

George leaned his elbows on his knees and dropped his head into his hands. 'I'm sorry, love, I've failed you. Instead of giving you a better life, I'm dragging you down.'

'What a load of nonsense you're talking, George Richardson! You've given me a wonderful life and you're the best husband in the world. I would willingly live in the coal shed if you were by my side. Besides, I don't think your brother Ken, or Lizzie, would think they've been dragged down! They're quite happy in their homes, and they have a few bob spare in their pockets every week, which we haven't. It isn't only the rent money we'd save, it's less for coal because this place takes more to heat, the window-cleaner would be half the price, there's all sorts we would be saving on.' Ann glanced sideways. 'You're not too much of a snob to live in a two-up two-down, are you, George?'

He tilted his head to look at her. 'I was born in one, Ann, and lived in one until the day I married you. I was happy there, with marvellous parents, good mates and good neighbours. My memories of those days are warm and rich. No, I am not a snob, far from it.'

'Then taking into consideration the fact that our money worries would be at an end, and we could even save for the holiday in Wales we've promised the children, would you have any objection to moving?'

He shook his head. 'If it was to the end of the world, Ann, I would follow you. But what makes you think it would be easy to find a house? It would have to be near, otherwise the children would have to change school and I don't think they'd like that.'

'We'll have a word with your friend on Saturday, eh? You see, I've got every faith in Mrs Lizzie.'

Chapter Fourteen

Lizzie had been well briefed before her visit on Saturday afternoon. She was to put on an act and pretend to be surprised when Tess presented her with the news. As she would have been had George not been so proud he couldn't keep it to himself. Mind you, she didn't blame him for that. If it had been her daughter she'd be strutting round like a peacock, telling everyone who wanted to listen. She grinned to herself as she knocked on the Richardsons' door. Even if they didn't want to listen she'd have made them. Pinned them down if that was what it took.

'Hello, Mrs Lizzie.' Tess had been on tenterhooks waiting, and beat her sister to the door. 'Wait until you hear what I've got to tell you. You'll be amazed and flabbergasted.'

'Ooh, it must be good, queen, 'cos it's a long time since anyone was able to flabbergast me. I can't wait to hear what it is.' Lizzie slipped her arms out of her coat. 'Just let me hang this up, then I'll be all ears.'

Tess was hopping from one foot to the other, and as soon as the coat was hanging on the hall stand she dragged Lizzie into the living room. 'Sit down and make yourself comfortable, 'cos I've got a lot to tell you.'

'Can I say hello to your mam and dad first, and Maddy? It's bad manners to walk in someone's house and then ignore them. If they got a cob on, which would be quite understandable, it would be me what gets thrown out, not you. And can yer imagine the sight I'd look, sitting in the middle of the road on me backside?'

'We wouldn't leave you there for long, Lizzie,' Ann said. 'And we'd all give a hand to help you to your feet.'

'Yer'd need a crane to do that, queen, I'm no lightweight.'

Maddy, who was sitting on the floor in front of the hearth, began to giggle. 'While we were waiting for the crane, we'd bring you a cup of tea out to keep you warm.'

'Now that's what I call real mag . . . magnin . . . oh, what do I call it, George?'

'Magnanimous is the word you're looking for, Lizzie.'

Tess lost her patience. 'Will you all stop talking, please? I've been waiting for Mrs Lizzie all day, and now I can't get a word in.'

Lizzie shuffled her bottom on the chair until it found the position that suited it, then she folded her arms. 'I'm all yours now, queen, waiting with bated breath for you to amaze and flabbergast me.'

As Tess told of her good fortune, Lizzie gave the performance of her life. Her facial expressions and her gasps of surprise and pleasure were just what the young girl was hoping for, and she certainly wasn't disappointed. It was a piece of superb acting, and if Lizzie could have seen herself she would have been highly delighted and taken the tram straight down to the Empire Theatre and asked for a job.

'Well I never,' she said when a very happy Tess had finished her tale. 'Yer've really amazed and flabbergasted me. What a clever girl you are. I can't find the right words to say what I think of it.'

'How about marvellous?' George said.

'Or wonderful?' Ann offered.

'Or stupendous?' was Maddy's contribution.

'I'll take all of those, and mix them with fantastic. Here's me, at my age, can't string a sentence together, and you're going to be in a magazine! I'll have to buy one when it comes out so I can show it to people and say you're a very good friend of mine. I might even go as far as to say we're related. I mean, there's not many folk I know what's related to someone famous, so I'll pile it on.'

'You can be my auntie if you like,' Tess said, getting into the spirit of things. 'That would be nice.'

Lizzie opened her mouth and pointed to her tongue. 'I hope this is listening, 'cos her days for swearing are over. If I hear her coming out with a rude word, I'll bite her and that will teach her a lesson.'

George chuckled. 'A painful lesson for you, Lizzie.'

'It's got to be, George! I mean, like, I can't be related to a famous person and go round saying, "Where's me bleedin' purse?" It doesn't sound right and doesn't go with me new-found status.'

Ann looked to the window. 'If you girls want to play out for half an hour, you'd better go now because it's beginning to get dark. And I want you out of the way for a short time while I have a private talk with Lizzie.'

Her face the picture of innocence, Tess asked, 'What will you be talking about?'

While George and Ann looked at her blankly, Lizzie roared with laughter. 'Oh, that's a cracker, that is! What is yer private talk going to be about!' She rocked back and forth slapping her knees. 'Tess, queen, ye're a bleedin' treasure.'

The girl had no idea what had brought on the laughter, but was glad Mrs Lizzie had found it amusing. She'd ask her sister when they got outside.

Maddy scrambled to her feet. 'Come on, Tess, I'll get the skipping rope and see if Nita and Letty want to play.'

'Wrap up warm, and don't go out of the street,' Ann warned. 'It won't be long before it's pitch dark.'

Tess came back into the room struggling into her coat. 'You'll still be here when we come back, won't you, Mrs Lizzie?'

'Give us a chance, queen, I've only just got here! If I left now I'd meet meself coming back! Besides, now I've parked me backside I won't be un-parking it for an hour or so or it won't have been worth the effort.'

Maddy was tittering to herself as she handed Tess a pair of navy woollen gloves. Her sister was funny, and the funniest thing was, she didn't know it! And she was a little love too! 'Put those on and we'll give next door a knock to see if Nita and Letty will come out.'

When they'd left, Lizzie wiped a hand across her eyes and said, 'Yer've got two smashing daughters, they're a credit to yer. If yer ever get fed up, just pass them over to me.'

'Not much fear of that, Lizzie,' George told her. 'We wouldn't part with them, not even for a day.'

'I think ye're awful bloody tight, George, but I can see yer point. Anyway, what's this about a private talk? Yer've got me curious now.'

'It's Ann who wants to talk to you, I'm just going to sit and listen.'

'You're involved as much as I am,' Ann told him. 'So if you have anything to say, or any questions, then speak now or forever hold your peace.'

George grinned. 'I will do that. Now, before Lizzie dies of curiosity, will you explain to her what you have in mind?'

'Right, here goes.' Ann took a deep breath. 'I was telling George about the difference in our rents, Lizzie, and how I think it's ridiculous for us to be struggling every week when we could make life a lot easier for ourselves. I love this house, and if I had a choice I would never leave. But it's come to the point where I have to be realistic and admit we just can't afford to live here now.'

'I've already told yer my views on it,' Lizzie said. 'All ye're doing is making the landlord rich while you are living on the bread line. I'm buggered if I'd live like that, but then I'm not you, so what I think doesn't really matter. I don't want to be the one to tell yer to do something yer don't really want to do, and then get the blame for it later.'

'I'm not asking you to tell us what to do, Lizzie, so you could never get the blame for our actions. All I was going to ask is, do you know of any empty houses in your area?'

Lizzie cast an eye at George. 'Is this what you want too?'

'I'll go along with whatever Ann wants to do. As long as the family are together, that's all I ask. I'm sorry it's come to us having to leave this house when Ann is so fond of it, but needs must when the devil drives. As long as she and the girls are happy, that's all I ask of life.'

When there was no response Ann leaned forward. 'Lizzie, we don't have a choice. I'm going to get deeper in debt every week. And Christmas is not far off, how am I to make it a happy one for the girls? There's only one way, and that's to cut down on our biggest outlay, which is the rent. So once again I ask, do you know of any houses that are empty in your neck of the woods?'

'No, queen, not at the moment. They do come empty from time to time, but right now I don't know of any. I do know one in our street is coming empty in the next two weeks, but I wouldn't recommend it to yer. The landlord is going to have a hard time trying to find anyone decent to live there.'

'Why is that? Is it broken-down or something?'

'On the contrary, it's one of the cleanest and best-kept houses in the street. It's not the house that's the problem, it's the family what live next door to it.'

'What's wrong with them?'

'It would be easier to tell yer what's right with them! The woman, Nellie Bingham, is a real troublemaker, and her husband, Joe, is a bully. Everyone steers clear of them because they're always looking for a fight. No one in the street has a kind word for them. That's why Peggy Caldwell is leaving, she can't stand it no more. And it's a crying shame because they're a lovely family and Peggy's got her house like a little palace.'

'Why doesn't the landlord throw the bad neighbours out?' George asked. 'Wouldn't that be better than allowing good tenants to leave?'

'Oh, we've gone through that with the landlord, 'cos no one wants Peggy and her family to leave. The whole street's up in arms about it. But according to the rent collector, there's not much the landlord can do because the Binghams pay their rent on the dot every week. He has written a warning letter to them, but it doesn't make a ha'p'orth of difference.'

'What's this Bingham woman's house like?' Ann asked. 'A pig sty, I suppose?'

'No, as it happens, she keeps the house clean. If she didn't, the landlord would have grounds for throwing the family out. There's two young boys, but they're all right, they don't cause any trouble. I feel sorry for them in a way, because they look really downtrodden. And who wouldn't with parents like that? Their mother has a terrible tongue in her mouth and is too quick to use her fists. And the father, well,

196

when he gets drunk, which is often, he'll pick a fight with anyone around.' Lizzie grinned and injected a lighter note to her voice. 'He's given us a few laughs over the years, mind, especially the night he was so rotten drunk he picked a fight with a lamp-post. He was punching hell out of it and swearing at the top of his voice. It brought the whole street out, and we all stood there laughing our heads off. It shows how drunk he was, he didn't see us and thought it was the lamp-post laughing at him! Well, that made him more mad, didn't it, and he kept on punching until his wife finally came out, told us all to sod off and dragged him in the house. It just goes to show what the booze can do to yer. It must deaden yer brain so that yer can't feel any pain. His hands must have been in a terrible state and I bet he'd have been in agony when he sobered up. But the lamp-post had the last laugh, because when he passed it on the Monday morning both his hands were bandaged.'

'So life in your street isn't without its laughs, then?' Ann asked.

'We have our moments, queen. Most of the people are good neighbours, friendly and willing to do a good turn. But they say there's a bad apple in every barrel and ours is the Bingham family.'

George could see his wife's mind working and said, 'Forget it, Ann, it's not for us.'

'I wish I could forget it, love, but I can't.' Ann turned her eyes to Lizzie. 'If we did take the house, would your rent man give us a chance of the next one that came empty? Then we wouldn't have to stay there for that long. I could put up with a bit of bother for a short time while I straighten myself out, money-wise. That would be a load off my mind.'

'I could ask the rent collector, queen, and I do get on well with him and the landlord, so I know they would be helpful if it was possible. But I can't promise yer how long yer'd have to wait for a house to come empty, and that's being truthful. I've warned yer about the Binghams, so it's up to you and George what yer want to do. But don't ever come to me and say I didn't tell yer how bad it is.'

Ann looked at her husband. 'What d'you think, love?'

'I'm not saying anything, except you might be going from the frying pan into the fire.'

'I know that, but at least I'd have enough money to pay my ways and put decent food on the table. I can't carry on the way I am or I'll make myself ill.'

George held up his hand. 'Then you do what you want to do, love, and I'll fall in with you. At least the children wouldn't have to change school, they'd only have the same distance to walk.'

'We won't breathe a word to the children until we have something definite to tell them. I'd like to see the house first, if that's possible, Lizzie. Or am I being cheeky?'

'Not at all! I'm quite pally with Peggy Caldwell, so she won't mind. And with a bit of luck the Binghams will be having one of their ding-dongs and yer'll know what ye're letting yerself in for. How about Monday night?'

Ann breathed a sigh of relief. If she had to choose between bad neighbours, and having a splitting headache every waking moment with worry about where the next meal was coming from, she'd pick the bad neighbours any day. 'Monday's fine, Lizzie, thank you. And don't worry too much about the Binghams, I think I'm capable of holding my own.'

George leaned his elbows on his knees and quirked a brow at Lizzie. 'What about the neighbours on the other side of this family?'

'Oh, the Hamiltons? They're an older couple with a grown-up son and daughter. The son, I think he's about nineteen, is a strapping lad, really well built and able to handle himself. The Binghams leave them alone because they know the son, and father, would give a good account of themselves.'

There came a knock on the front door, and as Ann went to open it she said, 'Not a word, until we have something definite to tell them. Otherwise they'll pester the life out of me.'

'Why can't we come to Mrs Lizzie's with you?' Tess asked, looking glum as she watched her mother putting her coat on. 'I'd like to see her house and the rose on the wallpaper, and I know she'd be happy to see me and Maddy.'

'I'll be staying for an hour or so, Theresa, and it'll be past your bedtime when I get home. Besides, there'd be nothing there for you, only two women having a natter. You'd be bored stiff.'

The girl put on her stubborn look. 'I wouldn't be bored, and I'd really like to come.'

'And you'd leave your old dad on his own, would you?' George asked. 'Sitting here all on my tod with no one to talk to or make me laugh.'

This had some effect. 'We could tell you all about it when we get back.' Tess had lost that look of determination. She wouldn't like her father to be sad, thinking his two daughters had deserted him.

'I don't want to go,' Maddy chipped in. There was something going on, she could feel it, and that was why her mother didn't want either of them with her. 'I'll stay in and have a game of cards with my dad.'

George saw the indecision on his younger daughter's face and took advantage. 'Anyway, don't you think your mother deserves a night out on her own? I don't think she's had one since the day Maddy was born, so it's nice for her to have a friend to visit.'

Tess frowned as she took in this information. Then, deciding her

198

father was right and she was selfish, she put her arms around her mother's waist and squeezed. 'I'm glad you've got Mrs Lizzie for a friend. Everyone should have a friend they can visit and talk to.'

'I'll tell her you send your love and are looking forward to seeing her on Wednesday night. And if the rose has anything to say, I'll tell you over breakfast tomorrow.'

When Ann reached the top of the road she could see a bus coming. It was tempting, but she mentally shook her head. The fare would be a penny, and she couldn't afford it. Anyway, the walk would do her good, it wasn't that far.

Lizzie was all smiles when she opened the door. 'Ye're just in time to meet my feller before he skedaddles off to the pub for his nightly dose of medicine.'

Ann got a surprise when she was introduced to Norman. He was a fine figure of a man, tall and well built, with a mop of curly ginger hair and laughing hazel eyes. Shaking his hand, she said, 'Lizzie's told me a lot about you.'

'It's all lies, lass, honest! According to her I'm a lazy so-and-so who won't do a thing in the house. She probably told yer the heaviest thing I've ever lifted is a pint glass of bitter.'

Ann laughed. 'No, she always speaks well of you.' She cast her eyes around the spotlessly clean room, which was warm and comfortable. 'You have a nice home, so I can't believe you're a lazy so-and-so.'

Norman scratched his head. 'Well, I cannot tell a lie, it's Lizzie what does most of the decorating. She's better at it than I am, yer see, although I do hold the ladder for her.'

'Take no notice of him, he's having yer on!' Lizzie said. 'I cut the paper and paste it, but he's the one what gets up the ladder. That's when the mood takes him, like. And the mood had better take him quick, 'cos this room is crying out to be redecorated.'

'I must be going deaf, because I've never heard any crying. Yer don't half exaggerate, Mrs Woman.'

'There's none so deaf as those what don't want to hear.' Lizzie began to shoo him towards the door. 'On yer way, light of my life, and leave me and Ann in peace.'

Norman turned at the door and winked. 'She's a terrible woman, my wife. But it was nice to meet yer, Ann, and I'll see yer again, no doubt.'

When Lizzie came back after seeing her husband out she was shivering and rubbing her arms briskly. 'I'll have to warm meself through, Ann, then we'll go up to the Caldwells'. Sit yerself down for five minutes.' Standing with her back to the roaring fire, Lizzie lifted her skirt and let out a moan of pleasure. 'Ooh, that's just the job, I can feel the heat going right through me to warm the cockles of me heart.'

She turned her head to look down at her legs and saw she was showing a couple of inches of her knickers and elastic garters. 'This was a habit of me ma's, and I used to get really embarrassed when I was courting Norman 'cos she would show more than a few inches of bloomers. I remember asking her one night not to do it when Norman came, and I can just see the look on her face when she told me, "Listen, queen, if ye're ashamed of me, meet him at the door and don't bring him in. 'Cos I'll tell yer straight, I'm not having a cold backside, Norman or no Norman." And here I am doing exactly what I asked her not to do. I bet she's looking down from heaven now and saying to the angel next to her, "Just look at that flamer! She used to call me fit to burn, and now she's doing the same thing. She must take after me, a chip off the old block, 'cos I always had a cold backside in the winter."'

Ann looked at the flames roaring up the chimney and mentally compared it with the miserable fire she'd left at home. And she promised herself that one day soon they'd be able to have a fire that not only warmed but comforted as well. 'Did your mother have red hair, Lizzie, or your father?'

'I'm the spitting image of me ma, God rest her soul. And I couldn't take after a better person, 'cos my ma was a real cracker. Loving and generous she was.' Lizzie dropped her skirt and walked into the hall to fetch her coat. 'She died a year after me da, which is ten years ago now, but never a day goes by I don't think of them. The best parents anyone could ever have.'

'I had good parents too!' Ann said. 'They were strict, though, particularly with my education. While most girls I knew were playing out, I was stuck with my nose in a book and a pencil in my hand. Still, it never did me any harm and I loved my parents dearly.'

'It's a pity yer education is going to waste. If yer could get a job teaching, all yer troubles would be over, yer'd be laughing sacks.'

'It's too long ago, Lizzie, nearly seventeen years. Teaching methods must have changed a lot in that time. The only way I'd get back would be to start my education all over again, from scratch, and I'm too old for that. I don't want to teach now anyway, I just want to be a good housewife and mother.'

'When I got married that was all I wanted to do.' Lizzie jerked her head. 'Let's go, I'll tell yer the rest on the way up.'

Ann stood on the pavement and watched her close the door. 'How far away from your house is it?'

'Near the top on the opposite side, number forty-seven.' Lizzie linked arms and they set off. 'I'll finish what I was telling yer, shall I?'

'Yes please, it'll take my mind off things. I'm feeling nervous.'

'Now that's daft, 'cos there's nothing to be nervous about. Yer either like Peggy's house or yer don't. If yer do, then yer have to decide whether yer could put up with the Binghams. It's as easy as that. Now, let me finish what I was telling yer. When I got married I never thought I'd have to work again, I was all set for being a lady of leisure. But Norman was on very low wages then, and we just about managed. Then when our Vera was born, we were living from hand to mouth until she started school. That's when I decided to get a job to help out. I tried for a part-time, but there was nothing doing. Then I got the chance of the job I'm doing now, and one of the neighbours said she'd mind Vera for an hour in the morning, see her to school and look after her when she came home. She was glad of a couple of bob a week, so it worked out fine for both of us. As yer know, I'm still working there even though we don't need the money any more. I'd be lost without it now, 'cos staying at home isn't for me, it would drive me round the ruddy bend.'

Lizzie steered Ann across the road and stopped outside a house that, even in the dark, looked well cared for. Lifting the knocker, she said, 'This is it, queen, and next door is where the neighbours from hell live.'

There came a rustle from inside, then the door was opened and a woman wearing a wide smile welcomed them. 'Come in, Lizzie, out of the cold.'

Ann blinked, dazzled by the brightness after the darkness outside. There was a fire roaring up the chimney, and the grate and hearth were shining. The wallpaper was very light, and the furniture well polished. These things she noted in the few seconds before she was shaking hands with Peggy Caldwell. 'It's very good of you to let me come, I hope I'm not putting you out too much?'

'Not at all, any friend of Lizzie's is welcome. Sit yerself down and I'll stick the kettle on.'

'Oh, please don't bother, I don't want to be a nuisance.'

Lizzie hooted. 'Ay, you speak for yerself, queen! I could just go a nice hot cuppa, and a custard cream if there's one going.'

Peggy was a small, plump woman, with a round happy face and mousy, naturally wavy hair. She was very neat and obviously took a pride in her appearance. Grinning at Ann, she said, 'She's not backward in coming forward is our Lizzie. Then again, I've probably had more cups of tea and custard creams in her house than she's had in here. So I'd better go and see if I can give her what she wants, or I'll never hear the last of it.'

When she went out to the kitchen, Ann was able to take stock of the room without seeming nosy. It was warm, comforting and welcoming. A room that was cleaned and polished with love and care. And she knew right away that she could live in this house and be happy.

201

Lizzie was watching her through narrowed eyes. 'I told yer she kept it like a little palace, didn't I?'

'It's lovely, Lizzie, it really is. I have a feeling about the house, I know I could live here.'

'Don't set yer mind on it so quick, queen, wait and see what Peggy has to say.' Lizzie raised her voice and called through to the kitchen, 'Where's all the family, Peg?'

'The children are over the road playing cards, and Jack's probably standing next to your Norman in the pub. He'd never be able to sleep without his pint.' Peggy came through with a tray set with cups, saucers, milk jug, sugar basin and a plate of custard creams. She set it on the table, which was covered with a deep maroon chenille cloth. 'I hope that makes yer happy, Mrs Ferguson?'

'Couldn't be happier, queen, couldn't be happier.'

The tea was poured out and they sat around the table. 'I told Ann yer might be moving house, Peg, and she was interested as she wants to move to a smaller house.'

'There's no might about it, Lizzie, we're definitely moving a week on Saturday.'

'It's a shame,' Ann said. 'You've got it beautiful, it's a credit to you.'

'It's not a case of wanting to, girl, it's a case of having to. I couldn't put up with the shenanigans from next door any longer. And that's something you've got to consider if ye're thinking of asking the landlord for the tenancy of this house. The family next door are out-and-out troublemakers, and it's only fair to warn yer.'

'Not the whole family, Peg,' Lizzie said, 'only the mother and father. The two lads are no trouble and yer can't blame them for what their parents get up to.'

'Ye're right, Lizzie, I've got nothing against Jack and Willy. In fact I feel really sorry for the poor beggars. They're fourteen and thirteen, and they stick together like glue because all the other lads in the street give them a wide berth. I might be wrong, but I think Jack leaves school at Christmas, and with a bit of luck his life might improve when he gets a job and he's mixing with other blokes. It'll give him confidence and bring him out a bit.'

'Does the mother keep them clean and dress them decent?' Ann asked, wanting as much information as she could get to tell George. Troublemakers for neighbours were one thing, but if they were dirty as well, she couldn't tolerate that. 'Or do they go around like tramps?'

'Oh, no! For all her faults, and she has many, Nellie Bingham keeps the house and the family clean and reasonably dressed. But that's the only thing in her favour. She's pulled some stunts in the five years she's lived next door, believe me, which hasn't made her very popular with folk.'

'What sort of stunts?'

'Depends on the mood she's in. She's never laid a finger on me or mine, but there's many a man and woman been at the receiving end of her fists. If she hits yer, yer know it 'cos she packs a mighty punch. If I ever knock on the wall to tell them to stop making such a racket, she doesn't take a ha'p'orth of notice and the fighting and shouting goes on. But she finds some way of getting her own back the next day. If it's a wash day, she'll wait until I peg me clothes on the line and then she'll throw her ashes over the wall and I'll end up having to wash the clothes again. So most of the time I hang me clothes on the ceiling rack in the kitchen. It's a bloody nuisance because the windows get steamed up with condensation, but at least me clothes are clean. If she's got a cob on when I haven't got washing out, she doesn't bother going to the midden with her trash, she just throws it over our wall.'

'I don't know how she's got the nerve,' Ann said. 'Is she a big woman?'

It was Lizzie who answered. 'That's the funny part about it, 'cos she's not the size of sixpennyworth of copper! She little and thin, but by God, she's wiry. And believe me, there's some strength behind her punches. Even her husband's had a few belters off her and he's a big bloke! He must be nearly twice her size, eh, Peg?'

'Yeah, but it's mostly flab with him. He drinks like a fish and he's got a big beer belly. I don't know how true it is, but I believe she was bragging in the butcher's one day that when he gets out of hand all she has to do is punch him as hard as she can in his tummy. Apparently that takes the wind out of his sails.' Peggy placed her empty cup on the tray and smiled at Ann. 'If we haven't already put you off this house, would you like to see upstairs?'

'I'd love to, if it's no bother.'

'I won't come with yer,' Lizzie told them, 'it's exactly the same as me own house. And Ann can tell me later what colour yer eiderdowns are.'

Peggy led the way, telling Ann to keep hold of the hand-rail because the stairs were narrow and steep. Downstairs Lizzie sat in contemplation. Her mind was divided on this issue. She'd like nothing better than to have the Richardsons living so near, and she could see Maddy and Tess every day. But it would be selfish to persuade Ann to move here, because living next door to the Binghams would be no joke. The language and the fighting would frighten the girls, they weren't used to it.

Lizzie's finger made patterns in the deep plush of the chenille tablecloth while she was telling herself not to interfere but say a little prayer tonight that whatever decision Ann and George made, it would be the right one.

Chapter Fifteen

'Are you sure about this, love?' George asked. 'It's a big step to take if you're not.'

'This will be a move of necessity, and of course I'm not sure we're all going to be happy about it. But we can use it as a stopgap until I get myself financially on an even keel and we can look around for another place.' Ann had just come back from Lizzie's and was dismayed to find George had let the fire go out because he thought it would be a waste of coal to put another shovelful on when they wouldn't be long out of bed. 'At least we'll be able to keep a decent fire in the grate and I won't be afraid of the rent man knocking.'

'And you really liked the house?'

'Mrs Caldwell keeps it lovely and clean, and it's warm and cosy. There's no hallway to speak of, like we have here, and of course no parlour or bathroom. But I don't have to tell you this, George, because as you said, you were born in such a house and you have very happy memories of it. I know I'd like the house because I felt at home in it. We wouldn't have to decorate because it's not long since the Caldwells did the whole house from top to bottom. And there'd be no need for scrubbing because it's spotless.'

'And what arrangements have you come to?'

'I said I'd let them know after I'd spoken to you. And the girls, of course, they'll have to be asked. If we're all in agreement, Lizzie said she'd come with me one day to see the landlord. He's got an office on Hawthorne Road, and she said when we've decided you can let her know and she'll take a tram down in her dinner break and meet me outside.'

'Whatever you decide is all right with me, you know that, love. And I can't see the girls having any objection. The fact that Lizzie lives in the same street will be enough for them, they'll be over the moon.' George cupped her face and his smile was tender and full of love. 'All I ask is for you and the girls to be happy.'

'I'd be a lot happier if we were to have good neighbours, but beggars can't be choosers.' Ann repeated all that Peggy Caldwell had told her about what she'd had to put up with from the Binghams over the years. 'She's only leaving because of them, she said she can't take any more.'

'Will you be able to take that sort of behaviour? We've always had such good neighbours.'

'I'll put up with it until something better comes along. I can be quite tough when needs be, George, and I'll not be browbeaten by a loud-mouthed bully. And although I'll have to pay the rent in advance for Willard Street, it's over five shillings less than this and that will be a godsend.'

'When will you tell the girls?'

'In the morning when they're having their breakfast. All being well you can tell Lizzie on Wednesday morning in work, and I'll meet her that day. I can't leave it any longer to find out for sure whether we can have the house, because I need to give a full week's notice to our landlord.'

'You're not leaving yourself much time for packing, are you? And how are you going to find the cost of hiring a removal van?'

'First things first, George. Once I know we've got the house, then I'll start to worry about those things. By hook or by crook I'll find the money we need, because I have to. My girls are not going to spend a miserable Christmas if I can help it. I want them to wake up on Christmas morning to find presents, fruit and sweets in their pillowcases, a lovely fire in the grate and good food on the table. Oh, and if I can stretch to it, we'll have a tree as well.'

George bent his head and made a silent vow that he'd find some way to help his dear wife's dream come true. Several ideas were running through his mind, but he kept them to himself in case they came to nothing. 'Shall we make our way to bed? It's turned eleven and that's late for us.'

'I doubt if I'll be able to sleep,' Ann said. 'My mind is in a whirl.'

'I'll hold you in my arms until you drop off. Clear your head of everything until tomorrow.'

'That's easier said than done, but I will try.' She took his hand and pulled him to his feet. 'I think the comfort of your arms is just what I need. Come on, love.'

George had taken to leaving the house a bit earlier in the mornings to give himself some time to check the previous day's figures in his books. And after seeing him off the following morning, Ann shouted up the stairs to tell the girls it was time to get up. They washed and dressed before they came down, giving Ann time to make their breakfast. And today, as she was keeping an eye on the toast, she was going over in her mind how she should approach the subject. Should she do it in a roundabout way, or straight to the point? In the end it was Tess who made it easy for her.

'Did you see Mrs Lizzie's rose, Mam?'

'Yes I did, love,' Ann lied, because she'd never given a thought to the rose. Anyway she hadn't been in the house very long. 'But it didn't even say a word.'

Maddy bit into her toast. 'Has Mrs Lizzie got a nice house, Mam? I wish we could have gone with you, I'd love to see it.'

'Yes, she's got a lovely little house. Very warm and friendly.' Ann was chewing on the inside of her cheek, telling herself she'd never have a better opportunity. She took a deep breath and tried to stop her mouth from trembling. 'As a matter of fact there's a house coming empty in her street, and I wouldn't mind taking it. What do you think?'

'Oh, yeah!' Tess coughed as a piece of toast went down the wrong way, and her eyes began to water. But it didn't stop her from spluttering, 'In the same street as Mrs Lizzie, that would be the gear!'

Maddy was watching her mother's face closely. Particularly her eyes, which told her more than words could. 'Are you really thinking of moving, Mam?'

'Only if we all agree. Your father is easy, he'll do whatever we decide. So really it's up to you. The house is the same as Uncle Ken's, no parlour and the toilet is at the bottom of the yard. But on the plus side, it's much easier to warm, and the rent is a lot less, so you would get pocket money again and we could afford a few luxuries.'

Tess was bobbing up and down on her chair. 'Say we're going, Mam, please? I'd love to live near Mrs Lizzie.'

'What about you, Madelaine?' Ann's eyes locked with her elder daughter's. 'You don't seem keen, are you not in favour?'

'I'll do whatever you want, Mam. And like Tess, I think it would be nice to live near Mrs Lizzie. And we'd still go to the same school, wouldn't we?'

'Same school, same doctor, nothing would change.' Ann thought Madelaine should be told a little of the truth. It was the least she deserved. 'Instead of having to scrimp and scrape every week, love, we could have a little more of everything. A week in Wales next year, perhaps, instead of four days.'

'Oh, goody!' Tess was really excited. 'When are we moving?'

'I haven't got the house yet, Theresa, so don't go telling people until we're sure. It's possible I'll know tomorrow night when you come home from school. Until then, though, not a word to anyone, even Nita and Letty. I want Mrs Wilkins to hear it from me, not from other people.' The worry over now, Ann breathed a sigh of relief. She hadn't been sure what to expect, what her daughters' reaction would be, and was dreading seeing disappointment on their faces. But they both seemed quite happy. Particularly Theresa, who was highly delighted. 'Don't dally over your breakfast, otherwise you'll be rushing at the last moment. And put all thoughts of moving out of your head until we know something definite.'

'I hope you get it, Mam,' Maddy said, 'if you've set your heart on it.'

'We'll see what tomorrow brings, love.' Ann poured a cup of tea out for herself. 'If all goes well, we've got a lot of work ahead of us if we want to be out of here in ten days' time.'

'I'll help with the packing, Mam, and so will Tess.'

'You bet!' Tess would have started packing now, so excited was she about living in the same street as Mrs Lizzie and her talking rose. 'We'll be a good help.'

Ann felt a surge of love for them. 'I know you will, because you're good girls. But hurry up now and eat your breakfast so you won't be late.'

George tapped his pencil on the top of his desk. He had seen the boss go into his office and was trying to pluck up the courage to follow him. George wasn't a resentful man, nor would he hold grudges. But seeing his wife so distressed was making him question why it should be so. He'd had a fairly good job which, although it didn't pay a good wage, was one he enjoyed and which enabled the family to have a decent standard of living. They weren't living in luxury, but neither were they living in poverty. Then suddenly, through no fault of his own, everything changed and the family were struggling. Whichever way you looked at it, it wasn't right that they should suffer because of an accident caused by the carelessness of another person. The injustice of the situation had been building up within him for several weeks now and had been brought to a head last night when he'd seen the state his wife was in. It was time now for him to share some of the burden.

George got to his feet quickly, not allowing himself time to dwell on it and perhaps lose his nerve. He threw the pencil on the desk and turned in the direction of Mr Fisher's office. He straightened his shoulders and walked briskly, purpose in his step. The front of the office was glass, and when he knocked Mr Fisher lifted his head, smiled and beckoned him in.

'Can you spare me a minute, I'd like to have a word?'

'Certainly, George, sit down. I hear good reports about you from Joe Brogan, he said you've taken to the job like a fish to water.'

'I'm glad I'm good at figures, otherwise I'd never have been able to take it all in so quickly. I'm getting my head around it now, but it's quite a responsible job keeping account of all deliveries and sales, and making sure the figures tally. And that's why I'm here, Mr Fisher, to ask if you could see your way clear to giving me a pay rise. I honestly believe the job warrants more than I'm getting, besides which, I can't keep a family on what you're paying me now.'

Gerald Fisher sat back in his chair and crossed his legs. He was roughly the same age as George, with dark colouring and a florid complexion. But he was carrying a lot more weight due to lack of physical exercise. 'I've been half expecting this, George, because Albert Hancock said the wage was too low for the work involved. So shall we say a half a crown a week rise, would that suit you?'

'Starting from when, Mr Fisher? You see, we're having to move to a smaller house because we can't afford the house we're in now, and we'll need money to hire a removal van. We're hoping to be given the tenancy of a two-up two-down off Hawthorne Road, and we'll know for certain tomorrow. If we're accepted as tenants then we'll be moving a week on Saturday, which doesn't give us much time to get the money together. And as I've never borrowed in my life, I have no wish to start now.'

Gerald Fisher bent his head as he laced his fingers and placed them on his desk. He was silent for a few seconds, deep in thought. When he looked up, he smiled across at George. 'Your rise will start from yesterday and will be included in this week's wage packet. And you won't need to hire a removal van, I'll get two of my drivers to do the job for you. Jim and Harry are good grafters, they'll have you moved out of your old house and into your new one in no time at all. It will have to be on the Saturday afternoon, though, as they'll have deliveries to do in the morning.'

George felt like pinching himself to make sure he wasn't imagining it. 'I don't know what to say, Mr Fisher, except it's very kind of you and I really appreciate your help. It will certainly be a load off my wife's mind.'

'It's the least I can do under the circumstances, George. And we'll discuss your wages again in a couple of months, eh?' Gerald uncrossed his legs and pushed his chair back from the desk. 'As soon as you know definitely that you've got the new tenancy, let me know and I can have a word with Jim and Harry.'

Feeling light-headed with relief at the way things had worked out, George got to his feet. 'I can't thank you enough, Mr Fisher, you've certainly eased the situation.'

'You've worked here a long time, George, and given good service, so I'll help when I can. Now you get back to your job, I have a meeting in an hour's time and I want to prepare myself for it. Give my regards to your wife and say I hope the move will be a good one and you'll be happy in your new home.'

When Lizzie brought his tea later in the morning, she noticed a change in George. He looked in a good mood, as though all his cares and woes had disappeared. 'What are yer looking so happy about, lad? Has yer fairy godmother waved her magic wand over yer?'

George felt mean not telling Lizzie the truth, because she'd been so kind to him and his family. A real friend. But he wanted everything to be signed and sealed before saying anything. 'I should be lucky enough to have a fairy godmother, Lizzie, then all my troubles would be over. But I do feel a bit better, I must admit. Ann and I had a good talk last night, and all being well, we should be a neighbour of yours pretty soon. She was putting it to the girls this morning, and if they weren't too upset by the prospect of moving, she asked if you could meet her tomorrow dinner time and take her to see the landlord.'

'Yeah, I told her I would!' Lizzie narrowed her eyes. 'I know she liked the Caldwells' house, and it is a little palace. But did she tell yer all about Nellie Bingham and her feller?'

George nodded. 'Ann told me the lot, the good and the bad. But we're prepared to give it a try and see how it goes. If our lives are made unbearable, then obviously we'll start looking for somewhere else. However, all the talk is a bit premature, because we may not get the chance of the house. The landlord might already have someone else in mind.'

'Well, all will be revealed tomorrow. Tell Ann I'll meet her outside the office at half twelve if she's still of a mind to go ahead. I've told her where the office is so she shouldn't have any trouble finding it.' Lizzie was about to walk away when she remembered something. 'Oh, tell her to bring her rent book with her in case they ask for it.'

'She's a couple of bob in arrears, Lizzie, for the first time in her life.'

'So what! There's not many people can say they've never been in arrears. And Mr Collins will be able to tell by the rent book that it's the first time. Anyway, I'm well in with him, so I'll use me powers of persuasion. You know, George, I'll pout me lips and flutter me eyelashes at him. No one can resist when I turn me charms on them.' She walked a few steps away, stopped, then came back. 'That's except my feller. If I was to flutter me lashes at him he'd ask if I had something in me eye.'

George chuckled. 'And if you pouted your lips?'

'Oh, he'd say I was a bit old to be sucking a bull's-eye.' With a wave of her hand Lizzie went about her business, leaving George to drink his tea and relish going over the good news Mr Fisher had handed him. He would have given anything for a cigarette at that moment, but they were one of the luxuries he'd had to forgo.

George kept his news to himself until the girls were in bed. They'd been so talkative, especially Tess, that no one had noticed his eyes were brighter than usual and his laugh came more easily.

'I've got something to tell you, love, that I didn't want to mention in front of the girls. So will you make a cup of tea and we can sit and talk in peace and quiet?'

Ann looked suspicious. 'I hope it's not bad news.'

'On the contrary, love, I think you'll be pleasantly surprised.'

'Then I want to hear it now, don't keep me in suspense.'

'I don't want to gabble it out, I want to take my time and savour every word. And I want to be able to see the expression on your face. For the first time since I had the accident, I feel as though I'm pulling my weight, and not leaving you to carry the burden. So make a cup of tea, love, and we can perhaps get ourselves organised to cope with the next week or so.'

Ann wasted no time. She put just enough water in the kettle for two cups and as soon as it started to whistle she whipped it off the stove and poured the boiling water into the dark brown earthenware teapot. After stirring the tea-leaves in the pot, she carried it through to the living room. 'It'll need to stand for a few minutes to brew. I'll get the cups.'

Five minutes later, a cup and saucer in her hand and sitting in a chair next to a fire that had long since given up the fight to stay alive, she said, 'This had better be good, George Richardson, after getting me all worked up.'

'Don't sit miles away from me, come here.' George patted the empty space on the couch. And when she was settled he began. 'I went in to see Mr Fisher this morning to ask for a pay rise. It's been playing on my mind for weeks now, that the whole thing was so unfair. I didn't expect him to see it my way, and thought he'd probably throw me out of his office with a flea in my ear. Anyway, he was all right about it and agreed to my getting a half a crown a week rise, starting from yesterday and included in this week's wage packet.'

Ann leaned forward to put her saucer on the table, then she flung her arms around him. 'Oh, that's wonderful news, George, I'm so proud of you.'

'Well, it's not much, but it's better than a kick in the teeth.' He was thanking God he hadn't lost his nerve over going to see his boss. 'And Mr Fisher's agreed to review my wage again in a couple of months. So that sounds hopeful for the future.'

'That's marvellous, it really is. And the half a crown will be a godsend

211

for the next two weeks, because we'll be counting every penny.'

'I haven't finished giving you all the news yet, love, there's more to come.'

'I'm on the crest of a wave now,' Ann said, her eyes willing him to leave her there. 'So I hope you're not going to bring me down to earth with a bump.'

'Far from it, I'll hop on the wave with you. You see, while I was giving Mr Fisher the sob story about the struggle we were having making ends meet, I mentioned we were moving to a smaller house. And guess what?'

'I'd be here all night guessing.' Ann began to gently pummel his chest. 'Come on, sweetheart, tell me!'

'He's going to arrange the moving for us.' George saw his wife's eyes widen in surprise and it made him feel so good to be able to give her news that would cheer her up. 'Once I let him know for sure that we are moving, and when, he'll organise one of the vans and two of the men. But it would have to be in the afternoon, they're out delivering Saturday mornings.'

Ann laid her head on his shoulder. 'It would appear we're having a run of good luck for a change. It took some guts for you to ask for a rise, but it paid off, and I'm glad. And I want you to thank Mr Fisher for offering to help out with one of his vans. The only thing is, how much will the two men charge for their time?'

'The boss didn't mention that, but I've got a feeling he'll fork out for the few hours' overtime the blokes work. I don't think it'll cost us a penny.'

'That would be fantastic! We're not going to be on Easy Street, but I can see a way of scraping through now. That's really taken a load off my mind.'

'And there's a chance that Tess's five shillings might come through before then.' George felt hopeful for the first time in months. 'As my mother used to say, "You never know your luck in a big city."'

Ann kissed his cheek lightly. 'Let's not expect too much right now. We don't even know whether we'll get the house or not yet. Better to just hope that when you come home tomorrow I have good news for you.'

George didn't remind her that he'd know before then. Lizzie wouldn't be able to keep a thing like that to herself.

Ann was standing outside the landlord's office in Hawthorne Road when Lizzie arrived. 'Have yer been waiting long, queen?'

'No, only about ten minutes. I'm a bundle of nerves, though, I can't stop shaking.'

'There's no need for that, queen, 'cos Mr Collins is a smashing feller. He's very understanding and will put yer at ease right away.'

'What if he's not in? He might have gone for his lunch.'

Lizzie clicked her tongue on the roof of her mouth. 'Ye're a bleedin' worry wart, queen, that's what yer are. Never meet trouble halfway, that's my motto. If yer see it coming, run like hell in the opposite direction.' She pushed open the door bearing the name 'Stanley Collins' in gold lettering, and with an exaggerated movement of her shoulders from side to side, she swayed in.

Ann followed, her heart in her mouth. She found herself in a small reception area, bare except for the counter running the length of the room, with a solitary brass bell on top. Lizzie pressed on the bell, then leaned on the counter as though she didn't have a care in the world.

A door in the far wall opened and a man came through. He was middle-aged, bald except for fringes of brown hair on either side of his head, and with a ruddy complexion. A suit of fine cloth and a neatly tied silk cravat said that this was a man of substance.

'Well, if it isn't the man himself,' Lizzie said, standing upright. 'It's not very often we have the honour of seeing you.'

'Lizzie, my dear, it's a pleasure to see you. And you look very well, I must say. But what brings you here on a Wednesday afternoon? I thought you'd be at work.'

'I'm on me dinner break, so I haven't got long.' She gave a cheeky grin. 'It's a pity I haven't got longer, 'cos I know yer fancy me like mad. And ten minutes in yer private office would do us both the world of good.'

The man chortled. 'I doubt very much if I would stand the pace, Lizzie, you're more than I could handle.'

Lizzie gave a long, loud sigh. 'That's the story of my life. Anyway, I haven't come about meself, I've brought a good friend with me who wants to ask yer something.' She put her hand on Ann's arm. 'This is Mrs Richardson, I work with her husband. Ann, this is Mr Collins.'

Stanley Collins extended a hand and his grip was firm. 'I'm pleased to meet you, Mrs Richardson. Any friend of Lizzie's is welcome. And what can I do for you?'

Ann licked her lips. 'I believe there's a house coming empty in Willard Street, and I would be grateful if you would consider my family as suitable tenants.'

He looked puzzled. 'I'm afraid you have me at a disadvantage, Mrs Richardson, because I know of no empty house in Willard Street. Perhaps the rent collector has some knowledge of it, but I'm afraid he's gone home for his lunch and won't be back until two o'clock.'

'It's not empty yet, Mr Collins,' Lizzie said. 'It's number forty-seven, the Caldwells' house. They're moving out a week on Saturday.'

'Ah, yes.' Enlightenment dawned and he nodded. 'I know about the Caldwells leaving and I'm very sorry, they've been excellent tenants. But I didn't dream you were referring to their house, Lizzie, not when you know who the neighbours are. Surely you're not recommending your friend to apply for that particular house?'

'Don't be having a bleedin' go at me, I'm not recommending nothing! I've told Ann all about the Binghams, even taken her to see Mrs Caldwell so she could tell her as well. I can't do no more than that. She'll tell yer herself, I've warned her not to come crying to me when things start getting tough.'

'I've been well warned, Mr Collins,' Ann said. 'But I really need to move to a cheaper house, it's vital. My husband met with an accident at work several months ago which resulted in him having to take a lighter job with a big drop in wages. It means I can no longer afford the rent I'm paying on my present house. If things become intolerable living next to the Binghams I may, in time, ask you for a transfer when a suitable house becomes vacant.'

Stanley Collins was telling himself that this was the voice of an educated woman whom Nellie Bingham would make mincemeat of. 'Why not wait for a little while, until we have a suitable property for you? I think you would be wise, because we've had so many complaints about the Binghams I believe you would have cause to regret your decision very quickly.'

All this was taking too long for Lizzie. If they carried on at this rate she'd be late back at work. 'If me mate says she wants the bleedin' house, Mr Collins, then that's her look-out. So is it yeah or nay?'

'As long as she understands the situation, then as you say, Lizzie, it's up to her.'

'Then for crying out loud, can we put a move on? The way ye're carrying on I'll be late and get me pay docked. Show him yer rent book, Ann, and then Mr Collins will explain what the rent is and when yer can have the keys.'

'We'd like to move in on the Saturday afternoon, once Mrs Caldwell's left.'

'In that case, yer can get the keys off Peggy, save coming down here. That's all right, isn't it, Mr Collins? She can bring the rent money down on the Monday morning and collect her rent book.'

He scratched his head in a very gentlemanly manner and smiled across the desk at Ann. 'Have you ever had the feeling that your presence is not really needed, Mrs Richardson? As though things would go ahead just as well without you?'

Lizzie banged a clenched fist on the counter. 'Don't be so bleedin'

sarky, Stanley Collins! Don't forget I knew yer when yer had nowt.'
She leaned across the counter and patted his cheek. 'I still love yer,
though, even though yer are too slow to catch a flippin' cold. Now put
a move on and sort me mate out, so I can get back to work while I've
still got a job to go to.'

'I was beginning to think of asking if you'd like my job? You'd no
doubt be better at dealing with awkward tenants than I am.' He saw a
hot retort ready to leave Lizzie's lips and held a hand up in surrender. 'I
know, speed is of the essence, so I will dawdle no longer. You have my
permission to move into number forty-seven Willard Street a week on
Saturday, Mrs Richardson.' He reached under the counter and produced
a form. 'And if you would sign here for me, that will suffice until you
bring in your first week's rent.'

'About bleedin' time,' Lizzie muttered. 'I bet he's late for his own
bleedin' funeral.'

This brought a smile to the landlord's face. It was a pity more people
like Lizzie didn't come into the office to pay their rent, instead of some
of the moaning so-and-sos he saw. They'd complain because the latch
on the entry door was hanging off, and ask him to send a man out
because they were too lazy to turn a screwdriver and do the job
themselves. This little exchange now had brightened up an otherwise
very dull day.

He watched the women pass the window, arm in arm, and chattering
away fifteen to the dozen. And he let out a chuckle as a thought entered
his head. He wouldn't dare say it in front of Lizzie, but wouldn't it be
an ideal solution if she let Mrs Richardson have her house, and she
moved in next to the Binghams? Tough as she was, even Battleaxe
Bingham wouldn't be daft enough to cross swords with the indomitable
Elizabeth Ferguson. His imagination took over and his chuckles
increased in volume. Now that was something he really would like to
see.

Ann was feeling a bit sad as she knocked on her neighbour's door.
Maisie had been a good friend over the years and she'd miss her.
She was the only one she *would* miss, apart from the old couple
over the road, because most of the people kept to themselves and
she hardly knew them except to exchange a greeting when they met
at the shops.

'Hello, Ann!' Maisie lifted her flour-covered hands. 'I'm in the
middle of making a steak and kidney pie for the dinner, so yer'll have
to excuse me. Come on in, I've only got to trim the pastry around the
edges, then it's ready to pop in the oven.'

Ann followed her through to the kitchen. 'I'm sorry to come when

215

you're busy, but there's something I've got to tell you and I'd rather you heard it from me than the girls.'

'Oh, ay!' Maisie was spinning a large, deep plate as she expertly cut away the overhanging pastry. Then she put the plate on the draining board and made three slits in the top of the pie with a large knife. 'There, that's done. I'll just rinse me hands and then I'm all yours.'

'That looks very appetising,' Ann said. 'Unfortunately for my family, I'm not the best pastry cook in the world.'

'Ah well, we can't all be good at everything.' Maisie dried her hands as they walked through to the living room. 'When it comes to making fairy cakes, I'm hopeless. They come out as hard as rocks.' She sat at the table facing Ann. 'What was it yer wanted to tell me, kid?'

This wasn't something you could lead up to, so Ann blurted it out. 'We're moving next weekend, Maisie, and I've only just found out for sure, so I couldn't let you know before.'

'Moving!' She looked shocked. 'What are yer moving for? Yer always said yer love living here!'

'I do, and I wouldn't be leaving if I didn't have to. But the drop in housekeeping money since George's accident means we just can't afford to stay here. So, sad though it is, there's little I can do about it.'

'Ah, I'm sorry, kid, I had no idea. We have a bit of a struggle but we manage to hang on by the skin of our teeth.'

'I can't even do that, I'm afraid.' Then Ann felt a pang of guilt. She seemed to be putting all the blame on her husband, and that wasn't fair. 'But it won't be long before our circumstances improve. George is getting a small increase in pay this week, and they're going to review his position again in a few months. And then Madelaine leaves school next summer, that will make a big difference.'

'Yeah, our Nita leaves the same time, and will I be glad?' Maisie leaned forward. 'Ay, she won't half be upset when she knows ye're leaving, and our Letty. I'll have a crying match on me hands tonight when I tell them.'

'They can come and visit us, we're only moving to Willard Street. And I know my girls will want to come and see them 'cos they're good friends. And it wouldn't hurt to come for a cuppa one afternoon when you're not going to the pictures. You could bring Freda and Arthur with you, the walk would do them good.'

'Do they know yet?'

'Not yet.' Ann pushed her chair back. 'I'm going over to tell them now.'

'They'll be upset.'

'Not if I tell them you're going to bring them down to see me. That will give them something to look forward to.' Ann planted a kiss on her cheek. 'That's for being a good neighbour. And I hope we'll never stop being friends.'

'No chance of that, kid.' Maisie stood at the door and watched Ann cross the cobbled road. 'I'll be down to see yer that often yer'll be sick of the sight of me.'

'It's all happened so quick I can't think straight. In a matter of two days I've been to see the house, been accepted as a tenant by the landlord, and broken the news to Maisie and the Critchleys. Telling them was the worst because I got a lump in my throat and I thought I was going to cry. We've been neighbours a long time and I'll really miss them.'

'Lizzie told me when she got back what happened at the landlord's office,' George said. 'So I went to see Mr Fisher and told him we were definitely moving next Saturday afternoon and would be grateful for his help. He told me to see Jim and Harry to give them the addresses and time. And as I was leaving the office, he told me he would pay the lads overtime for doing the job.' He grinned and twirled his moustache. 'We did pretty well between the pair of us today.'

'Lizzie can take the credit for what happened at the office, she was a blinking hero! Honest, the way she talked to Mr Collins you wouldn't dream he owned her house and most of the others in the street. She took over, the poor man didn't have a chance! But you could see he had a lot of respect for her, even though she did say, "About bleedin' time! I bet he's late for his own bleedin' funeral."'

The girls had been sitting quietly, drinking in every word. Now Maddy gasped, 'She didn't say that, did she, Mam?'

'She jolly well did, and he was tickled pink! I didn't get the tenancy of the house, Lizzie did! I wasn't even asked one question.' There was laughter as Ann related some of the things her friend had said. 'You've got to take your hat off to her, she's priceless.'

'I'm glad we're going to live in the same street, Mam, 'cos I do love Mrs Lizzie,' Tess said. 'She always makes you laugh and feel happy.'

Ann nodded. 'She's a real character, a breed apart. She certainly proved a friend today the way she sorted things out. Everything's organised now, all we have to do is start packing.'

'There's one other thing, love,' George said. 'We'll have to tell our Ken and Milly. We can't just up sticks without telling them.'

'Oh, good heavens, I've had so much on my mind I forgot them! I'll go down tomorrow and see Milly. I was going to call to Mrs Caldwell's to ask for the measurements of the windows so I can cut these curtains to fit, so I'll call to Milly's while I'm down there.' Ann tilted her head. 'I could leave it until tomorrow night if you'd like to see the house, love?'

There were loud calls from the girls saying *they'd* like to see the house, so George shook his head. 'We can't all walk in on the woman, it wouldn't be right. You go on your own in the afternoon, love, and call to our Ken's while you're down there. They only live about three streets away, it's not far.'

'When are you going to start packing, Mam?' Maddy asked. 'Me and Tess can help.'

'We'll start in your bedroom when you come home from school tomorrow. Clothes you've outgrown we can give to the rag-man, and the others we'll stack neatly on top of the dressing table until I can find something to pack them in. I could do with a few big boxes, 'cos there's all the bedding as well as the clothes, and all the ornaments. Plus the crockery, cutlery, pans, brushes, bucket and mop, and heaven knows what else. There's loads to think of.'

'I'll come down to the Vale with you on Saturday,' George said. 'And we'll ask in the shops if they've any large boxes. Tea chests would be ideal, but where you'd get them from I don't know. And I imagine they'd be expensive.'

'Ooh, isn't it exciting, Maddy?' Tess couldn't sit still on her chair. 'My tummy is jumping up and down and going around and around.'

Her sister grinned. 'Is it doing all that at the same time?'

Ann's head was splitting with the thought of all she had to do in the next eight days. But she couldn't help smiling at her younger daughter. 'D'you know what, Theresa, the only emotion I don't feel is excitement. But I'm sure it won't be long before it joins all the others.'

Chapter Sixteen

Ann picked up her rent book from the sideboard when a knock came on the door. It would be the rent collector, who came at half past ten every Friday morning without fail. He was so punctual you could set your clock by him. She wasn't relishing facing him this morning, though, for not only was she giving a week's notice, she was only able to pay a shilling off the five shillings' arrears. He was a nice, quiet bloke, always polite and friendly. And as she made her way along the hall, Ann whispered to herself, 'Let's hope he believes me when I tell him I'll definitely make the arrears up next week.'

'Good morning, Mrs Richardson.' Bob Sinclair stood with his collection book open at the right page, and his fountain pen at the ready. He was middle-aged, with sandy hair, blue eyes and a healthy complexion from working in the fresh air most days of the week. He was a family man with two grown-up sons and one daughter. 'Weather's not too bad this morning, a bit on the cold side but better than it's been.'

'No, it doesn't feel as cold as yesterday, but when you're polishing and mopping it's hard to tell.' Ann passed over her rent book with the money inside. 'Bob, I've got something to tell you and I'd like to get it off my chest quick. I want to give the landlord a week's notice. We're moving next Saturday. But I'll clear the arrears next Friday, I promise. I wouldn't leave with a debt hanging over my head, I'd never sleep.'

Bob marked the book and handed it back to her. He'd known for some weeks now that Mrs Richardson was struggling, so the news came as no surprise. He was sorry, though, because they were nice people and good tenants. 'You won't need to pay any rent next week, only the arrears, so that should be a help.'

'How d'you mean, I won't need to pay any rent? We'll be living here all week, until the Saturday.'

'You pay your rent a week in advance, Mrs Richardson. If you remember when you took the tenancy you were asked for a week in advance. So the money I'm taking off you today is next week's rent. As long as you're out of this house before the following Monday, you will only need to pay me the four shillings' arrears when I call next Friday.'

It seemed too good to be true and Ann didn't want to get her hopes up. 'Are you pulling my leg, Bob?'

'Good heavens, no! If you look at the rent book I've just marked, you'll see the date I've written in is next Monday's, the start of your week. I'm surprised you didn't know that.'

'Well I didn't! You probably think I'm as thick as two short planks, but I honestly thought the rent I paid you was for the week you came. Oh, I do hope you're right.'

He chuckled. 'I wouldn't last long in this job if I was giving money to people who weren't entitled to it. No, you can rest assured that next Friday I'll only be holding my hand out for four shillings.' He closed his book, keeping a finger in the place he was up to. 'I'll be very sorry to see you go, very sorry indeed. You were always in, so I didn't have to come twice like I do with some people. And you always had the correct money ready, which is a help.'

'I should have moved weeks ago, instead of getting myself into debt, but I couldn't bear the thought of leaving this house. The girls were born and brought up here, and it holds a lot of memories. But memories don't put bread on the table, Bob, nor do they pay the rent or the coal man. So I've got to learn to live within my means. And the house I've managed to get in Willard Street has been cared for and doesn't need a thing doing to it. So I'm learning to live with the idea. And I've got a good friend living in the street and my in-laws live nearby.'

'Well I wish you luck in your new home. But I'll see you next Friday, same time.'

As he moved away, Ann couldn't resist asking, 'You are sure about the rent, aren't you? I'd hate to spend it and then find myself in trouble.'

'I'm positive.' Bob nodded to the rent book in her hand. 'Read the first page and you'll see the terms of your tenancy. But you must be out of the house on the Saturday. If you're still here on the Monday Mr Cosgrove will be down on you like a ton of bricks.'

'We'll be out, the removal van is already booked. And thanks, Bob, you're an angel. I'd kiss you if it weren't for giving the neighbours something to talk about.' Ann closed the door on his chuckle and hummed as she walked through to the living room. She sat at the table and opened her rent book. On the back of the front cover the terms of tenancy were printed. And yes, her rent was paid weekly in advance. She would never have thought of it because it was over fifteen years since they'd moved in. But casting her mind back now, she could remember going down to the office for the keys and having to pay a week's money over the counter.

Ann held the rent book to her chest. What a blessing it was, the answer to all her problems. Wait until she told George, he'd be over the moon.

'What's to eat, Mam?' Maddy asked, throwing her coat over the arm of the couch. 'I'm starving.'

'Poached egg on toast,' Ann called from the kitchen. 'How does that sound?'

'Sounds good to me!' Tess threw her coat on top of her sister's. 'My tummy's rumbling.'

'It's almost ready, so sit yourselves down.' Ann was smiling when she carried the plates through and she was humming softly. 'Golden toast and runny egg, just the way you like it.'

'You look happy, Mam,' Maddy said. 'Has something nice happened?'

The girls knew nothing about the rent arrears and Ann thought they were too young to be told such things. 'I've made up my mind that I'm not going to worry about the packing or anything else, it only gives me a headache. I'll just go at my own pace, doing so much each day. And with your help I know we'll be well organised when next Saturday comes.' She went out to get her own plate. 'I'm going down to Willard Street, as you know, and to see Auntie Milly. So I'll walk part way with you.'

Maddy gave her sister a nudge. 'Haven't you got something to tell our mam?'

'Ooh, er, I nearly forgot.' Tess, her eyes wide, leaned across the table. 'Miss Bond asked if you would call in to sign a paper?'

'It's a contract, Mam, from the magazine,' Maddy explained. 'You have to sign it for Tess, with her being too young.'

'In that case I'll come to the school with you, it's not far out of the way. But just in case I'm not back when you get home from school, I'll give you a spare key, Madelaine. I'll try to be back, but you never know what crops up and I don't want you hanging around in the cold.'

Tess saw moving to Willard Street as a big adventure. It was all she thought about and she'd told everyone in her class, and Miss Harrison. Right now she was swinging her legs back to kick the bottom of her chair, and egg yolk was running down her chin. 'Saturday tomorrow, Mrs Lizzie will be coming. I hope she's had an argument with the rose and makes us all laugh.'

'Theresa, you've got egg yolk on your chin, go and wipe your face.'

'I've only got one more mouthful, Mam, I may as well eat it before I wash my face, otherwise it will be a waste of time.'

Ann shook her head. You really couldn't argue with that. 'Hurry up then, I don't want us to be late and me having to run to keep up with

221

you. My legs aren't as young as yours.'

Tess giggled. 'Me and Maddy will give you a piggy-back.'

'Ay, you speak for yourself!' Maddy feigned indignation. 'If Mam jumped on my back I'd collapse. Anyway, we'd never get to school at that rate.'

'And we'll never get there if you two don't stop talking.' Ann lifted her dirty plate and used a hand to push herself up. 'Now get a move on so I can wash the plates before we go out. I can't abide coming home to dirty dishes.'

'I don't know why you worry, Mam,' Maddy said, 'when no one can see them.'

'No, but I know they're there and that's enough for me. So come on, get moving.'

'I just need you to sign this contract, Mrs Richardson, on behalf of Theresa.' Miss Bond opened a drawer in her desk and took out a large envelope. The contract she drew from the envelope consisted of three pages. Ann read it through before signing, but all it said was that the magazines were buying the rights to print the article by Theresa Richardson and for that they were paying her the sum of five shillings. It would be printed in fifty thousand copies on the twenty-second of December.

'Fifty thousand copies!' Ann gasped. 'So fifty thousand people will read Theresa's work, isn't that wonderful!'

'More than that,' Miss Bond said. 'Magazines are usually read by more than one member of the family before being passed on to friends. I think you could easily double that number.' She pointed to a line on the bottom of the third page. 'Will you sign your name there, and underneath write "on behalf of Theresa Richardson".'

Ann didn't hesitate, thinking of the calls she had to make. 'I must remember to tell our friends in Wales so they can buy a copy.'

She was getting to her feet when the headmistress took another, smaller envelope from the desk drawer. 'This is the postal order for five shillings. It's made out to you so you'll have no problem drawing it at any post office.'

Ann sat down heavily. Surely she was still in bed and all this was a dream? But Miss Bond looked real enough as she leaned across the desk inviting Ann to take the envelope from her outstretched hand. 'This is a surprise, I wasn't expecting it so soon.'

'My friend brought the envelopes this morning. And apparently the editor of the magazine said they would consider reading anything that Theresa writes in the future. That must make you feel very proud of her.'

'Yes, I am proud of her. But I'm also very proud of Madelaine, because it was she who taught Theresa how to read and write. When Theresa was off school so often through sickness, I tried to teach her, giving her lessons every day. But since I'm her mother she tried too hard to please, and was afraid of getting her sums wrong or spelling a word incorrectly. And it was Madelaine who realised you couldn't be a mother and a teacher at the same time, and she had the courage to speak out. Thank God she did, because Theresa's health was suffering, as was her education. So my younger daughter's progress in every aspect of life is through Madelaine's love for her sister, and her patience and sense of fun.'

'And the love and devotion of her parents. It's plain to see she adores both you and your husband.' Miss Bond could see tears weren't far off and sought to terminate the visit. 'Theresa told me you were moving house and I wish you good fortune in your new home.' She walked with Ann to the door. 'Thank you for coming in.'

With the envelope still in her hand, Ann felt as though she was walking in a trance. She never thought they'd make it money-wise, but now, in just a few hours, it seemed her worries were at an end. It was unbelievable, and if it wasn't for the envelope clutched in her hand, she would probably think her imagination was playing tricks on her. It was only as she neared Willard Street that she pulled herself together, and the envelope was pushed into her pocket before she lifted the knocker on Peggy Caldwell's front door.

'Hello, girl, I wasn't expecting you!'

'I promise I won't intrude after today, Peggy, but I wondered if you could give me the measurements for the curtains. Mine will be too long so I'll have to turn them up. The nets should be all right, though, 'cos it doesn't matter if they hang over the window ledge, no one will see them.'

'I've just made meself a pot of tea, so come and sit down, have a cuppa to warm yer up and we can have a natter.'

Peggy left her visitor to close the door while she bustled through to the kitchen to see to the tea, and as soon as Ann walked into the room she felt at home. She sat down and the warmth enveloped her. It was much lighter and brighter than the living room in Hanford Avenue, having a window at both ends of the room, but there was more to it than that. This room seemed to glow with cheerfulness.

'Here, that should warm you up.' Peggy put a cup down on the table and a plate with a buttered scone on. 'Ye're in luck, I made a batch of these this morning. There's nothing my feller likes better than a scone with thick butter on.' She went back to the kitchen and returned with her own cup of tea. 'I pinched a scone before, so I won't have one now.

But you tuck in and pretend ye're at yer granny's.'

'I've been looking at the curtains and I don't think there's much difference in the length to the ones I've got up now. Maybe a couple of inches, that's all, so I won't bother altering them.'

'A couple of inches is neither here nor there,' Peggy said. 'Mine are about twelve inches from the floor, so yours should be a nice length. The lino in every room is in good nick so you won't have to worry about floor covering. I'll give it a good scrub so it'll be nice and clean for yer to move into.'

Ann looked surprised. 'You're not taking the lino with you?'

Peggy pulled a face and shook her head. 'It's not worth it, girl, 'cos if we tried to lift it it would tear and crack. My feller agrees, it wouldn't be fit to put down in the house we're going to. The landlord has agreed to let us have the keys on Thursday, so I'm going to get new lino fitted before we move in.' She could see Ann was pleased and grinned. 'They say once yer've got yer floor covered and yer curtains up, that's the biggest worry over. So I won't mind if yer want to bring yer curtains down one day and put them up.'

'You really are very kind, Peggy, and I'll take you up on your offer. What day would be best for you?'

'Whenever suits you. But yer can't take them down too soon and leave yerself without covering on yer windows. Yer don't want everyone looking in at yer.'

'Our parlour is at the front of the house, and we never use it. There's four curtains on the windows which are never drawn, so anyone passing wouldn't notice the difference. Even if they did, what would it matter? I've told my friends we're leaving and they're the only ones I worry about. The four curtains would do both of these windows, so I'll put them in the dolly tub tonight and I'll have them washed, dried and ironed in a couple of days.' She put a hand to her mouth as a thought flashed through her mind. 'What am I talking about! How can I hang curtains with no ladder to stand on!'

'Have no fear, Peggy's here!' A wide grin covered the bonny face. 'We've got a ladder in the yard. It's as old as the hills, but safe enough if I hang on to it while you're putting the curtains up. Where there's a will there's a way, girl!'

Ann sighed with contentment. 'What say I come on Wednesday, and I'll bring the curtains, the nets and all the wires?' When Peggy nodded, Ann said, 'D'you know, Peggy, this has been a lovely day.'

Milly Richardson opened the door and gaped. 'Blimey, look what the cat dragged in! What brings you to this neck of the woods?' She stepped aside to let her sister-in-law pass. 'Yer've caught me with me feet up listening to the wireless, while me sink's full of dirty dishes. If my feller saw me he'd call me for all the lazy sluts under the sun.'

'I've got a surprise for you.'

'I hope it's more interesting than the play I've been listening to.' Milly switched the wireless off. 'It's supposed to be a murder mystery, but anyone with half an ounce of sense will have guessed it's the butler what done it.'

Ann pulled a chair out and sat down. 'My news isn't as exciting, I'm afraid, there's no skulduggery involved.'

'Couldn't yer make something up to break the monotony? Life doesn't half get dull.'

'How about me telling you that we're moving house?'

Milly snorted, 'Blimey, can't yer do better than that?'

'Only if I tell you a lie. You see, we *are* moving house, Milly, I'm not pulling your leg.'

Her sister-in-law scratched her cheek as she studied Ann with eyes narrowed to slits. 'If ye're telling me the truth, what brought this about?'

Ann had no intention of telling her about the struggle they'd had over the last few months, not the full story anyway. 'George and I discussed it a month ago because the money situation was a bit tight, and we talked of looking for a smaller place. He's had a pay rise recently which will ease things, but when a friend told us of a house coming empty in Willard Street we decided to apply for it so we'd have money to spare every week. I went to see the landlord yesterday and he agreed to let us have the house. So we're moving in a week tomorrow.'

Never one to mince her words, Milly said, 'It's about time yer came to yer ruddy senses. Yer want to start getting out and enjoying yourselves. Yer only live once, yer know, so yer'd best make the most of it.' Again she scratched her cheek. 'Doesn't Lizzie Ferguson live in Willard Street? Was it her what told yer about the house?'

'I didn't know you knew Lizzie,' Ann said. 'You've never mentioned her before.'

'I've never set eyes on the woman, it was Ken who told me. He met her at yours when he went to help bring the bed down. He knows her husband well, they're boozing buddies. He said Lizzie's a smashing woman, full of beans and very funny.'

'She's all that and more. From the day George had his accident she's been a very good friend to me, and the girls absolutely love the bones of her. If I was ever in a fight, it would be Lizzie I'd like in my corner.'

'Wait until I tell Ken, he'll get a surprise. Mind you, I bet the first thing he says is that he'll be able to go for a pint with his brother now.' Milly was beginning to take to the idea of having relations so near. It would be somewhere to go for a cuppa and a chat, and that had to be better than listening to a lousy play on the wireless. 'What time are yer moving in on Saturday, 'cos we'll give yer a hand. Ken works till twelve, but I could help out.'

'It'll be in the afternoon after Mrs Caldwell has moved out. George has to work in the morning anyway, so we couldn't go any earlier.'

Milly's facial expression changed several times before settling into one of shock. 'Ye're not moving into Peggy Caldwell's house, are yer?'

'Yes, number forty-seven.'

'Next door to Nellie Bingham's lot?' Milly's voice reached a high pitch. 'Yer want yer bumps feeling, Ann, 'cos she'll shred yer into little pieces and spit yer out. Everyone around here knows Nellie, and everyone keeps well clear of her. They cross the road when they see her coming because if yer as much as look sideways at her, she'll ask yer what ye're looking at before belting yer one.'

'I know all about the Binghams, Milly.' Ann sighed. She might have known the day had been going too well. Something had to come along to spoil it. 'Both Lizzie and Peggy have warned me what to expect. Even the landlord tried to put me off. But I like Peggy's house, it's been well cared for and is spotlessly clean. I might look as though I couldn't stick up for myself against a bullying neighbour, but believe me, I'll give as good as I get. I certainly won't be put off a house I want because of her. Anyway, if it gets too rough we can always look for another house. I don't think we'll have to, but if push comes to shove there's always that to fall back on. We don't have to be tied there for life.'

'Well, you know yer own mind best, girl, so go ahead and do what yer want. And we'll give yer a hand next Saturday, so count us in. If ye're too busy to slip down and let me know what time yer want us, tell Lizzie and she can give us a knock. It's one way of getting to meet this paragon of virtue.'

Ann laughed. 'If Lizzie heard that, she'd laugh her socks off. That's after she'd asked you what it meant. But you'll find out for yourself when you meet her. She'll be coming to give a hand and I guarantee she'll have you in stitches the whole time. Plus doing twice as much work as any of us.'

'It'll give me something to look forward to,' Milly said. 'I enjoy a good laugh. I've often thought how nice it would be to have me own court jester. Yer know, like the kings used to have in days gone by. I wouldn't be cruel to them, not like the kings were. They used to chop their heads off if they didn't make them laugh! I wouldn't go that far, a kick up the backside would be my limit.'

'I've got another surprise for you. It won't make you laugh, but I think you'll be pleased.' Ann went on to tell of Tess's good fortune in having one of her compositions printed in a magazine, and felt amply rewarded by Milly's facial contortions. 'And she was paid five shillings for it.' The envelope was brought out of her pocket and waved aloft. 'I've got a postal order here, made out to me 'cos I had to sign the contract, with Theresa being too young.'

'Well I declare!' To say Milly was surprised would be an understatement. She loved Tess dearly, but if she was honest she'd have to say she'd never expected the girl to get anywhere because of her always being sickly and acting childish. Yet here she was, miles ahead of everybody else in the family, who had never achieved anything like this. 'Well, she's knocked spots off every one of us, and I'm so pleased because it couldn't have happened to a nicer girl. I bet she's over the moon. I know Ken will be, and the kids, because they think the world of Tess. And Madelaine of course, they don't make fish of one and flesh of the other. It's just that Tess has always been so frail and that made her sort of special.'

'She's thrilled about this move. Anyone would think we were moving to a palace,' Ann said, remembering Theresa's face with egg yolk running down her chin. 'I hope the gilt doesn't wear off the gingerbread too quickly.'

'Keep her away from the cow next door, I believe her language is enough to turn the air blue. Yer don't want the girls listening to that sort of thing.'

'Don't worry, I'll make sure of that! If she as much as lays a hand on either of my girls I'll get the broom to her. I believe she's only small, so I should be able to hold my own.'

Milly huffed. 'Don't forget, girl, poison comes in small bottles.'

'So does perfume. Perhaps we'll be able to change her from a wicked devil to a sweet-smelling angel.' Ann reached for her coat, which she'd slipped off when she came in so she'd feel the benefit of it when she went out into the cold. 'I'd better make an effort, I'd like to be home for the girls because it gets dark early now and I worry about Madelaine standing on a chair to light the gas.' She slipped her arms into her coat and buttoned it up to the neck. 'If I can't get down before, I'll do what you suggested and ask Lizzie to give you a knock and tell you what time the van is likely to arrive at Willard Street. We would be grateful for your help, Milly.'

'We'll be there, kid, don't worry. If we all muck in, yer should be settled in no time.'

Lizzie stepped off the tram on Friday night after work, and made her way to the corner shop. She pushed the shop door open and rubbed her hands when she felt the warmth fan her face. 'Good evening, Bertram, I hope ye're in good form.'

'Oh God, here she comes.' Bert Green winked across to his wife, who was serving a customer at the side counter. 'Lizzie's being polite, Lily, which means she's after something. Would you like to serve her and I'll see to Mrs Bentley?'

'Oh, ay, soft lad, what d'yer think I am? I've got a nice quiet customer here that won't give me no trouble, and you want me to swap her for Lizzie Ferguson! I'd need me flippin' head testing.'

'That's charming that is,' Lizzie said, looking suitably put out. 'If that's the way yer feel about it I'd better take me bleedin' custom elsewhere, where I'll be appreciated.'

'Oh no, there's no need for that, Lizzie, that's very thoughtless of yer. Yer know me and Lily are saving up to be rich and are counting every penny. And your pennies are as good as anyone else's, so just tell me what yer want and I'll give yer me full attention.'

Lizzie was dying to laugh. Either she or Bert were going to get their eye wiped and she was hoping it wouldn't be her. 'Have yer got any tea chests?'

The shopkeeper thought she was having him on and he burst out laughing. 'A laugh a minute you are, Lizzie. Now tell us what yer really want.'

'I've asked yer once, and I'll ask yer again. Have yer got any tea chests?'

By this time Lily had stopped serving so she could listen, and her customer was so interested she forgot what she'd come in for.

Bert tried to keep his patience. 'Come on, Lizzie, stop messing about, I've got shelves to stack. Just tell us what yer want.'

'I'll say it once more, Bert Green, and if yer don't give me an answer I'll come behind that counter and clock yer one. Now I'll say it slowly so yer've no excuse for pretending yer don't know what I'm talking about. Have . . . you . . . got . . . any . . . tea . . . chests?'

'Lizzie, we sell everything under the sun, except tea chests.'

'I don't want yer to sell me one, yer daft nit, I want yer to lend me one!'

By this time Lily and her customer were in stitches. Well, there was nothing better to warm you up on a cold night than a good belly laugh.

'D'yer mean yer've no intention of buying anything, ye're on the cadge?'

'Now, Bert, keep yer hair on. When yer tell me I can borrow one of them tea chests I've seen in yer stock room with me very own eyes, then I'll tell yer whether I'm going to buy anything or not.'

'That's blackmail! All you've got to do is say yer'll buy something if I lend yer a tea chest. But if I'm soft enough to say of course yer can borrow one of me tea chests, you could turn round and buy a flippin'

228

ha'penny box of matches! How soft you are!'

Lizzie knew this was all just talk, that in the end she'd get what she wanted. And she was fully aware that Bert knew. And his wife and the customer she'd been halfway through serving when all this started, they knew. But a little bit of haggling did no harm and gave everyone a laugh. 'Ye're wrong on all counts, Bert. Yer see, I was going to ask you for the loan of two tea chests, not one. And I wasn't going to buy a ha'penny box of matches, I was about to purchase five Woodbines for my feller. So there, smart-arse!'

'I'd give in gracefully if I were you, Bert,' Lily called. 'Because yer don't stand a snowball's chance in hell of winning.'

'Don't yer think I know that? But I can't get over the cheek of it! I mean, I'd have loaned her one of the chests as a friendly gesture, but the greedy woman's not satisfied with one, she wants two!'

Lizzie's voice was as sweet as honey when she said, 'But I'm not asking for the impossible, Bert, am I? I mean, yer've got two chests in the storeroom standing there doing nothing! I'd be doing yer a favour, really, by getting them out of yer way for a week.'

'A week! Yer want them for a whole week? I use them chests, Lizzie Ferguson, I keep stock in them.'

'Eight days really, Bert, I won't lie to yer. But before yer tear out what little hair yer've got on yer head, let me explain. Yer see, they're not for me, they're for a mate who's moving into Peggy Caldwell's house next Saturday. And she could turn out to be a good customer for yer, Bert, 'cos she's got two kids who like sweets.'

'They won't be customers for long, though, will they? They'll be out of there after a week when Nellie Bingham starts her shenanigans. There's not much point in me doing a favour to someone I won't have time to get to know.'

Lizzie, who had been leaning on the counter, now stood to attention. 'My feller will be wondering where his dinner is. So make it snappy, can I borrow those two chests or not?'

'Oh, I suppose so, or I'll never hear the last of it. But how are yer going to get them to yer friend's house? They're bloody big things, yer know, and they're heavy.'

'That's for me to worry about, but by hook or by crook I'll get them there.' Lizzie gave him a beaming smile. 'You're a cracker, Bert, one of me very favourite men. I knew yer wouldn't let me down. Now yer can give me ten Woodbines for my feller and quarter of mint imperials for meself. While he's puffing, I'll be sucking.'

It was Saturday afternoon, and when the knocker sounded Tess was off her chair like a shot from a gun. 'This will be Mrs Lizzie, I'll go.'

There was a smile of pleasant anticipation on her face when she opened the door. But at the sight that met her eyes the smile faded as her mouth gaped. Mrs Lizzie was standing on the path, but on the pavement outside there stood a battered old pram with a huge tea chest on top. And holding on to the chest on either side were two young boys about the same age as herself.

'Don't stand there with yer mouth open, queen, or yer'll be catching flies. Go and ask yer mam and dad to give us a hand, will yer?'

George heard the familiar voice and came to the door with Ann and Maddy on his heels. He looked from Lizzie to where the pram stood. It was worn and battered and one of the back wheels was buckled. Laughter in his voice, he asked, 'You haven't wheeled that thing, have you, Lizzie? It's falling to pieces!'

Lizzie bristled. Her shoulders were in motion and her jaw set. 'Well I didn't carry the bleedin' thing on me back, George. Now, do yer want the tea chest, or don't yer want the ruddy tea chest?'

Ann pushed her husband aside. 'Oh, yes, Lizzie, I'd be made up with it! But you shouldn't have pushed it all this way. If you'd told me I would have come down and helped you.'

'The two lads have done all the hard work, all I did was try to keep the ruddy thing in a straight line. Now if yer'll give a hand to get it in, the lads are going back to pick another one up.'

Ann gasped. 'You mean you've managed to get two of them?'

'I don't do things by halves, queen, it's all or nothing. I've got them on loan from one of the local shops, and I promised he'd get them back in good nick. Now come on, all hands to the pumps so the lads can get away.'

One of the lads said, 'Me and Billy can carry it in between us, Mrs Ferguson.' And showing off in front of Tess and Maddy, he pulled himself to his full height and added, 'They're not that heavy, we can do it easy.'

'Oh well, let's clear the way for the workers then.' Lizzie grinned when she saw young Billy eyeing Tess up. 'Outside everyone, so they can get in.'

The family trooped out to give the boys room, and as they heaved the chest off the pram, the older boy, fourteen-year-old James Cobden, winked at Lizzie. 'Don't let anyone pinch the pram, Mrs Ferguson.'

'Blimey, son, yer'd have to pay someone to take it away!'

George and the girls followed the lads down the hall to tell them where to put the chest, while the two women stayed on the path. 'Lizzie, you're an angel, they'll solve all my problems. But what made you think about getting them?'

'I asked George if yer had any packing cases and he said yer were going round the shops this afternoon to cadge some cardboard boxes. So I thought, to hell with that, yer needed something stronger than cardboard boxes. Yer'll get everything in the two tea chests so they'll be easier to unpack.'

Ann put her arms around her and kissed her. 'Lizzie, what would I do without you? You really are an angel.'

'Listen, queen, when yer say that, would her mind looking up to heaven so He can hear yer? I might need references to get a place up there when me time comes. As they say, self-praise is no recommendation, so I'll need a little help from me friends.'

Chapter Seventeen

At last the day had arrived and Ann had been very busy since the crack of dawn. All the packing had been done except for the few dishes they'd need for their lunch. The house looked lonely and sad with all the pictures, mirrors and ornaments packed away, and Ann couldn't help feeling sad herself. She'd known a lot of happiness and love with her husband in this house, and with the children when they came along. It was going to be a wrench walking out of the front door for the last time.

She was taken away from her thoughts when the girls burst into the room. 'We've gone through every room, Mam,' Maddy said. 'Looked in every nook and cranny and there's nothing been left behind.'

'You've both been very good, I couldn't have managed without you. Now all I've got to do is clean myself up a bit and comb my hair.'

'I'll get the mirror for you, Mam.' Tess was white-faced with excitement. 'It's only standing in the hall, I can put it back again when you've finished with it. You can't titivate yourself up if you've no mirror to look in.' She ran into the hall, and when she reappeared she was bent double under the weight of the heavy old mirror which had once belonged to Ann's parents. 'Give us a hand, Maddy, to stand it on the mantelpiece so our mam can see herself in it. She wants to look her best when she meets her new neighbours.'

God love her, Ann thought, she's in for a shock. But there's no point in telling her now and spoiling the day for her. The time to face trouble is when it comes, not before. She took a comb from her handbag and went to stand in front of the fireplace. Her hair was hanging down past her shoulders because she hadn't bothered with it this morning, there were more important things needed doing. She ran the comb through it several times to untangle any knots, then made a middle parting from her forehead to the nape of her neck. Then she took the hair from one side and began to plait it, ready for twisting into a bun. She could see the reflection of the girls in the mirror, sitting quietly watching her. Maddy because she'd nothing else to do. She'd said goodbye to her friends last night, even though she'd see most of them in school on Monday. Tess was leaning forward, interest in her eyes. And Ann felt a bit guilty when she remembered she'd once told Theresa she would teach her how to plait her hair, and never had. Her daughter mustn't have been so keen anyway, otherwise she would have asked.

Ann was laying the plait on her shoulder when she happened to glance in the mirror again. This time the expression on her younger daughter's face caught her attention. It reminded her of the times they'd looked in a shop window and Theresa had seen something she liked but which they couldn't afford. It wasn't an expression of greed, more like a longing. Then remembered words suddenly came back to run through Ann's mind. 'You'd look much prettier if you wore your hair loose, Mam.' And another time, 'None of the women in the street have hair this long. You could get it cut, though, and then you'd look nice.'

Ann stared at herself in the mirror as she fingered the loose hair waiting to be plaited. Then a further look at her daughter's reflection in the mirror brought her to a quick decision. They were moving into a new house; perhaps it was time for her to move on to something different. Off with the old, on with the new. 'Madelaine, I don't suppose you can remember where we packed the scissors? Would they be easy to get to?'

Tess stared at her mother and the hair she was fingering. And she sprang to her feet. 'I know where they are, Mam, they're in the canvas bag on top of one of the chests. I'll soon find them for you.'

Maddy looked puzzled. 'What d'you want them for, Mam?'

'You'll see.' Ann grinned when Tess came flying in with the scissors in her hand. And she could tell her daughter knew what she had in mind. 'I would like my hair cutting, but I can't do it myself, it would be all skew-whiff. So, any offers?'

Maddy gasped. 'You're not cutting your hair off, are you, Mam? What are you doing that for, our Dad will go mad!'

'No he won't, because I mentioned it to him once before and he seemed quite pleased. So who'll volunteer to give the first snip?'

'I'll do it, Mam.' Tess sounded eager. 'I've never cut hair before but I'll do my best.'

Maddy's eyes rolled. 'You should get it done properly, at the hairdresser's. I'd be frightened of making a mess of it.'

'I don't have time to go to the hairdresser's, nor do I have the money to spare. And now I have made up my mind, I would like it doing before we move. So who is best at cutting in a very straight line?'

Tess had to admit defeat. 'Maddy can cut straight, my lines go all wonky.'

But her sister didn't like the idea. 'Mam, I don't want to get the blame if it looks a mess.'

'If it looks a mess it will be my own fault, Madelaine, you won't get the blame. If we just decide what length would suit me best, all you need to do is cut it even all round. I'm willing to take a chance, so won't you?'

Maddy took a deep breath then let it out slowly. 'If it's what you want, then on your own head be it. I'll get a newspaper to put the hair on, save it going on the floor.'

George stood back in amazement. 'Who is this pretty young lady? I've never seen her before, girls, is she a friend of yours?'

Tess giggled. 'Doesn't she look nice, Dad?'

George stared at his wife, who looked years younger. Her hair was cut in a bob, just below her ears, and it had fallen into soft waves. 'Your mother looks more than nice, she looks very lovely. The style suits her.'

Ann felt both relieved and satisfied. 'Madelaine's made a very good job of it, don't you think? I've told her she should consider hairdressing when she leaves school.'

'I didn't want to do it, Dad, in case I made a mess of it.' Maddy was chuffed with herself now her work had been given the seal of approval. 'I was frightened of her not liking it and asking me to stick it back on again.'

Tess's infectious giggle rang out. 'If you'd had to stick all the hairs back on, Maddy, it would have taken you a hundred years.'

'I think your sister has done an excellent job, very professional. I think I'll let her cut my hair in future.' George looked around the room. 'I see you've got everything organised, love, you must have worked very hard.'

'Oh, I didn't do it alone, I had two willing workers. But doesn't the place look lonely and bare? It doesn't look like our home any more.'

'Not having regrets, are you, love?'

'I'll feel sad when I'm walking out of the door, but that's only natural after all these years. I wouldn't be normal if I didn't feel sad. But I don't have any regrets because I think life is going to be better for us. We'll be able to get out and enjoy ourselves. Like going to the pictures or a ferry ride across to New Brighton. It's a long time since we did things like that.' She nodded her head. 'Yes, George, life will be a lot easier for all of us.'

'Well, what's the agenda for this afternoon?'

'As we planned. When I've put your dinner out, me and the girls are going to make our way down to Willard Street. We've had something to eat and our dishes have been washed and packed away. You're staying behind until the van comes and I hope you'll keep an eye on the men, see they're careful with the furniture and those chests with all the

235

breakables in. Then when the house is empty, make sure the doors are closed back and front. You won't be able to go out and come back in again, as you know, 'cos I gave the keys to the rent collector yesterday. The men did say they'd bring you down in the van, didn't they?'

George nodded. 'There's no problem there. Lizzie told me to tell you if the Caldwells are still in the throes of emptying their house when you get there, then go down to hers and she'll make you a warm drink. Oh, she's had the coal man throw a bag of nuts in the coal shed, so you'll be able to light a fire as soon as we move in.'

'She thinks of everything does Lizzie. I'll be forever in her debt.'

'Oh, that's not all! She's ordered her milkman to leave you a pint every morning, starting from today. And we're all invited down for something to eat at tea time. She won't be thanked, either! I did try and she went all uppity on me. I can't take her off, I'm not good at that sort of thing and wouldn't do her justice, but this is what she said: "Yer can't drink yer bleedin' tea with no milk in. And all yer'll be getting for yer tea is harmless, 'cos I'll be too busy helping and I can't be in two bleedin' places at once."'

Laughter was heard in the room for the first time that day. 'Oh, I do love Mrs Lizzie,' Tess said. 'Even if she does use naughty words.'

'They don't sound naughty coming from her,' Maddy said. 'You can't help but laugh.'

'I agree, but I wouldn't like to hear them coming from your mouth. So while you may laugh, you may not copy.'

'Too bleedin' true!' The words sounded so strange coming from her husband's lips, even Ann couldn't stop the gurgle of laughter that erupted. But when she saw the girls doubled up, she tried to be firm.

'Really, George, that's no way to talk in front of me and the children. Please don't encourage them.'

'Yes, dear.' George sounded suitably contrite. 'I'll do what Lizzie does. When you've gone, I'll give myself a jolly good talking-to. I could even end up giving myself a good hiding, but that's rather debatable because I'm not as brave as Lizzie.'

So when Ann walked out of eighteen Hanford Avenue for the last time, her daughters linking her either side, there were smiles on the three faces. The sadness was to come later.

'There's Lizzie talking to Mrs Caldwell, and there's no sign of the removal van.' Ann began to quicken her pace. 'Let's run.'

Peggy Caldwell was in the act of handing the keys over to Lizzie when she saw Ann and the girls hurrying up the street. 'I'm glad you caught me, girl, I was hoping to see yer to wish you all the best.' She handed over the keys and beamed. 'Let me guess. You're Madelaine,

236

and you are Tess. Your mam and Mrs Ferguson have told me all about you. And I hope yer'll be very happy in yer new home.' Pulling on a pair of navy woollen gloves she said, 'I've mopped right through, Ann, so all yer have to do is put the furniture down. And there's still some life in the fire so yer won't be cold.' With one last look up at the house that had been her home for many years, she straightened her shoulders and sniffed up. 'I'll come down and see you, Lizzie, once I've settled in.'

She was walking away when Ann touched her arm. 'You couldn't have been kinder, Peggy, and I'm grateful for all you've done. I hope you settle in all right and find happiness in your new home. Where are your family, by the way?'

'Oh, they left ages ago to be there for the van arriving. And if I don't put a move on they'll stick the furniture any old how. You know what men are, they've no idea. My feller would put the wardrobe in the living room if it was left to him.' With a wave of her hand she was off, and she never looked back even though the group stood watching until she'd turned the corner.

'She's upset,' Lizzie said. 'And it's a crying shame. I could throttle a certain person with me bare hands.'

'Why is it a crying shame, Mrs Lizzie?' Tess asked. 'The lady wouldn't be moving if she didn't want to.'

'She didn't get on with a neighbour, queen, that's why she's left.'

Ann thought it time to intervene. 'And how are you, Lizzie?'

'Fair to middling, queen, fair to middling. But d'yer think we can go inside now, 'cos I'm bleedin' freezing and I can feel me chilblains starting up.'

'Then let me invite you into our new home. You'll be our first visitor and we couldn't wish for anyone better.' Ann climbed the step, unlocked the door and stepped inside. 'Welcome, Mrs Ferguson.'

The girls were shy for all of two minutes. Then they both started talking at the same time without stopping for breath. 'This is a nice room, Mam, nice and bright,' Tess said. 'It's just like Auntie Milly's house. Is it the same as yours, Mrs Lizzie?'

'The curtains look better in here than they did in our other house,' Maddy said, her eyes everywhere. 'And the lino is a nice light colour. Can we go upstairs, Mam, and see where we'll be sleeping tonight?'

Ann rubbed her forehead. 'Yes, but don't go running around or you'll have the neighbours complaining. And if your hands are dirty don't touch the wallpaper.' She closed her eyes at the clattering on the bare stairs. 'I hope that doesn't start Nellie Bingham off, I couldn't stand an upset today.'

'She won't hear that, queen, 'cos the stairs are on the wall next to yer other neighbour, Mrs Flannery. And yer won't get any trouble from her, she's a smashing woman and all her family are the same.' Lizzie pointed to the wall where the fireplace was. 'That's the wall that separates yer from the Binghams, and yer can bet yer sweet life she'll be raking the grate out at six tomorrow morning, just for spite. She'll make such a racket yer'll think all hell has broke loose, but it'll only be her having her little joke.' Lizzie leaned back against the door and folded her arms. 'My advice would be not to get mad and do the same back to her, 'cos if yer do yer'll just be asking for trouble. Anything you can do she can do twice as bad. And she can keep it up longer too! All day if the mood takes her.'

'She must be a bad . . . bad . . .' Ann floundered as she sought the right word. But help was close at hand.

'The word ye're looking for, queen, is "bugger". There's other words I can think of, but you stick to "bugger", 'cos it's mild compared to some of the names she's been called.'

'We'll all be dead beat after working so hard today, so if she wakes us up at six o'clock in the morning I might ask you to write some of those names down for me.' Ann cast an eye on the dying fire. 'I haven't a poker or shovel, so I hope the van comes before that breathes its last breath. And while I think on, I'll pay you for the bag of coal you so kindly had delivered for me. And you must have given those boys something for bringing the chests, so I'll settle up now. Out of debt, out of danger.'

'George paid me for the coal this morning, when he got his wages. And as for the lads, they wouldn't take nothing,' Lizzie lied. She'd given them thruppence each, and they'd gone to first house at the Carlton on Thursday night. They couldn't get in without an adult, so they'd asked a stranger to take them in and were over the moon. 'So yer don't owe me nothing, queen, only civility.'

'I can't even offer you a seat! Would you like to sit on the stairs while we're waiting?'

'No, I'm going to nip down and make a pot of tea for us. I've got a big basket so I'll fetch some cups and milk and sugar. It'll warm us up and help pass the time.'

Tess was down the stairs first, followed closely by Maddy. 'Can I come with you, Mrs Lizzie? Say yes, please, 'cos I'm dying to see your wallpaper with the roses on.'

Her sister gave her a dig. 'And me! You're not going without me!'

'Girls, behave yourselves,' Ann said. 'Mrs Lizzie has enough on her plate without you two hanging on to her.'

'Not at all! They can help me carry the basket back. Many hands make light work.'

Ann had her hand on the front door, ready to open it, when there was a rap on the knocker and she nearly jumped out of her skin. 'Who on earth can this be?'

'There's a good way of finding out, queen, just open the bleedin' door!'

Ann slowly opened the door, half expecting the dreaded Nellie Bingham. But the woman standing outside was wearing a friendly smile and so the door was opened wide. 'If it's Mrs Caldwell you want, I'm afraid she doesn't live here any more.'

'Yes, I know, love. I live next door.' The woman was pointing to a door which was so close to her own Ann could have reached out and touched it. 'Me name's Dolly Flannery and I'm not being nosy, I just knocked to see if yer'd like a pot of tea while ye're waiting.'

Lizzie elbowed her way to the front. 'That's nice of yer, Dolly, but I'm on me way down to make a brew.' She waved a hand as she made the introductions. 'Dolly, this is Ann Richardson. And these two sweethearts are her children, Maddy and Tess.'

They were squashed like sardines in the tiny hall. The houses weren't built with hallways, you stepped straight from the street into the living room. But Mr Caldwell had built a makeshift hall to give them some privacy when the front door was opened, and to keep out the draught.

Ann stepped down on to the pavement and beckoned the girls to follow. 'It's rather a tight squeeze in there. You're welcome to come in, Mrs Flannery, but there's nowhere to sit, I'm afraid.'

'No, I won't come in 'cos I know ye're expecting the furniture van. But if yer want anything just knock on the wall for me. And by the way, everyone calls me Dolly.'

Ann smiled. 'That's very kind of you, Dolly. I hope we can be friends.'

The girls were too shy to speak, but when Lizzie stepped down to join them, they were drawn to her like a magnet and linked an arm each. 'We'll be back in fifteen minutes, queen, and I'll bring a shovel so yer can keep the fire going.'

'Right, I'll have a little scout around to get to know where everything is. I'll see you later.' Ann was closing the door when she heard Lizzie's voice. 'How's your feller, Dolly, keeping all right, is he?'

'Yeah, he's fine, Lizzie, touch wood.'

Ann was feeling happy as she made her way through to the tiny kitchen. 'Well, I've met one neighbour who seems nice and friendly, that's a good sign. And I've got Lizzie, the woman who anyone could get along with. Good company and as straight as a die.' She spoke aloud as her eyes took in the scrubbed shelves, draining board, woodwork and floor. You could eat your dinner off any of the surfaces.

And the window was clean inside and out. Peggy Caldwell was obviously a good housewife and Lizzie was right, it was a crying shame she'd been forced to leave. She'd make sure the same thing didn't happen to her. If she had to toughen up, then toughen up she would. No bully was going to get the better of her!

Maddy and Tess had been standing by the window keeping watch, and when the van pulled up outside they became very excited and were clapping their hands and jumping up and down. 'It's here, Mam!'

'All right, just keep calm. I think it would be best if you girls stood outside to give the men more room to manoeuvre, otherwise we'll all be under their feet. So hurry up and put your coats on and stand outside by the window.' Ann hurried to open the front door to find George standing with one man, whom he introduced as Jim, and the man she could see letting the back of the van down was Harry. 'Come in and have a look around, so you'll know the lay-out. The girls are going to wait outside to give you more room.'

Lizzie was standing in front of the fire, and when Jim clapped eyes on her he started to laugh. 'Blimey, Lizzie, is there no getting away from yer?'

'That's nice, coming from someone who's supposed to love the bones of me. Even promised me undying love if I left my feller for yer,' Lizzie huffed. 'Ye're fickle, Jim, that's what yer are. Just like all bleedin' men who'll promise yer the earth when they're on the cadge.'

'Now that's not fair, Lizzie, tell the truth. I swore I'd leave me wife if yer'd come away with me, but yer turned me down flat.'

Lizzie was in her element. Having a bit of a laugh and warming her backside at the same time, you couldn't beat it. 'Yeah, I can't tell a lie, yer did ask me to run off with yer. But yer see, Jim, I've got a weak constitution and I couldn't face the thought of living in a tent. If yer'd been Rudolph Valentino now, I would have given the offer some serious consideration, 'cos his tents are like palaces. They have slaves to wave fans at yer when it's hot, and gas fires to keep yer warm in the winter.'

Harry was standing outside waiting for his mate when he heard gales of laughter. He poked his head around the door and called, 'Ay, I've promised to take the wife to the pictures tonight, so come on, let's be having yer.'

At that moment, Jim moved to reveal Lizzie in all her glory. 'Oh my God,' Harry groaned. 'I might have known it was talk a bit. If we miss the pictures tonight, Lizzie Ferguson, then you can come and tell the missus why.' He turned his head to look back into the street. 'Ay, come on, there's gangs of kids hanging around the back of the van.'

And so work started in earnest. George wasn't allowed to help with the heavy stuff in case he did himself an injury, but he made himself useful and kept on the go, while his wife and Lizzie were in the kitchen unpacking the chests. The number of children gathered around had grown to about twenty, and although there was a lot of shouting and pushing and pulling, on the whole they were well behaved. Amongst them were James and Billy, who had helped Lizzie push the pram with the crates on, and they were soon recognised by Tess, who waved a hand in greeting. This made the boys feel very important as they edged their way to where the girls were standing in front of their window. And although there wasn't a word passed between them, they each made for the sister they had their eye on. It was fortunate that both boys didn't fancy the same one.

Next door, Nellie Bingham was standing at her bedroom window watching what was going on. She couldn't see very well, unless she pressed her nose against the window, because she had to squint sideways. And there were so many kids there they were blocking out her view of the furniture being carried in. She wasn't very happy about this because she wanted to see everything that went in so she would know the kind of people she'd have to deal with. Her two sons were out there, Jack and Willy, but the silly buggers wouldn't be able to tell her anything, they were leaning against the wall on the opposite side of the street. A fat lot of good it had done sending them out with instructions to note everything that went in next door. And another thing getting her goat was that Lizzie Ferguson was in there helping! She'd soon wormed her way in, the cheeky cow.

So, feeling frustrated at seeing so little, Nellie decided to make her way downstairs to stand on her front step. But, being so short in stature, even standing on the top step didn't give her the advantage of a better view because she couldn't see over the heads of the kids. She started to get worked up, and signs that she was almost ready to explode were beginning to appear. If her sons had been able to see her flared nostrils and quivering chin, they would have legged it out of the street altogether before the ructions started.

Jim and Harry had lifted the sideboard out of the van when they heard a commotion. They heard a young boy's voice cry, 'Take yer hand off me, missus, I was here first.'

'Don't give me no lip, lad, or yer'll wonder what hit yer,' Nellie said, her fingers digging into the boy's arm. 'Now get over to the other side 'cos ye're blocking me view and I can't see a bleedin' thing.'

'Ay, leave him alone, he was here before you,' James Cobden said, seeing the young boy's face creased in pain. And of course, he was being brave in front of Maddy. After all, he was fourteen now and leaving school at Christmas. 'Take yer hand off him or I'll go and get his mam.'

There were murmurs from the other children too, but that didn't stop Nellie. 'Sod off, you, and go and get his bleedin' mam. Bring his dad as well, see if I care.' She dug her fingers deeper into the young boy's arm, causing him to yelp. 'I want to see what's going on and ye're in the way, so scram before I belt yer one.'

Jim and Harry were still holding on to the sideboard, but at a nod from Jim it was lowered to the ground. He rubbed his hands together as though dusting them, then asked, 'Did yer buy a ticket for the front stalls, missus?'

'Don't you be so bleedin' funny or yer'll be laughing the other side of yer face. These buggers live down the street so they can sod off to where they belong. I live next door and I'm titled to stand by me own house.'

By this time, George, Ann and Lizzie had come to the front door, and several neighbours from opposite who'd been watching behind their net curtains came out to stand in the street. Their children were amongst those around the van, and although no one would like to lock horns with Nellie Bingham, they wouldn't stand by and see their children harmed.

'Oh, ye're titled, are yer? I'm sorry, I didn't know that. What is yer title? Is it Lady, or is it Your Royal Highness?' Jim was grinning, as were the onlookers, and this really stoked the fire. But Jim wasn't to know of the little woman's reputation. 'Do we kneel before you, or would a bow be sufficient?'

Jack Bingham gave his younger brother, Willy, a dig, and the two of them legged it hell for leather down the street. If they'd stayed just a few more seconds they would have seen their mother take a flying leap at Jim. Her arms and legs flailing, she landed several blows and kicks before he came out of shock and tried to restrain her. But she was like a mad woman and Harry rushed to his mate's aid. He'd thought it was funny at first, but this little woman obviously didn't see the funny side. George made an attempt to help, but Ann and Lizzie held him back. 'Keep out of it,' Lizzie warned, 'or yer'll never hear the end of it. She's a bleedin' maniac that one, and best left alone.'

But to the children and watching neighbours, it was all very high drama. And when Jim took one of Nellie's arms, and Harry the other, everyone felt like cheering but knew they'd be made to pay for it if they did. So when the men lifted her three feet off the ground, not a word was spoken by the children as they moved aside to make a pathway for her to be carried through. She was set down on her step, but the men didn't release her arms because she was still struggling, shouting threats and swearing like a trooper. A minute passed and she still hadn't let up, and Harry began to lose his patience. If he was home too late to take his wife to the pictures he'd have another battle on his hands. Not one like this, of course, but his wife would sulk for a week. 'When yer've quite finished with yer little tantrum, we'll let go of yer.'

'I'll get yer for this, I'll take the poker to yer,' Nellie spat. 'I'll soon sort you two out, yer pair of bleeders.'

Jim raised a stiffened finger and wagged it in front of her face. 'You just listen to me. I've never hit a woman in me life, but I'm sorely tempted to give you a go-along because ye're not like any woman I've ever known. Ye're certainly no lady, and that's a fact. So do yerself a favour, go inside and shut this door. Any more shenanigans out of yer and I'll put yer under me arm and take yer to the police station. I'll ask them to charge yer with assault and public disorder. They'll keep yer in the cells overnight, and that should calm yer down.' He pushed her gently backwards and pulled the door shut.

With straight faces, the two men made their way back to the sideboard. Once there, they doubled up with laughter. With tears running down his face, Jim looked at George. 'Why didn't yer warn us, George? I'd have brought me boxing gloves if I'd known.'

'I'm sorry about that, lads, I really am. We were told she was a bully, but I had no idea she was that bad. It looks as though we're going to lead a very hectic and noisy life.'

'I thought it was hilarious,' Jim said. 'I wouldn't have missed it for the world. But ye're going to have yer hands full with her, George, and I don't envy yer, 'cos she's a little spitfire.' He picked up his end of the sideboard. 'Come on, Harry, the show's over.'

Tess was white-faced. 'Ooh, she's a very bad lady she is. I'm never, ever going to speak to her, I don't like her.'

'Yer won't be the only one,' Billy said. 'No one in the street speaks to her, she's horrible.' Billy Cartwright was six months younger than his mate, James, and he wasn't due to leave school until next summer. He was a nice-looking boy with auburn hair, brown eyes and a fresh complexion. Tall for his age, he always looked neat and clean. 'They don't half have rows in their house, yer'll probably hear them through the wall.'

It was then that George's brother and his wife came on the scene. They could tell there was tension in the air, with people standing in groups, unsmiling and nodding their heads. 'What's been going on here?' Ken asked. 'There's something up.'

'A pound to a penny Nellie Bingham's involved,' Milly said knowingly. 'Her mother should have poisoned her when she was a pup.'

Maddy was the first to spot them and she ran towards them, James Cobden following close enough to be her shadow. He was a tall lad for his fourteen years, with blond hair, blue eyes and a deep dimple in his chin. 'Oh, Uncle Ken, you've just missed a fight,' Maddy said, still in a state of shock. 'The woman next door was kicking and punching the two men who brought our furniture. Mr Jim threatened to take her to the police station and said she'd have to spend the night in the cells.'

'Who is it ye're talking about?' Ken asked, thinking his brother and Ann wouldn't be very happy, they weren't used to fights in the street. 'And who started it?'

'I bet it was Nellie Bingham,' Milly said, hoping to be proved right. 'Wouldn't yer think she'd have kept out of the way for one day?'

'It was Mrs Bingham.' The vision of her being carried through the air, kicking and screaming, would stay with James forever. It was about time someone put her in her place, she was a menace. The women in the street were afraid of her, and the men felt they couldn't exchange fisticuffs with a woman, it wouldn't be right, even if she was a devil. 'The two men lifted her up in the air and put her in her house. They said if she came out again they'd take her to the police station.'

'Come on, Milly, let's go and see what's going on.' Ken weaved his way around the van and the children, with Milly hanging on to his sleeve. 'Our kid's not going to like this sort of carry-on, he'll do his nut.'

His wife was going to say they'd been warned, but thought it wiser to keep her mouth shut. It did no good to rub salt in an open wound.

The two workmen were coming out of the door and Jim took one look at Ken and said, 'No mistaking you, ye're George's brother. He's just being saying yer didn't live far. Pity yer didn't get here in time for the big picture, it was an eye-opener.'

Ken nodded as he passed them. 'So I've heard.' He walked into the living room, which was a replica of his own, and found George, Ann and Lizzie hard at it. Now the sideboard was in place, there was room for the cutlery and crockery that had been unpacked, so Ann was handing it over to her husband with instructions as to where it should go. 'All right, our kid? I hear yer've had a very warm welcome.'

George grinned. 'I didn't know whether to laugh or cry. If you'd seen it at the pictures you wouldn't know whether to describe it as a comedy or a drama.'

Lizzie came through from the kitchen. 'Where the hell d'yer think you've been? Half the work's done now, and you stroll up as cool as a bleedin' cucumber as though there's all the time in the world! I bet yer were hoping it was all finished and yer could sit down and smoke a fag while drinking a cup of tea. Well I've got news for yer. Yer can get that bloody jacket off, and if yer hands aren't dirty in ten minutes I'll want to know why. We'll have no skivers here.'

Ken was chuckling as he reached for his wife's arm. 'Milly, this is the bigmouth I was telling yer about what works with George. Her name's Lizzie, she never stops talking and she thinks she knows everything. Lizzie, I'd like yer to meet the wife.'

'Hello, queen, it's nice to meet yer. I don't know what to say, really, except yer have my deepest sympathy. Anyone what lives with the queer feller deserves a medal.'

'I agree with yer, Lizzie, he's not easy to live with,' Milly said, turning her mouth down at the corners. 'Take today, for instance, he knew we were expected round here to help, but he insisted on a flippin' big dinner. He won't discommode himself for no one, brother or no brother.'

'Shame on you, Ken.' Ann was smiling as she came through with her arms full of bedding. She knew Milly was piling it on. 'If you've come to work, then these are to go in that cupboard in the recess. It is clean, so all you have to do is lay them out neatly. Sheets, pillowcases and towels on the middle shelf, anything else on the bottom. I want the top shelf leaving for ornaments and such-like.'

Milly took off her coat, looked around, then asked, 'Where can I put this?'

'There's some hooks under the stairs, you can put it there.'

'Give it here, queen, I'll hang it for yer.' Lizzie had come prepared for work, with her sleeves rolled up, a scarf covering her head and wearing a wrap-around pinny. 'Take that bedding off Ann, then we can get more stuff out for yer. We haven't done so bad, the pans and frying pans are all on the shelf, the kettle's on the stove and the teapot on the draining board. One of the tea chests is nearly empty, so with an extra pair of hands we should be able to get it out of the way in no time and that'll give us more room out here.'

'That's you sorted out, love,' Ken said. 'Now what can I do?'

'I've been helping Jim and Harry with small stuff,' George told him. 'Perhaps you could do the same. The likes of chairs, small tables, mirrors and plants. It all helps.'

They set to and worked hard, without interruption, for the next half-hour. Then Lizzie walked through with a spring in her step. 'One chest empty, one more to go. I'll get the lads to take this one back to the shop and we can get cracking on the other.'

James and Billy were standing by the girls, and with them was the little boy who'd had his arm pinched by Nellie Bingham. He was only about eight, and Tess had felt sorry for him and beckoned him over. 'Did she hurt you?'

'Yeah, not half! I bet I've got bruises, and me mam will kill me. She'll say I shouldn't have been here in the first place.'

'No she won't,' Tess said, feeling the boy had been hurt enough, never mind his mother killing him. 'I'll come to your house with you and explain to your mother.'

'His mam won't hit him.' Billy ruffled the boy's dark curly hair. 'She loves the bones of him, doesn't she, Peter?'

Before the boy could answer, Lizzie popped her head out of the door and called, 'James and Billy, will yer do us a favour and take one of the chests back? But come round the back and carry it down the entry, save getting in the men's way.'

'I'll come with you.' Maddy was tired of standing and wished it was all over. 'My legs are stiff standing in one spot.'

'I'm coming too!' Tess said. 'That's if we can find which entry door is ours.'

'That's all right, we know which it is. Me and Billy only live a few doors down.'

While the chest was being manoeuvred out of the kitchen door, Maddy and Tess pressed their noses to the back window. They saw the table was in the middle of the room and their mother was spreading their chenille cloth over it. The sideboard was set against a wall and the two fireside chairs were in position either side of the hearth. Apart from little things like ornaments, the only thing missing was the couch. 'Ooh, er, it won't be long now,' Tess said. 'And doesn't it look nice and bright?'

Maddy nodded. 'We should be able to go in soon. But shall we go with the boys to take that big box back to wherever it's going? It would be better than standing around.'

With a girl on either side, the boys looked as happy as Larry as they carried the chest between them. They felt they'd found new friends. Pretty ones at that! And they didn't half talk posh.

Chapter Eighteen

'Come on, George, have some more stew, there's plenty over.' Lizzie stood behind George's chair using both hands to carry the huge iron pan, which was blackened by years of standing on the fire hob with clouds of sooty smoke billowing round it. 'I'm sure yer can find a bit more room in yer tummy.'

'Lizzie, I'm so full I can hardly breathe.' He patted his bulging stomach. 'But it was a very tasty meal and I thoroughly enjoyed it.'

Lizzie tutted as she turned to Ann. 'What about you, queen?'

'My seams are about to give any minute, I'm absolutely stored.'

Maddy waved an open hand. 'Don't ask me, Mrs Lizzie, I'm nearly bursting.'

'Me too!' Tess said. 'I couldn't eat another mouthful.'

Lizzie looked across the table. 'What about you, Norman? Have yer got room for a bit more, or are yer full?'

Her husband shook his head. 'I'm bloated, sweetheart. If I had another spoonful I wouldn't be able to drink me two pints, there'd be no room for it.'

'Oh, we can't have that, can we! That would be the end of the bleedin' world if you had to miss yer ruddy pints.'

His smile covered everyone around the table. 'Anyone would think I was a boozer. But it's me darling wife what pushes me out of the door every Saturday night, and d'yer know why? It's because I'm always sweet-tempered when I've had a drink, and she can worm anything out of me. At least that's the only way I can account for what she tells me on the Sunday morning. I'm supposed to have promised her this, that and the other, things I wouldn't have dreamt of promising if I'd been in me right mind.'

'Stop moaning,' Ann said, jokingly. 'You don't know how lucky you are if you get meals like this every day. I don't know how you managed it, Lizzie, because you couldn't have got home from work until half twelve, and you've been helping us since one o'clock.'

'I'm organised, yer see, queen. I got the stewing meat on me way home last night, and the spuds and veg. And I prepared everything, so all I had to do when I came in today was put it on the stove. Oh, and I threw in a cupful of barley for good measure. I brought it to the boil and then turned it on to a low light and let it simmer all afternoon.'

'Well, it was lovely.' Ann got to her feet. 'Me and the girls will do the washing-up, so give me the pan and I'll put it on the stove for you to finish off tomorrow.'

'We won't eat it tomorrow, queen, 'cos our Vera and her husband are coming and I've bought mutton chops for the dinner.' She looked undecided for a few seconds before saying, 'Don't be offended, but could you eat it tomorrow? There's enough left for the four of yer, and it would be a shame to throw it away.'

Ann glanced at George to see if he would give her a sign, but his expression gave nothing away. She hadn't got the Sunday dinner in yet and had been intending to slip down to the shops before they closed at seven. But it would be a shame to waste the stew that was over, and she didn't want to hurt Lizzie by refusing. 'It would be a sin to throw it away, it's delicious. If you're quite sure, then we'll be glad to have it. If I don't have to cook tomorrow it will give me the full day to put everything away where it should be.'

Lizzie looked pleased. 'I'll put the pan lid on for yer to take it home.'

'Thank you, you're an angel.' Ann cast her eyes on her daughters. 'Come on, Madelaine and Theresa, help clear the table and we'll wash up.'

'While ye're doing that, queen, I'll make a brew for us.'

Norman made a move to stand up. 'You sit down, love, I'll make the tea.'

Lizzie gaped. 'Yer what! You'll make the tea! What's wrong with yer, are yer sickening for something? If you put yer hand on the handle of that teapot it would fall off with shock.'

Norman settled himself back in his chair and winked at George. 'I only offered 'cos I knew she wouldn't let me.' He took out his packet of Woodbines and held it across the table. 'Help yerself, and we can relax with a smoke while the women do the work.'

So the men sat puffing away, quietly getting to know each other by talking about their jobs and their favourite football team, while the kitchen was a hive of activity and chatter.

'Did Auntie Milly like your hair, Mam?' Maddy asked, putting plates away after Tess had dried them. 'Did she think it suits you?'

Ann laughed. 'D'you know, she'd been there an hour before she noticed it. I think the shenanigans of Nellie Bingham outshone my new hairstyle. But when she finally did notice, she said it really suited me. At first she thought I was pulling her leg when I told her you'd done it, Madelaine, so you must have done a good job. Don't be surprised if she asks you to trim her hair before the week is out.' Ann lifted her hands from the soapy suds and rested them on the edge of the sink. 'She wasn't the only one who took a while to notice either, 'cos Tilly Mint here,' she jerked her head to where Lizzie was standing waiting for the kettle to boil, 'she didn't mention it until Milly did!'

'Young Tess didn't give me time to notice, queen, 'cos the first thing she said to me was, "D'yer like me mam's new hairstyle?" I was going to pass comment, but thought yer might be insulted by the words that were on the top of me tongue. If I'd said the short hairstyle took ten years off yer, it would sound as though yer looked as old as Granny Grunt before. But it does suit yer, queen, and it does make yer look a lot younger.' The water in the kettle began to boil and Lizzie reached for a piece of cloth to cover her hand before picking it up. 'Tea will be ready in five minutes, so put a move on 'cos me throat's parched.

Norman had been told about the incident with Nellie and Jim, but he came back to it when they were all seated around the table having their drinks. 'It wasn't what yer'd call a house-warming party, was it? Yer must be asking yerself if yer done the right thing by moving here.'

George put his cup down in the saucer, wiped the back of a hand across his moustache and smiled. 'To tell you the truth, when she first started I thought it was a joke. Then I was shocked, because I've never seen anything like it in my life. And I was concerned for Jim, who got the worst of it. But he took it very well and actually thought it was funny. So I decided to do the same as him and see the funny side. And I think that's the best approach for us. We should ignore her if possible, if not, laugh at the things she does and don't let her get us down. She's definitely got a screw loose, there's no doubt about that. She actually wanted everyone to move out of the way so she could have a ringside seat to see everything that was being carried into our house. And she didn't care if the whole street knew! I felt like asking her if she'd like an inventory of every stick of furniture we had.'

'There's one incident yer don't know about, 'cos I've been keeping it to meself until now so yer could all hear it at the same time.' Lizzie sat back, folded her arms and hitched up her bosom. 'Wait till yer hear this,' she said in a voice lowered to enhance the mystery. 'D'yer know when the boys were taking the first tea chest out the back way? Well, the girls were with them, and I watched them walking down the entry to make sure they could manage. Then after I'd closed the entry door, I turned to walk back up the yard when I heard a noise from next door. It sounded like something being dragged along the ground, like a chair or stepladder. I thought the queer one was up to something, so I stood very still, hidden from view by the lavvy. There were a few more sounds, then everything went quiet so I moved away from the lavvy, and yer'll never guess what I saw. The cheeky bitch was standing on something and was looking over the wall into your yard. And she had her arms on the wall as though she intended to make an afternoon of it! I don't know who got the biggest shock, her or me! It must have been her 'cos she tried to get down before I could call her all the nosy buggers going. But in her haste she must have knocked over the chair she was standing on, and she was left with her arms on the wall and her feet on fresh air! It's the first time I've ever seen Nellie Bingham lost for words, but if looks could kill, I'd be a dead duck now. Anyway, I could hear her feet scraping on the wall, trying to find a foothold, and I started laughing. I told her she'd got herself up, she could get herself down, but, being a good-living woman, if she was still there at tea time I'd take her a cup of tea out. And to rub salt in the wound, I said I could see she was in a predicament, like, and wouldn't be able to hold a cup, so I offered to hold it for her while she had a drink. And when I was walking away I told her that yer always get paid back for doing wrong, and she was getting paid back for being such a nosy cow.'

When the laughter had died down, Ann wiped the tears away before saying, 'The woman is unbelievable! There's definitely something radically wrong with her for expecting to get away with half the things she does.'

'She's round the bend, doolally, and that's why she gets away with it. Folk are afraid to tangle with her 'cos she'd clock yer one sooner than look at yer.' Lizzie's head was nodding. 'A few people have had a go at her for the things she does, but they came off worst and have never tried since.'

'What happened to her, Mrs Lizzie?' Tess asked. 'Did she manage to get down off the wall?'

'I stood by your kitchen wall, out of sight, and I heard her feet scraping on the bricks. Then she must have fallen off because she let out a yell. The air was blue, and she screamed, "It was her fault, the bleedin' mare! Just wait till I get me hands on her, she'll be sorry she was ever born. I'll scratch her bleedin' eyes out, see if I don't."'

Maddy looked concerned. 'She wouldn't hurt you, would she?'

'No, queen, I'm the one woman in the street she wouldn't lay a finger on. She tried it once, she wouldn't do it again. Yer see, a few years ago I caught her battering one of the neighbours' kids, a boy of seven, and the poor lad was terrified. So I pulled her away and told the lad to run home to his mam. The next thing I knew, she made a flying leap and jumped on me, her two hands around me neck. Well, I wasn't going to stand for that, not when I'm twice the size of her, so I put me hands around her waist and lifted her off the ground, as high as I could. She wasn't so sure of herself then, and she loosened her hands. I stood her down, told her to grow up and act her age, and started to walk away. The silly bugger didn't know when to leave well alone and jumped on me back. By this time half the street was out, some shouting at her to leave me alone, and others telling me to give back what she was giving. I couldn't shake her off, she was hanging on like grim death, nearly choking me. So I backed up against a wall and pressed as hard as I could, squashing her against the brickwork. It did the trick because she couldn't breathe properly and had to let go.' Lizzie's eyes went around the table. 'Now wouldn't yer think she'd have given up after all that? Oh no, not Nellie Bingham, she had to have another go. She came at me with her hands curved like claws, intending to scratch me face. But I got in before her and belted her one. I knocked her to the ground and she sprawled there calling me fit to burn. The neighbours were clapping and cheering, which didn't improve her temper, but she made no effort to retaliate. And for a week after she was walking around with a beautiful black eye.'

'Lizzie, would you teach me how to box, please?' Ann asked. 'I think I'm going to be in need of a few lessons.'

'Don't try it, queen, 'cos yer won't win. If yer take my advice, have a good laugh when she tries to wind yer up and let her think yer don't care. Once she sees she's not getting to yer, she'll give up and pick on someone else. I told Peggy Caldwell dozens of times to do that, but she wouldn't.'

'What I don't understand is, where was her husband this afternoon while all this was going on?' George asked. 'And her two children?'

'I saw the two boys legging it as soon as their mother started. They're not bad lads and I think they're ashamed of her. As for her feller, yer never see him on a Saturday afternoon until tea time, and then he's half kalied. Where he goes God only knows, 'cos all the pubs around here close at two and don't open again until six. He must know a very obliging pub landlord who lets some of his regulars have a stay-behind. I believe that does happen. It's a mystery where he gets the money from, though, 'cos he's out again at eight and rolls home rotten drunk about half ten.'

'He must have a good job to be able to afford to live like that,' Norman said. 'I know I couldn't do it, and me and the wife both work.'

'Even if I had a job that paid well, I'd have better things to spend my money on than beer. I enjoy the odd pint now and again, but I can't see the point in getting drunk.' George couldn't stand seeing anyone so inebriated they made an exhibition of themselves. Particularly if they had children at home who were going without decent clothes and food. 'The breweries wouldn't get very rich on my money, I'm afraid.'

'You deserve a pint tonight, though, love, you've worked very hard,' Ann said. 'Why not go with Norman for an hour?'

Her husband shook his head. 'No, I wouldn't leave you and the girls on your own tonight in case our neighbour decides to kick off. Perhaps another time, eh, Norman, when things are settled down and we've got the measure of the land?'

'Ye're welcome to join me any time. And yer wouldn't be amongst strangers 'cos your brother would be there. He's a good laugh is Ken, gets on with everyone.'

Ann glanced at the clock on top of the mantelpiece. 'Lizzie, would you think it rude of us if we love you and leave you? It seems terrible to eat and run, but I've got to make the beds up and see to the curtains for the girls' bedroom. You don't mind, do you?'

'Not at all, queen, I know yer've got loads to do. I'd offer to help but I think I'd only be in the way, not knowing what goes where.'

'You've done enough for us, Lizzie, and we're very grateful. But you must be worn out, going to work for half a day, then straight up to ours for more work. If I were you I'd get my feet up on the couch and listen to the wireless.'

'I might just do that, queen, 'cos me legs are tired. And the corn on me little toe is practically talking to me, saying it's about time I took me shoe off and gave it a break.'

Tess had kept her question bottled up, but now they were getting ready to go home she was prompted to ask, 'Does the rose still talk to you, Mrs Lizzie?'

'Of course she does, sweetheart, but only when I'm on me own.' Lizzie turned and pointed to a pink rose on the wallpaper. It was a foot above the sideboard and was bigger than the roses clustered around it. 'We'll have a good natter tonight when I'm on me lonesome. I've got a lot to tell her about the goings-on today, and I bet she'll have plenty to say about Nellie Bingham. She's never seen the woman, but I keep her up to date with the news and she knows everything that goes on. She has some very good suggestions on how to deal with Nellie, but if I carried them out I'd either land meself in clink or at the end of a rope.'

'I'll wait until we're settled in properly and then decide how to cope with our neighbour,' Ann said. 'If she continues to make a nuisance of herself she'll find that two can play at that game. One thing I am sure of, she'll not drive us from that house.' Her expression softened when she looked at her elder daughter. 'Would you get our coats, please, Madelaine, and we'll leave Mr and Mrs Ferguson in peace.'

'Yer've no need to rush on account of us,' Norman told her. 'Have another cup of tea and give yer dinner time to settle.'

'No, but thank you all the same. I want to get the beds made up because I think it'll be an early night for all of us.'

Maddy handed the coats out, then walked to where Norman was sitting and kissed him on the cheek. 'Thank you for having us.'

Not to be left out, Tess did the same. 'Mrs Lizzie is my very best friend, and now you're my best friend too!'

Lizzie could see the joy on her husband's face as she gathered the two girls to her. 'We couldn't ask for better friends.' She kissed the tops of their heads. 'I'll nip up and see yer in the morning, make sure ye're all right. It'll be early, about half ten, 'cos I have to be back for our Vera coming. But if yer need me before then, just give me a knock.'

The family were just a few doors from their home when they saw a woman leave a house on the opposite side of the street and hurry towards them.

'Sure, I've been keeping watch for yer, so I have. I wanted to catch yer before yer got to your house.' The woman, her voice with a lovely Irish lilt, spoke softly, her eyes darting as though on the look-out. 'Me name's Bridget Hanrahan and I live in number forty-two. I happened to look out of me window about an hour ago to see if there was any sign of my two boys. They were an hour late for their tea so they were, and wasn't it meself that was worried to death? Anyway, I saw Nellie Bingham sneak out of her house with a shovel in her hand, and knowing what a divil the woman is, didn't I stand there and watch what she was up to? Whatever it was she had on her shovel was thrown on yer step and she scurried away like a thief in the night. It's one of the woman's favourite dirty tricks, throwing dog dirt or horse manure on the step of some poor soul she's taken a dislike to. But to do it to you, on yer first day in yer new house, well, it's to be hoped that God pays her back for being so wicked.'

George found his voice. 'D'you mean she's thrown dirt on our doorstep?'

'That's what she's done, right enough. And I didn't want yer stepping in it and spreading it through yer house. I'll not be wanting yer to think I'm a nosy biddy who spends her life spying on people, because mostly I keep to meself. But I'll not have yer thinking that all yer neighbours are like the mad woman who lives next door to yer.'

Ann gulped before she spoke. 'Thank you, Mrs Hanrahan, it's kind of you to be concerned. I'll have words with Mrs Bingham about it.'

'Oh no you won't!' George sounded very determined. 'As you said before, two can play at that game. We'll deal with this my way. But perhaps you'd rather not be seen to be involved, Mrs Hanrahan, and would prefer to leave now?'

'Sure, I'm not frightened of the woman, Mr, er, Mr . . .?'

'George Richardson. And this is my wife Ann, and daughters Maddy and Tess.'

Bridget smiled a greeting before telling them, 'My husband Paddy

253

is six foot four, and a foine figure of a man, so he is. A gentle giant most of the time, but let anyone upset me or the boys and he's like a raging bull. No, I don't fear the Binghams, but as Nellie has eyes and ears like a hawk, I think it would be best if I leave you to quietly do what yer have in mind. But I'll not lie and say I won't be peeping from behind me curtains.' She stepped down on to the cobbled street. 'The best of luck to yer, me darlings, and goodnight and God bless.'

The family waited until she'd entered her house and closed the door. Then George put a finger to his lips. 'Not a word, be as silent as mice.'

The light from the street lamp showed there was a mound of dog dirt on the step, and Ann would have vented her feelings if George hadn't gripped her arm. He slipped the key silently in the lock and threw open the front door. 'Step up on to the top step,' he whispered, 'and not a sound when you get inside.'

He didn't close the door after himself, not wanting to make the slightest of noises. 'Maddy, the shovel is standing in the kitchen, bring it to me, please. And Tess, the paper we used to wrap the crockery in, it's in a cardboard box under the sink. Will you pick out two pieces of newspaper that haven't been torn, please?'

'What are you going to do?' Ann asked, fearful of him getting involved with a mad woman.

'I'm going to give her back that which is hers.'

'Oh, George, what if she sees you?'

'I'll take a chance. Even if she does, she'll still get that dirt on her step, of that I am determined. And while I can shovel it easily off our step, she won't be so lucky. I intend to put the newspaper down over it and hit it with the shovel so it sinks in and spreads. Then perhaps she'll think twice about doing the same thing again.'

Maddy handed him the shovel. 'I'll come with you, Dad, just in case.'

'No, love, you and Tess stay here with your mam. I'll be quieter and quicker on my own. One minute, that's all I'll be.'

The girls went to stand next to their mother and she put an arm around each of them. 'Keep very quiet so we can hear if trouble starts.'

George was true to his word. After one minute he came back grinning all over his face. 'D'you know, I got a kick out of that. And I'll get a bigger kick when I hear her scrubbing the step in the morning. She'll need plenty of elbow grease to get it white again.'

'She'll pay us back,' Ann said. 'We won't get away with it. I bet you any money she'll think of something twice as bad.'

'Whatever she does, we do back. That's the only way to deal with a bully. Once they see you're afraid of them, they'll pick on you even more. If we're to get any peace in this house, we've got to start as we mean to go on.' George lowered himself on to his fireside chair. It had been a long day and his back was aching. 'If she throws ashes over the wall when you've got your washing out, do the same to her. Anything she does to annoy you, do it back to her. Just make sure the argument is conducted over the wall and not in the street where she can get at you, because you wouldn't stand a chance.'

'Some life it's going to be.' Ann sighed deeply. 'Having to worry every day what she's going to do next. I'll be frightened of my own shadow.'

George beckoned his daughters to come and sit near him in front of the fire. It was no use worrying the life out of them, it wouldn't be fair. 'Let's all make up our minds that the woman who happens to live next door to us isn't going to make us unhappy. Ignore her if we can, laugh at her if we can't. But never be rude to her, girls, because that would bring you down to her level, and we don't want that.'

'I'm not going to stand by and let her have a go at our mam,' Maddy said with feeling. 'I won't be rude, but I'll tell her what I think in a ladylike way.'

'Me too!' Tess narrowed her eyes and clamped her lips tightly together, to show she meant business. 'Miss Harrison said we must never let anyone bully us, we must report them to her or Miss Bond.'

A picture of the headmistress flashed through Ann's head and she saw the funny side. 'It would take someone like Miss Bond to sort Nellie Bingham out. One of her stern, looking-down-her-nose, withering looks would have anyone quaking in their shoes.'

'Shall we make up our minds now, and agree that we're not going to let anyone mar the pleasure of our new home?' George asked. 'You said a Mrs Flannery called to see if you needed help, Ann, so she sounds friendly. And Mrs Hanrahan really put herself out by watching for us coming home to warn us. That's two people who you could make friends with. And last but not least we've got Lizzie living near.'

'And me and Tess have made friends with James and Billy,' Maddy said. 'So that's another two.'

George nodded. 'There you are, you see! More good than bad, I would say. So let's not think about Nellie Bingham unless we have to, let's be happy in our new home.'

The girls' nods were enthusiastic, but Ann's was less so as she asked herself what her parents would have made of all this. They'd have been horrified. She took a deep breath and wondered what tomorrow would bring.

'Wait for me, Dolly.' Ann quickened her step to catch up with her neighbour. 'We may as well walk to the shops together.'

255

'I'm walking to Stanley Road for what I want.' Dolly Flannery had turned out to be a good friend. Never a day passed that she didn't knock to see if Ann needed anything. She was bonny in figure and face, was Dolly, with thick sandy hair, eyes that changed from green to hazel and a fresh, healthy complexion. She crooked her arm now for Ann to link. 'D'yer feel like going that far, or are yer shopping local?'

'No, I'll walk with you. It'll do me good to stretch my legs and get some fresh air into my lungs. There's a better selection there, anyway.'

Dolly raised her brows. 'Heard nothing from the queer one?'

'No, and I'm keeping my fingers crossed that it stays that way. We've been here nine days now, and there's been no trouble since the day we moved in. Except for the unearthly racket she makes when cleaning the grate out. She rattles the poker between the bars so hard I'm surprised the whole street doesn't hear her. And she'll bang on the wall for no other reason than to annoy us. And this is at half six every morning without fail. George said we don't need to set the alarm clock, she's just as reliable.'

'There's always a lull before the storm, girl, so don't drop yer guard. That affair with the dog dirt, she won't have forgotten that, mark my words.' Dolly's bonny face creased. 'It was dead funny, though, wasn't it? The whole street got to hear about it and they all had a good laugh. My Frank laughed so much I thought he was going to choke.'

'You've got a boy and a girl, haven't you?'

'Yeah, but they're both working and out all day. David is fifteen and Wendy fourteen. She only left school in the summer and got herself a job in Vernon's round the corner. The pay's not much, but it's the same everywhere. David doesn't earn much more because he's an apprentice joiner, but to hear the pair of them talk yer'd think it was their money keeping the wolf from the door. They're good kids, though, never given me a minute's worry and I love the bones of them.'

They were passing Sayer's cake shop when Ann had a thought. She'd given Lizzie her rent money to pay in to the office with her own, and she'd seen the coal man this morning and paid for a bag of nuts and a bag of slack. She had no other debts to worry about, and for the first time in heaven knows how long, she was starting Monday with fourteen shillings and sixpence in her purse. 'Would you like to come for a cup of tea this afternoon, Dolly? I'll buy a few cakes and invite Mrs Hanrahan over.'

'That would be nice, girl, I'd like that. And you can come to mine another day and I'll mug yer to a cake. And Bridie Hanrahan, as well. Give us something to look forward to and break the monotony.'

'Come in the shop with me then and choose which cake you'd like.

Me, I'm having one of those cream slices with the cream oozing out of the sides.'

'Make that three, girl, 'cos they're me favourites. And I know Bridie's got a sweet tooth.'

When they'd finished their shopping they walked home at a leisurely pace. It was a cold, crisp day, and the wind whipped their cheeks a rosy red. It was an hour before the girls would be home from school for their lunch, plenty of time for Ann to make some sandwiches with the brawn she'd bought. And for dinner she'd bought a sheet of ribs which would go down well with the family. 'I've finally got the house straight, with everything where it should be. It's taken me a week but now I know exactly where to put my hand on anything.'

'D'yer like the house, girl? D'yer think yer'll settle?'

'I love the house, Dolly, so do George and the girls. The only bugbear is next door, I'm on edge all the time waiting for her to start something.'

'Don't let her get yer down, 'cos that's what she's after. She gave Peggy Caldwell a dog's life 'cos she knew Peggy wouldn't fight back. Her husband, Jack, would have done, he'd have marmalised Nellie Bingham, but Peggy wouldn't have it. She'd rather up sticks than have any bother. I flaming well wouldn't move house for some little jumped-up big-mouth, but then we're all made different, aren't we, girl?'

When they reached Dolly's house, Ann said, 'About two o'clock, then, is that all right?'

'Fine by me.'

'I'll nip over to Mrs Hanrahan's now, while I've got my coat on.' Ann waved goodbye and picked her way over the cobbles to a house opposite. And while she waited for an answer to her knock, she admired the white step, the shining red-raddled windowsill and the gleaming windows. All the women in the street kept their houses very neat and tidy, except for a couple of exceptions. But Ann had been told these houses belonged to families where the father was out of work and they were having a struggle to put food on the table. 'Hello, Mrs Hanrahan, I hope I'm not interrupting you?'

'Not at all, me darlin', come in out of the cold.'

'I won't if you don't mind, the girls will be home soon and I want to build the fire up. It's really cold out and they'll be wanting a warm. What I came for is to ask if you'd like to come for a cup of tea this afternoon? Dolly's coming, and it would be a good chance to get to know each other.'

'Sure, I'd like that, right enough! With not another soul in the house, isn't it meself that's talking to the four walls all day? And it isn't often I get an invitation to tea, so I'm beholden to yer, Mrs Richardson. What time would yer like me, and could yer tell me if it's evening dress I

257

should be wearing, or can I come as I am?'

Ann grinned. 'Unless you've got a diamond tiara tucked away somewhere, you can come as you are. Is two o'clock all right?' When Bridie nodded, Ann turned to cross the street, only to find herself facing the bold Nellie, who was standing on her step with her arms folded and a sneer on her face. 'Oh dear, I hope this doesn't mean trouble.'

'Pretend yer haven't seen her, me darlin', and take yerself off home.'

Her head down, Ann would have done that. But Nellie wasn't having any. Bored with no one to talk to, she'd been thinking of how she could liven herself up when she happened to glance through the window and saw Ann talking to Bridie. And this, she thought, was the chance she'd been waiting for to get her own back for the mess they'd made on her step. The fact that she herself was to blame didn't enter her head. They'd made a fool of her and she wasn't going to let this opportunity pass to show them they would do well not to trifle with her. Stepping down to the bottom step, she shouted, 'Oh ay, Mrs Hoity-Toity, getting well in with yer neighbours, are yer? I would have thought they weren't bleedin' posh enough for yer. Or are yer slumming, so you and that bastard of a husband of yours can have a good laugh at them tonight, eh?'

'That's enough, Nellie,' Bridie said. 'Get back inside yer house and leave Mrs Richardson to go about her business.'

'I'll go back in when I'm good and ready, you Irish cow, and not before. Just keep yer soddin' nose out of it.' Nellie walked to the edge of the pavement and stepped down to make her way across the street, her arms still folded and her sneer intact. And it was her whole cocky manner that caused Ann's fear to turn to anger.

'How dare you talk like that to Mrs Hanrahan and myself.' Ann walked forward and met her neighbour in the middle of the road. This caused Bridie to come to the edge of her step, ready to intervene. 'What gives you the right to think you can do what you like with the people in this street?'

Nellie was shorter than Ann, so she had to stand on tiptoe to bring their faces together. 'Oh, aren't we all lah-de-bleedin'-dah! Proper swank come to live next to us. Well let me tell yer, missus, I do what I like and I say what I like. Yer don't impress me with yer fancy talk, and if yer don't shut yer gob I'll knock yer bleedin' block off.'

'I dare you!'

Bridie was off the step like greased lightning, expecting Ann to be sent flying and wanting to be there to catch her before she was really hurt. But while Nellie pulled her arm back ready to lash out, believing her new neighbour would be a walk-over, Ann was quicker. She thrust her arms forward, and with her open hands on the woman's chest, she pushed her backwards with such force Nellie was in danger of losing

258

her balance. 'Get back in your house before I really lose my temper,' Ann said, all the while pushing, safe in the knowledge that her arms were longer than Nellie's and kept her out of reach of the hands that were itching to do her an injury. 'And if you've nothing better to do than interfere in the lives of your neighbours, can I suggest you spend some time washing your mouth out with carbolic soap?'

Bridie didn't know whether to laugh or cry. The expression of total surprise on Nellie's face was really comical, but the Irish woman had known her too long to believe Ann would come out of this unscathed. So she pulled one of Ann's arms away and slipped between her and Nellie. 'That's enough now, ladies. Sure, there's not a worse sight than to see two women fighting like dockers, and that's the truth of it. Away home with yer now, Ann, before the girls are in from school.' She stood her ground until Ann walked towards her house and inserted the key in the lock, then she turned to face a raging Nellie. 'And I suggest you go in, me darlin', before yer have all the neighbours out. Sure, yer cause more trouble in this street than everyone else put together, so yer do.'

Nellie's face was deep red with rage and the veins on her neck were bulging. 'Did yer hear what the bitch said? That I should wash me mouth out with carbolic soap? Well she'll not get away with that, I can tell yer. Next time she sets foot in the street I'll have her. A good doing-over is what she wants, the stuck-up bleedin' snob.' Then, because the woman she was raging against wasn't there, she turned her wrath on Bridie. 'Anyway, why don't yer mind yer own business, yer nosy cow? It's got nothing to do with you, so bugger off before I belt yer.'

'Ah, I think yer've more sense than to do that, Nellie, 'cos my family wouldn't take kindly to yer laying a finger on me, and that's the truth of it. And I'll give yer another warning to think on about. Mrs Richardson has quite a few friends in this street, so she has, and I'm one of them. So you keep up this stupid one-sided fight with Ann, and five women will be watching out for yer. And even you, with yer vile temper, wouldn't like to chance yer luck with five of us.' With a nod of her head, and her heart beating fifteen to the dozen, Bridie returned to her own house and closed the door.

Ann was shaking as she dropped into a fireside chair and gripped the arms. She couldn't let the girls see her in this state so she'd better buck herself up. She wasn't going to mention the incident that had just taken place, nothing would be gained by it. As the minutes ticked by she became calmer, asking herself how she'd had the nerve to actually meet Nellie Bingham head on. She was glad she had because there comes a time when you have to stick up for yourself rather than slink away like a coward. But it was the first time in her life she'd ever put a hand on another human being in anger, and she wasn't proud of herself. Anyway, she wasn't going to tell the girls, or George. He'd have a fit if he knew.

The clock chiming twelve o'clock brought Ann out of her chair. Her daughters would be home in fifteen minutes and she had to make sandwiches. And the fire needed raking out a bit and a few cobs of coal added. She wasn't shaking now, but her insides were turning over. She hoped she never had to go through anything like that again.

Bridie and Dolly arrived at the same time, and seeing their smiling faces cheered Ann up. Her daughters hadn't noticed she wasn't as talkative as usual, they were too busy telling her about a new girl who was starting on Monday and whose father had brought her in a car for her interview with Miss Bond. It had never been heard of before, none of their friends had cars, and they were so full of it they wouldn't have noticed if their mother had grown two heads.

'Come in, ladies, and welcome to my home.'

'D'yer know, I feel proper posh,' Dolly said. 'It's the first time I've ever been invited to afternoon tea. I've had plenty of cups of tea off the neighbours, like, but never by invitation.'

'Well now, Dolly me darlin', this is yer lucky day. For it's meself that's inviting you and Ann to afternoon tea next Monday. And the following week it's yerself that can do the honours.'

'Ay, isn't it a shame that Lizzie goes out to work?' Dolly hung her coat on a hook behind the door before making herself comfortable in George's favourite chair. 'She wouldn't half liven up the proceedings.' She cocked a brow at Ann. 'Mind you, it's a good job she wasn't here before, otherwise there'd have been skin and hair flying. I saw it all from my window, Ann, and for a minute I thought of joining in. But as Bridie just told me, yer didn't need any help.'

'The tea's made, so I'll bring it through and then we can talk.' The tray was set with Ann's best china, and there was a fancy paper doily on the plate under the cream slices. 'Come and sit at the table so yer don't have to balance things on your knees.'

Bridie took one look at the cream slices and licked her lips. 'How did yer guess they were me favourites, me darlin'? Sure, me mouth's watering at the sight of them.'

'Yer can thank me for that,' Dolly said. 'I knew yer had a sweet tooth.'

Ann poured out the tea and handed the cups over. 'Help yourself to sugar, ladies, and a cake. And before we go any further, can we forget Nellie Bingham for the next hour or so? I didn't tell the girls about her, and I'm not going to tell George, so I'd be grateful if you would keep what happened under your hats. And don't let her spoil our afternoon.'

Bridie reached for the cake with the most cream in and was about to take a bite when she said, 'I know I'm a greedy glutton, me darlin's, but where cakes are concerned I can't help meself.' With a look of pure bliss on her face, she sank her teeth in and sighed with pleasure. 'Sure, wouldn't I rather have one of these than a pan of scouse any day?'

'Ye're right, yer are a greedy bugger,' Dolly said, a blob of cream on her nose. 'So yer've invited two greedy buggers into yer house, Ann.'

'I'll get my own back when I come to yours,' Ann said. 'Just make sure the girl in Sayer's gives you the three biggest cream slices in the shop.'

The conversation was friendly and the three women talked as though they'd been friends for years. 'It's only a few weeks off Christmas,' Dolly said. 'Have yer started getting things together yet, Ann?'

'Not yet, I haven't had the money with moving house. But I was thinking of going into town one day this week and having a look around. The girls need new dresses, they're the biggest item, so I thought I'd get them first. One this week, another next week. Once they're off my mind I can start on presents. I want this to be a good Christmas for us, with plenty of food on the table, a tree in the corner and lots of decorations.'

'Would yer not be trying Paddy's market first? Sure, yer get twice as much for yer money there,' Bridie said with conviction. 'Have yer never been, me darlin'?'

Ann shook her head. 'No, I haven't.'

'Yer don't know what ye're missing, girl!' Dolly contributed. 'They sell everything under the sun and are very cheap. If yer like, I'll take yer on Thursday and yer can judge for yerself.'

'I'll come with yer,' Bridie said. 'Sure, don't I love the hustle and bustle of the market and looking for bargains. I might just see something that takes me fancy.'

'I'd love to.' Anne was delighted to have made two friends. 'I'll look forward to it.'

Chapter Nineteen

'This is the spare key, Madelaine. In case I'm not home in time for you coming from school, you can let yourselves in.' Ann put the key on the table by her elder daughter's plate. 'I'll try to be home in time, but I can't guarantee, so better to be sure than sorry. I'd hate you to be hanging around in the cold.'

'It's nice you've got friends to go out with, Mam,' Maddy said. 'You didn't have any real friends in Hanford Avenue, did you?'

'Of course I had friends! There was Auntie Maisie and the Critchleys, I was very friendly with them. But most of the people there were more reserved than they are here. Not that there's anything wrong with that, but it is nice to stand and have a chat when I go to the shops.'

'And have afternoon tea, Mam,' Tess said. 'You never had that before.' She chewed on the inside of her cheek, a far-away look in her eyes. 'I wish I could go to the market sometime, would you take me?'

'I'm going with Lizzie on Saturday afternoon, 'cos it's the only time she has off. But I believe it gets very crowded then, with it being pay day. I don't think you'd like to be pushed and shoved, would you?' Ann saw the look of disappointment and felt guilty. Theresa seemed to be getting stronger, with no sign of the coughs and sneezes which usually plagued her all winter long. But was she strong enough to stand up to the hundreds of people who Lizzie said visited the market on a Saturday? 'I'll tell you what, Theresa, I promise to take you and Madelaine one Saturday before Christmas to buy your presents. How would that suit you?'

'Oh, that would be lovely, Mam! I won't spend my pocket money on sweets, I'll put it away so I can buy presents.'

'I've still got your five shillings, Theresa, I managed without touching it. So you'll have plenty to buy what you want.'

'No, I said you could have that money, Mam, so you keep it.' Tess looked sideways at her sister and gave the matter some thought. 'What you could do is give me and Maddy a shilling each and you keep the rest. With our pocket money, we'd have plenty to buy presents for each other and you and our dad.'

Maddy swivelled in her chair and hugged her. 'That's a lovely thought, Tess, and I love you for it. But you earned that money, you should keep it.'

'No, Theresa is right,' Ann said. 'A shilling each it shall be. And so no one is left out, I'll buy five Woodbines for you to give to your father. He'll be highly delighted.'

'What would you like for Christmas, Mam?' Maddy asked.

Ann grinned. 'How about a new couch? Would your shilling run to that?'

Maddy didn't answer the question right away. What she was thinking was how much her mother had changed in the last few months. The change was more noticeable in the two weeks they'd lived in this house. She looked much younger with her hair short, much prettier. And she laughed a lot, was far more easy-going. 'Mam, I know we've got a terrible neighbour who must get on your nerves, but apart from her, you seem to be much happier living here.'

'I am, Madelaine. I've got a feeling this house is going to be very lucky for us. I thought that the first time I walked in, when Mrs Caldwell was here. The house seemed to welcome me, and I took to it right away.'

This caught Tess's imagination. 'How did the house welcome you, Mam?'

'It's hard to put into words, love, it was just a feeling of well-being. Like a warm glow in my heart, as though the house was opening its arms to me.'

Maddy pushed her chair back and picked up her plate. 'We'll have to make a move, Tess, or we'll miss the bell.'

'Yes, okay.' Tess got as far as the kitchen door, then turned. 'Can I write to Wales, Mam, and tell them about our new house?'

'I wrote to them the day before we moved, Theresa, so they know about the house. Still, you can write and tell them how we've settled in. But not a word about the terror next door.'

'I thought you said it was quiet on a Thursday,' Ann said, elbowing her way through the crowds. 'If this is quiet I'd hate to see it when it's busy.'

'Wait until you see it on Saturday,' Dolly laughed. 'Yer'll be going home with bruises in places yer didn't know yer had.'

'It's mostly second-hand stuff the crowd are after today, me darlin', 'cos most people are skint and happy.' Bridie held on tight to Ann's arm so they wouldn't become separated. 'The stalls selling new stuff don't do a lot of business. Come Saturday, it'll be the other way round.'

Although there was plenty of jostling, the crowd on the whole were good-natured. And the stallholders' voices, each trying to outdo the other, called out to attract potential customers to their stalls. They were very good-humoured and funny, and Ann found herself enjoying the experience. 'Come on, ladies,' one stallholder called, 'where else can yer buy jumpers for one and eleven? Yer couldn't knit the flippin' things for that! And there's no dropped stitches in them, either!'

'Are those jumpers all right?' Ann asked. 'Seems too good to be true.'

'Ay, I'll have yer know the jumper I'm wearing was bought off that stall,' Dolly said, putting on a haughty expression. 'And it's as good as yer'll get anywhere in town for twice the price.'

Ann looked more closely at the stall. 'He's got girl's dresses as well. Will you come with me to have a look? If they're no good there's no harm done.'

Bridie pulled her to a halt about two yards from the stall. 'If yer see anything yer think yer'd like for the girls, me darlin', let Dolly do the haggling. Sure, she'd win an argument with the good Lord himself, so she would.'

Ann looked puzzled. 'How d'you mean, haggling?'

'Nobody pays the asking price 'cos it's always higher than the stallholder really expects. He always puts a higher price on so when he drops it yer think he's given yer a bargain. But he can spot a beginner a mile away, and he'd take one look at you and up the price.'

Dolly's head was nodding. 'She's right, girl! Give me the wire if yer see something yer like, then leave the rest to me.'

As they neared the stall, Ann could see a line of girls' cotton dresses on a makeshift clothes rack. They looked all right too, and she soon spotted two pretty ones that would fit her daughters and would be lovely for Christmas. 'The blue and the pale green, Dolly, I like both of those. Ask him how much and if he'll get them down so I can feel the material. It's no good buying them if they're going to look like dish-cloths after they've been washed.'

Dolly favoured the stallholder with a beaming smile. 'How much are those dresses, sunshine?'

'All different prices, queen, depends what size yer want.'

'The blue one, with the frill around the neck and sleeves. What are yer charging for that?'

'Seeing as I like the look of yer, darling, I'll let yer have it for four and six. It would cost yer more in shoe leather looking for somewhere yer could get it cheaper. Best buy in Liverpool, they are, even if I do say so meself.'

'Get it down for us and stop the bleedin' blarney.' Dolly tutted. 'Yer must think I came over on the banana boat.'

'What! A good-looking woman like you!' The stallholder was lifting the dress down with the help of a long-handled iron hook. 'No, I think yer came over on one of those airyplane things from Hollywood. And I bet one of the passengers mentioned me name to yer, and that's why ye're here.' He had a cheeky grin on his face when he laid the dress down in front of Dolly. 'All the film stars know me, yer know. Oh ay, I had Joan Blondell in last week to buy one of me better-class dresses. Made up with it she was, and gave me a tanner tip.'

'My God, sunshine, yer haven't half got the gift of the gab. And all the time yer talking ye're telling yerself yer've got another sucker on yer fishing line.' Dolly fingered the material of the dress as she tapped her foot against Ann's. 'What d'yer think, girl? D'yer think me daughter would like it?'

This was the first time Ann had ever been to a market, and she was amazed at the price of the dress and the decent quality of the material. She always bought the girls' clothes from one of the most expensive shops in Liverpool, and she was telling herself now that it was no wonder she was always short of money. What a fool she'd been! 'I like it, it's very pretty and the colour would suit her complexion.'

Ann didn't know what was coming next, but Bridie did and she waited with bated breath. This was part of the enjoyment of a day out with Dolly.

'How much did yer say?' Dolly stared the man out. 'Three and six, was it?'

'Was it hell! Listen, missus, yer haven't got cloth ears, yer know very well I said four and six. I'm practically giving it away at that price, it cost me nearly that much.'

'Sod off, sunshine, or yer'll have me crying in a minute.' Dolly could see by Ann's expression that she would be prepared to pay the four and six as she thought the dress was worth it. But the man would go to sleep with a smile on his face if anyone paid him what he asked for. 'Do us a favour, sunshine, and reach that green dress down, I can't make up me mind which one I like best.'

'God, ye're just like my missus, she can never make up her mind either.' The stallholder's voice was good-natured, with a laugh in it. He reached for his hook then smiled at Dolly. 'Except when I hand her me wages. That's one time she never says, "Ooh, I can't make up me mind whether to take them, Bert."'

While his back was turned, Dolly went into a huddle with Ann while Bridie kept her ear cocked. 'What d'yer think, girl? If yer like them, which one d'yer want to get today?'

'I'd get them both if I had enough money on me,' Ann whispered back. 'I've only brought five shillings with me, and a few odd coppers for the tram.'

'I'll help yer out if ye're stuck, me darlin',' Bridie said. 'Yer can pay me back when yer get yer wages.'

'I could pay you back as soon as we get home.' Ann was thinking of Theresa's five shillings. She could put it back on Saturday. 'I've got enough to pay you today.'

'Well, do yerself a favour and keep yer mouth shut,' Dolly told her as the man came back to them with the green dress.

'That's a size smaller than the blue one, so it mightn't fit.'

'It would,' Ann said, her head lowered and speaking out of the side of her mouth. 'Both would be perfect fits.'

'I'll take the two,' Dolly said. 'If I can have them for three and six each.'

'No can do, missus, sorry. I've got a wife and kids at home to keep. And the funny thing about them is, they like to eat and run around with shoes on their feet.'

'Spare me the gory details, sunshine, I've got enough trouble trying to keep me own family from starving to death.' Dolly pretended to ponder for a few seconds, then said, 'I'll give yer three and eleven each for them, and that's me last offer. Take it or leave it.'

This was the price the man had had in mind from the beginning and he was delighted to be selling two dresses on a Thursday. But it wouldn't do to tell the customers that. 'Yer drive a hard bargain, missus, but seeing as yer've got a big family, I'll let yer have them for that.' He reached for a paper bag. 'I'm all heart, yer see. A sucker for a sob story.' He put the dresses in the bag and handed it over. 'That's seven and tenpence, if yer please.'

Dolly turned to Ann. 'Lend us that five bob yer said yer had, girl, and I'll pay yer back when my feller gets his wages.'

'Got a good job your feller, has he, missus?'

Dolly's body shook as she roared with laughter. 'Yeah, he's a pilot of one of those airyplanes yer mentioned. Smart uniform and peaked hat, he's a proper toff. He married below himself, yer see, but he's never thrown it up in me face 'cos he loves the bones of me. But, funny thing, he's never had no Joan Blondell on his plane or he'd have told me. Jean Harlow and Gary Cooper, yes, but never no Joan Blondell. And he knows what she looks like 'cos he's seen her at the pictures and thinks I'm the spitting image of her.'

The stallholder snapped his fingers. 'I thought yer reminded me of someone but couldn't for the life of me remember who. Of course, yer haven't got blonde hair, blue eyes and a sylph-like figure. But yer've got everything else she has, like one head, two arms and legs and ten fingers and toes. So there is some resemblance.'

'Ay, you, don't be getting personal, talking about me arms and legs.

267

If my feller heard yer, he'd be landing his airyplane in Scotland Road and coming to duff yer up. So mind yer manners if yer please.'

'Only having a laugh, missus!'

'I know that, sunshine, it's what makes the world go round, isn't it? Anyway, I'll be seeing yer when I've got a few bob to spend.'

Ann was over the moon. She had two dresses for the price she usually paid for one. 'Dolly, you're an angel. That's the girls fixed up for Christmas. I'll give yer the three shillings as soon as we get home. But I don't want them to see the dresses until Christmas morning, so if they're in from school would one of you hide them in your house for me?'

'I'll take them, me darlin', and put them on top of the wardrobe,' Bridie said. 'My two boys never rummage, so they'll be quite safe.'

They wandered around the stalls, and Ann couldn't believe her eyes. Men's shirts and socks, jumpers and cardigans, all at unbelievable low prices. 'I'll get everything I want from here, they're so cheap.'

'I won't be buying much until I get me tontine,' Dolly said. 'Then I can buy everything in one go. At least, almost everything.'

'What's a tontine?' Ann asked. 'It's a new word to me.'

'A woman in the next street runs it and it comes in handy. You pay in a shilling a week and get two pound ten shilling back the week before Christmas. Yer get a free week at Christmas, and the woman keeps a shilling for herself.'

'As Dolly said, it comes in handy, so it does,' Bridie said. 'Sure, if yer were saving a shilling a week at home, yer'd be dipping into it all the time. This way, yer pay every week and she'll not let yer draw it out no matter what hard-luck story yer give her.'

'Can anyone join?'

'Of course they can, girl! I'll give yer the wire when it starts up.'

Ann nodded her head while thinking what a sheltered life she'd led. They say you live and learn, well, she'd left it a bit late but she was certainly learning now.

Maddy and Tess had just turned in to their street when they stopped in their tracks. The street seemed to be alive with women running from one side to the other and others dashing out of entries and running into houses. And small groups were gathered at intervals down the whole length of the street, the women with serious faces and speaking in low tones. 'There's something very wrong, here,' Maddy said. 'I wonder what it is?'

'Perhaps someone's been murdered.' Tess gripped her sister's arm as her imagination took over. 'You never know.'

'Don't be silly, no one's been murdered.' Maddy didn't know any of the families from this end of the street, apart from Mrs Lizzie, of course, but she was at work. So she didn't like stopping at any of the groups they passed as they slowly made their way home. But it felt eerie, and a premonition that something was drastically wrong sent a shiver through her whole body. Perhaps someone had died, or been taken to hospital? Then she shook her head, telling herself that neither of those things would bring every woman in the street out of her house.

'Why don't you ask someone, Maddy?'

'I will when I see someone I know. But don't worry, Tess, I'm sure it's not anything really bad.' Then Maddy saw a woman whose face she recognised as living opposite to them, and who had smiled at her a few times. So she hurried across the cobbles, pulling Tess with her. The woman was with two other neighbours, and it was awkward because Maddy didn't know any of their names. But if she didn't ask, she'd never find out. 'Excuse me, but could you tell me why all the women are out in the street? Is there something wrong?'

'Yes, sweetheart, a little girl has gone missing. We've searched everywhere and can't find her. Her mam's out of her mind. The child's only four and heaven only knows where she's got to. Yer probably know her, it's Emma Wilson from two doors down.'

'The little girl with long blonde ringlets?' Maddy was horrified. 'How long has she been missing?'

'Over an hour now. Her mam said they heard the rag and bone man in the street and Emma tormented her for some rags so she could get a balloon off him. The child hasn't been seen since.'

'Perhaps she's in someone's house?' Tess said. 'She might be showing off her balloon.'

'We've tried every house in the street, sweetheart, and every yard, but there's no sight or sign of her. And we've been up and down every entry half a dozen times, and down to the shops. The child seems to have just vanished. Anyway, the police have been told and we're expecting a bobby any minute now.'

'What about the field in Province Road? She might be playing there.'

'She wouldn't go that far on her own, sweetheart, she never wanders away from home and her mammy.'

'We'll put our school things in the house, and then go and look in the field. She might just be there, it's worth a try.' Maddy moved so fast she almost pulled her sister over. 'Come on, it'll be dark soon and then they'll never find her.' She was putting the key in the lock when she noticed Tess walking away. 'Where are you going? Wait for me!'

'I'm going to ask Mrs Bingham if she's seen Emma. I bet no one has asked her 'cos they don't like her.'

'Tess, our mam won't like you doing that. Now come back and we'll go out together.'

'No, I won't be a minute, I'll just give her a knock.' Tess wasn't going to be put off and was rapping on the Binghams' door before her sister could stop her.

'What d'yer want?'

The scowling face of Nellie was enough to send a shiver down the girl's spine, but she stood her ground. 'Have you seen little Emma Wilson, Mrs Bingham?'

'What the hell are yer asking me that for? Now go back home where yer belong and don't be bothering me again.' Nellie began to close the door. 'I've got more to do with me time than be messing with the likes of you. Now get lost.'

'She's gone missing, you see, and I just thought you might have seen her.'

The door was opened wider. 'How d'yer mean, she's gone missing? And if she has, what makes yer think I know where she is?'

'Well, every woman in the street has been looking for her, they've searched everywhere and can't find her. She's been missing for over an hour now and the police are coming.' Nellie came to the edge of the step and poked her head out. Looking from left to right, she muttered, 'Why didn't her bleedin' mother keep an eye on her?'

'She only went out to get a balloon off the rag man, and her mam hasn't seen her since. The neighbours say she's out of her mind with worry.'

'The rag man, eh? Has anyone looked for him?'

'They never said. But they've looked in all the entries and didn't see anyone.'

Nellie reached for her coat off the hook behind the door. 'Come with me, girl, and we'll try places no one else has thought of looking.' When Tess dropped her head, she said, 'I'm not going to eat yer, girl, so come on.'

Maddy was by her sister's side in a trice. 'I'll come with you.'

Without looking left or right, Nellie walked with some speed. She might be wrong, but if the rag man had evil intentions towards the child, he wouldn't walk the streets with her because she was known to too many people. And even if his cart would fit, he wouldn't take her down an entry because they were open both ends and he'd be spotted in no time. Of course she could be wrong and the rag man might have nothing to do with the child going missing, but she had a hunch and if she didn't follow it up she might regret it.

'Where are we going, Mrs Bingham?' Maddy asked, fearing they were going further away from their street. 'She won't have come this far.'

'She wouldn't on her own, no, but she might if someone said they were taking her for a walk. Anyway, it's better to be lookin' than standing around doing nowt. The child might be in a strange place and frightened out of her wits.'

'But where are we going?'

'There's an entry along here which would be wide enough for a cart. And it's blocked off at one end so not many people use it. It's worth a try.'

The girls were afraid now, hearing that Emma might have gone off with a stranger. They'd thought she'd wandered off on her own and got lost. But Mrs Bingham's words filled them with dread.

Nellie came to a halt and put her arms out to stop the girls from going any further. 'Stay here and keep quiet.' She walked on a few steps, stopping just before the opening of a wide entry. She popped her head around the corner and her hand went to her mouth. The cart was there, and the rag man had his back to her, talking to the little girl, who was crying and asking him to let her go home to her mam. The man had the front of his raggedy coat open, and Nellie knew he was exposing himself to the child.

She walked back to the two waiting girls and said, 'One of yer stay with me, the other go back to Willard Street and fetch someone back quick. Tell them we've found the child and to get here as fast as they can.'

Tess's face lit up. 'Ooh, you've found her! Can I go to her?'

'Keep quiet,' Nellie hissed. 'The rag man has got her and I want some of the women to help me catch him. You,' she pointed to Tess, 'run faster than yer've ever run in yer life. I want to teach this bastard a lesson.'

They watched Tess fly like the wind, then Maddy asked, 'What are we going to do?'

'I'm going to sneak down behind him and take him by surprise. With a bit of luck I'll be able to hold him until someone comes to give me a hand. One thing's for certain, he'll not get that bleedin' cart past me. But if he tries to make a run for it, I can't follow him 'cos I want to stay with the little girl till her mam gets here. So that's where you come in. Run after him, shouting at the top of yer voice as though the bleedin' devil was after yer, just to make people notice. He mustn't get away 'cos he's evil and will do it again to another child unless he's taught a lesson.' Nellie looked briefly into the girl's deep brown eyes, then turned her head. 'Give me half a minute, then pop yer head around the corner and see what's going on. Can yer do that?'

'Of course I can! I'll do anything to help you!'

Nellie was blazing inside at what she knew the rag man was doing to a small, innocent child. Thank God the little girl was too young to know what the dirty swine was doing, but that didn't excuse him. And if she could help it, this child wasn't going to have her innocence taken away from her and live her life thinking all men were filthy perverts. 'No, I'll manage.' It took Nellie all her time to keep the anger out of her voice. 'You stay here and keep a look-out. Yer sister should be here soon with help.' While Maddy watched, Nellie crept down the entry towards the man, who was busy talking to the child, telling her not to cry, he wasn't going to hurt her, he only wanted to show her something and then she could go home to her mam. The sound of his own voice drowned out any slight noise Nellie might have made on the cobbles, so when she grabbed him from behind by the neck of his shirt and coat and pulled him backwards with every ounce of strength she possessed, he was completely off his guard and unprepared for the attack. He tottered backwards, his arms waving madly in an effort to find something to help him stay upright. But there was nothing to get a grip of, only fresh air, and before he could pull his senses together he found himself lying flat on his back with Nellie sitting on his stomach.

'What the bleedin' hell d'yer think ye're doing, missus! Gerroff!'

'Yer'll soon find out what I'm doing, don't worry. By the time me and a few other women have finished with yer, yer'll rue the day yer were born.' After making sure the man's raggedy coat was covering his nakedness, Nellie beckoned to Maddy, who was wide-eyed with wonder and admiration. 'Come and get the child and take her to her mother.'

Maddy kept close to the wall, as far away from the man's arms as possible. He was trying to shift Nellie, who was only half his size and weight, but she stayed put. And when the thought of being torn limb from limb by a gang of women made him desperate enough to punch her on the side of her face, she pulled her arm back and belted him with such force he could see stars. 'Go on, girl, get out of this place.'

Little Emma, her face red with tears and her body shaking with heart-rending sobs, stretched out her arms. 'I want me mam.'

Maddy picked her up and held her close. 'I'll take you to your mam now, darling, so don't cry.' She looked down at Nellie. 'Will you be all right on your own, Mrs Bingham?'

'I'll be all right, and this feller's going nowhere. Now take the child to her mother.'

Maddy took half a dozen steps, then turned her head. 'I think you're very brave, Mrs Bingham, very brave indeed.'

Nellie wasn't used to compliments and didn't know how to respond.

In a gruff voice she said, 'On yer way, girl.'

Maddy reached the top of the entry just as Tess led an army of women to the scene. Amongst them was Emma's mother, Edna Wilson, who was weak with relief. She took her daughter from Maddy and smothered her with kisses. 'I thought I'd lost yer, baby, that I'd never see yer again.'

The group crowded into the entry and the sight that met their eyes was one they'd never forget. 'My God, I've never seen the likes in me life,' one woman said. 'She's a bloody hero!'

'Yer never spoke a truer word, girl,' said another. 'Let's go and give her a hand.'

The first woman led the way. 'We should string the bugger up.'

With fifteen women surrounding them, Nellie thought it was safe to get up, and she held out her hands for assistance. It was then the women saw the man's open trousers and several kicks were aimed at him before a policeman came up behind them.

'All right, ladies, I'll take over now. That's enough, I said.' He pushed his way through the angry crowd, thinking it was his job to maintain law and order, until he saw the reason for their anger. If that little girl he'd just seen with her mother had been his daughter, he would have wanted to kill the man, never mind kick him. But he couldn't allow his personal feelings to affect his work. 'If you'll all go home now, I'll take the gentleman down to the police station and he'll be dealt with there.'

'Gentleman, did yer say!' One irate woman, Fanny by name, shook her fist. 'To class him as a gentleman is an insult to every decent man on earth.'

'Ye're dead right, Fanny!' A neighbour of the Wilsons', Jane, minded young Emma sometimes when her mother wanted to go to the shops and the weather was bad. And the woman loved the little girl as though she was her own. She now put her face close to the policeman's. 'If it hadn't been for this woman here,' she jerked her head at Nellie, 'God knows what would have happened, he might have killed the poor mite.'

The man took his helmet off and mopped his brow. 'Yes, you did a good job, missus, but what made you look here?'

'It was when I heard she'd gone out to get a balloon off the rag and bone man. Yer see, I'd seen the cart in the street, from me window, like, and I noticed it wasn't the rag man what's been coming since I moved into the street. I never gave it any thought at the time, till I heard the girl had gone missing.' Nellie was trying to distance herself from the hands that were wanting to shake hers, and the arms wanting to hug her. Shows of emotion were something she couldn't handle. 'This is the only wide entry around here that's bricked up at the end. It never gets used because the people in these houses use their front doors to get to the shops, it's easier.' She looked down with contempt at the man, who had managed to cover himself and was now pulling his cap down to hide his face as much as possible. 'And he needed an entry. He wouldn't have got far walking the child.'

'That was good thinking on your part.' The policeman smiled down at her. 'The sergeant will want to take some details from you, so could I have your name and address, please?'

'Bingham, forty-nine Willard Street.' Nellie's words were abrupt. 'And now I'll have to get back, I left a pan on the stove.' She walked away, a lonely figure with her head bent.

The women stared after her, they couldn't make her out. Then Edna Wilson, her daughter pressed close to her chest, ran after her. Half of the women followed, leaving the others to see what happened to the rag man. 'Mrs Bingham, wait a minute, I haven't thanked yer proper for what yer did.'

'I don't want no thanks, the child's all right, that's enough for me.'

'But she might not have been except for your quick thinking.' There were murmurs of agreement from all the neighbours. 'I was out of me mind with worry, and God knows what the swine would have done to Emma if you hadn't found them. None of us would have dreamed of her going with the rag man, and we'd never have thought of that entry. I will never forget what yer did as long as I live.'

'I only did what any woman would have done under the circumstances. And now yer've got yer baby back, keep yer bleedin' eye on her in future.'

'Oh, I will, I won't let her out of me sight.' When Edna stopped trying to keep up with Nellie and came to a halt, the neighbours stayed with her. 'She's a funny ossity, isn't she? She won't even let me thank her.'

'She's a funny one all right,' Fanny said, 'but I take me hat off to her. There's not many women would tackle a grown man like she did, considering it wasn't her child.'

'She's always been a loner, and a troublemaker.' Jane pulled on one of the long hairs sprouting from a wart on her chin. 'I thought this might have made her more friendly, like, and she'd get along with everyone. But it seems I was wrong and she doesn't want to get involved with her neighbours. Still, no matter what tricks she gets up to in future, I might rant and rave at her but she'll always be a brave woman in my eyes and I'll never forget what she did today.'

'I never will, if I live to be a hundred,' Edna said, kissing her daughter's tear-stained face. 'I owe a lot to her and I'll never fight with her again. If she starts off, I'll just turn the other cheek. For all I know, she might have saved my daughter's life.' She began walking again. 'I'll get the length of my feller's tongue when he finds out. He'll call me fit to burn for not keeping an eye on Emma. And I'll have to tell him in case the police call.' She let out a deep sigh. 'He doesn't understand that I'd need eyes in the back of me head to watch her all the time.'

'That's men all over,' Fanny said. 'It would be a different tune if they were the ones what had the babies. Men can't stand pain. If my feller has a toothache he moans that much yer'd think he was dying. Silly buggers, the lot of them.'

'To think all this was going on while I was strolling around the market.' Ann shook her head as though she couldn't believe what the girls had told her. 'I'd have been home like a shot if I'd known. The child's mother must have been out of her mind.'

'She was, Mam, she was crying her eyes out.' Tess hadn't been allowed to go down the entry so she had no idea what the man had been up to. 'And if it hadn't been for Mrs Bingham, we might never have found Emma.'

'How did she come to get involved?' Ann asked. 'None of the neighbours bother with her.'

'I knocked on her door and told her.' Tess didn't care if she got told off because, after all, if she hadn't told the woman next door, then little Emma might still be missing. 'Maddy told me you wouldn't want me to, but I'm glad I did.'

'I went with her, Mam, Tess didn't go on her own.' Maddy was quick to defend her sister. 'And it's a good job she thought of it because Mrs Bingham was brilliant.' She had already told them how Nellie had floored the man and sat on him until help came. 'I was afraid for her 'cos she's only little and the man was as big as you, Dad!'

'Well, events proved Tess did the right thing,' George said, while wishing he'd been here to confront a man who would scare a wee child so, and frighten the mother out of her wits. 'And they also proved that there's some good in most people. For all the crazy, annoying tricks Mrs Bingham plays, she has a good heart. And surely that makes up for her wrong-doing.'

Just as Ann stood up to gather the dinner plates in, there came a knock on the door. 'Oh dear, of all the times to call, when the place is a mess. Clear the table quickly, girls, while I see who it is.'

Lizzie didn't wait to be asked in. She brushed past Ann, saying, 'I know ye're probably in the middle of yer dinner, but I can't wait to hear what's gone on. I've heard bits and pieces off some of the neighbours, but they said Maddy and Tess saw the whole thing.' She winked at George. 'Can't get away from me, can yer, lad?'

'Have you had your dinner already?' he asked, always happy to see the woman who could bring a smile to the most miserable of faces. 'You've been quick.'

'I threw me dinner down and left my feller halfway through his.' The girls came through from the kitchen and Lizzie beamed. 'I believe you two were in the thick of it from beginning to end, and I like to get the whole story instead of bits and pieces. So sit yerselves down and tell Mrs Lizzie all about it.'

The girls were in their element, and took it in turns to tell what they'd seen and the part they had played. And Lizzie, clicking her tongue on the roof of her mouth, and shaking her head, added to the drama. 'It was like something you see at the pictures, Mrs Lizzie,' Maddy said. 'Mrs Bingham sneaking up on the man from behind, it was really exciting. But little Emma was crying and asking for her mam, and that was sad.'

'I wish I could have got me hands on him, the dirty swine.' Just in time she remembered Jane had told her the girls hadn't seen what the man was up to, Nellie Bingham had seen to that. And here was she, nearly letting the cat out of the bag. 'I hope the police give him a good hiding, that's what he deserves.'

'I think Mrs Bingham frightened the life out of him. She sat on his chest, and when he tried to punch her, she gave him a real belt on his chin.'

'Eh, she's a real turn-up for the books, isn't she?' Lizzie said. 'Everyone is saying she's a hero, but apparently she wouldn't even let anyone thank her or shake her hand. She's a strange woman, and although I've called her all the names under the sun, I must say she turned up trumps at the right time.'

'I like her,' Tess said, surprising everyone. 'She probably doesn't like being the way she is, but she can't help it! I didn't like being the way I was when I was sick all the time, but there was nothing I could do to make myself better.'

'Ye're right, queen, of course yer are. I mean, look at me, I'm a good example! D'yer think I wouldn't like to be all sweet and honey if I could? With a face like Garbo and a figure like Jean Harlow? Blimey, I wouldn't call the King me auntie.' Then Lizzie's coarse laughter filled the room. 'Ay, if I had the face of Garbo and the body of Jean Harlow, my feller would think he'd died and gone to heaven. He wouldn't be going to the bleedin' pub every night, he'd be frightened to take his eyes off me in case I waltzed off with someone else.'

'And if I had the looks of Ronald Colman, Lizzie, I'd be the one to waltz you off.' George fingered his moustache, saying, 'This is the only thing I've got in common with him.'

Tess put her arms around Lizzie. 'I love you just the way you are, nice and cuddly.'

'Just as well, queen, seeing as ye're stuck with me like this.' She nodded her head and put on a sad face. 'I was only talking about this last night to that rose on me wallpaper. She wasn't a bit sympathetic. Told me to grin and bear it, and make the best of a bad job.'

Chapter Twenty

'George, wake up, we've slept in.' Ann shook her husband's shoulder urgently, then slipped her legs over the side of the bed. 'Come on, move yourself.'

'I didn't hear the alarm,' George grunted, struggling to sit up while rubbing the sleep from his eyes. 'Are we very late, or just a few minutes?'

'Twenty minutes, so get your skates on.' Ann draped a cardigan over her shoulders and shivered as her feet touched the cold lino. 'Put an extra vest on, 'cos it's freezing.' She crept down the stairs without making a sound. It was too early for the girls to get up, they might as well stay in the warm bed until their father was ready for work.

There was a plate of toast and a cup of tea waiting when George came in from the kitchen after having a swill. 'I'd have given anything for an extra half-hour in bed this morning, I was in a deep sleep.'

'Never mind, there's only six days to go, then you've got three days off for the holiday. It's lucky Christmas has fallen at the weekend this year, so you get that extra day off.'

George munched on a piece of toast. 'I never thought I'd say it, but I miss next door raking her grate out. I don't always hear the alarm, but she made such a racket you couldn't help but hear. I wonder what's made her go quiet all of a sudden?'

'I don't know the reason, but she stopped the early morning racket the day after that little girl went missing. But she still gets up to mischief. Never a day goes by that she doesn't throw something over the wall, or call names after me when I walk down the street. I'm not the only one she picks on either, she has a go at most of the women.'

'Is she getting you down, love?'

'Not at all! I just let her get on with it. In fact nobody answers her back now, so she ends up talking to herself.'

'I wonder what sort of a Christmas her family's going to have? I doubt there'll be much fun in that house.'

'Oh, now, I think you could be wrong. I know she's been paying money into the sweet shop, 'cos I've seen her getting her card marked. And Bridie saw her buying paper decorations and tinsel, so she must decorate the house for Christmas. Another thing, she looks after her boys, they're always clean and well dressed.'

George emptied his cup before pushing his chair back and getting to his feet. 'She's a hard one to understand, that's for sure. But I'm beginning to think Tess was right when she said the woman can't help the way she is. Perhaps something has happened in her life to trigger it off, who can tell? Anyway, as long as she's doing us no harm, as far as I'm concerned it's live and let live.'

'You're going to be late, George, you'd better hurry.'

'I've decided to hop on a bus to Stanley Road and get the tram from there. It's only a penny, and not worth my trying to make up the time. I can't walk as quick as I used to so I'm going to mug myself and go to work in style.'

'I don't know why you don't do it every day,' Ann said, helping him on with his coat. 'We're not as strapped for cash now, it wouldn't break the bank.'

'We'll see how things go after the holiday.' George bent to rub noses with her. 'I'll see you tonight, love.'

Ann watched him walk down the street, then closed the door and made for the stairs. It was time to get the girls up.

'While Maddy's doing her homework, Mam, can I go outside with my skipping rope?' Tess asked. 'I won't go away from the door.'

'Make sure you don't, because it's dark out. Your dad will be home soon and we'll be having our dinner.'

'I'll come in with him.' Tess took the skipping rope from a shelf under the stairs. 'I'm going to try cross-overs, so if you hear a scream you'll know I've tripped myself up.'

'I won't be long doing my homework,' Maddy told her. 'Then I'll show you how to do it without tripping up and breaking your neck.'

Tess shook her head. 'I'd rather practise on my own so I don't get laughed at if I make a fool of myself. I'll have you a bet that by the time you come out I'll be able to do one cross-over at the very least.' After wrapping a scarf tightly around her neck she pulled on a pair of navy woollen gloves. 'If I can't, it won't be for the want of trying.'

As Tess closed the door behind her and stepped down on to the pavement, she spotted Mrs Bingham's elder son walking up the street. His head was bent and he would have passed her without a glance, but Tess stood in his path. 'Hello! My name's Tess and I live in this house next to yours.'

'I know.' His voice was gruff, and although it couldn't be seen in the darkness, his face was red with embarrassment. 'I've seen yer in the street.'

'You could have let on,' Tess said. 'We should be friends, being neighbours. What's your name?'

The boy didn't know how to take her. None of the people in the street talked to him or his brother, and he couldn't tell if she was being funny. But from the light of the street lamp, he couldn't see any sign of sarcasm on her face. And he was dying to tell someone his news. 'Me name's Jack. I leave school on Friday, and I've just been for an interview for a job.'

'Oh, that's good!' Tess sounded really interested. 'How did you get on?'

A tall lad for his age, with mousy-coloured hair like his mother, he seemed to grow in stature and there was pride in his voice. 'I got the job and I start work after Christmas.'

'Ooh, isn't that marvellous! I bet you're very pleased and excited.'

'Yeah, I am.' Jack was relaxed now, and he could tell the girl was genuinely interested in what he was telling her. 'I'm starting as an apprentice with a firm of decorators in Stanley Road, so I won't have far to travel to work.'

'I bet your mam will be over the moon, 'cos you'll be able to do her decorating for her.'

The boy's eyes narrowed at the mention of his mother. He knew she wasn't liked in the street, and there were times she did things that made him ashamed. But he loved her dearly and wouldn't hear a bad word said about her. 'I'd do anything for me mam, she's a smasher.'

'So is my mam, and I'd do anything for her.' Tess saw a familiar figure approaching, and wanting everyone to be friendly, she said, 'Here's my dad. Tell him your good news, Jack.'

But the lad turned on his heels. 'Me dinner will be ready. I'll see yer.' He was letting himself into the house next door before Tess could say anything to stop him.

George put an arm across her shoulders and whispered, 'You're a bit young to be courting, my dear.'

'I wanted him to stay and talk to you, but he just skedaddled.'

'Tell me about it inside, love, because I'm frozen through to the marrow.' George left Tess to close the front door while he made a bee-line for the fire. 'It's bitterly cold down by the docks. The wind is fierce and there were times when I thought my fingers were going to drop off.'

'Give me your coat and I'll hang it up,' Ann said. 'You could do with buying yourself one of those hats that have side pieces to cover your ears.'

'You mean like Sherlock Holmes?' George chuckled. 'I can just hear the men if I walked in with one of those on my head. I'd be a laughing stock.'

Ann tutted as she walked through to the kitchen to put the dinner out. 'I wouldn't care what they said about me, as long as I was warm.'

Maddy looked up from her exercise book. 'They didn't laugh at Sherlock Holmes, Dad.'

'I think he moved in different circles to me, love. He was a detective, not a docker.' Out of the corner of his eye, George could see Tess moving from one foot to the other, a sure sign she had something to say. 'And you, young lady, what was it you wanted to tell me about the boy next door who took to his heels when he saw me?'

'His name is Jack, Dad, and he's very shy, that's why he ran off. He leaves school on Friday and he'd been for an interview for a job.'

Ann came in, a tea towel in her hands. 'Have you been talking to one of the Binghams?'

'Yes, and he's very nice. I told him my name, and that I lived next door, and he said he knew 'cos he'd seen me in the street.' Tess didn't think she'd done wrong, and went on, 'And guess what? He got the job and starts after Christmas. Isn't that great?'

Ann wasn't so sure. 'Did you speak to him first, or did he approach you?'

'Oh, I spoke to him first. He would have just walked past me if I hadn't. I mean, he is our neighbour and we should try and be friendly.'

Maddy closed her book and put it on the sideboard. The conversation was more interesting than arithmetic. 'What would you have done if he'd kept on walking and didn't stop? Would you have done a flying tackle on his legs to bring him down?'

Tess giggled. 'Of course not! Anyway, he did stop, and I think he was glad to have someone to tell about his new job. He's very pleased with himself.'

'You really shouldn't have done that, Theresa, knowing how difficult his mother is,' Ann said. 'We should have as little to do with the family as possible.'

'I don't agree with you over that, love,' George said. 'He's only a lad, you can't blame him for what his mother is.'

Tess went on the offensive. 'He loves his mother, he said she's a smasher and he'd do anything for her. And I told him I love you, Mam, and would do anything for you.'

Ann had no answer for that, so she went to the kitchen to put the dinners out. But all the while her ear was cocked.

'How did he come to tell you that about his mother, sweetheart?' George asked. 'I hope you weren't discussing Mrs Bingham with him?'

'No, I wouldn't do that, Dad! He's going to be an apprentice painter and decorator, and I said his mam would be over the moon 'cos he could do all the decorating for her. And that's when he said he'd do anything for his mam 'cos she's a smasher.'

'Then he's a good son and I admire him for it. And I'm glad you broke the ice, Tess, it would be nice if the children could be friends, even if the parents can't.'

Ann's head appeared around the door. 'It's not a case of the parents not getting on, George, and you know that! I'd be more than happy to be friends with Mrs Bingham, but it takes two, you can't have a one-sided friendship.'

'I know that, dear, I wasn't implying that you were in any way to blame for the situation. But I don't think the two boys from next door should suffer in any way for what their mother does. And I hope Tess, and Maddy, treat them as they do their other friends. That's if the boys want it that way, of course.'

'Let's discuss it another time, shall we? The dinner will be dried up if I don't serve it now, so sit at the table everyone and I'll bring the plates through.'

The set of her younger daughter's face told Ann she should steer clear of any mention of the Binghams. Theresa had a very stubborn streak, and if she thought something was right then nothing on God's earth would make her change her mind. But there was no harm in her, she didn't have a wicked thought in her head and would never upset anyone. All she asked of life was that everyone around her should be happy.

'Madelaine is going to write the Christmas cards out tonight for Wales, so I'll post them in the morning to make sure they get them in time. And I bought a few to send myself. There's your Ken and Milly, Lizzie, Dolly, Bridie, and I mustn't forget Maisie and the Critchleys in Hanford Avenue. Once they're out of the way I'll start putting the decorations up.'

The conversation Tess was having in her head petered out as the excitement of Christmas crept in. After all, her mother was always very fair, and she hadn't said definitely she mustn't speak to the boys next door. Still, it might be better not to mention that she'd made a card and intended to put it through next door's letter-box on Christmas Eve. 'If me and Maddy get our cards done early, can we start putting the bunting up tonight?'

'Ooh, I don't know about that. The picture rail will need dusting first, but that won't take long. It's just that I'm no good at knocking nails in to hang the paper chains on. I'm hopeless with a hammer when I have to stretch. And I'm certainly not going to ask your dad, not after he's worked a full day, he'll be too tired.'

'I admit I don't fancy doing the whole lot,' George said. 'But I wouldn't mind making a start and finishing it off tomorrow night.'

'I'll do the picture rail after we've had our dinner, Mam,' Maddy said. 'I can put a clean cloth over the brush head and reach it easy.'

Tess wasn't going to be left out. 'I'll hold the paper chains, Dad, so they won't get torn.' She clapped her hands in delight. 'Ooh, won't we be posh? And we'll be even posher when we get the tree. When will that be, Mam?'

'Not till nearer the weekend, love. They're pretty expensive to buy right now, but they go down a lot in price as it gets near to Christmas.'

'I was wondering what you thought about asking our Ken and the family around on Christmas night?' George raised his bushy brows. 'We've been invited there every year and I think it's about time we returned the favour. So how about it, Ann? You wouldn't have to go overboard with food and drink, just a bottle of sherry and lemonade for the children.'

Both girls' eyes were wide with anticipation as they waited to hear what their mother had to say. It was true they went to Uncle Ken's every Christmas Day, and they always enjoyed themselves. Except their mother, who would never have a drink and never looked in the party mood. And although she had changed a lot lately, had she changed enough?

'I think that's a good idea, love! I'll see Milly tomorrow and ask her. You're right, it is time to pay them back for all the years they've played host to us.'

The happiness of the two girls knew no bounds. 'What about Mrs Lizzie?' Tess wanted to know. 'Can she come with her husband?'

'I'm afraid she can't, love, because her daughter comes for Christmas Day with her husband and the baby.' Ann had been keeping a secret for over a week now, and it had been really hard at times. Seeing her children so happy now was her undoing, she couldn't keep it to herself any longer. 'But she is coming on Boxing Day, in the afternoon, and staying for tea.'

'Yippee!' Maddy threw her arms around her sister. 'This is going to be the best Christmas ever, Tess, aren't we lucky?'

'Excuse me, girls, but would you eat your dinner, please? You can get as excited as you like after, but right now I want to see every bit of food disappear from those plates into your mouths and on its way to your tummies.'

George looked puzzled. 'When did you ask Lizzie? She never mentioned it to me.'

'I'm sure there's lots of things Lizzie gets up to without telling you, George.' Ann grinned. 'I mean, she's not married to you, so she doesn't have to account to you for every single thing she does. And I asked her on the quiet last Saturday, when we took the girls to the market to buy their presents. So now all has been revealed, I hope you're happy?'

'I'm delighted, my dear. We have two days of lively fun to look forward to.' George pushed his plate away and licked his lips before running the back of a hand over his moustache. 'And we must have the room looking nice and jolly for our visitors, so we'll make a start when we've had a drink and the dishes are washed.'

Tess ate with gusto, her bottom swivelling on the chair. Today had been a lovely day.

It was Christmas Eve and Ann had everything prepared for dinner the following day. She was really pleased with herself for being so organised. The children's presents had been wrapped ready to go in a pillowcase that would be hung on the grate after they'd gone to bed. With the dresses, there would be writing materials for Theresa, an underskirt for Madelaine, a bag of assorted sweets each, and an apple and orange. And George's new shirt and pullover, also wrapped in bright red and green paper, would be placed under the tree, which the girls had decorated the night before. It looked very attractive with coloured balls dangling from its branches and lengths of silver tinsel hanging down. In fact the whole room looked very festive, with paper chains criss-crossed from one side to the other, and balloons bouncing in each of the corners.

Ann saw her daughters passing the window and hurried to open the door. Their faces were whipped to a rosy red with the chill wind, and they looked the picture of health. It was months since Theresa had shown any sign of sickness or a cold, and Ann was keeping her fingers crossed that those worrying days were over. 'Come and get a warm by the fire, you both look perished. But don't put your hands too near or you'll get chilblains.'

'This room looks lovely, Mam,' Maddy said. 'It's like walking into a grotto. The only thing missing is a Father Christmas.'

'I'm dead excited.' Tess threw her gloves and scarf on the couch. She was half expecting to be told to put them away properly, but her mother never said a word. 'I can't wait for it to be morning and we all get our presents.'

'I've been very busy today, so busy I was meeting myself coming back at times,' Ann told them with more than a little pride. 'The turkey is ready for the oven, and the potatoes and vegetables are in pans just waiting to have the gas lit under them. I'll have to get up early because the turkey will take hours to roast.' She suddenly put a hand to her mouth. 'Oh, aren't I stupid! Here's me praising myself to high heaven

285

and I haven't got the stuffing for the bird! How could I have forgotten to put that on my shopping list! Oh dear, I'll have to run to the shops and get a packet. A turkey is no good without the stuffing.'

'I'll go to the shop for you, Mam,' Tess said, reaching for her scarf and gloves. 'It won't take me five minutes to run there and back.'

'No, it's starting to get dark out, I'll go myself.'

'Mam, I'm not a baby! I can go on a message without getting lost or forgetting what I'm supposed to buy.' A mutinous expression came to the pretty face. 'The shops are packed with people, and so are the streets.'

While Ann hesitated, she thought of what George would say. He'd tell her that Theresa was old enough now to be given some responsibility. She would never grow up if she wasn't allowed to. 'Okay, but run all the way there and back, and do not speak to anyone.'

Tess wrapped herself up again before holding out her hand for the money. 'What exactly is it I have to ask for?'

'It's a packet of Paxo sage and onion stuffing. I usually make my own with fresh sage, but it's too late for that now. I'm not sure how much it'll be, but here's sixpence and you should have change out of that.'

'D'you want me to come with you, Tess?' Maddy asked. 'I don't mind, I like seeing the people hurrying and scurrying with their Christmas shopping.'

'No, I'm going on my own.' With a nod of determination, Tess fled from the house before any more advice was forthcoming. Anyone listening would think she was incapable of going on a message on her own.

The shops were indeed very busy with last-minute shoppers hoping to get a bargain. The butcher's and greengrocer's were doing a roaring trade selling off their perishable goods at a fraction of the usual price to cut their losses. Better that than having to throw them away after Christmas.

Tess waited patiently for her turn to be served. She quite enjoyed it really, because it was warm in the shop and the customers were all happy and talkative. With their biggest worries over now, the women were looking forward to the next morning, when their children would be shrieking with delight as they opened their presents. For some, whose fathers were out of work, it might only be an apple, an orange, some nuts and a comic. But even they would be a luxury to kids whose parents were hard up, and would be received with noisy pleasure.

When it was her turn, Tess asked for a packet of sage and onion stuffing and passed over the silver sixpence. The coppers she got in change were stuffed down her glove before she left the shop so they'd

286

be safe. Once outside, the cold air hit her and she shivered. Best to run all the way home and warm herself up. She hadn't gone far before she saw the familiar figure of Mrs Bingham walking in front of her. The woman was weighed down with a heavy basket over one arm, while her other was holding so many things they were in danger of falling. Particularly the loaf of bread that was slowly slipping away from her.

Tess quickened her steps to catch up. 'Can I help you carry something, Mrs Bingham?'

Nellie glanced sideways, afraid to move in case she dropped one of the many things she had in her arms. She should have made two journeys, but she didn't know she wanted so much until she got in the shops and saw things on the shelves that she'd forgotten. Anyway, suffice to say she wasn't in the best of tempers. 'No, I can manage.'

But an abrupt voice wasn't going to put Tess off. 'We live next to each other so I can easily carry some of those things for you, it wouldn't be out of my way.'

Nellie's footsteps didn't even falter. Her one aim right at that moment was to get home before her arms dropped off, with everything she'd paid good money for. 'I've told yer, I can manage. Now on yer bike and leave me alone.'

The young girl kept up with her. 'My teacher in school is called Miss Harrison, and she often tells us that we should be good Samaritans and always offer to help someone who needs it. We should never stand by, waiting to be asked. And if Miss Harrison saw me walking next to you, with only one small packet in my hand, and you weighed down, she would be very disappointed in me.'

Nellie stopped in her tracks. Apart from her aching arms, her feet were cold and the corn on her little toe was beginning to give her gyp. She was not in the mood to be kept back by a chit of a girl. There were strong words on her tongue when she turned her head, but although her mouth went through the motions, the words were never uttered. For one look into eyes that were innocent and honest brought a pang of guilt. She wouldn't admit to herself that she was giving in, though, only that she'd be home a lot quicker if she let the child have her own way. 'Take the loaf from under me arm, then, that will be a help.'

Tess eased out the badly squashed loaf. 'It's all bashed in, Mrs Bingham, but you'll be able to get it back into shape when you get home. Now let me take this bag off you, that should make things lighter.'

'Leave that where it is, girl, it's got spuds in and is too heavy for yer.'

But Tess already had the bag in her arms. And although it was indeed very heavy, she managed to say, 'I'm stronger than I look, you know. I can carry this easy.'

Nellie thought she'd gone far enough and had no intention of talking to the girl. So when Tess asked if she was looking forward to Christmas, did she have a tree and were her sons getting any presents, every question was answered with a grunt. But it didn't put the girl off, she just chattered away until they'd passed her house and stopped at the one next door.

'Knock on the window, girl, I can't get to me keys. But don't put the bleedin' thing in or we'll be in a right state over the holiday.'

It was Jack who answered the door, and his jaw dropped at the sight. He just stood there, thinking he was seeing things, until his mam spoke. 'Don't stand there looking gormless, let me get in. And take that shopping off the girl.' Nellie disappeared from sight, but her voice stayed as loud as ever. 'And don't be all bleedin' night about it, 'cos the draught's just blown yer dad off his chair.'

Jack reached for the bag of potatoes. 'How come ye're carrying me mam's shopping?'

'Well, I only had this little packet to carry and your mother was overloaded. So I offered to help, and here I am.'

The bag of potatoes on the floor, the boy held out his hand for the loaf. 'Blimey, that's in a bad way, isn't it? It looks as though it's had a battering.'

'Your mam had it tucked under her arm, that's how it came to be squashed. Anyway, Jack, are you looking forward to tomorrow?'

'Not particularly, it's just another day.' This wasn't quite true, but Jack thought it was time he began acting like a grown-up. After all, he'd left school now and was starting work next week. Then he had another thought. If he acted too grown up, Tess might not talk to him any more, and he wouldn't want that because she was the only one in the street who acknowledged he even existed. 'I'm looking forward to me presents, of course, and me dinner. But there's not much doing after that, is there? It's not worth going out 'cos there's nowhere open.'

'We're having a party,' Tess said, showing off. 'My mam's got a bottle of sherry for the grown-ups, and lemonade for us youngsters.'

Nellie's voice thundered, 'Jack! Will yer shut that door at the same time as yer shut yer bleedin' gob! We're freezing in here.'

Jack could feel the colour rising upwards from his neck, and he said a silent prayer the girl would leave before his mother said anything more to embarrass him. But he was surprised to see Tess giggling behind her hand. 'She's really funny is your mam. You must have loads of laughs with her.'

'She won't be laughing if I don't shut this door,' Jack said. 'Thanks for helping her. I'll see yer.'

'Tell your mam I said a happy Christmas.'

'Yeah, and you too. Ta-ra.'

Ken stepped back with a look of pretend amazement on his face. 'Well I never! Will yer look at these two, Milly, they look like princesses.'

Her face a glowing pink with all the excitement, Tess did a twirl to show off the new pale green dress. 'Aren't I proper posh?'

Not to be outdone, Maddy pushed her sister aside. 'And how about me in my blue creation? Am I not a picture of elegance?'

'As I said, yer look like two princesses. All yer need now is Prince Charming to come along and whisk yer off yer feet.' Ken noticed his daughter watching him with raised brows. 'Perhaps three knights in shining armour would be the thing, then yer'd have one each.'

'How come yer didn't tell me I looked like a princess?' Joyce asked.

'There was no point in me telling you that yer looked like a princess when ye're a real one, now was there?' Ken spread out his hands. 'I mean, after all, I am the King. So it stands to sense me daughter would be a princess.'

Billy decided to get in on the act. 'That makes me a prince, then, does it? I always knew I was different from the other boys in our class.'

'How did you know that, Billy?' Tess asked. 'Was it because of the crown you had on your head?'

'When you've all finished flattering each other, can I take the visitors' coats?' Ann asked. 'Then we can sit down and relax.'

'Give them to me,' Maddy said. 'I'll take them upstairs and put them on the bed.'

'Hang on a minute, I've got something in me pockets.' Ken put a hand in each of his deep pockets and brought out two bottles. One was a half-bottle of whisky, the other a pint bottle of bitter beer. 'These are for me and me kid brother to help us get drunk.'

'Ay, we run a respectable house here, Ken Richardson.' Ann put on her schoolteacher's stern expression. 'No rowdiness or drunkenness. When you leave here you will be stone-cold sober, with all your wits about you.'

Ken chuckled. 'Over my dead body! It's Christmas, a time for celebration, and me and our kid are going to celebrate.'

'Take no notice of him, Ann, he's having yer on,' Milly said. 'If he gets drunk he can crawl home on his own. I'll walk on with the kids and pretend we don't know him.'

'You're heartless, woman!' Ken settled himself on the couch, next to his brother's chair. 'What d'yer think of that, our kid? Me own wife would leave me in the gutter and walk away.'

'If that was where yer fell down, then I'd leave yer there.' Milly sat beside him and linked his arm. 'But I'd come for yer in the middle of the night when there was no one around to see what a drunk I was married to.'

While the four children sat at the table exchanging details of the presents they'd received, Ann made herself comfortable in the fireside chair facing her husband across the grate. 'I don't know about anyone else, but I couldn't eat anything yet. I'm still bloated after the big dinner we had.'

'None of us can be hungry, so relax, Ann.' Milly kicked off her shoes and stretched her legs. 'Let's sit and talk, give ourselves a chance to wind down after the hectic morning we've had. I was hoping with the kids being older they wouldn't have us up at some unearthly hour, but it wasn't to be. Six o'clock Joyce was shaking me shoulder asking me what time it was. And no amount of coaxing would get her to go back to bed for another hour.'

'Why don't we all have a drink? George, would you do the honours, please?'

Ann's words brought silence to the room. Even the children were stunned. And George thought his ears were deceiving him. Then he decided his wife must mean their guests, because never in their whole married life had Ann ever taken an alcoholic drink. 'Er, yes, I'll do that, my dear.' He pushed himself out of the chair. 'Would you like a glass of your own whisky, Ken?'

'Yeah, if you have one with me. Put a drop of water in mine, but not enough to drown the taste.'

'Milly, will you have a sherry?'

'I don't mind if I do, George, thank you.'

'Right!' Rubbing his hands, he made for the kitchen. 'And lemonade for the children.'

Then Ann dropped her bombshell. 'I'll have a sherry, please, George.'

Ann had sipped on the first glass of sherry, pulling a face as the taste was not to her liking. But she enjoyed the warm glow it brought to her body. She was happy and talkative as she later set the table with the help of Milly, laughing freely at Ken's many jokes and surprising everyone when she added some of her own. They weren't particularly funny jokes, certainly not thigh-slapping, side-splitting like Ken's, but everyone laughed because this behaviour was so unlike her. Gone was the stiff and starchy manner which was all anyone outside her family had ever known. When she laughed her head went back and the sound that came was of genuine enjoyment. Milly was pleasantly surprised, but Ken was flabbergasted. He'd always felt a bit sorry for his brother, being married to someone so prim and proper who acted and looked years older than she really was. But he was getting his eye wiped today and quickly changing his opinion of her. He could now see how George had fallen for her all those years ago. And as for George himself, he couldn't take his eyes off her.

'That was a very good spread, Ann, I really enjoyed it.' Milly looked at the table, which an hour ago had been filled with a variety of sandwiches, cakes, jellies and biscuits, but which was now practically bare. 'I'm afraid yer haven't got much over for tomorrow.'

'I'm glad there's nothing left, it shows you all enjoyed it. Besides, I've bought enough in for tomorrow because Lizzie and her husband are coming. And Dolly and Bridie will be calling in with their husbands for a drink. They're not coming until about eight, though, 'cos I haven't enough food to feed the five thousand.'

'Why didn't yer ask Lizzie today?' Ken looked really put out. 'We'd have had a ruddy good laugh with her.'

'She's got her family today, otherwise she'd be here.'

'Then invite us tomorrow night,' Ken said. 'I love winding Lizzie up, and she wouldn't half liven the place up.'

His wife gave him a dig. 'Yer hard-faced thing! Don't yer think Ann's got enough on her plate without seeing your ugly mug again?'

Ann had done a quick calculation. 'That would mean ten adults and four children. This room isn't big enough for that number. And besides, we wouldn't have enough drink in.'

'Those problems are easily solved.' Ken waved a hand in the air as if it were of no importance. 'The four children can go to ours and play cards, or ludo, whatever. They won't come to any harm. And as for the drink, I can always get me hand on that. Me and the landlord are like this.' He crossed two fingers. 'All I have to do is knock on the side door and he'll give me what we want.'

But Tess wasn't well pleased with those arrangements. 'But I want to see Mrs Lizzie, to show her my new dress.'

'She's coming in the afternoon, so she'll see your dress then. You wouldn't have to go to Auntie Milly's until after tea.' Ann still wasn't sure. 'It's going to be a crush, though, we can't seat ten in comfort. And as for drinks, I know Lizzie, Dolly and Bridie only drink milk stout. We got a dozen bottles in, but I don't know whether that'll be enough.'

'Don't look for trouble, love,' George said. 'If it comes to the push you can sit on my knee. In fact I'd rather like that.'

Ken could see his sister-in-law was weakening. 'It'll be a good night, Ann, I promise.'

'Oh, I have no doubt,' Ann said. 'By the way, d'you or Milly know Dolly Flannery and Bridie Hanrahan?'

Ken looked at his wife, and when she shook her head he said, 'We might know them by sight, but their names don't ring a bell. Why?'

'I was just curious.' In her mind's eye Ann could see Bridie and Dolly. Two women who were the funniest she'd ever known. Ken would be hard put to get the better of either of them. 'You'll like them, they're nice, quiet, respectable people.'

Maddy and Tess stared at their mother in amazement. Mrs Flannery and Mrs Hanrahan were indeed very nice ladies, and very friendly. But by no stretch of the imagination could you say they were quiet. Especially Mrs Flannery, who spoke and laughed loudly, and could out-swear Mrs Lizzie.

Ken wasn't particularly keen on the words 'quiet' and 'respectable'. It probably meant they were miserable and dull. 'Still, Lizzie will be here and she'll have the party going in no time. We'll have a smashing night.'

Ann could feel her husband's eyes on her, but she avoided them because she didn't want to give the game away. Let Ken find out for himself that she hadn't been exactly truthful about her friends. 'Yes, you're right. I think we can safely say it will be a smashing night.'

Chapter Twenty-one

Billy and Joyce were walking between their mam and dad when they turned into Willard Street. They were on their way to pick up their cousins to take them back to their house so the grown-ups would have more room for the party. And Billy and Joyce didn't mind being left out, because they were going to have a little party of their own. Their mam had left enough set out in the kitchen to keep them going for a few hours. There were crackers to pull, so they'd all have paper hats, as well as food, fruit and sweets. And lemonade, of course, because you couldn't have a party without that.

They were three doors away from their destination when Ken brought them to a halt. 'Listen! That's Lizzie's laugh, I'd know it anywhere.'

'I thought we were early,' Milly said. 'But they must have started without us.'

'No, Lizzie doesn't need a party to enjoy herself.' Ken began walking. 'I hope the other neighbours don't sit like corpses all night and spoil it for everyone else.'

His wife tutted as she lifted the knocker. 'Don't start crying until ye're hurt, Ken, look on the bright side, for heaven's sake.'

Tess opened the door and was so excited she kept them standing outside while she showed off the bangle she had on her wrist. 'Look what Mrs Lizzie bought me, isn't it lovely? Mine's green to match my dress, and Maddy has a blue one to match hers.'

Ann came up behind her. 'For goodness' sake, Theresa, couldn't you wait until they were inside to show them? They must be freezing.'

Lizzie was sitting like a queen on a throne in Ann's fireside chair. 'Well, look what the cat dragged in! I don't mean you, Milly, or the kids, I wouldn't insult yer. It's your feller I'm talking to. The one what doesn't know his arse from his elbow, or a nut from a screw.'

Ken looked to where Norman was sitting on the couch. 'How d'yer put up with her, Ginger? It's a wonder yer hair's not white having her bossing yer around.'

'Ay, just watch it!' Lizzie said. 'And if yer don't mind, seeing as it's Christmas and we're having a party, would yer mind calling him by the name he was christened?'

293

With a straight face, Ken extended his hand. 'Compliments of the season, Norman, and all the best. Now I can't promise I won't forget after I've had a few drinks and go back to calling yer Ginger, but I'll do me best.'

Tess was reluctant to put her coat on, she wanted to stay with Mrs Lizzie. But when Billy told her they had the makings of a party at his house, she cheered up and was chatting away happily when she left with Maddy and her two cousins. That was after Maddy had shown off her new blue bangle, which made her feel very grown up. After all, she'd be fourteen and leaving school in the summer, and that wasn't far off.

The kids had only been gone a few minutes when there was a ran-tan on the knocker. 'I'll go,' Ann said, 'it'll be the neighbours.'

Ken's eyebrows shot up when he heard a voice booming, 'All the best, girl, and may yer have many more years so I can write the date of yer party in me diary. That's if we enjoy ourselves, like, 'cos as I said to Frank, if we don't I wouldn't be arsed coming again.'

Dolly seemed to burst into the room. 'Merry Christmas, everyone.' She spotted Lizzie ensconced in the best chair in the room, and shook her head. 'Trust Lizzie to bag the best seat. I bet yer've been camped outside all night to make sure yer were here first.'

'Seasons greetings, me darlings.' When Bridie came in followed by her husband, Ken's brows nearly touched his hairline. For at six foot four, and built like a battleship, Patrick Hanrahan was as fine a figure of a man as you'd ever see. And his handshake had Ken grimacing and thanking God he'd only need to shake hands with this giant once every year.

Dolly's husband, Frank, was completely different to his wife, being quietly spoken and mild-mannered. He was the same height as her, five foot seven, but standing next to the Irishman made him appear a lot smaller. He was carrying six bottles of milk stout, which he handed to George. 'They're for the ladies. My wife doesn't get going until she's had a few bottles of that.' He gave a shy grin. 'As yer know, she's usually very quiet, but she'll liven up when she's had a few.'

George chuckled. 'I noticed she was the quiet type, but she won't be shy when she gets used to everyone.' He pointed to the bottles he'd been handed. 'Thank you for these, but you shouldn't have bothered, because we've already got a dozen bottles.'

'Yer'll not have a bottle left by the end of the night, I promise,' Norman called. 'Lizzie's like Dolly, very partial to a bottle of milk stout . . . or two or three.'

'Put them in the kitchen, George, and now everyone is acquainted let's all make ourselves comfortable,' Ann said. 'It's going to be a tight squeeze for seats, I'm afraid. Some of us will have to sit on the wooden chairs.'

'If yer take my advice, me darlin', I'd not be putting Paddy on one of those. If yer did, yer could be using it for firewood in the morning 'cos it would be smashed to smithereens.'

'I say let the women sit at the table.' Lizzie used the arms of the chair to push herself up. 'We can pull the neighbours to pieces while the men get themselves drunk. I know enough about men to know they won't begin to enjoy themselves until they've had a few pints down them and on the way to being tiddly.'

'I'll pour the drinks.' George waited until the five ladies were seated, then asked what they would like. They all said milk stout, except Ann, who chose sherry. She couldn't imagine drinking a full bottle of stout, and anyway she'd taken a liking to sherry.

With the men settled in the fireside chairs and on the couch, with pint glasses in their hands, they began to get to know each other. Their first subject was the merits of Everton and Liverpool football teams. The second pint took them to discussing their jobs. They would stop now and again when there were roars of laughter from the table, and smile at each other as much as to say, it doesn't take much to amuse the womenfolk. But when the laughter turned to shrieks, they all cocked their ears.

Dolly was in full flow, recounting bygone days when she was a schoolgirl. 'There was this man that lived in our street who had a wooden leg. All the kids used to make fun of him and shout "Peg Leg Pete!" after him. Many's the bleedin' hiding I had off me mam when she heard me calling after him. Told me I'd be laughing the other side of me face when I grew up and had a wooden leg of me own.' Nodding her head and hoisting her bosom, Dolly took off her mother. '"Don't forget, God sees and hears everything what goes on. And it would be the price of yer if He heard yer mocking the poor man. He might decide to give you a wooden leg so yer can see what it feels like to be made fun of."'

'Yer mother was right, Dolly Flannery, so she was.' Although it was over thirty years since Dolly was a young girl, Bridie was feeling pity for the poor man. 'Sure, isn't it a sin to mock a man who is afflicted?'

Dolly's laughter filled the room. 'Bridie, if yer think me mam, God rest her soul, was an angel, wait until I tell yer what she did.' Leaning her bonny arms on the table, she went on, 'I came home from school one day, I must have been about eight, and me mam said she'd had the house to pieces looking for the hammer. A nail had come out of the woodwork and the back curtains had fallen down. I can see her now, standing in the middle of our living room and scratching her head, wondering what she could do. She'd tried hitting the nail with a shoe, but it had no effect at all. Then she said to me, "Go and ask Harry to lend me his wooden leg to hammer the nail back in." I thought she meant it and I must have gone as white as a sheet. "Go on, move yerself. And don't forget to say please." Now, because she was in such a temper and likely to belt me one, I was between the devil and the deep blue sea. I could either defy her and get a crack, or knock on Harry's door and get a crack off him.'

'With his wooden leg,' Milly said, hugely enjoying the proceedings. 'And that would have hurt more than yer mam's hand.'

Dolly, pausing for effect, noticed the men were sitting on the edge of their seats listening to what she was saying. So she piled the drama on. 'I ran into the street, sobbing me heart out and wishing me dad would come home from work and save me from a fate worse than death. I could see me mam watching me through the window, so I started to walk up the street to where this Harry lived. Me knees were knocking, me hands shaking and the tears were running down me cheeks. Then I had an idea. I wouldn't ask Harry if we could borrow his wooden leg, I'd ask for the loan of a hammer. So, feeling very clever, I lifted me hand to knock on his door. I was just inches away from it when I felt a hand grab me by the scruff of the neck and pull me backwards. It was me mam, and I could tell by the smile on her face she'd been pulling me leg all along. "That gave yer a fright, didn't it?" she said. "I hope it's taught yer a lesson, yer stupid article. Perhaps next time yer see Harry yer'll give him a smile instead of shouting names after him." And d'yer know, I never once called after him after that. And if any of me mates did, I used to chase them.' Dolly's mouth was dry with all the talking, and she drank her milk stout in one go. 'So there yer have it. The story of Peg Leg Pete.'

'After all that,' Ann said, 'how did your mother manage to knock the nail in?'

'The nail had never come out! Me mam had staged the whole thing to teach me a lesson. And her and me dad spent the whole night laughing at me for being stupid enough to believe she really wanted to borrow the wooden leg. The whole street got to know and me mates pulled me leg something shocking.'

'My mam sent me out once for a pennyworth of elbow grease.' Milly chuckled at the memory. 'The man in the corner shop nearly split his sides laughing. I felt a right nit.'

'When I first started work,' Norman said, 'I was as green as a cabbage, didn't have a ruddy clue. The bloke I was put to work with was a right character. Nothing to look at, mind, he was tall, as thin as a rake and his face had this grey pallor. He reminded me of someone who'd risen from the dead. Anyway, one day he asked me to run back to the factory and ask the foreman for a bubble for the spirit level. And like a bloody fool I did as he asked. I didn't doubt him for a minute, 'cos he wasn't one for telling jokes. Well, the boss's face was a picture. He didn't know whether to laugh or tell me off for being away from the job. Anyway, he sent me off with a flea in me ear, and it was only when I got outside his office that I heard him laughing so much he must have done himself an injury.'

'I often think of the old days in Ireland, when I was a youngster,' Bridie said. 'We were very poor, but so was everyone else, so we thought nothing of it. I have fond memories of those days, so I have. We often went hungry, but when yer have a loving family and many good friends, sure, the rumbling of yer tummy doesn't seem so bad at all.'

'Why did yer leave Ireland, Paddy?' Ken asked. 'It must have been a wrench leaving your family behind.'

'There was no work there and people were starving. My mam and dad were only in their early fifties when they died, and I swear they died because they'd lost the will to live. There was poverty all around, so there was, and no sign of anything better in the future.' For his size, Paddy had a quiet voice, and with the lovely lilt of Irish mixed in with a Liverpool accent, it was pleasing to the ears. 'When me and Bridie got married we stayed on to look after her mother. The poor woman was sick, and there was no one else to care for her. Our two boys were born in Ireland, but they remember little of it now. Anyway, when Bridie's mother passed away, there was nothing to keep us there. No future for our children. So we scraped together enough money for the fare to England. We've made a good life for ourselves and the children, but sure, haven't we left a bit of our hearts in the dear Emerald Isle? No matter how far in the world yer travel, yer never forget the place where yer were born, and that's a fact. Even the bad times yer remember with fondness.'

'We were poor when I was a kid,' Lizzie said, a finger circling the dimples in her elbows. 'I can remember being hungry and having holes in me shoes. But most of all I can remember the laughs we used to have. My ma was a real case, always had a smile on her face and no money in her purse. But somehow she always managed to have a dinner of some sort on the table.' Her eyes went from the women around the table to the men. 'I don't know whether I should tell yer this, 'cos me ma, God rest her soul, would turn in her grave if she heard. But it's an incident I've never forgotten because it made me realise more than anything what me ma had to go through to keep us fed and clothed. As yer know, Friday is always a hard-up day for everyone, what with getting paid on a Saturday. Well, one Friday I got home from school and me ma was in a right state. She didn't have a slice of bread in the house, never mind a dinner. She'd tried to borrow off the neighbours, but they were as skint as she was. Anyway, she tells me not to take me coat off 'cos I was going to the shops with her. I can remember as plain as day asking her how she could go shopping when she didn't have a bean. And she chucked me under the chin and said, "Ask no questions, girl, and yer'll be told no lies. And while we're out, you keep yer mouth closed no matter what I do."'

Lizzie sighed and laced her fingers before laying her arms flat on the table. 'She did no more than march me down to Irwin's shop and stood at the counter as bold as brass with her basket over her arm. My knees were knocking, but me ma had a smile pasted on her face. And as true as I sit here, she asked for a large loaf, two ounces of margarine and a quarter of brawn. I was hoping the ground would open and swallow me up. I mean, how was she going to pay for the stuff? Anyway, as the assistant was putting the things in the basket, me ma moves away from the counter and says, "Bloody hell, I've dropped me shilling! Get on yer knees, girl, and find it for us, it can't have gone far." So there was me, on me hands and knees, looking for something I knew wasn't there. And I was joined by the girl assistant, who was very kind and sympathetic. She couldn't see any sign of this missing shilling . . . well, she wouldn't, would she? Then the manager came over to see what was going on, and me ma told him, with tears in her eyes, that the shilling was all the money she had in the world. I can still see him patting her on the shoulder and telling her not to worry because the shilling must have rolled under one of the counters. Then he got down on his knees as well. And after ten minutes, when even customers were helping by this time, he must have felt a right nit and told me ma she could take the groceries as they were bound to find the shilling when they were brushing up after the shop closed.'

'Ay, your ma had a head on her shoulders,' Ken said. 'I think what she did was very clever. Very funny too, 'cos it must have looked hilarious with the manager and everyone on hands and knees looking for a bob that never was!'

'Oh, not everyone was on their hands and knees, Ken. Me ma just stood and watched! And on the way home, with the goods safely in the basket, she looked down at me and said, "I couldn't get down on me knees, Lizzie, 'cos I've got a bleedin' big hole in the sole of me shoe. And after all, I do have me pride."'

Amid the laughter that followed, Norman said, 'Yer must take after yer ma, Lizzie, 'cos you can get blood out of a stone.'

'You can't leave it there, Lizzie,' Ann said. 'What was the outcome?'

'Well, as soon as me dad got in with his wages on Saturday dinner time, she was off like a shot, with her basket over her arm. She didn't ask me to go with her this time, so I only know what she told me. The manager was very apologetic and said they'd searched high and low and couldn't find the shilling. He asked if she was sure it was a shilling she'd dropped, as they'd found a sixpence which had rolled under the counter.'

Paddy's deep chuckle rumbled. 'And did yer ma tell him she could have sworn it was a shilling but she could have been wrong?'

'No, she said she'd told enough lies and wasn't about to add to them by saying the sixpence was hers. So she told the manager that she was sorry to have caused such a nuisance, and it was her own fault for not being more careful. And she paid him the money she owed for the few groceries he'd let her have.' Lizzie leaned towards Ann and pointed a stiffened finger. Then, wagging the finger, she repeated what her ma had said. '"Not one word do yer say to yer dad, understand? He'd have me guts for garters if he found out."'

'And you never told anyone, Lizzie?' George asked.

'Not a soul until now. But I learned a lesson that day which has stayed with me all me life. My ma had no intention of fiddling the shop out of the money, she did it out of desperation. All so she could put food in our bellies. Times are hard now for some poor buggers, but they were a damn sight worse in those days.'

'I can remember when I was a lad there were a few times I went around barefoot 'cos me ma couldn't even afford a pair of second-hand shoes from the market,' Frank told them. 'She used to take in washing and scrub floors to earn a few coppers. Me dad was a docker, and it was worse on the docks then than it is now. He was lucky if he got two days' work in, which barely paid the rent. If it hadn't been for me ma, we'd have been thrown out on the street and ended up in the workhouse.'

Lizzie nodded. 'The women were the mainstay of the families in those days, God bless them. That's why very few lived to a ripe old age, they were worn out with work and worry.' Then she banged a clenched fist on the table. 'This is supposed to be a bleedin' party, George, what's happened to the drinks?'

'They're on their way, Lizzie.' George caught his brother's eye. 'Come on, our kid, give us a hand. The sooner they get their drinks, the quicker they'll be drunk enough to enjoy themselves.'

Half an hour later Paddy was persuaded to give a song. And he chose one that was very popular called 'Maggie'. He had a powerful voice, and the haunting melody and sad words had Lizzie wiping away the tears. Under her breath she croaked, 'This bleedin' song always makes me bawl me eyes out.'

There was a ripple of applause for Paddy when he'd finished, and requests for an encore. But he wasn't to be coaxed. 'Let one of the ladies give a turn now.'

His wife whooped. 'Paddy Hanrahan, yer know I've got a voice like a foghorn, right enough, so don't be expecting me to make a fool of meself.'

Lizzie could see by Ann's face that they didn't have a snowball's chance in hell of getting her on her feet. Then she had a bright idea. 'I know, the ladies will all sing together and the men can harmonise. Come on, girls, on yer feet and we'll do the job properly.'

'Lizzie, I don't know any songs,' Ann wailed. 'I've never sung a song in my life.'

'Oh, yer'll know this one, queen, it's the song the drunks sing when they're being thrown out of the pub at closing time.'

Dolly was all for it. 'Come on, girls, let's show the men how it's done.' She pulled a face at Bridie. 'Even the voice of a foghorn isn't going to get yer off the hook, Bridie. And you, Milly, I don't care what yer voice is like, get on yer feet. As for you, Ann, yer have no choice. As the hostess ye're obligated to entertain yer guests.'

The table was quickly pushed back and the women formed a group. There was some whispering, then Lizzie said, 'On the count of three, girls. And if yer forget the words, just hum.' Then she waved her hand as though she was carrying a baton. 'Now!'

> 'There's an old mill by the stream – Nellie Dean,
> Where we used to sit and dream – Nellie Dean,
> And the waters as they flow, seem to murmur soft and low,
> You are my heart's desire, I love you – Nellie Dean.
> Sweet – Nellie – Dean.'

The men harmonised all the way through the song, and they did it well. 'I think we stole the show there, gents, don't you?' Ken's face was flushed with the effects of beer and the warmth in the room. And he was thoroughly enjoying himself. 'Let's have another song. What shall it be this time?'

George made his way over to his wife. She had kept up valiantly with the other ladies and was both surprised and pleased with herself. 'You did well, love, and you seem to be enjoying yourself.'

'George, I'm having the time of my life. Who would ever have thought I'd stand up in front of people and sing? Well, I won't say "sing" because that would be flattering myself. I was humming most of the time until I got used to the words.'

'You look lovely,' he said softly. 'And I can't resist a kiss.'

Ann's hand went to her mouth and her eyes widened. 'You can't kiss me in front of all these people! What will they think?'

'They'll think I'm a man who loves his wife very much.' George cleared his throat before facing the neighbours. 'My wife is of the opinion it shouldn't be done in public. But I am of the opinion a kiss should be given when the need is there. So, if you'd kindly close your eyes, folks, I'd like to kiss my wife.'

There were whistles and cat-calls, and Ann's face was the colour of beetroot. But the action found favour with the ladies. 'Can yer imagine my feller kissing me like that?' Lizzie folded her arms, a sure sign she meant business. 'I bet he'd rather kiss the bar counter in the pub than kiss his wife. The woman that he married and said he loved. And what about those promises to look after me in sickness and in health? Ay, and what about the bit that said yer had to honour me with thy body?'

Norman was in stitches. 'How can I look after yer in sickness when ye're never ruddy well sick, missus? And as for honouring yer with me body, how can I do that when yer turn away as soon as I get down to me singlet?'

'Ay, now, that's enough!' Lizzie bristled. 'There's no need to start getting personal just 'cos yer can't be arsed getting up to give me a kiss.'

Norman was up like a shot. 'Never let it be said that my loved one is going short in the romance department. Come here, wench.'

Frank looked across at Paddy. 'I think we'd better make the effort, otherwise our dear wives will take exception to being left out. And when Dolly gets a cob on, she usually reaches for the rolling pin. Unless the poker is nearer to hand, like, 'cos she's not really fussy.'

Paddy got to his size sixteen feet and held his arms wide. 'Bridie, me darlin', would yer not be giving yer loving husband a kiss?'

Frank didn't have to move from the spot, because his wife came to him. Putting her hands around his waist, she lifted him off the floor. 'Ah, we can't leave you out, can we, light of my life? Give us a kiss and make it a real sloppy one.'

'Ay, we'll have none of that,' Lizzie said, her arms wrapped around her husband's waist. 'Ann runs a respectable house.' She began to laugh. 'What a pity she hasn't got respectable friends to go with it.'

'Would yer mind speaking for yerself, Mrs Woman?' Bridie stuck her nose in the air. 'I'll have yer know that me and me husband are altogether respectable, so we are. Yer could take us anywhere and we'd fit in.' Hanging on to Paddy's arm, she lifted her hand and waved grandly, as she'd seen royalty doing on the Pathé News at the picture house. 'We're at ease with the wealthy, the hoi polloi and even tramps.'

'We don't belong with the first two,' Dolly said. 'That leaves us with the bleedin' tramps! Isn't that nice, coming from someone who's supposed to be a friend?'

'Don't be getting yer knickers in a twist, Dolly.' Lizzie eased herself from Norman's arms. 'Come on, George, ye're the slowest bartender I've ever seen. Get yer skates on and dish out the drinks. Then we can have another sing-song instead of standing here all lovey-dovey like lovesick sixteen-year-olds.'

Ken was following his brother to the kitchen to give him a hand with the drinks, and when he was passing Lizzie he asked, 'What song are we having next, girl? Just so I can tune me vocal cords, like.'

'I thought a lively one this time, Ken, to get us all going. How about "Wait Till The Sun Shines, Nellie"?'

'Just the job that, girl! Sound as a pound! I know all the words to that so I'll give yer a solo if yer like.'

'No, we'll all sing it together, lad. It's that sort of song, yer see. If yer were singing it on yer own, we'd all join in anyway 'cos we know the words. But later on yer can sing a nice romantic one for Milly, she'd like that.'

'Like it!' Milly's mouth gaped. 'If my feller ever did, or said, anything romantic, I'd think he was sickening for something. I don't get a kiss when he comes home from work at night, like Ann does. All I get is, "What's for dinner, girl?" Or, "What the blazes have yer done with the ruddy *Echo*? And don't say it's under the cushion 'cos I've looked and it's not."'

'Same here, girl,' Dolly said, her head nodding knowingly. 'Sometimes all I get is a flippin' grunt, and that's if I'm lucky.'

'Yer've brought them up wrong,' Lizzie said. 'Yer haven't got them house-trained like Norman is. And ye're too late to start now, 'cos once they're in the habit, yer'll never change them if yer live to be a hundred.' She gazed at Dolly and burst out laughing. 'Mind you, if all ye're getting is a grunt, life can't be very exciting for yer, so yer probably wouldn't want to live to be a hundred anyway.'

'Here's the drinks, ladies.' Ken handed the glasses out. 'Drink it up and then we can make ourselves happy singing about the sunshine.'

Next door, Nellie Bingham was in a dark mood. She'd sit for a minute and then get up and pace the floor, shaking her fist at the wall, through which they could hear the singing and laughter. Her husband, Joe, was there, which was unusual. And Joe sober was a very different man to Joe the drunkard. He had a book open on his knee, but although his eyes were on the page, he wasn't reading. He could hear the jollity coming from next door, but it didn't worry him. It was Boxing Day, a day when most people in the street would be celebrating with their

302

families. No, the noise didn't worry him, but his wife's behaviour did. And the boys were sitting so quietly he knew they were on edge.

'Why don't yer sit down, pet, and the four of us can have a game of cards to pass the time away.'

'How can yer concentrate with that racket going on? I think they've got a bleedin' cheek, singing their heads off without a thought for anyone else. I've a good mind to knock on their door and tell them what I think of them.'

'They're entitled to have a party at Christmas, Nellie, that's what most folks do. There's no reason why we can't have a drink and play a hand of cards, instead of sitting like stuffed rabbits.' Joe kept his voice low so as not to antagonise his wife. 'Come on, pet, sit yerself down and have a drink. I'm sure the boys would like a game of cards.'

'Yes we would, Mam,' Jack said. 'Wouldn't we, Willy?'

His younger brother nodded. 'It would be better than sitting here doing nowt.'

Just at that moment the singing and laughter from next door increased in volume, and Nellie took off. 'That's it, I'm not putting up with that no more.' She picked up the poker, intending to knock on the wall, but Jack had jumped to his feet and he caught hold of her wrist. 'Don't do it, Mam.'

'Let go of my arm, Jack, or I'll belt yer one.' Nellie didn't mean it, she didn't even know what she was saying. She wanted to hit out at someone, and next door were the ideal targets. 'I said let go!'

'That's enough now, from both of yer.' When Joe stood up, the book fell to the floor. 'Can we have one night when there's no fighting or arguing?'

'Me and me mam never argue, Dad, and I know she wouldn't belt me one. But I don't want her knocking on the wall just 'cos they're having a bit of a party.'

'A bit of a party, did yer say? Sounds like a bleedin' big party to me, they're making enough noise to wake the dead.' Nellie tried to free her hand. 'We don't have to put up with it and I'm going to let them know.'

'Will yer listen to me, Mam,' Jack pleaded. 'That girl next door, Tess, is the only one in the street that's treated me decent. None of the other neighbours look at me or Willy, but she went out of her way to talk to me. And she was nice and real friendly. She told me they were having a party, she was really looking forward to it. So don't spoil it for them, Mam, please? And don't spoil it for me either, because it's a nice change to have a friend in the street.'

Nellie dropped her head and let the poker slip from her fingers. 'She's only a kid.'

'I know she's only a kid,' Jack said. 'But she's a nice kid.' He could see the tears well up in his mother's eyes, and said, 'Don't cry, Mam, please.'

The next minute Nellie was in her husband's arms and he was gently patting her back. 'Come on, pet, there's no need for those tears. Yer know we all love yer more than anything in the world.'

Sobbing loudly, Nellie said, 'I don't know what comes over me, Joe, I just can't help it.'

'We all understand, sweetheart, so dry yer eyes and Willy will get the cards out while Jack fixes us all a drink. And we'll sit around the table like a family should, and have a laugh every time I lose a hand at cards.' He bent his head and whispered, 'I do love yer, yer know.'

'And I love you, Joe. Sometimes I wonder how yer can put up with me.'

When Jack came back with a glass of sherry, Nellie took it from him, saying, 'You and Willy are good lads, and I am proud of yer even if I don't always show it.'

Chapter Twenty-two

Ann wrapped the woollen scarf tightly around Tess's neck, then brought the ends together to cover her chest. 'Are you sure you feel well enough for school, Theresa? You look very peaky to me.'

'I'll be all right, Mam, honest. I don't want to stay off school, because I'll be behind the rest of the class then.'

'One day in bed would do you more good! The wind is bitter and there's still a bit of snow and ice about. I'm sure Miss Harrison would understand.'

'No, Mam! I want to go to school!' Tess was getting agitated. She did feel rotten, but didn't want to give in to it. The thought of going back to the days when she was never in school made her determined to fight the cold she could feel coming on. Perhaps it would go away in a day or two. A lot of the girls in her class had coughs and sneezes, and they didn't stay home in bed. 'I'll be all right, honest!'

Maddy was standing by, all wrapped up and ready to go. 'We're going to be late if we don't put a move on. Let Tess come with me, Mam, and I'll see her at playtime. If I think she's not well I'll tell Miss Harrison.'

Ann sighed. 'Just one day at home could prevent you from getting worse and having to spend a week in bed. But seeing as you're determined, and against my better judgement, I'll give in. But you have to promise me you'll tell the teacher if you don't feel well.'

'I promise.'

Maddy held on tight to her sister's arm, because it was very slippy underfoot, and being ever protective, she didn't want her to fall and get hurt. And as Ann watched them walking down the street, she thanked God for her elder daughter. Maddy had never once complained or shown any resentment over Theresa getting so much attention. In fact she fussed over her sister like a mother hen. Ann knew in her heart that as soon as the playtime bell sounded, Maddy would be out searching the playground. And as she closed the door she told herself that where Theresa was concerned, Maddy had more sense than she herself had. All the years of wrapping her sickly daughter in cotton wool, not letting the wind blow on her, had only made it worse for the child by weakening her resistance to any bugs that were in the air.

Ann made for the kitchen and the washing-up. After that the dolly tub would be brought out to soak the clothes and bedding waiting to be washed. And as she worked, she talked to the empty kitchen. 'I did what I thought was best for her, but I was wrong. She'd have been stronger and tougher if I hadn't kept her in every time she sneezed.' She took her hands out of the soapy water and rested them on the side of the sink. Looking out of the window on a sky that threatened either rain or more snow, she said, 'Everything I did was with the best intentions because I love her so much. And Madelaine, of course, but she is very seldom sick. I don't think she's had more than two days off school since she started.'

A knock on the front door had her wiping her hands down her pinny as she hurried through the living room. She hoped it was no one she had to ask in, because she hadn't tidied up yet. The fire was lit, but she hadn't polished the grate.

'Hello, Dolly! Goodness, you are early this morning.'

Dolly didn't wait to be asked, she just pushed her way in and made straight for the fire. 'I thought I'd get to the shops early and get it over with. I've got a bleedin' tub full of clothes to start on when I get back.' She put her basket on the floor while she held her hands out to the flames. 'It's a corker out there, girl, cold enough to freeze the you-know-what off a monkey.' There was a look of pure bliss on her face when the warmth started to seep through to her body. 'Bleedin' lovely that is.' Then she bent down and took a magazine from the basket at her feet. 'I'm sorry I haven't given this back before now, girl, but I've been doing the rounds with it. I hate people who brag, but I haven't half done my share this last week, I can tell yer. Everyone I know has seen Tess's story, but if I think of someone I've left out I'll borrow it again.' Her chubby face creased into a smile. 'Ay, yer should have seen the airs and graces I put on when I told them it had been written by the daughter of a friend of mine. Talk about toff wasn't in it. I even cleaned me bleedin' nails so I could point to where they had to read. It's not often I've got anything to brag about, so I made the most of it. Ye're not just a friend, ye're me very best friend whether yer like it or not, so there! But joking aside, young Tess is very clever on the quiet. Yer should be proud of her.'

'I didn't want her to go to school this morning because I think she's getting a cold, but she would have it that I let her go.' Like Lizzie, Dolly Flannery always seemed to be in a good temper. She was never without a smile and could make a joke out of anything. Her very presence lifted Ann's spirits. 'Would you like a quick cuppa before you go to the shops?'

'No thanks, girl, I'll go while there's not many people about to save hanging around waiting to be served. Is there anything I can get yer, save yer going out? It's deadly trying to walk out there, ye're slipping all over the ruddy place.'

'We're having left-overs for dinner, but I need a loaf and a quarter of corned beef for the girls' lunch and George's carry-out. That's if you don't mind?'

'I don't mind, girl, it's no skin off my nose, 'cos I'm going to the shops anyway.'

'I'll get my purse and give you the money.'

'Nah, pay me when I get back. I'm so flush these days with both kids working I don't know meself. But if that cuppa's still on offer, I'll take yer up on it and rest me weary body for half an hour before I go back to the drudgery of wash day.'

'You take care, now,' Ann warned. 'Watch where you're walking.'

The chubby face beamed. 'If I'm not back in an hour, yer'll know I've gone arse over elbow and yer'd better send for the lifeguards. Oh, and tell them to send nice-looking ones, I don't want no ugly buggers lifting me up. I've got me pride.'

Ann was smiling when she closed the door. To think she'd been worried about missing Hanford Avenue! She'd made friends so quickly here her days had been filled, and she wouldn't go back now for any money. She missed Maisie and her family, but they'd exchanged visits a few times, and as Maisie said, they would always be friends.

Her movements brisk, Ann finished the dishes, put four pans of water on the stove to boil for the dolly tub, then tidied and dusted the living room. She was just finished, and standing back to make sure there was nothing she'd missed, when the knocker sounded. This couldn't be Dolly, there hadn't been time for her to get to the shops and back. Throwing the duster in the cleaning box under the stairs, she went to answer the door.

'It's only me, me darlin'.' Bridie was so well wrapped up, only her nose and eyes were visible. 'I'm off to the shops and wondered if you wanted me to get yer anything. It's not fit weather for man nor beast, and it's meself that would be sitting in front of the fire if me bread bin wasn't empty.'

'Dolly called about fifteen minutes ago, on her way to the shops, and she's getting me the few things I need. But thanks, Bridie, I appreciate the offer.'

'I'll see if I can catch up with Dolly, me darlin'. If we hang on to each other, sure we've more chance of staying upright.'

'I rather think Dolly is hoping she falls,' Ann laughed. 'I've had strict instructions to call out the lifeguards if she's not back within the hour. Oh, and they've got to be nice-looking lifeguards, 'cos she's got her pride.'

Bridie chuckled. 'That woman is a case, so she is. But I'd not be having her any other way, and that's the truth. Yer know exactly where yer are with Dolly. What yer see is what yer get, like it or lump it.'

'I'm making a pot of tea for when she gets back, and you're very welcome to join us.'

Bridie nodded. 'Just the job, me darlin', just the job.'

Ann was looking through the window and she had the door open before they could knock. She waited until they were in the living room before asking, 'Well, no slip-ups? All in one piece I see?'

Dolly did contortions with her face before she was satisfied she had the right expression to do justice to the tale she was about to tell. 'Ye're never going to believe this! But I'll have to sit down to tell yer, 'cos I'm all overcome.'

Without another word, they all sat down. Bridie and Ann faced Dolly across the table, and they waited as she stared into space. In the end, Bridie burst out laughing. 'It looks like a fortune-tellers' meeting and we're waiting for Dolly to tell us what's in store for us.'

'Ay, girl, if I'd known what was going to happen to me today, I'd have put me best blue fleecy-lined bloomers on.'

Ann held back the laughter. 'Why, whatever on earth happened?'

'A miracle, girl, a bleedin' miracle. I got to the corner of the street and it was that slippy I thought I was going to fall. And I would have done if two strong arms hadn't held on to me. And when I looked up to see who my saviour was, I came over all funny and thought I'd died and gone to heaven.' She gazed up at the ceiling and put her hands together as though in prayer. 'Forgive me, God, I nearly said "bleedin' heaven" then. But as quick as a flash I told meself it wouldn't put me in Your good books, so I didn't say it. And I hope that when the day comes and I have to face my Maker, You have a blinking good memory.'

'The good Lord will need more than a good memory, Dolly Flannery,' Bridie said, trying to look stern. 'It's a sense of humour He'll be needing, and a very forgiving nature.'

'Don't be getting yer knickers in a twist, Bridie, I have no intention of facing me Maker just yet. And I'll make me apologies to Him in bed tonight, when I'm saying me prayers.'

Ann remembered the tea. 'Oh, crikey, the tea will be stiff. Not one word out of either of you until I get back.' And silence reigned until they each had a cup of tea in front of them. 'I didn't have time to look for biscuits, you'll have to do without.' She folded her arms and sat back in the chair. 'And now, Dolly, let's hear what you've been up to.'

'I haven't been up to nothing, girl, 'cos as I told Victor, I'm a married woman.'

'Who the heck is Victor?'

Dolly clicked her tongue. 'He's the bloke what stopped me from landing on me backside! Very tall and handsome, with eyes the colour of the sky on a summer's day, and a strong, rugged face. And dressed to the nines he was, with a posh overcoat and a grey trilby set at an angle, like yer see on the pictures. And he took a liking to me right away, I could see. He introduced himself and asked me name. Then he asked if I'd like to have dinner with him tonight at the Adelphi Hotel. Sadly I had to tell him I wasn't a free woman, I was already took by me husband. He was dead upset and begged me to leave me husband and walk off into the sunset with him. A life of luxury I'd have, waited on hand and foot and wanting for nothing. But I stood firm and told him I couldn't walk out on me husband and kids. And I told him I'd have to go because me dolly tub was full of dirty clothes. He tried again to coax me, but I wasn't having any. So I held out me hand to shake his and say goodbye, and d'yer know what he did? He lifted it to his lips and kissed it.' She rubbed the back of her left hand. 'I'll never wash this hand again as long as I live.'

'I didn't know you were ambidextrous, Dolly,' Ann said, tongue in cheek. 'I've never noticed.'

Dolly put her folded arms under her bosom and hoisted it up so she could lean across the table in comfort. 'What was that yer called me, girl?'

'Before I tell you, can I ask if you're left-handed?'

'Am I heckerslike! I'm as right-handed as you are!'

Kicking Bridie under the table, Ann said, 'No you're not, because when I shake hands I use my right hand.'

'And what d'yer think I shake, pray? A bleedin' leg?'

'I'm just curious, that's all. I mean why are you never going to wash your left hand when it was the right one that Victor kissed?'

Dolly leaned back and her arms appeared from under the rather large bosom. She held her hands in front of her face and chuckled. 'I told yer I didn't know me arse from me elbow. But it was a good story, don't yer think? Makes a day look less miserable when yer can have a laugh. I made it up while I was waiting for the man to cut your corned beef. If yer'd been getting half a pound instead of a quarter, I'd have had more time to spice it up a little. Yer know, something like yer see on the pictures, where a couple bump into each other when they're turning a corner and it's love at first sight. Romance blossoms just by looking into each other's eyes, and they know they're made for each other.'

309

She pressed both hands to her tummy to stop it from shaking while she chuckled. 'Love at first sight, me backside! How d'yer know when yer meet someone for the first time whether they've got sweaty feet or bad breath?'

'It was a very good story, Dolly. In fact it's meself that would go as far as to say it was one of yer best.' Bridie couldn't stop laughing inside as her imagination ran riot. In her mind's eye she could visualise Dolly slipping on a patch of ice, her arms waving in the air, and a man rushing forward to help. Only Dolly's seventeen stone was too much for him and he ended up on his back, vowing never to try and be a gentleman again because it didn't pay. 'And when I tell Paddy tonight he'll laugh his head off. I might even embellish it a little to make it more interesting.'

Dolly's eyes became slits. 'Are you two having a bleedin' laugh at my expense?'

Ann feigned horror. 'Good heavens, of course not! Why would me and Bridie want to laugh at you?'

'It's these bleedin' long words ye're using that I've never heard in me flaming life! Like, what is Bridie going to do to me story when she's telling Paddy? All I could understand was that it had something to do with me belly, and I think it's getting a bit too personal for my liking. I mean, what's my belly got to do with Paddy?'

'Sure, I never mentioned yer belly, me darlin', yer must have misheard me. What I said was that I might embellish it a little to make it more interesting.'

Dolly tapped her fingers on the table. 'Embellish, eh? Well, would yer kindly explain to me what it means, so I can try it on me unsuspecting husband?'

Bridie thought long and hard, her eyes rolling from side to side as she tried to find the right words to explain. Then her smile came. 'It means to add something nice.'

'Go 'way! Well, yer live and learn, don't yer? So in bed tonight, if my feller is feeling frisky, which is once every blue moon, like, I can safely tell him to embellish it?'

Ann had just taken a drink of tea, and when she roared with laughter it spurted out and just missed Dolly by inches. 'Oh, I'm sorry about that, but if I'd tried to swallow it I'd have choked. You'll have to warn me in future, Dolly, when you're going to say anything outrageous so I can be prepared.' She saw the gleam in her neighbour's eye and knew what was coming. 'Before you ask, ambidextrous means someone who can use both hands equally well.'

'Well, I've learnt a valuable lesson today, girls,' Dolly said, 'and I'm going to share me new-found knowledge with me husband. Tonight in bed, after I've told him to embellish, I'll tell him to be ambidextrous at the same time.'

'What would yer do with the woman?' Bridie asked, pretending to be shocked. 'Sure, yer'd be afraid to take her anywhere, so yer would.'

A wicked gleam came to Dolly's eyes. 'Afraid to take me anywhere! Me what's ambidextrous and can embellish like no one's business? Yer don't know how lucky yer are having a friend like me.'

'Oh, we know that, right enough, me darlin',' Bridie said, getting to her feet and pushing her chair back under the table. 'We know when we're well off.'

Dolly pulled a face. 'The party's over, is it? Back to the bleedin' grind. Life's a bugger, isn't it?' She levered herself up, then thought of something to keep them there a little longer. 'Ay, I never hear anything about the queer one next door. How are yer getting on with her?'

Ann spread her hands and shrugged her shoulders. 'I never see the woman! She takes off occasionally and makes a racket, but she's a lot quieter than she was. And she doesn't throw so much over the wall now. Theresa talks to the eldest boy if she's in the street when he comes home from work, and Madelaine will if she's not with one of her mates. According to them both he's a nice boy but rather shy. I had to laugh at Theresa when she saw him coming home from work for the first time in long trousers. She said he looked real grown up and very handsome, and she'd told him so.'

'I think your Tess could melt the heart of the divil himself,' Bridie said. 'She has a way with her that's rare in young girls today. Most of them are too old in the head for their age.'

'I'm going,' Dolly said with determination. 'Sitting here thinking about me washing isn't going to get it done.' At the door she turned. 'Let me get this straight now. It's embellish and ambidextrous, right?'

When both women nodded, she grinned. 'I'll use them on my feller in bed tonight and I'll let yer know how I get on. If I've got a cob on me don't ask, 'cos it'll mean it was one of those nights when he had a splitting headache.'

One look at Tess when she came home was enough to tell Ann her daughter was worse than she'd been that morning. 'I should never have let you go to school, you're not fit.'

Maddy unwound her scarf and threw it on the couch. 'Miss Harrison said to tell you that Tess has been coughing and sneezing, and she's got a temperature. She said it would be advisable to keep her home for a few days. There's four other girls in her class off with the same thing.'

Ann helped her daughter off with her coat. 'I'll make a bed up on the couch where you'll be nice and warm. But sit at the table for now and try to eat the sandwiches.'

'I'm not hungry, Mam.'

'Try and eat them for my sake, love. Even if it's only one, that would help. I'll make a rice pudding for you this afternoon, you'll enjoy that.'

'Shall I pour the tea out while you're making the couch up for Tess?' Maddy asked. 'I've only got twenty minutes.'

'That would be a help, love.' Ann put a hand on her elder daughter's shoulder. 'Do you feel all right, Madelaine? No sign of a cold or the shivers?'

'No, I feel as fit as a fiddle! But I'd say half the girls in our class have got colds. The one who sits next to me, Miriam, has done nothing all morning but blow her nose. I just hope she doesn't pass it on to me, I don't want to stay off school now because I need a good reference for when I go after a job, and good timekeeping is important.'

'Yes it is, love, but I don't think you need have any fears on that score, you must have a good record for attendance and punctuality.'

'I'll never get a job with my record,' Tess moaned, sitting on the couch and looking very dejected. 'I'm off school more than I'm in.'

'There's two years for you to make up for lost time, and you'll do it,' Ann said with conviction. 'You've gone seven or eight months without any problems, and as Madelaine said, half the school have got colds so you're not on your own this time.'

When Ann went upstairs to fetch some bedding, Maddy patted the chair next to her. 'Come and sit here and try to eat a sandwich.'

Tess felt as though her body was filled with cement, it was so heavy. And her headache was making it difficult to keep her eyes open. She sat next to her sister and rested her head on the table. 'Why does it always happen to me?'

'Don't start feeling sorry for yourself, Tess, or you'll make yourself really miserable. And to make Mam happy, try and eat a sandwich. And while you're doing that, I'll tell you how lucky you are.' Maddy waited until her sister had picked up a piece of bread, then continued, 'I know I don't get colds or have to stay off school, but neither have I ever had a story I've written printed in a magazine! That's a real achievement, Tess, better than anything I'll ever do.'

Her sister seemed to perk up and take an interest. 'Yes, I am lucky, aren't I?' But she wasn't going to be selfish and sing her own praises. 'I'll never be as clever as you, Maddy, you shine in every subject and can knock spots off me.'

'Seeing as I'm two years older than you, I'd be in a pretty pickle if I didn't know more than you do! You can learn a lot in that time and in the end you'll probably leave me standing.'

Tess leaned sideways to give her a hug. 'I'll never leave you standing, Maddy, never! You're my big sister and I love you.'

Upstairs, Ann pulled the eiderdown off the bed and folded it in four to put over her arm. Then on top of that she put two pillows. When she got to the top of the stairs she found she couldn't see her feet, and with both arms full couldn't use the banister to help negotiate the steep stairs. So she called down, 'Madelaine, would you catch these two pillows for me, please, before I trip and break my neck?'

'I'll come up, Mam!'

'No, stand at the bottom and I'll throw them to you.' Ann was pleased to see Theresa eating, even though she didn't seem to be enjoying it. 'You'll be nice and warm and comfortable on here. Better than in your bedroom where the draughts nearly blow you off your feet.'

'Can't I sleep in my bed tonight? I don't want to leave Maddy on her own, she'll be cold without me to cuddle up to.'

Ann plumped up the pillows and spread the eiderdown over the couch. 'You should really stay in the same temperature if you want to get better. But we won't talk about that now, we'll see what your dad has to say.'

Maddy could see her sister wasn't well pleased, so she quickly tried to take her mind off the subject. 'While I'm at school, bored to death with a history lesson, you'll be as snug as a bug in a rug.' Then, as though she'd just had a brain wave, she said, 'Hey, what about doing some writing? You've got plenty of paper and pencils, so you've no excuse and it will help you pass the time.'

'Ooh, I wouldn't know what to write about and my head's all fuzzy.'

'It won't be after our mam gives you a Beecham's Powder and you've been lying down for a while. And I know what you can write about, you've talked about it often enough.'

'What's that, Maddy?'

'Mrs Lizzie and her talking rose.' Maddy was smiling encouragement. 'But you can't use Mrs Lizzie's swear words, though.'

That brought a smile to the flushed face. 'That would be nice. Mrs Lizzie wouldn't mind, would she, Mam?'

'Mind! She'd be over the moon! Very honoured in fact.' Ann opened the door of the cupboard in the recess at the side of the fireplace and brought out a clean nightdress. 'I'll put this on the fireguard to warm through. Now drink your tea, Theresa, and I'll get you settled down. I haven't got a Beecham's Powder in, so I'll have to run to the corner shop. You'll be all right on your own for five minutes.'

'I can bring one in on my way home from school, Mam, save you going out.' Maddy was getting herself wrapped up against the cold wind outside. 'I'll run all the way home.'

313

Ann thought of how worried she would be leaving her younger daughter in the house on her own. What would happen if a spark flew out of the hearth and the rug caught fire? 'That's a good idea, you can get a packet while you're at it.' From her purse she took a shilling. 'I don't know how much they are but that should be plenty.'

Maddy bent and put the silver coin in her shoe. 'It'll be safe there.' She kissed Tess on the cheek. 'I hope you feel better by the time I get home.'

Nellie Bingham heard her neighbour's door open and flew to the window. She moved the curtain aside and pressed her forehead against the glass pane. It wasn't that she was being nosy, but she had no one to talk to all day, so taking an interest in the goings-on in the street was her pastime. She saw Maddy step down on to the pavement and heard Ann saying, 'Don't forget the Beecham's, love, Tess needs them to bring her temperature down.'

Once Maddy was out of sight, Nellie let the curtain drop back into place. She returned to the rocking chair at the side of the fireplace, thinking the young girl next door must be sick. This brought back memories that had torn her apart for the last six years. She tried to keep them at bay because they hurt so much, but every now and again something happened to trigger them off. Rocking the chair gently back and forth, she stared at the flickering flames as the tears ran unchecked down her cheeks.

George was in a happy frame of mind when he came home that night. He had some good news which would delight his wife. The broad smile on his face when he let himself in faded as soon as he saw his daughter lying on the couch. His eyes went to Ann. 'What's wrong with Tess, is she ill?'

'She's got a heavy cold, but she's not on her own because a lot of the children have come down with it. I've given her a Beecham's and she's had a dish of rice pudding.'

George hung his coat up before sitting on the edge of the couch. 'I won't touch you, pet, because my hands are freezing. D'you feel any better since you had the Beecham's?'

'Yes, Dad, my head isn't so full. And I ate every bit of the rice pudding and really enjoyed it. Especially the skin off the top, that's my favourite.'

'If I'd been here you would have had to share it with me,' Maddy said jokingly. 'I love the skin as well.' She glanced at her mother. 'D'you think it's worth me getting a cold, Mam? Is there room on the couch for two?'

314

'There's many a true word spoken in jest, love, so think on.'

When Ann went to the kitchen to put out the dinners, George followed her. 'I had a bit of good news today, love. Mr Fisher called me into his office and told me I'd been given a half a crown rise to start from this Saturday.'

She put her arms around his neck. 'Oh, that's marvellous news. You definitely deserve a kiss for that.' And her kiss held all the love she had for him. 'The way things are going we should be able to have a full week in Wales this year.'

'That's what I was thinking. Let's tell the girls, eh? Maddy will be delighted and it will cheer Tess up. It will give us all something to look forward to.'

Willy Bingham stamped his feet to keep the circulation going. He was frozen to the core, but he wanted to meet Jack coming home from work to tell him their mam had been crying. He'd asked her why she was crying but she'd just said she felt out of sorts. He knew this wasn't true, but at thirteen years of age he wasn't capable of finding the words that might comfort her and stop the crying.

'What are yer doing out here on yer own? Why aren't yer in by the fire?'

Willy jumped when his father came up behind him. 'I was waiting for our Jack.'

'Get in the house before yer turn into a block of ice.' When his son seemed reluctant, Joe asked, 'What's wrong, son?'

'Me mam's been crying and I didn't know what to do. Something must have happened to upset her and I was waiting for our Jack so I could go in with him.'

'Yer should be used to yer mam by now, and yer know she can't help it.' Joe Bingham sighed for the life that might have been. He put his arm around his son's shoulders and pulled him close. 'If it's company yer want, let's go in together.' He turned the key in the lock and shouted, 'I'm home, love.'

'In the kitchen! I'm just seeing to yer dinner.'

Joe ruffled his son's hair. 'Get that coat off, son, and sit near the fire. Yer must be frozen standing out there.' He chucked the boy under the chin before making his way to the kitchen. 'Everything all right, love?'

Nellie kept her back to him. 'Same as usual. The bleedin' weather would get yer down.'

'Willy said yer seemed out of sorts, is that right?'

'No, I'm all right,' Nellie told him quietly. 'It's been one of those days when I don't seem to be able to buck meself up. But I'll get over it, it's a case of having to.'

315

'I'll tell yer what, I'll stay in tonight. Instead of going to the pub I'll get a couple of bottles of beer in and we can have a game of cards. How does that sound?'

'Yer'd get more pleasure out of going to the pub than yer would staying in with me. I'm not fit company for anyone.'

'I'd rather stay in with you and the boys. They enjoy a game of cards, and they'll be glad of something to do, because they don't get out much.'

Nellie knew this was a gentle reminder that they hadn't been the best of parents to their sons for a long time. 'Yes, you stay in and we'll play cards. I'd like that.'

Lizzie arrived unexpectedly about eight o'clock. 'I just slipped out to the corner shop for a quarter of mint imperials, and Fred, behind the counter, said Tess was sick. Why didn't yer send Maddy down to tell me?'

Ann gawped. 'How did Fred know?'

'I told him, Mam!' Maddy said. 'Well, he asked me who the Beecham's were for and I could hardly tell him to mind his own business.'

Lizzie bustled to the couch. 'Ah, yer poor thing, what's wrong with yer?'

'I've got a cold, but it's only going to last a few days.' Tess was pleased to see her favourite friend. 'I'm glad you've come, Mrs Lizzie, 'cos I want to ask you something.'

'Hang on a minute, queen! Let's get this cold sorted out. How d'yer know it's only going to last a few days? Are yer in the know with someone?'

Tess giggled. 'I've told it I'll be good and do as I'm told, but it must be gone by the weekend 'cos I want to go back to school on Monday.'

'Oh, I see.' Lizzie nodded as though impressed. 'I'll have to tell my feller to put his foot down and have a good talk to himself. He's coughing and sneezing like mad, but it hasn't stopped him going to the pub. Even the rose passed remarks about it. "There can't be much wrong with him if he can go out boozing, so he'll get no sympathy from me." That's what she said, queen, if I never move from this spot.'

'It was the rose I wanted to ask you about, Mrs Lizzie. Our mam said you wouldn't mind, that you'd be over the moon, honoured even, but I thought I'd better ask. I mean, it's only manners to ask, isn't it?'

'Well now, it all depends what ye're asking for, queen. Like, if yer asked someone for a loan, they might tell yer to sod off. Whereas if yer asked them to a party, then they would be over the moon, and honoured even.'

'It's neither, Mrs Lizzie. I just wanted to ask if you'd mind if I wrote a story about your rose. It was Maddy's idea, and she said to call it "Mrs Lizzie's Paper Rose". I've started on it already, but I'll stop if you don't like the idea.'

Lizzie was already preening. 'Yer mean a story like the one yer wrote, what got put in that magazine?'

Tess thought for a few seconds, then said, 'Well, it's a different kind of story, and it won't be put in a magazine.'

'How d'yer know it won't, queen? I bet yer never thought the other one would be, did yer? Yer never know yer luck in a big city, is what my old ma used to say. And I don't half fancy seeing me name in print.' She raised her head and looked down her nose. 'I'd strut down this street like a bleedin' peacock. And it would be God help my feller, 'cos I'd be murder to live with.'

'Don't get carried away, Lizzie, it's only a little story about a rose on your wallpaper. It won't propel you to stardom.' George could see how Tess had brightened up and believed Lizzie was a better tonic for her than any medicine. 'Mind you, as your ma used to say, you never know your luck in a big city.'

'That's what she used to say, George, but she never found any bleedin' luck, 'cos she never had two ha'pennies to rub together.'

'I'll try and have it finished for when you come on Saturday, Mrs Lizzie, and you can tell me what you think of it.'

'I'll do that, queen, with pleasure. But don't forget, in your story Mrs Lizzie has got to be tall and slim, and very beautiful.' She glared at George when he burst out laughing. 'Well, smart-arse, a girl can dream, can't she?'

When Saturday came, Ann was as eager as Tess for Lizzie's knock. She thought her daughter's story was absolutely brilliant. As she'd said to George the night before, it was a God-given talent their younger daughter had and they should nurture it. No one would believe it had been written by a young girl, not yet twelve years of age, as she lay on the couch with a runny nose. It was very funny, yet there was pathos there as well. And Theresa had described Lizzie perfectly. The way she walked, talked and chuckled. You could actually see her in your mind as you read. Ann thought it was brilliant and was so proud. But then it was her daughter, so she was biased. It needed someone not so close to give their verdict.

When the familiar figure passed the window, Ann beat Maddy to the front door. 'Well, this is a welcoming committee!' Lizzie looked pleased. 'Have yer come into money?'

Ann pulled her inside. 'We've all been on pins waiting for you.

Theresa wouldn't read the story to us until you came. We've all read it of course, but we wanted to hear her read it aloud.'

Tess was sitting on the couch with just a small blanket over her knees. She looked a bit pale but the sniffles and shakes had gone. 'I told you, didn't I, Mrs Lizzie? Saturday and I'm nearly over it. I'll be in school on Monday.'

Ann helped her friend off with her coat. 'Now sit down in my chair and make yourself comfortable while Theresa performs for us. No, performs isn't the right word, but it doesn't matter, it'll have to do.'

There was no shyness about Tess, nor was there any sign of showing off. She read from the sheet of paper as though it was something she did all the time. When she was talking about Lizzie she used one voice, then changed to a higher one for the rose. And when there were bursts of laughter, she would pause until it died down. Eyes were not on Tess, though, they were on Lizzie. Her expressions matched those described in the story. She held her head high, chuckled loudly, nodded when she recognised something she'd said, and didn't see or hear anyone else but the young girl who was holding her spellbound.

There was a ripple of applause when Tess had finished, her face glowing with pride. 'Was that all right, Mrs Lizzie?'

'I'm lost for words, queen! Speechless, as they say. Ay, and I didn't half like what yer said about me hair being the colour of the sun. Makes me sound as though I've got a halo around me head.' Lizzie left the chair to give Tess a kiss. 'No kidding, queen, I never imagined anything so good. If yer don't grow up to be a writer, I'll eat me bleedin' hat.'

'I didn't know you had a hat, Mrs Lizzie,' Maddy said. 'I've never seen you in one.'

'I haven't, queen, but if push came to shove, I could buy one. There's a stall at Paddy's market what sells second-hand ones for a couple of coppers. Some of them are green with age, like, and yer can't tell what colour they've been, but I wouldn't mind, I'm not that proud.'

'Ooh, you shouldn't wear anyone else's hat, Mrs Lizzie.' Tess pulled a comical face. 'You never know who had it before.'

'As I've said, queen, I'm not proud. I mean, what's a couple of fleas between friends?'

318

Chapter Twenty-three

The winter was a long one, lasting until the end of March. People could be heard complaining that it was the worst winter they'd known, with lots of rain and wind, and skies so dark they made you feel miserable. But in the first week of April it seemed as though someone had waved a magic wand and suddenly there was spring in the air, bringing the smiles back to people's faces. The street became alive again, with neighbours standing on their doorsteps chatting and being brought up to date with news and goings-on. They were able to discard their heavy winter clothes, with mufflers and gloves being stored away until the following winter. Even though Lizzie warned, 'Keep yer winter undies on, queen, 'cos yer know the old saying about never casting a clout until May is out.'

Then May came, and with it the sunshine. The nights were light so the children were allowed to play out longer . . . boys with their ollies and kick-the-can, and the girls skipping or playing hopscotch. Tess had mastered the art of skipping now and it was her favourite game. But Maddy felt she was too old for childish games, and her only reason for going out was to see James Cobden. He was working now, and thought of himself as very grown up in his long trousers. He was a nice-looking boy, tall, fair-haired, blue-eyed and sporting a very attractive dimple in his chin. And when Ann had been concerned about his knocking on the door one night and asking if Maddy could come out, she was soon won over by his good manners and neat appearance. After all, they were only kids, and they never moved away from the house, so what harm could come of it?

And it was a regular occurrence now for Tess to stop Jack Bingham on his way home from work and have a chat. He wasn't so shy with her now; working with men had brought him out a lot. But although she'd tried, Tess couldn't get near to his mother. She always said hello whenever they met, had even knocked to see if their neighbour wanted any messages, but a grunt was the only answer she ever got. This saddened the girl, because she liked everyone to be happy and friendly. But she wasn't going to give up trying, because she sensed that in Mrs Bingham's heart there was a lot of unhappiness.

'Only two months to go, and I'll be nearly fourteen and leaving school.' Maddy was leaning against the wall outside their house, talking to James and Billy. 'And we've booked for a week's holiday in Wales, so I've also got that to look forward to.'

'You're not the only one, Maddy, so don't be swanking,' Tess said, letting the skipping rope fall loose over her feet. 'I've got a birthday around the same time as you, and I'm going on holiday as well.'

'And you've got something else to look forward to,' her sister told her. 'I'll be giving you a penny pocket money when I start work.'

'Aren't yer going to look for a job before yer go on holiday?' James asked. 'Yer'd be soft not to, 'cos if yer don't, all the jobs might be taken. There's a lot of kids leaving school and they won't all find work.'

'We've talked about that. I don't want to miss the holiday, but neither do I want to miss the chance of finding work. Dad said I should leave it until next month, then have a word with the headmistress and ask her advice.'

'If yer get a job in a factory, yer'd be off those two weeks anyway, 'cos they all close down.' Billy was leaving school himself in the summer, but he'd already been promised a job as an apprentice carpenter with the firm his dad worked for. 'I'm dead lucky getting a job with me dad. I'll only be working two weeks and then I've got the two weeks off.' He kicked the wall with the toe of his shoe. 'Mind you, I won't get paid for them weeks, worse luck.'

'I won't be getting paid either,' James said, pulling a face. 'Yer've got to have worked there a year before yer even get paid for one week.'

'Count yourself lucky you've got a job with prospects,' Maddy said. 'You'll be on decent money when you've served your time.'

'Yeah, in six years' time!' James knew she was right, because his mam and dad were always drumming into him how lucky he was. 'It's a long time to wait.'

The Binghams' front door opened and Jack stepped down on to the pavement. 'Hiya, Jack!' Tess put the two wooden handles of the skipping rope into one hand. 'Are you going out somewhere?'

'Only to the corner shop.' The lad looked embarrassed when he saw the other two boys. 'Me dad wants a packet of ciggies.'

'Hello, Jack,' Maddy said. 'You know James and Billy, don't you?' He nodded. 'I've seen them around.'

Maddy gave James a sly kick and a knowing look. It had the required effect. 'Hello, Jack, I believe ye're working now?'

'Yeah, doing a bit of painting and wallpapering. Or at least I'm trying to.' His discomfort was obvious. 'I'd better go, me dad will be waiting for his ciggies.'

'I'll come with you,' Tess said. 'It'll give me something to do.' Before he could object, she fell into step beside him. 'Did you get on all right in work?'

'Yeah, I quite like it. Not that I'm doing much, all they've got me doing is rubbing paintwork down and scraping paper off walls. But I'm keeping me eye on what's going on all around me, taking it all in, like. Me dad said I'll learn a lot by just watching the skilled men.'

'And what does your mam say? Does she say your dad's right?'

Jack chuckled. 'Me mam said this time next year she expects me to be good enough to decorate our living room. I hope she's right, 'cos I'd like to do it for her.'

'I've tried to make friends with your mam, but I don't think she likes me.'

Jack stopped in his tracks. 'Why, what's she said to yer?'

'That's just it, she hasn't said anything! She won't talk to me! I don't know how she can't like me, 'cos I haven't done anything to upset her.'

Jack dropped his head and was silent for a while. When he looked up he said, 'If I tell yer something, will yer promise not to tell anyone?'

'I'll try not to tell anyone, but sometimes my mouth runs away with me. If it's a secret, though, I will keep it to myself.'

'Well, me mam hasn't always been the way she is now. She used to be full of fun, and never had a fight or anything with the neighbours where we used to live. She used to always be singing and laughing. Then something terrible happened and she's never been the same since.' His voice broke and it was a while before he could bring himself to speak. 'I was eight at the time, and our Willy seven. We had a baby sister who was five. Her name was Enid.'

Tess's voice was high with surprise. 'You've got a sister?'

He shook his head. 'She died the week she was to start school. Me mam thought it was just a cold she had, but it turned into pneumonia and she died.' He heard the girl's sharp intake of breath and wondered briefly if he was doing the right thing. But he wanted her to know why his mother acted the way she did. Often over the years, when his mam had been fighting and screaming in the street, he'd wanted to tell everyone how she'd suffered so they'd understand. But until now he'd never been able to find the right words. 'Me mam was out of her mind, and me dad, 'cos they thought the world of her. So did me and Willy, she was our little sister and we loved her. But me mam took it bad, and it turned her head. That's why we moved here. Me dad thought she would get over it quicker if she wasn't being reminded of Enid all the time. It made no difference, though, 'cos she's never got over it.'

The tears were rolling down Tess's face. 'Only five, and she died! Oh, the poor little thing. And your poor mam, I feel so sorry for her.

And for your dad and you and Willy. It must have been terrible for all of you.'

'Me dad never used to drink until Enid died. But losing her, and then seeing me mam going out of her mind, he started drinking to forget.' Jack seemed to shake himself mentally. 'Anyway, now yer know why me mam does funny things sometimes and me dad often gets drunk. But she'd go mad if she thought I'd told yer, so don't mention it to a soul. Okay?'

'I'm glad you're my friend, Jack, and I'll try harder than ever to make friends with your mam. I've promised I won't tell anyone what you've told me, and I'll keep that promise.' Tess made a cross over her heart. 'Cross my heart and hope to die, if this day I tell a lie.'

Lizzie came up one night, two weeks before the schools broke up, and she was bristling with excitement. After first making claim to the rocking chair, which was her favourite, she said, with a note of importance, 'I come bearing two lots of news, so park yerselves comfortable and pin back yer lugholes.'

Tess sat on the floor at the side of her best friend. 'I'm all ears, Mrs Lizzie, and I hope what you have to tell us is going to make us laugh.'

'Not the first part, queen, that's more serious than funny. And it's for Maddy, if she's interested. If she's not, then there's no harm done.'

Maddy sat forward, all ears and expectancy. 'What is it, Mrs Lizzie, out with it. Don't keep me in suspense.'

'How would yer like to work in a shop, queen?'

George and Ann looked across at each other. What on earth was their friend up to now?

'I hadn't thought about working in a shop, Mrs Lizzie,' Maddy said, her frown saying she was now giving the possibility some deep thought. 'What sort of a shop?'

'One that sells everything, from a gas mantle to a loaf of bread. Sweets, cigarettes, cakes, babies' dummies, firewood . . . oh, I could go on all day. It would be easier to tell yer what they *don't* sell, 'cos as far as I know, they stock everything under the sun.'

'Is there a reason for you asking this, Lizzie?' Ann was hoping her daughter could get an office job, she was clever enough. But to say so now would make her sound like a snob. And anyway, it was up to Madelaine to choose what she would like to do.

'Of course there's a reason, queen, I'm not just talking to hear the sound of me own bleedin' voice, even though it is a sweet sound.' Lizzie grinned. 'No, it's just that I know Bert will be looking for an assistant soon, and I immediately thought of Maddy. It's near home so there'd be no tram fares to fork out, and it's pleasant enough work.'

322

'How d'you know he'll be looking for an assistant?' Ann asked. 'Has he told you?'

'Doesn't need to, queen, 'cos I've got eyes in me head. I reckon Lily is about five or six months pregnant so she won't be able to carry on much longer. And Bert certainly couldn't manage on his own, 'cos it's a busy shop.'

'My God, Lizzie, you do have your eyes to business, don't you?' George shook his head in wonder. 'You don't miss a thing.'

'Yer wouldn't get far in life if yer went around missing things, George. Now if I went around with me eyes shut, I wouldn't have noticed Lily was expecting. And then Bert could have offered the job to someone else and Maddy would have missed the chance. Perhaps she doesn't fancy working in a shop, and in that case there's nothing lost.'

'I wouldn't mind working in that shop,' Maddy said, looking decidedly perky. 'I like Mr and Mrs Green, they're so nice and friendly. Every time I go in the shop they're both cracking jokes with the customers, even when they're up to their eyes. Yes, I'd like to work there. But how would I learn the prices of things when they sell so much?'

'It wouldn't take yer long, queen, 'cos yer've got a good head on yer shoulders. Anyway, Bert has a price on nearly everything so that customers know exactly what they're paying.'

Ann thought it was time to bring her daughter down to earth before she got too interested. 'Don't be thinking the job is yours for the asking, Madelaine, because I'd hate you to build your hopes up and then be disappointed. Mr Green may already have someone in mind. Someone a little older with shop experience.'

Tess saw the light leave her sister's eyes and quickly said, 'He might not, though! And he wouldn't get anyone better than Maddy even if they were a hundred years older.'

'Before we do any more talking, can I ask what you think, George and Ann? If the job was up for grabs, how would you feel about Maddy working in the shop?'

'That's entirely up to her as far as I'm concerned,' George said. 'Better to work where she thinks she'd be happy than take any job that comes along.'

Ann could feel her daughter's eyes on her and didn't want to be the one to put a damper on the subject. 'I've no objection to Madelaine working there if that's what she wants. But nobody knows whether there's a job going or not! Seeing as Mr Green hasn't mentioned wanting an assistant, she can hardly go and ask him to consider her for the position.'

'I'll put the feelers out,' Lizzie said, setting the chair in motion. 'I often go in their stock room to have a cuppa with Lily, so I'll wheedle it out of her in a roundabout way. Now I know Maddy is interested I'll see what I can do this week. I can't promise anything, but I'll do me damnedest.'

'When you came in, you said you had two lots of news,' Ann reminded her. 'Shall I ask what the other item is, or should I keep my mouth shut?'

'I'm going to tell yer whether yer mouth's open or shut. Yer'll probably tell me to get lost when yer know what it is, but God loves a trier, and yer can't say I'm not a trier.'

George chuckled as he twisted the ends of his moustache. 'Don't tell us you've found a job for Tess in the fish shop?'

Tess shivered and pulled a face. 'Ooh, I wouldn't want to work in the fish shop, 'cos all the fish are dead.'

The more Lizzie laughed, the faster the chair rocked. 'Are they, queen? Well, I didn't know that! Mind you, I've often passed the shop window and thought the fish lying on that cold slab didn't look well. I thought they looked a bit green around the gills, but I never knew the poor buggers were dead.'

Once again Ann thought she'd better change the subject before her sensitive daughter decided she'd never eat another fish. 'Lizzie, what *is* your other piece of news, or do we have to drag it out of you?'

'I don't know quite how to put this, queen, but I'd say it was good news for me, but bad news for me very best friends the Richardsons.'

'Oh dear, it sounds ominous,' George said. 'Perhaps we'd be better not knowing.'

But Lizzie was having none of that. 'Ye're going to sit and listen whether yer like it or not. I'll bleedin' sit on yer if necessary.'

'Oh, not that! Anything but that, I beg you!'

'George, will yer stop arsing about and get off yer knees? I can't stand to see a grown man grovelling. Sit on yer chair and behave yerself. The time to get on yer knees and plead is when yer've heard what I've got to say.' Lizzie waited until he was seated, then said, 'Yer know this holiday ye're going on, to Wales? Well, I was wondering if the house ye're going to could take another one?'

'Who is this other person?' Ann had a gut feeling, and she was praying she was right. 'Do we know them?'

'It's me, yer silly sod! Who else would it be?'

The two girls screamed with delight and threw themselves on to the rocking chair, nearly sending it flying. 'Ooh, Mrs Lizzie, that would be marvellous!'

'Watch it, girls, or I won't live to tell the bleedin' tale!' Lizzie pulled down her skirt, which was riding high up her thighs. 'Get off, I'm showing all I've got!' She looked across to see George and Ann laughing their heads off. 'Is that laughter I hear, or hysterics?'

'It's pleasure, Lizzie,' Ann told her. 'We'd love you to come with us. I'll write to Gwen in the morning and catch the dinner-time post. She does have a spare room, and I don't think she'd let it with us going, but best to find out. We'll know for certain in a couple of days.'

'What about Norman?' George asked. 'Doesn't he want to come?'

Lizzie shook her head. 'Yer know my feller won't go far from the pub. It's what he likes, and I say everyone to their own taste. He doesn't mind being left for a week, he's big and ugly enough to look after himself. It was him what suggested I go with yer.'

'I'm glad he did, it'll be lovely having you with us.' Ann meant every word of it. This woman had made such a difference to her life she would never forget her. Gone were the days when she was robbing Peter to pay Paul, they now lived comfortably and had a few bob over every week. And they had made many friends. But their best friend would always be Lizzie, who gave so much and asked for little in return. 'You'll get on like a house on fire with Gwen, she's just your type. Always laughing and cracking jokes.'

'Does she swear?'

'Not so you'd notice, why?'

'Well, you know me, queen, I can't abide folk that swear. Especially women. They sound as common as muck. I can't help being a snob, it was the way I was brought up.' Her face deadpan, Lizzie got to her feet. 'Anyway, that's two missions successfully carried out. Now I'd better get down to that bleedin' shop before the bugger puts the shutters up. I'll see what I can get out of Lily and let yer know.' She was near the front door when there was a banging on the wall. 'Don't tell me the queer one's up to her tricks again?'

'No, she's not!' The words were out before Tess could stop them. Oh, how she wished she could tell them the truth. 'Mrs Bingham's not bad now, is she, Mam?'

'Not as bad as she used to be, love, I admit. Just now and again she takes off.'

'Well I like her, and I feel sorry for her.'

Lizzie ran a finger down Tess's cheek. 'That's right, queen, it's far better to like people than to hate them. For hatred brings no reward.'

Bert was bending down behind the counter when he heard the shop doorbell tinkling. He looked up and groaned when he saw who was closing the door behind her. 'In the name of God, Lizzie, I was just going to put the bar on, I'm closed!'

'If yer were closed, Bert, I wouldn't be standing here, would I? I'm clever, but even I can't walk through bleedin' wood.'

'Is that you, Lizzie?' A voice came from the stock room. 'I've just made us a pot of tea, come on through.'

Then Bert made a remark that was to make Lizzie's mission much easier. 'Blimey! She'll be asking yer to come to bed with us next!'

'Yer'll be needing someone to sleep with yer before long,' Lily called, ''cos it won't be long before I'm taking meself off to the spare room.'

Lizzie lifted the hinged part of the counter and made her way through to the stock room. 'Am I right in thinking he's been a naughty boy and put yer in the family way?'

They heard Bert curse as he bumped into something in his haste to get to the stock room. 'Ay, I heard that, Lizzie Ferguson! Don't you be trying to cause trouble between man and wife.'

Lizzie lifted her hands and feigned horror. 'Me cause trouble! Me what's quiet and shy, who never says a word out of place? Me what's the most peaceable customer what comes in your shop? I'm cut to the quick, Bert Green.'

'Aye, with bells on! Yer'd cause trouble in an empty house, you would.'

'D'yer hear that, Lily? Next he'll be saying it's my fault ye're in the family way!' Lizzie wagged a finger at the grinning shopkeeper. 'Why don't yer be a man and admit yer've been a naughty boy?'

'It takes two to make a baby, so I can't put all the blame on him.' Lily made room for Lizzie to sit next to her on an upside-down orange box. 'Anyway, we've been married ten years, so it's about time we started a family.'

'Yeah, I'm made up for yer, Lily, and you, Bert. If I'd known I'd have brought a bottle of sherry to celebrate.'

'What d'yer mean, if yer'd known! I bet yer've known since the very minute of conception, Lizzie, 'cos nothing escapes those eyes of yours.' Bert was feeling on top of the world. They hadn't told any of the customers yet, so he was glad it was out in the open and he could stick his chest out and show how happy and proud he was. 'Me and Lily are delighted. We've put off starting a family because of the shop, but we're not getting any younger and we don't want to go through life childless. The shop is important because it's our livelihood, but so is a family.'

'Yer'll be looking for someone to help yer in the shop, then?'

'Yeah, I'll be keeping me eye open. Lily wants to work for another month or so, but I'll have to look around before then or I'll be left in the lurch. One person couldn't run this shop even if they had ten feet and ten pairs of hands.'

Lizzie couldn't believe her luck. Norman was always saying how jammy she was, that if she fell down the lavvy she'd come up with a ruddy gold watch. And she had to admit she seldom disappointed herself. 'Will yer be wanting someone with experience?' She kept her voice casual. 'Yer know, someone what's worked in a shop before?'

'It would be a help, but it's not essential. As long as they're honest, pleasant, good at adding up and will get along with the customers. If I get someone with all those qualities I'll consider meself lucky. Oh, and as long as they're not a slow coach, 'cos yer need to move like greased lightning in this place.' Bert caught her eye and grinned. 'Ay, ye're not thinking of yerself, are yer, Lizzie? 'Cos if yer are yer can forget it, I'm not a glutton for punishment. We'd have the whole street in, standing gossiping all day, and I'd never make any money. And the idea is that me and the wife want to save up for our old age. When I'm too old to run the shop I want to have a few bob to retire with.'

'Go 'way, who d'yer think ye're kidding? I bet you and Lily have got a long stocking stashed away somewhere. This place must be a little goldmine.' Lizzie took the cup Lily held out to her. 'But yer work hard for yer money, I'll say that for yer. The pair of yer are on the go from morning till night. And yer need the patience of a saint with some of the customers yer get in. If yer not salting some money away for yer old age, then yer want yer bumps feeling.'

'I wouldn't like to be doing this when I get old,' Lily said. 'In fact I couldn't! Me feet are nearly dropping off some nights, and once the bar's on the door, the most I can do is flop in a chair and that's me lot.'

'Then yer want to start taking it easy, what with the baby and all.' Lizzie took a sip of tea and pulled a face. 'Flippin' heck, there's no bleedin' sugar in me tea! Yer know I take two spoonfuls! I know I've told yer to salt money away for yer old age, but I didn't mean at my expense.'

Bert passed the sugar bowl over. 'All right, Lizzie, don't get out of yer pram, I'll pick yer dummy up.' He watched her put two heaped spoonfuls of sugar in her tea, then stirred it for her. 'I dunno, yer get waited on hand and foot when yer come here.'

'Well now, in repayment for all yer kindnesses to me, I might just be able to do yer a favour in return.' Lizzie's haughty pose came into play, and her little finger was stretched to curve outwards from the handle of the cup, like she'd see them do in the pictures. Mind you, the film stars weren't sitting on an upturned orange box in a little stock room at the time, but that was only a minor detail. 'I know a young girl what has all the qualities yer mentioned. She's very pretty, with a good sense of humour, has a brilliant head on her shoulders and I can vouch for her honesty.' Her eyebrows were raised and her eyes were so intent on looking down her nose she appeared to be cross-eyed. 'She's the daughter of my very best friend, and her sister is a writer what has had a story published in a very well-known magazine.'

Lizzie looked so comical Bert and Lily were in stitches. This was why she was always welcome at the end of a day when they'd been rushed off their feet; she made them forget how tired they were. 'If she's as posh as you sound, Lizzie, she wouldn't last five minutes in this shop. Yer know what the customers are like, they'd pull her leg something shocking.'

'I never said she was posh! She does speak nicely, her mother sees to that, but a snob she ain't. Anyway, I don't even know whether she'd want to work here, it was just a thought that came to me.'

'Do we know her, Lizzie?' Lily asked. 'Does she live local?'

'Yeah, only up the street! It's Ann Richardson's daughter, Maddy. As nice a girl as yer'll find anywhere, and she leaves school the week after next.'

'I know who yer mean,' Bert said. 'She is a nice polite girl, but is she the right sort for the shop? Or, to put it another way, is the shop right for her?'

'I'll tell yer what, Bert.' Lizzie drained her cup before handing it to him. 'Before any more is said, 'cos we're not really going to get anywhere just talking between ourselves, why don't yer have a word with the girl? That's if she's interested, of course. I'll ask her to pop in tomorrow if yer like, or, better still, I'll bring her down tomorrow night when ye're closing up. That way yer won't be interrupted with customers wanting to be served.'

'Wouldn't do no harm, Bert,' Lily said. 'She does seem a nice girl, and yer need someone who's on the ball and not afraid of being on the go all the time. And above all, as Lizzie said, she's honest.'

'Okay, it's worth a try. At least she wouldn't have any travelling to do, so no reason for her being late for work.' Bert nodded his head. The more he thought about it, the more interested he became. 'You bring her down tomorrow night, Lizzie, and we'll take it from there.'

Lizzie stood outside the shop and heard the bar being put across the inside of the door. Then she began to rub her hands together and did a little jig. 'Not a bad night's work,' she muttered aloud. 'A job for Maddy and a holiday for meself! I don't think the girls will be in bed yet, so I'll nip up and tell them what's been said. Then I'd better get home before my feller comes in, or he might get his hopes up and think I've run off with the coal man.'

Maddy and Tess were walking up the street the following day on their way home from school when Nellie Bingham passed them with a basket over her arm. 'Hello, Mrs Bingham,' Tess called. 'I'll go on a message for you if you like?'

The answer she received was a shake of the head as the little woman carried on walking with her eyes on the ground.

'You'd think the least she would do is answer you,' Maddy said. 'All she had to do was thank you and say she preferred to do her own shopping.'

'I don't mind,' Tess said. This was the first time she'd ever kept a secret from her sister, and she would dearly love to confide in her so she'd understand why their neighbour behaved as she did. But it wasn't her secret to share, it was Jack's. 'I still like her, and one day she'll be my friend, I know she will.'

Maddy knocked on the front door before putting an arm across her sister's shoulders. 'If she isn't, it won't be for want of trying on your part.'

Ann stood aside to let them pass. 'Did you have a word with Miss Harrison about working in the shop, Madelaine?'

'Yes, and she said shop work can be very rewarding, as I'd be in contact with lots of people. And the experience would be good for me, building up my confidence. She also said there was no reason why I couldn't move on if I decided it wasn't what I wanted, and suggested I attend night school to learn shorthand and typing. She said there would always be work for secretaries.'

'That's a very sensible suggestion.' Ann nodded, in total agreement with Miss Harrison. 'I believe you should give that some thought. There's nothing wrong with working in a shop, Madelaine, but there's nothing wrong with being ambitious, either.'

'I know that, Mam, and I will think about it. But at the moment the idea of working in a shop appeals to me, so I'll give it a try. That's if Mr and Mrs Green think I'm suitable.'

'Ooh, I'd love to work behind the counter in a shop,' Tess said. 'I'd be very polite, asking people what they would like and putting things in their baskets for them. It would be more exciting than working in a stuffy office.'

'Work is not all about enjoying yourself, Theresa, it's about making a living and earning a wage. If you happen to find work you enjoy, then that is a bonus.'

'Then our dad is lucky, isn't he, 'cos he enjoys his job.' A frown creased Tess's forehead. 'At least I think he enjoys it, he's always laughing when he tells us funny stories about the men he works with. And Mrs Lizzie, of course, and what she gets up to.'

'I was only thinking the other day that if it hadn't been for your father's accident, we would never have met Lizzie,' Ann said. 'I was worried to death at the time because we didn't know how badly hurt he was, but when I look back and remember how helpful she was to us, I realise that some good came out of the accident. She's a true friend.'

'I'm glad she's coming on holiday with us, we'll have a marvellous time.' Maddy was standing in front of the mirror over the fireplace, combing her hair. She was trying it in different styles so she would look her best when she went down to the shop tonight. 'Do I look better with a middle parting, Mam, or a side parting? Which makes me look more grown up?'

'You suit either way, Madelaine, but you shouldn't be trying to make yourself look older. Enjoy your childhood and don't be wishing your life away. When you get to my age you'll be doing whatever you can to make yourself look younger.'

'All you had to do to make yourself look younger was to cut your hair.' As Tess spoke to her mother she was eyeing her sister's thick lustrous black hair. 'You've both got better hair than me, I've hardly got any.'

Maddy spun around. 'You've got nice hair, Tess! Come here and let me comb it for you. See if I can make you look like a film star. Who would you like to look like . . . Janet Gaynor or Lillian Gish?'

Tess giggled. 'Can you do me ringlets, like Shirley Temple?'

'If you learn to sing and dance like her, I promise to put rags in your hair so you get the curls.'

'Madelaine, I think you should change out of your gymslip to go and see Mr Green. Put your blue dress on and a cardigan.' Ann wasn't too keen on the whole idea of her daughter being a shop assistant, but if she was going for an interview she wanted her to look her best. 'First impression is important.'

'Yes, I'll do that, Mam.' A mischievous glint came to Maddy's eyes. 'If you wore lipstick I'd ask if I could borrow it.'

'You certainly would not!' Ann turned to see both daughters giggling, and knew she was having her leg pulled. 'It will be a long time before you're ready to paint your face.'

'When I'm going to my first dance, that's when I'll wear lipstick.' It was obvious Maddy had already given this much thought. 'I'll be old enough then.'

'It's too early for you to be even thinking about it. You're not fourteen yet!'

'I will be in a couple of weeks.'

'And I'm twelve in a couple of weeks,' Tess said. 'But I won't be asking if I can wear lipstick, Mam, 'cos I know I'd look daft, and you wouldn't let me anyway.'

'I haven't forgotten about your birthdays, and I was wondering if

330

you'd each like to invite one of your friends for tea?'

Tess clapped her hands in glee. 'Oh, goody, a party!'

'No, Theresa, not a party as such, just afternoon tea. You could invite one of your friends from school.'

'Mam, could I invite James?' Maddy asked. 'He's a friend, and I'd rather ask him than anyone else. And Billy Cartwright, if you wouldn't mind.'

Ann was on the point of refusing, but changed her mind. Far better for her daughters to bring their friends home so she could get to know them properly. 'I suppose so. And we'll have to invite your cousins, Joyce and Billy, we couldn't leave them out.'

'What about me, Mam?' Tess was wearing her stubborn expression. 'Aren't you going to ask me who I want to invite?'

'Of course I am, love! I wouldn't leave you out!'

Tess was expecting opposition and her fears caused a tone of defiance to enter her voice. 'I'd like to invite Jack and Willy, from next door.'

Ann's jaw dropped for a second. 'I beg your pardon! That's quite out of the question, Theresa, and you know it.'

'Why? You said we could invite a friend, and Maddy's asking James and Billy, so why can't I ask who I like?'

'I'm not going to argue with you, Theresa, so let's leave it at that. Invite one of your friends from school, or two if you wish.'

'I don't want to ask anyone from school! Jack and Willy are my friends, so why can't they come? After all, it's my birthday, and I should be allowed to invite who I like.'

'I don't want the Bingham boys in my house. And I'm sure your father will agree with me when he comes in.'

'They're not bad lads, Mam,' Maddy said, seeing the distress on her sister's face. 'In fact they're quite nice. They can't help the way their mother is.'

'I don't want to hear any more on the subject, Madelaine, so leave things be.'

'But that's not fair!' Tess was near to tears. 'You're taking it out on the boys because you don't like their mother, and that's mean.' With that she ran up the stairs and they could hear the door bang behind her.

Ann looked bewildered. 'What on earth's got into her? But she can sulk as much as she likes, I will not have the Bingham boys in this house.'

'I'm sorry, Mam, but I agree with Tess,' Maddy said. 'The party is for both our birthdays, and if I can invite who I like, then she should be able to. She gets on well with Jack and Willy, they're her friends.'

Ann was surprised. It was very seldom that either of her daughters answered her back and she was at a loss how to react. 'Madelaine,

331

everyone in the street shuns the Binghams, with good reason, yet you and Theresa expect me to befriend them? You're really asking too much of me.'

'Because other people shun them it doesn't mean it's right. Or that we should do the same thing. It must be awful for those two boys with no one speaking to them. They've never harmed anyone.'

'We'll discuss it later when your father's here. Now go upstairs and tell Theresa to come down and stop being childish.'

When Maddy came down, however, it was without her sister. 'She won't come, Mam, no matter what I say. You know how stubborn she can be. And she said she doesn't want any dinner 'cos she's not hungry.'

'What an obstinate child she is. Well I won't be blackmailed into giving her her own way, so she can stay up there until your father comes in. Let him deal with her.'

'I'll go and sit with her for a while,' Maddy said. 'Keep her company.'

'Where are the girls?' George asked. 'I didn't see them in the street.'

'They're both upstairs. Theresa refuses to come down because she's taken a fit of the sulks because I won't give her her own way, and Madelaine is keeping her company.'

'What brought this on?'

'I suggest you go upstairs and ask Theresa yourself, while I'm putting the dinner out. See if you don't agree with me when I say that what she wants is out of the question.'

Ten minutes later Ann was standing at the foot of the stairs wondering what they were talking about and why it was taking so long. 'Will you come down now, your dinner's ready.'

George appeared on the tiny landing, and looking down at his wife said, 'Will you put the dinners in the oven for five minutes, love, I want to talk to you.'

'Won't it wait until we've eaten? The dinner will get all dried up in the oven.'

George turned and looked back into the bedroom where his two daughters were sitting on the bed. 'I won't be long. Come when I call you.' He closed the door so no words would carry up to them, then came down the stairs two at a time. 'Let's sit and sort this silly argument out, love, before things are said that aren't meant but can't be taken back.'

'I don't see there's anything to sort out. I've made my position clear, but Theresa is being childish and stubborn. I suppose she's told you who she wants to invite to the birthday party?'

'Yes, she has.' George took one of his wife's hands and held it between his. 'And I don't feel as strongly about it as you obviously do.

It is not your party, or my party, but one for the girls. And I believe they should ask the friends they wish to ask. Whether we agree with their choice doesn't really come into it.' He let out a deep sigh. 'I really don't think you or I have the right to brand two young boys as being unfit to be friends with our children when we don't even know them. They've never done anything to annoy or harm us, have they?'

'No, but their mother is enough to tell us what the family is like. I don't think they are suitable friends for Theresa, and I'm surprised you're taking her side in this.'

'I'm not taking sides, love, just saying what I think is right. And from what I've heard, Theresa feels very strongly about it. You know she hardly ever speaks ill of anyone and likes everyone to be friendly and happy. Apparently she's taken a liking to Jack and Willy from next door, and I for one am not going to tell her they aren't good enough for her. And I don't think you should, either. She's a very loving girl, very tender-hearted, and I wouldn't want her to change one little bit.' George rubbed a finger over the back of his wife's hand. 'I think you should trust Tess in her choice of friends, and I think you should give the lads next door the benefit of the doubt.'

It was Ann's turn to let out a deep sigh. 'I started to realise I was being too hasty when Madelaine took Theresa's side. You are right, and the girls are right. It was wicked of me to think badly of the boys without knowing them. I'll go up and tell Theresa I'm sorry and I would like her to invite her friends from next door.'

George leaned forward and kissed her. 'I remember when I was little, my dad used to sing a song that never failed to make me cry. I think it was called "And a Little Child Shall Lead Them". Our Tess reminds me of that child.'

Chapter Twenty-four

Maddy linked Lizzie's arm as they walked down the street. Her heart was thumping like mad at the prospect of being interviewed for her first job. 'I'm shaking like a leaf, Mrs Lizzie. I hope I don't go all tongue-tied and make a fool of myself.'

'Of course yer won't, queen, yer'll be fine! I'll be there, and I'll make sure they don't eat yer.' Lizzie glanced sideways. 'Tess looked as though she's either got a cold or she's been crying. Or was I imagining things?'

'She was upset over something.' Maddy thought of telling a white lie and making light of it, but she didn't really want to lie to this woman. 'If I tell you, will you promise not to repeat it? I don't think my mam would be happy for me to tell tales out of school.'

'I'll not say a word, queen, yer have my promise on that.'

'It was nothing to cry about, really, but Tess does get upset easily.' Maddy went on to tell the tale. 'I admired her for sticking up for her friends, and I said so. And our dad must have agreed because he had a word with our mam while we were upstairs. I don't know what was said, but our mam came up and said she'd been wrong, and that Tess could invite anyone she liked to the party.'

'I should think so too! I feel sorry for those lads, the poor buggers always look lost, as though they haven't got a friend in the world.'

'They've got a good friend in Tess, Mrs Lizzie, 'cos she's very loyal to her friends. Anyway, it's all been sorted out to everyone's satisfaction. I invite James and Billy, and Tess is asking the Bingham boys.'

'And that's how it should be. What's the good of having a birthday party if yer can only invite yer enemies?' They were outside the side entrance to the shop when Lizzie chuckled. 'She's strong-willed is yer sister, and she sticks to her guns. Good luck to her.'

'Don't you think you should be saying good luck to me?' Maddy's tummy was doing somersaults as Lizzie knocked on the door. 'I'm going to need it.'

They could hear boxes being dragged away from the back of the door before it opened. 'Come in, Lizzie, if yer can get in. There's no room to breathe in this hall.' Bert Green noticed the frightened look on the girl's face as she passed him, and his heart went out to her. He could still remember how he'd felt when he'd gone for his first job interview. Not only had he been afraid of being thought stupid and not getting the job, but he'd been embarrassed because he was wearing short trousers. His mam had said she couldn't afford to buy him long kecks until he started work and was bringing a few bob in. He could laugh about it now, but to a fourteen-year-old boy it wasn't funny. 'Mind yer don't scratch yer legs on those boxes, sweetheart, or yer'll end up with loads of splinters.'

Maddy had hold of the back of Lizzie's coat and was hanging on tight until a voice croaked, 'Have a heart, queen, ye're bleedin' choking me!'

Bert chortled. 'That's one way of shutting yer up, Lizzie! I've thought of many ways over the years, but Maddy's got a winner there. Hang on, girl, and perhaps we'll be able to talk without interruption.'

Being called by her first name calmed Maddy's nerves somewhat, and she was able to smile and say, 'Ooh, I don't want to choke Mrs Lizzie, so shall I just put my hand over her mouth to stop her from talking?'

'Holy suffering ducks!' Lizzie pulled her coat free. 'I was fighting for me breath there!' She glared at Bert. 'Don't you be teaching her all the wrong things, or her mam will have yer life. She's come to see if yer'll let her work behind yer counter, not kill the customers off.'

'Oh, I didn't want her to kill yer off, Lizzie, I can't afford to lose a customer. I just thought perhaps a little bit of torture, if yer see what I mean.'

'Will yer let the girl in, please?' Lily called from her speck on the orange box. 'Before she thinks we're all stark staring mad and takes to her heels and runs away.'

Maddy gazed around the storeroom, which was bursting at the seams with items of every size and description. There was everything in the room except chairs. 'I'll stand up, Mrs Lizzie, you can sit on the orange box with Mrs Green.'

'I've got a better idea. Why don't yer take Maddy through to the shop, Bert, and let her have a look around.' Lizzie parked her backside next to Lily and folded her arms. 'Yer'll be able to hear yerselves talk in there, without me and Lily butting in. Ask each other questions and see how yer get on. And don't you be afraid to speak out, queen, 'cos Bert won't bite yer head off. He can be quite nice when he puts his mind to it.'

'What d'yer mean? I'm always nice! I'm the nicest, most loving person ye're ever likely to meet, and Lily will vouch for that, won't yer, sweetheart?'

Lizzie got in before his wife could answer. 'Oh, we all know how loving yer are, smart-arse, we've only got to look at yer wife to see that.'

Bert thought the conversation was leading down a road which was unsuitable for young ears, so he cupped Maddy's elbow and led her through to the shop. 'This is it, sweetheart, nothing to write home about, is it?'

'It looks different without any customers in.' Maddy's eyes were everywhere. There must be hundreds of items here, she thought, but everything seemed very organised. Shelves were neatly stacked, and the line of small drawers running under the shelves all had labels on to say what they contained. There was pepper, nutmeg, packets of custard powder, headache powders, gravy browning, tacks and curtain hooks. They were just the ones Maddy could take in before she realised Mr Green was talking to her.

'This end of the long counter is used only for food stuffs, like tea, sugar, bacon and cooked meat. The other end is for newspapers, sweets and ciggies. That side counter is where we keep the trays of bread and cakes, and under the window, as yer can see, is where the firewood is kept, well away from the food. We sell small bags of coal and paraffin as well, but that's all kept in the back yard.'

Maddy was looking at the many cards tacked to walls around the shop, from which were hanging babies' dummies, hair nets, combs and nail files. 'Mrs Lizzie said you sell everything under the sun, and she was right.'

'Even Lizzie hasn't seen everything. There are things we don't put on display so as not to embarrass customers. Things like fine-tooth combs and sassafras oil. We're very diplomatic when we serve those, 'cos people don't want their neighbours to know the kids have fleas. Not that there's anything to be ashamed of, most kids get them once they start school. I know I did, and I can remember me mam rubbing sassafras oil on me hair and me screaming me head off 'cos it didn't half sting. The best of it was, she kept doing it even when she'd got rid of the blinking fleas!'

Maddy giggled. 'Me and Tess don't have any fleas, but our mam puts the oil on once a month, just to be on the safe side.'

When she smiled, Bert thought what a pretty girl she was. She was neatly turned out and very well spoken too, which was unusual in that neighbourhood. But she wasn't stuck up or lacking in humour. And working in a shop you needed to have an ever-present sense of humour combined with the patience of a saint. 'Well, sweetheart, what are your thoughts on the matter? D'yer think yer'd like to work here?'

337

The nod and the wide smile came with, 'Oh, I'd love to! That's if you'd have me?'

Bert put a finger to his lips and moved quietly towards the stock room door. And there stood Lizzie, her head on one side and a hand cupped round an ear. 'If yer can't hear properly, missus, why don't yer come in and join us?'

Lizzie waltzed in, not the least ashamed of having been caught out. 'I'm just making sure the girl's all right. She's one of me best friends, so yer'd better watch yerself with her, Bert Green, or yer'll have me to answer to.' She winked at Maddy. 'How far have yer got?'

It was the shopkeeper who answered. 'Not as far as we would have been if you hadn't decided to poke yer nose in. I think I'll just stand back and let you do the honours, Lizzie.'

She rewarded him with a beaming smile. 'Now ye're talking sense, so I'll continue with the interview. Maddy, queen, would yer like to work in this shop with Bert and Lily?'

The girl couldn't keep a giggle back. Was there no end to what Mrs Lizzie would do? 'I'd like to very much, if Mr Green thinks I'm suitable.'

'Of course he thinks ye're suitable, queen, he's not daft. He knows a good thing when he sees one. So I'll leave yer with him now to sort out the hours and wages. And don't forget to tell him ye're going away for a week's holiday, so he knows where he's up to.'

When Lizzie had gone back to her seat on the orange box, Bert grinned. 'She's a corker, isn't she? But she's a good woman, and her heart's in the right place.' He took a Fry's Cream chocolate bar from a glass display and handed it to Maddy. 'Split this with yer sister.'

Maddy backed away from him. 'No, I can't take that, you'll never make a profit if you give things away.'

'Oh, you and me are going to get on fine. Try telling my customers I've got to make a profit to live, and they call me all the tight-fisted so-and-so's they can lay their tongue to. But I want yer to take this and share it with yer sister. Yer might never get the offer again.'

Maddy slipped the bar into the pocket of her cardie. 'Thank you, that's very kind of you.'

Bert leaned both arms on the counter. 'Now let's get down to business. The hours would be half eight until half five, six days a week, with an hour off for dinner. We open on a Sunday as well, but we wouldn't expect you to work then unless it was an emergency. The wages would be five shillings a week to start, with a rise when yer've got some experience and can be left to serve on yer own without any help from me or Lily. Now how does that sound to yer?'

'That sounds fine, Mr Green, but you do know I don't leave school for another two weeks, don't you? And then, as Mrs Lizzie said, I'm going to Wales for a week with my family. Would that be all right with you, or can't you wait that long?'

'The wife said she'll carry on as normal for the next month, so we'll manage. But what yer could do, if yer mam will let yer, is come in for an hour after school, or on a Saturday, just to get the feel of the place and familiarise yerself with where things are. I'd give you a couple of coppers for it, of course, I wouldn't expect yer to do it for nothing.'

'I'd like that, Mr Green, and I'm sure my parents will have no objection.'

'Then let's go and put Lizzie out of her misery, shall we?' As they turned towards the stock room, Bert put a hand on Maddy's arm. 'If this hadn't turned out as it has, yer know she would have clocked me one, don't yer?'

The girl grinned. 'In that case, she should now give you a big, smacking kiss.'

'Blimey,' Bert said softly, 'I don't know which is the worst of the two evils.'

It was the Sunday before their holidays, and Maddy and Tess were eagerly waiting the arrival of the guests to their shared birthday party. Both were wearing new cotton dresses which Ann had bought as presents, and they'd had strict instructions not to get them dirty as she didn't want to have to wash them before their holidays. And under the dresses they were wearing the underskirts Lizzie had bought them. There was a band of lace on the bottom of the skirts, and Tess kept twirling around to show off the lace.

The table was set with sandwiches, cakes, jellies and trifles, and in the centre, on a glass stand, was a cake iced in white with red lettering wishing them a Happy Birthday and with both their names underneath. It was the first real party the girls had ever had and they were in high spirits.

The first to arrive were their cousins. Billy was fifteen and had been working for over a year, and his sister, Joyce, had left school the same day as Maddy. She'd got a job in the British Enka, and was full of it when she passed the girls their presents of boxes of Cadbury's chocolates. 'Me and me mate have got jobs working together, Auntie Ann, and we're made up. We start on five and six a week, and get a sixpence rise when we've been there a year.'

'Holy smoke, will yer give yer mouth a rest?' Billy said. 'We've had this since she went for the interview and she's driving us all nuts.'

'I bet you were the same when you started work, son,' George said. 'I know I was.'

A knock on the door had Tess racing to answer it. When she saw

James Cobden and Billy Cartwright there was disappointment in her voice. 'Oh, it's you. Come on in.'

The boys had their best clothes on and their hair sleeked back. And the presents they passed over were nicely wrapped, showing a woman's touch. The girls couldn't open the gifts quick enough, and tore at the paper. They gave a shriek of delight when they saw the small cases containing comb and mirror. 'Oh, thank you, they're lovely!' Much to the boys' embarrassment, Tess gave them both a hug, while Maddy blushed and said to her mother, 'Look, Mam, aren't they nice?'

'Don't forget your manners, Madelaine. Do the boys know your cousins?'

'Ooh, sorry!' Maddy waved a hand. 'Billy and Joyce, meet James and Billy.'

Her cousin was quick to correct her. 'I get Bill now off the men in work and me mates.' His voice was still breaking and went from high to gruff. 'There's only me mam and our Joyce call me Billy, and I'm fed up telling them I'm a working man now, not a schoolboy.'

Tess was on tenterhooks. 'Mam, can I go and knock for the boys next door?'

'Certainly not, Theresa! They'll be here when they're ready, unless something's cropped up and they can't come.' The words were no sooner out of her mouth than the knocker sounded. 'There you are, I told you they'd come when they were ready.'

But her daughter didn't hear, she was already opening the door. 'I thought you weren't coming, you're late.'

'It's his fault.' Jack pulled a face as he jerked his head towards his brother. 'He spilt tea on his shirt and me mam made him get changed.'

'Well, you're here now, so I forgive you. Come on in.'

The brothers looked so shy and uncomfortable, George took pity on them. He approached them with his hand outstretched. 'I haven't had the pleasure. You must be Jack, and you're Willy.' He shook their hands before quickly reeling off the names of the other guests. 'And this is my wife, Mrs Richardson.'

Ann smiled. 'I'm glad you could come. Now, it's going to be a tight squeeze at the table but I'm sure you'll manage. Make yourselves at home and tuck into the food while I put the kettle on. For those who don't want tea, there's lemonade.'

Willy tugged on his brother's jacket, saying, 'Shall we give them now?'

Jack was wishing the ground would open and swallow him up. They'd lived in the street for over five years now, and this was the first neighbour's house they'd been in, and the first time in company. He nodded to his brother and they both reached into their pockets and brought out small packages that had been nicely wrapped but were now crumpled. Their faces the colour of beetroot, they handed a package to each of the sisters, Jack to Tess, and Willy to Maddy. And in unison, their voices cracked, they said, 'Happy birthday.'

Not for a moment had Ann expected the boys to bring presents, and she sat down on the arm of the couch and looked on with interest. She was as surprised as her daughters when the wrapping was opened to reveal pretty scarves in voile, patterned with dainty flowers on a white background. The flowers were a different colour on each of the scarves, so there'd be no mix-up over which belonged to whom.

'Oh, they're beautiful,' Maddy said, fingering the soft material. 'I was going to say you shouldn't have bothered, but I'm glad you did because they're lovely. Thank you very much.'

But words weren't enough for Tess, she had to hug each of the brothers. 'It's a lovely present, and I'm going to take it with me on holiday. I can wear it on my head when the sun gets too hot, then I won't feel dizzy.' She held the scarf out for her cousin's inspection. 'Isn't it lovely, Joyce?'

'It certainly is!' Joyce said, full of envy. 'I'll invite you to my birthday party if yer promise to buy one of them for me.'

'You're not having a birthday party!' Bill said. 'Yer told me mam yer'd rather have new clothes for the holiday.'

His sister tutted. 'Ye're a proper spoilsport you are! I was only kidding, soft lad!'

'They're very pretty, and a nice present,' Ann said. 'Did you choose them, Jack?'

Jack had thought long and hard about this, in case anyone asked. He knew there wasn't a person in the room who liked his mother, apart from Tess, and he was inclined to say he had bought them himself. But to do that would mean he was ashamed of his mother, and he would never be that. 'No, my mam bought them. We didn't know what to get so she said she'd find something she thought they'd like.'

'Then she has very good taste and Theresa must thank her when she sees her.'

'Oh, I will!' In the mad scramble for chairs, Tess had managed to put herself between Jack and Willy. 'The very first time I see her.'

James was in his element sitting next to Maddy. He thought he'd hopped in lucky, not realising the girl had never had any intention of sitting next to anyone else. 'Me mam said yer served her in the shop on Friday, and she said yer did all right.'

'And why wouldn't I?' Maddy's look of indignation soon turned to a smile. 'She was easy to serve, your mam. She must shop there very

341

often because she knew where everything was and pointed me in the right direction.'

Ann and George sat on the couch listening to the chatter. It seemed everyone wanted to talk at the same time, except the Bingham brothers. But with Maddy and Tess drawing them out, with the help of Joyce, they began to relax and join in the laughter. And like the others, they tucked into the food with gusto.

'I think we're surplus to requirements, love,' George whispered. 'Shall we leave them to get on with it and pay Lizzie a visit?'

Ann looked uncertain. 'D'you think it wise? Will they be all right?'

'There are four very sensible children sitting at that table, Ann, and they'll make sure nothing goes wrong.'

'Oh well, if you're sure.' Ann got to her feet and had to raise her voice to be heard over the noise. She had never quite realised that eight children could make such a racket. 'Your father and I are going down to Lizzie's for an hour. So I'm relying on you to be on your best behaviour. And that means all of you.'

After loud reassurances, she followed her husband out of the front door. 'Why did you say there were four sensible children around the table? What's wrong with the other four?'

'I don't think any of them would do anything stupid, like throwing jellies and trifles at each other. But Madelaine is very adult for her age, so are Bill, James and Jack. They are more grown up in the head than the others and will keep them in check. So let's enjoy ourselves at Lizzie's for an hour while the kids make their own enjoyment.'

Next door, Nellie and Joe Bingham could hear the shrieks of laughter coming through their wall. 'I'm glad the boys are making friends, it's what they need,' Joe said. 'And it was good of yer to help them with the presents, love, they were made up with them.'

'Elevenpence ha'penny each those scarves were, 'cos I wasn't going to buy anything cheap and give the neighbours something to talk about.'

'Nellie, don't yer think ye're being unfair to the neighbours? Next door have never done us no harm, and they did invite the boys to their party.'

Just then they heard Tess's high-pitched laughter, and Nellie said sadly, 'Our Enid would have been nearly eleven now, and I miss her as much now as I did the day she died. Never a day goes by that I don't think of her, and wonder what she'd be like.'

'And yer think I don't?' Joe reached for her hand. 'Just because I'm a man doesn't mean I'm not crying inside. But for the sake of the boys we have to try and put it behind us. They shouldn't suffer, or be made to feel second best, that wouldn't be fair.'

342

'I do me best, Joe, I can't do any more. But there isn't a mother breathing that wouldn't feel the same as I do if they'd lost a child. When Enid died, part of me died with her, and I still can't come to terms with it, even after all these years. Every time I see a mother with a daughter I get jealous and hate her for still having her child when I don't have mine. Sometimes I feel so bitter I go into a rage, and that's when I cause trouble and take it out on strangers, who think I'm crazy.'

'I understand that, Nellie, but the boys need your love as much as Enid would have done. All children need to know they are wanted and loved.'

'I do love them, Joe, and I do try to show it. And I am getting better, even though it is slow and yer might not notice.'

He squeezed her hand. How he worried about her too! She was as thin as a rake and a bag of nerves. There was little to see of the girl he'd married. The girl who had attracted him because she was loving, full of life and always had a smile on her pretty face. He sighed. 'We'll get there, love, just give it time. Yer know I've cut down a lot on me drinking, and I don't go out every night now. That's because I don't want to let the boys down by coming home plastered and picking fights with anyone in the street who gets in me way. So I'm trying as well, and if we hang in together, love, we'll get there in the end.' He hung his head, not wanting to meet her eyes when he said, 'D'yer remember what I used to call our little girl? Smiler, 'cos she always had a big smile on her face. Well I bet right now she's looking down from heaven and wondering why her mam and dad never have a smile on their faces any more. It probably makes her feel sad. So I think, for her sake as well as the boys', we should both make an extra effort, don't you? Then all our children will be happy.'

His words brought tears, as he'd known they would. But better to get them out than keep them locked inside building up the longing, sadness and anger in her heart.

Tess wanted to knock next door on the Monday to thank Mrs Bingham for the scarves, but she'd been warned by her mother that she mustn't make a nuisance of herself. The boys had been thanked for the presents, and that was enough. But it wasn't enough for the young girl, who kept Jack's secret alive in her heart. She wanted to get close to the woman to comfort her and share her grief.

Maddy had gone down to the shop after tea, as she'd been doing for the last week, working from half past five until eight o'clock. So Tess was alone playing outside the house with her skipping rope. She was hoping Mrs Bingham would put in an appearance, because her mother couldn't shout at her if she just spoke to the woman in the street. That wasn't being a nuisance. And the girl's wishes bore fruit when the door opened and Nellie stepped down on to the pavement.

Tess waited until she came abreast then fell into step beside her. 'I want to thank you for the beautiful scarf, Mrs Bingham, I really love it.'

'I'm glad yer liked it,' Nellie grunted, not slowing her pace. 'I'm in a hurry to get to the shop before it closes.'

'I'll walk with you, to keep you company.'

Tess had laid a hand on the woman's arm and Nellie pulled away as though she'd been burned with a red-hot poker. 'I'd rather go on me own.' She hurried away leaving Tess feeling sad and hurt, but without resentment in her heart. It was going to take a long time for Mrs Bingham to like her, but the day would come, she was sure. So the young girl walked back the short distance to her home and knocked on the door. There was no pleasure playing out now, she'd go in and listen to the wireless with her mam and dad.

Nellie, meanwhile, had entered the corner shop to be confronted by Maddy. She would have walked out, but if she did there'd be no tea for their breakfast because all the other shops were closed. 'A quarter of loose tea, please.'

'I'd like to thank you for the lovely scarf, Mrs Bingham,' Maddy said. 'I'm really pleased with it.'

'So yer sister said. Now can yer serve me, 'cos the family are gasping for a drink of tea.'

As she walked to the drawer where the pre-weighed bags of tea were kept, Maddy wondered what it would take to make this woman, if not friendly, then at least polite. It wasn't surprising that no one in the street spoke to her; she certainly gave them no encouragement. 'Thruppence, Mrs Bingham, please.' Maddy passed the tea over and held out her hand for the money. 'Thank you.' Then, as the little woman turned to walk away, Maddy thought of her sister's persistence with their difficult neighbour, and wondered if Tess had a point when she said the woman couldn't help the way she was. So as Nellie put her hand on the door, the girl called, 'Ta-ra, Mrs Bingham.'

She didn't get an answer, but contented herself with saying that at least she'd tried. And before she had any more time to dwell on the subject, Mrs Lizzie was standing in front of her. And her beaming face was in stark contrast to the woman she'd just served.

'Won't be long now, eh, queen? Five days from now we'll be in Welsh Wales!' Lizzie rubbed her hands together in glee. 'I can't wait, me bag's packed already! My feller said I'm like a child the way I'm going on about it.'

'I'm excited myself, Mrs Lizzie. I'm dying to see Mrs Gwen and Mr

344

Mered again, and the chickens. And all our friends at the farm too! You'll love them, I know you will.'

'If I don't, I'll ask for me bleedin' money back,' Lizzie said jokingly. 'Ay, d'yer think I'll click with one of the farmers?'

Maddy giggled at the thought. 'I'll tell your husband if you do. I mean, I wouldn't mind the coal man, or the milk man, 'cos that would be like keeping it in the family. But a Welsh farmer, well, that's different.'

'What's this about a Welsh farmer?' Bert had come up behind Maddy and she nearly jumped out of her skin. 'Is Lizzie leading yer astray, girl?'

'Oh, ye're there, are yer?' Lizzie pulled tongues at him. 'I was just saying, I've packed all me long evening dresses in case I meet a rich, handsome farmer. Always be prepared, that's what I say.'

'I see yer point, Lizzie, a long evening dress would go down very well on a farm. Especially mucking out the pig sty.'

'Yer know, Bert, whatever romance yer've got is in yer backside. I don't see meself mucking out the bleedin' pig sty, I see meself sitting on a horse, overseeing things, if yer know what I mean, like. Lady of the manor, no less.'

'I don't know about my romance being in me backside, but I do know that's where your brains are. Lady of the manor, riding a blinking horse, and I don't think! The horse would take one look at you and bolt, never to be seen again.'

'Bert, yer weren't invited to join in this conversation, so will yer scarper and leave me and Maddy with our dreams? Go and make some other customer miserable.'

Before he left, Bert whispered loudly in Maddy's ear, 'Yer must be suckers for punishment, taking this one on holiday with yer. I'd have thought yer'd have been glad to be rid of her for a week.'

Lizzie was ready for him. 'Ay, well yer know what thought did, don't yer? Followed a muck cart and thought it was a wedding. And the silly bugger even got a cob on 'cos he hadn't been invited.'

When Maddy's clear laughter filled the air, Bert looked across at his wife and they smiled at each other. The looks they exchanged said how nice it was to have a young one in the shop, because there wasn't a customer who didn't have a smile on their face.

Chapter Twenty-five

'In the name of God, where have all the people come from?' Lizzie glared at a woman who had elbowed her out of the way. The station platform was crowded, with hardly enough room to turn. 'I've never seen so many in me life, even on the beach at New Brighton.'

George nodded in agreement. 'I'll never understand why every factory has to close down the same two weeks. If they staggered them, it wouldn't be so bad.'

'We'll be lucky to get seats on the train when it comes in,' Ann said. 'There'll be a mad scramble to get on.'

'I think it would be a good idea if the girls and I leave you and Lizzie with the cases while we fight our way on. We'd stand more chance without having to lug the cases, and we might be lucky in grabbing a few seats. The girls could sit on them while I come for you and the luggage. We might not get one each, but we could take turns in sitting. I don't fancy standing all the way.'

'That's a good idea, Dad,' Maddy said. 'We're quick and can slip in between the people easy, can't we, Tess?'

'Oh yes, we can duck and dive.' Tess's face was flushed with excitement. She didn't care if she had to sit on the floor as long as the train took her to Wales. But her mam and Mrs Lizzie couldn't sit on the floor, that wouldn't be ladylike. 'I bet we get some seats for you.'

But Lizzie was having none of that. George was far too polite to push people out of the way, while she wasn't. 'Sod off, George, I'd stand more chance than any of yer.' She bent her arms so her elbows were sticking out. 'No one would get past them.'

Just then the train chugged in and there was a massive surge. Lizzie told the girls to grab hold of the back of her dress and to hang on tight and not let anyone push her out of the way. George picked up the small bag which held their underwear, and told Ann, 'You stay put, love, until I come for you.' With that, he quickly pushed himself forward until he was behind Tess and they were at the edge of the platform waiting for the passengers alighting from the train to fight their way through the heaving throng.

'If this is what a bleedin' holiday is, then yer can keep it.' Lizzie fell into one of the seats. 'I'll stay at home in future.' She waved the girls into seats in the narrow compartment. 'Sit down quick before someone nabs them.'

'I'll leave this on a seat and go and get Ann.' George threw the small bag down and wiped the sweat from his brow. 'You're right, Lizzie, it's more like hard labour than a holiday. But things will improve, I promise.'

They were lucky to end up with four seats because the train was packed to overflowing, with parents and children squatting on the tops of cases, or on the floor of the corridor outside which ran the full length of the carriage. Maddy and Tess shared a seat, taking turns to sit on each other's knees. And they were getting more excited as each chug of the train took them nearer to their friends in Wales.

'Was it as bad as this last time yer came?' Lizzie asked, finding that if she wanted her feet to touch the floor she had to sit forward in her seat. 'It would have been enough to put me off.'

'No, it wasn't nearly as bad. But then we came on a Monday and travelled home on the Friday, so we missed most of the crush.' George grinned at her. 'You look all hot and bothered, Lizzie, your face is the colour of beetroot.'

'I was sweating like a pig before, but I'm beginning to cool down now. Mind you, as I'm getting rid of one complaint, another one's cropping up. Can't yer hear me tummy rumbling with hunger? I'm bleedin' starving.'

'You won't be when we get to Mrs Gwen's, she'll have a big meal waiting for us,' Tess said. 'Your tummy won't be rumbling then, it'll be groaning with being too full.'

'Don't say any more, queen, or yer'll have me mouth watering.' Lizzie noticed the train had left the built-up area behind and was travelling through the countryside. 'Ay, that's more like it. Look at those green fields and the trees.' She hoisted up her bosom, and much to the amusement of the other people in the carriage said, 'Nature in the raw, that's what it is. Just like God intended it to be. I'll swap it any time for our back jiggers and the smell from the gas works.'

'I doubt that, Lizzie, you'd miss all your friends and neighbours,' Ann said. 'When we were in Wales last year, I said I'd like to live there. But as George said, you have to be born into it. At our age it's too late to appreciate the outdoor life, especially in the winter when the snow's thick on the ground and you can't get around. No dashing to the corner shop if you find you've run out of tea, or sugar. Or if your gas mantle goes for a burton, then you'd be left sitting in the dark.'

'I'm way ahead of yer, queen.' Lizzie was thinking of other things which would be missing from her life. 'I wouldn't see me granddaughter very often, and my feller wouldn't last no time if he didn't have his pub to go to. He'd be dead before I had time to say, "Hey, Norman, get a load of that mountain, isn't it lovely?"' She smiled at the woman in the seat facing, who was trying to hold her laughter in. 'Well, it's true, isn't it, missus? When yer get to our time in life yer can't change yer habits. I like me quarter of mint imperials and my feller would be lost without his nightly pint of bitter ale. When I was a baby in me pram, I used to have a dummy. But my feller used to spit his dummy out, and his mam told me the only way she could stop him crying was by giving him a bottle of brown ale. And he's been partial ever since.'

The two girls giggled as they conjured up a vision of the quiet man who was Mrs Lizzie's husband. Listening to her talk, you would think he was a man who rolled home drunk every night, while he was just the opposite and she loved the bones of him.

'I'm sure Norman would be very pleased if he could hear you,' George said. 'You give the impression he's a drunkard.'

Lizzie opened her mouth in horror. 'Go 'way! Yer don't think that, do yer, missus? Nah, yer must have known I only said it in fun. I mean, no baby could hold a bottle of beer to his mouth, could he? Unless of course he had a clever mother what put the beer in his baby's bottle, which is what his mam did. It worked a treat, she said. He was the most contented baby in the street, never cried and slept most of the time.'

And Lizzie continued to keep her travelling companions, and other passengers, amused for the entire length of the journey.

The station master at Hope station was expecting them, and his face widened into a beaming smile when they stepped from the small local train. Hurrying forward to help with the cases, he said, 'It's a treat to see you again, welcome back. I've had strict instructions from Gwen to look after you. So if you'll wait until I make sure all the doors are closed, and I give the driver the signal, then I'll help you with your luggage.'

'Well, fancy that now! Treated like we were some high-falutin' dignitaries.' The holiday was taking on a new meaning for Lizzie as she saw the station master wave his flag and blow his whistle. 'It's not often I get spoilt, but I could soon get used to it.'

When she was introduced to the station-master-cum-porter-cum-ticket-collector, Lizzie gave him her most ladylike greeting. Holding her hand out like Lady Bountiful, she said, 'I've heard all about you from my friends, and I'm delighted to make your acquaintance.'

George nearly swallowed his Adam's apple trying to keep the laughter back. 'She's being on her best behaviour. She can be a tinker when she gets going.'

'Then she'll be in good company with Gwen.' Acting now as the ticket collector, the man took their tickets before picking up the cases. 'I'll carry these, Mr Richardson, if you'll take the bag.'

Tess was skipping beside him. 'Is Goldie coming for us, Mr Porter?'

'She is that, sweetheart, as soon as I blow my whistle.' He looked down into the eager face. 'You look better than you did last time you came, and you've grown quite a bit.'

Maddy wasn't going to be left out. 'What about me? I've left school now and I've got a job in a shop.'

'My word, that's good, isn't it, bach? Quite the little lady you are, and a very pretty one.' Once outside the station gates, he put the cases down and blew on his whistle. 'They'll be here before you can say Jack Robinson.'

When Lizzie saw the horse-and-trap coming towards them, she was almost lost for words. Almost, but not quite. 'Well I declare! It's just like yer see on the pictures.'

Farmer Tom jumped down from the trap and was very enthusiastic in his greeting. 'The wife and children have got me motheaten. I'm to tell you they're expecting you first thing in the morning. They wanted to come with me now, but I said you'd be tired after the journey.' He grinned at Lizzie. 'You'll be the Mrs Lizzie the girls write about. If all they say is true then we're in for an entertaining week.'

'Take no notice of them, I'm as quiet as a mouse and wouldn't say boo to a goose.' Lizzie had been giving the trap the once over, and the step leading up to it. Sure as eggs she'd show her knickers if she had to climb up that. 'Will we all get in there? Pity the poor horse if he's got to pull the lot of us.'

Maddy and Tess were stroking Goldie, and the horse was nodding her head and neighing, as though to say she remembered them and was glad to see them. 'Goldie is strong, aren't you?' Tess had her arms around the horse's neck and was kissing her. 'She's as strong as an elephant.'

'Well I'm getting in last,' Lizzie said with a determined nod of her head. 'I'm not letting the world see all I've got.' And she stood and watched as George helped his wife and children up the step. Then came her turn, and what a performance that was. In her desire to keep the secret of her knickers to herself, she waved Tom away. 'I'll manage, you go and sit up front with the horse.' The farmer did move away, but not very far because he had an idea she wasn't going to get up that step without help. And although Lizzie didn't know it, the porter was still at the station gate taking it all in so he could tell his wife. And he had plenty to tell her about the antics of the woman who put one foot on the step and then tried to reach the side of the trap to pull herself up. When that didn't work, she turned around and tried getting up backwards. It was so hilarious everyone was in stitches. I mean, he told his wife later that day, there was nothing for her to grip to lever herself up, only fresh air. So around she turned again. And this time she put her hands on the floor of the trap, thinking she could use that to pull herself on to the step, but her bosom and tummy got in the way. Red in the face, she growled, 'Damn, blast and bugger it! It's this flaming bust of mine! When I look down I can't see me feet!'

Tom came from his hiding place, his eyes wet with tears of laughter. 'Let me help you, Lizzie, it'll be a lot quicker.'

'Yeah, okay. If I'm left to meself the bleedin' holiday will be over before it starts.' Lizzie could see the funny side herself, but until she was sitting in the ruddy trap she wasn't going to let her laughter out. Her eyes went around those sitting comfortably and watching her struggles. 'Before yer say anything, I'll tell yer meself. I haven't got me fleecy knickers on, I'm wearing me best cotton ones, and they're blue. That'll save yer the trouble of straining yer necks.' She jerked her head at the farmer. 'Come on, Tom, give us a hand to get in this contraption. And watch where ye're putting yer flaming hands or I'll clock yer one.'

Gwen Owen had been keeping watch, and she was at the gate when the trap came to a halt. The girls were first to reach her, then Ann and George. Hands were shaken and hugs and kisses exchanged. Then George said, 'I'll give Lizzie a hand to get down.'

'Oh, yer've come, have yer? I thought yer were going to leave me here for the whole week, save the trouble of getting me back on again.' Lizzie was looking down at that one step which was the cause of her trouble. 'D'yer think I could make it if I came down backwards?'

George rubbed his chin and looked deep in thought. 'You could try, Lizzie. Me and Tom will stand here and catch you if you fall.'

'Listen to me, soft lad. If I fell on yer I'd flatten the pair of yer.'

Gwen could tell a soul mate when she saw one. So going to the back of the trap, she said, 'Hello, Lizzie, I'm Gwen. And I used to have the same trouble as you getting in and out of the trap. The best way is to come down sideways, with Tom in the trap holding one hand, and George at the bottom holding the other.'

And it worked like a dream. In less than a minute Lizzie was on the ground and glaring at George. 'Why didn't you think of that, yer daft ha'p'orth? Yer see, it proves what I've always said. That a woman's got far more nous than a man.'

Gwen linked her arm. 'Come on in, I bet ye're dying for a drink.'

Tom put the cases in the hall, then as he was leaving he whispered in Gwen's ear loud enough for all to hear, 'From what I've seen, Mrs Owen, I think you're in for a very hectic week with lots of laughter on the menu.'

'D'yer know, Farmer Tom, I think ye're right. It'll be like a holiday for me and Mered.'

And Tom was right about the laughter. For at the dinner table that night, Lizzie's plight was told, and acted out, by Maddy and Tess. And of course George threw in his twopennyworth. But the loudest laughter came from the woman herself, Lizzie. Looking across the table to where Mered was wiping his eyes, she told him, 'They've left something out. They haven't told yer about me new cotton knickers, which are sky-blue pink with a finny-haddy border. They haven't got no pocket in, though, 'cos I didn't see no point at my age. I mean, a pocket in me navy blue fleecy knickers what I went to school in, well that pocket came in handy to keep me ollies in. But I gave up playing ollies when I got married.'

Tess came to stand beside her chair and put an arm around her. 'You were a tomboy if you played marbles, Mrs Lizzie, 'cos it's not a girls' game.'

Lizzie swivelled in her chair and lifted her skirt above her knees. 'See them, queen? Well, they're not housemaid's knees what I got from scrubbing floors. They're from kneeling in the gutter playing ollies with the lads, with me backside stuck up in the air and me tongue hanging out of the side of me mouth.'

The dinner took two hours that night, because there was more laughing done than eating. And just over half a mile away, there was laughter around the farmer's table as he related the antics of Lizzie. The children laughed so loud it was a wonder it wasn't heard in the railway cottage, where the station-master-cum-porter-cum-ticket-collector lived with his wife. But then they wouldn't have heard it, because they were too busy laughing themselves.

Next morning, when Gwen was clearing the breakfast dishes, she asked, 'Would yer mind if I came to the farm with yer today? Save me being stuck in the house talking to meself.'

'You're more than welcome, Gwen,' Ann told her. 'I'll help you with these dishes and they'll be done in no time.'

'I'll help as well, queen, seeing as that was the best breakfast I've ever had in me life.' Lizzie felt full to bursting. 'I thoroughly enjoyed it, Gwen, thank yer.'

'You can't wash the dishes, Mrs Lizzie, you're coming to help me and Maddy feed the chickens.' Tess had that no-nonsense look on her face. 'You haven't seen them yet, and you've got to meet Nelson and Cagney. Mr Mered said he would leave the food ready for us, and they'll be hungry by now.'

'Oh well, that's me told, isn't it, queen?' Lizzie, who had only ever been near a dead chicken, didn't know whether she fancied feeding live ones. 'Are you coming, George?'

'I wouldn't miss it for a big clock, Lizzie. The poor chickens don't know what they're in for. Let's hope you don't frighten them so much they stop laying, or we'll get no breakfast tomorrow.'

'Take no notice of him, Lizzie,' Gwen said, a huge tray between her hands stacked with the dirty dishes. 'Our chickens don't frighten so easily.'

'Do they all lay eggs?'

'Only the hens. We keep half hens and half cocks.'

'You've still got Nelson and Cagney, haven't you?' Tess asked. 'And Clarissa?'

Gwen had been well primed by Mered for this, and she didn't flinch. 'Yes, they're all still here.' Knowing how sensitive the girl was, it had been decided not to tell her that Clarissa had graced someone's Christmas dinner table. Nor that Nelson and Cagney had only been saved because neither Gwen nor Mered would have the heart to tell Tess that the birds she mentioned in every one of her letters were no longer in the land of the living. 'You might not recognise Cagney, 'cos he's grown quite a bit.'

'Ooh, I can't wait to see them! Come on, Mrs Lizzie, we've had a big breakfast and it's not fair to keep the chickens waiting for theirs.'

Lizzie took one look at the squawking birds behind the barbed wire and shook her head. 'Yer'll not get me in there for love nor money. If you're daft enough to go in, then you go, but I ain't budging from here.'

George winked at the girls. 'Come on, let's show Lizzie how brave we are.'

Tess thought she'd recognise the birds, but they all looked alike to her now. So she called, 'Nelson, come on, Nelson.' And sure enough, the biggest bird in the coop came close to her, squawking its head off. 'Maddy, you feed him while I find Cagney.'

'I think that's him at the back, Tess,' George said, spreading the seed over a wide area. 'It seems he's still as shy as he was last year.'

Tess took a handful of seed from the bucket and made her way

353

through the flock. 'Come on, Cagney, it's me again. You remember me, don't you?'

Lizzie began to feel guilty. She was being put to shame by two young girls! Well, she couldn't let that happen, could she? Never let it be said that Elizabeth Ferguson was a coward. 'Open the gate, George, and let me in. But don't yer leave me, mind, you stick by me side the whole time. I don't half like eating a chicken leg, but I don't want one of them doing a tit-for-tat and eating one of *my* bleedin' legs.'

'Especially not today,' Maddy said, giggling. 'Not when you've got your best sky-blue-pink-with-a-finny-haddy-border knickers on.'

Gwen grinned when she heard the laughter. 'She's a real case is Lizzie. I bet there's never a dull moment when she's around.'

'She might not look it, Gwen, and she might not sound it, but she's an angel. I don't know what I'd have done without her when George had his accident. She was a tower of strength then, and she's been my friend ever since.'

'That's what you call a friend.' Gwen pointed to the large Welsh dresser. 'The plates go on there, sweetheart.' She looked around to make sure there were no more dirty dishes before pulling the plug out of the sink. 'I can't wait for Brenda to meet her, she'll be in her apple-cart. There's nothing she likes better than a good laugh.'

Ann folded the tea towel and put it over the bar behind the door. 'She'll get plenty of those today, I guarantee it.'

'Ay, this is the life, isn't it?' Lizzie said as they strolled up the lane towards the farm. 'My feller doesn't know what he's missing. He'll be sitting watching the clock right now, waiting for the bleedin' pubs to open.'

'Everyone to their own taste, Lizzie,' George said. 'If that's what Norman likes, then who are we to disagree?'

'Ay, maybe so. But if I have my way he'll be coming with us next year. That's if yer'll have us, that is.'

'We'll have you any time, Lizzie, you know that,' Ann said. 'To use your own expression, we all love the bones of you.'

'Ah, that's nice of yer, queen.'

They were nearing a bend in the lane when they heard young voices, and the two girls took to their heels. 'It's Grace and Alan!'

'Are we near the farm, then, queen?'

'Yes, Lizzie, it's just around the corner. The next time you see the girls they'll either be in the pig sty or in a field with Goldie.'

Brenda was waiting at the door and hurried to the gate to greet them. Her welcome was warm and genuine. There were hugs and kisses for Ann and George, and a tilting of the head when she stood in front of

354

Lizzie. 'And this is your good friend who had a slight problem with our trap?'

'A slight problem, did yer say?' Lizzie went into her dramatic pose. 'Ay, missus, I'll have yer know that your trap was the cause of me losing me modesty.'

George chortled. 'What modesty was that, Lizzie?'

'The modesty I would have had if it hadn't been for that flaming trap!' The sun was shining on Lizzie's red hair, turning it into a golden glow, and bringing her freckles into prominence. 'It was no joke, I was mortified.' She grinned at him. 'If yer don't know what mortified means, George, look it up in the dictionary like I did.'

Brenda put her arms around her and gave her a hug. 'Mortified or not, you are more than welcome. Now come in the house and have a cool drink of home-made lemonade. Then we'll show you around the farm before Tom comes home for his dinner.' She took Lizzie's arm. 'Tom warned me not to mention blue cotton knickers, but what's a pair of knickers between friends, eh?'

'Them's my sentiments exactly, queen. We'd all be in Queer Street without them, walking around with bare backsides. I mean, how would I feel if I got run over by a tram and was taken to hospital with no knickers on? I wouldn't be just mortified, I'd be bleedin' mortified.'

After a cool drink and a sit-down, Brenda took them on a tour of the farm. And Lizzie, who'd never been near a live animal in her life, except for the moggy next door, was thrilled and excited about everything she saw. She even picked up the courage to stroke Goldie. But she gave the pigs a miss because as she said, they were dirty beggars and she couldn't understand how Maddy and Tess could pick them up and pet them.

It was the pigs that started the laughter as they sat around the big farm kitchen table having their lunch. 'I didn't mind yer chickens so much, Gwen, 'cos they keep themselves pretty clean. But I have to say, Tom, those bleedin' pigs are filthy buggers. What yer should do is put nappies on them. I mean, they don't care where they do it, do they? Or who's watching?'

Tom was tucking into a slice of home-made mince pie, and he nearly choked as a piece of meat went down the wrong way when he laughed. 'You reckon that would be an improvement, do you, Lizzie?'

Lizzie's eyes narrowed. 'I'm not thinking straight, am I? Silly cow that I am, I forgot it would be Brenda what had to wash the nappies. No, yer best bet, Tom, is to put paper out for them to wipe their backsides on.'

Grace and Alan couldn't take their eyes off Lizzie, they'd never known anyone like her. There was no swearing in their house, unless there was a catastrophe like the tractor breaking down, or their mam forgetting she had a batch of cakes in the oven and they were so burned they were only fit for the animals. It wasn't that they'd never heard swear words, mind you, there were women in the village who could turn the air blue. But coming from Mrs Lizzie it was funny, because her face was doing contortions at the same time and you couldn't help laughing.

'Those pigs you're talking about happen to be my friends, Mrs Lizzie,' Tess said. 'And they can't help being dirty beggars.'

Her face dead serious, Lizzie held out her hands. 'Yer mean I'm yer friend, and Curly and Pinky are yer friends too?'

The girl nodded. 'Yes, you're all my friends.'

'That puts me in me place, doesn't it? My feller's always telling me I've come down in the world, but I didn't think I'd come that far down. And I'll tell yer what, queen, much as I want to be yer friend, ye're not getting me in that sty while I'm wearing me best blue cotton knickers.'

Tom raised his brows before saying casually, 'If yer want to see around all my fields, Lizzie, I could take you in the tractor, save you walking.'

'Oh, that's nice of yer, Tom!' She missed the meaningful glances being exchanged and George's look of apprehension. 'Yeah, I'd like that. Will the others be walking behind?'

'They'll have to, because I can't get them all on the tractor.'

Lizzie thought that was a splendid idea. She could act like Lady Muck, waving her hand to everyone. And when Tom said they could take photographs, well, there was no stopping her imagination from running riot.

'Dad, could me and Tess have one taken standing on the tractor, with Mrs Lizzie behind the wheel?' Alan asked. 'That would be great!'

'And me and Maddy, Dad?' Grace was thinking it would be a miracle if Mrs Lizzie managed to get on the tractor, but in case she did, it would be nice to have a photograph to look back on. She'd left school now but hadn't got a job yet. Not that she'd tried hard, she wanted to leave it until her friends from Liverpool had been.

'What about little old me?' Gwen asked. 'I know I'm no oil painting, but I wouldn't break yer camera.'

'We'll all get in on the act if Tom has no objection.' George had very grave doubts that photographs would ever be taken of Lizzie on the tractor. The trap was bad enough, the tractor would be ten times worse. But it should be fun.

Lizzie eyed the tractor with a look that gave nothing away. 'Is that it?'

'Yes, you'll have a good view sitting up there.' Tom reached for the iron bar on the side of the machine and used it as a lever to pull himself on to the very high step. 'You'll like it up here, Lizzie, you can see for miles.'

Lizzie crooked her index finger and beckoned for him to lean closer. 'Yer know what yer can do, Tom? Yer can sod off! I'd need a pair of wings to get up there and I've left mine at home on top of the wardrobe.'

'You could do it, Lizzie, if you tried,' George said. 'I'll give you a push from behind.'

'Ay, buggerlugs, yer can just keep away from my behind. It's private property that is.' She could hear the giggles and laughter, and this made her determined to get on that bloody tractor if it killed her. 'Come down, Tom.'

'Ah, aren't you going to join me? I was looking forward to seeing you sitting next to me.' Tom jumped down with ease. He'd been driving a tractor since he was Alan's age and it was second nature to him. 'I am disappointed, Lizzie.'

'Oh, I'm not going to disappoint yer, lad, just yer wait and see.' Lizzie was dying to laugh, but she'd wait until she was perched up there looking down on them all, and then she'd laugh her bleedin' head off. 'Brenda, have yer got a stool I can borrow?'

Alan was quick to answer. 'I'll get it for you, Mrs Lizzie. Come on, Tess.' The pair were back in less than a minute and the stool was put in front of Lizzie.

'Now can yer all see that white cloud over there? Well I want yer all to line up on the other side of this bloody contraption, with yer backs to me, and keep looking at that cloud until I tell yer to turn round.'

As Gwen was to tell her husband that night, the next fifteen minutes were the funniest she'd ever known. They could hear Lizzie puffing and panting, and her language was colourful to say the least. First it was the bleedin' stool wobbling, then her dress was too bleedin' tight for her to bend her leg, and whoever made the bleedin' tractor was tuppence short of a shilling and if she could get her hands on him she'd bleedin' pulverise him.

When Brenda could stand it no longer, she put a finger to her lips to warn the others to be quiet and crept around the machine. She came back holding her tummy and saying, 'You wouldn't believe it. Her dress is around her waist, she's sitting on the step so she can't turn to get in the cab of the tractor, and the stool's fallen over so she can't get back out.'

'Oh, the poor woman! I'm going to give her a hand.' Gwen started to walk, while calling out, 'It's only me, Lizzie, and if ye're shy, just remember yer've got nothing that I haven't got.'

'No need to, queen, I don't need no help.'

They all turned around and their mouths gaped when they saw Lizzie sitting in the tractor, waving to them. And the smile on her face said it all: 'There yer are now, clever buggers, yer can laugh the other side of yer faces now.'

'How on earth did you manage it?' Ann asked. 'I never thought you'd make it in a month of Sundays.'

'I'd tell yer, queen, if there were no men here. But I can't say in front of them that I took me knickers off and threw them over the steering wheel so I could pull meself around. Then I was able to kneel on the step and the rest was easy. But I won't tell yer in case I embarrass the men.'

'You're not sitting on my seat without any knickers on, are you, Lizzie?'

'Of course not, soft lad! I put them back on again, didn't I? And the only one what saw me doing me contortionist act was a bleedin' cow, and he ain't going to tell no one.'

That episode was the start of a week of sunshine, laughter and friendships sealed. A week that everyone was sorry to see the end of.

George put the case down in the middle of the living room. 'Well, home sweet home again. But what a marvellous holiday it's been, eh?'

Ann put her arms around his waist. 'Wonderful. Absolutely wonderful.'

'Mrs Lizzie didn't half enjoy it,' Tess said. 'She's coming again next year.'

'It was even better than last year.' Maddy was wishing the holiday was just beginning and they could go all through it again. 'I can't wait to tell James about it.'

'I'll be telling Jack,' Tess said. 'But not the part about the knickers.'

'Theresa, I wish you wouldn't be so friendly with Jack, he's too old for you.' Ann turned from her husband. 'Besides, you know what a funny ossity his mother is. It's not natural the way she behaves and I don't want you getting too friendly with any of them.'

Tears were quick to sting the back of the girl's eyes. She wanted to blurt out that the only thing wrong with the woman next door was that her heart had been broken. But she didn't, because she'd made a promise. 'Well I like Jack, he's my friend and I'm going to keep on talking to him.'

'All right, leave things be,' George said. 'We've just come back from a wonderful holiday and I don't want to spoil the memory. If Tess wants to talk to the boy, and I see no harm in that, let her do so. And can we now close the subject, please?'

Tess tossed her head, that stubborn look on her face. If only Jack hadn't asked her to make that pledge, everything would be different. Her mam and everyone in the street would understand and sympathise, and they'd go out of their way to be friends with the woman next door. Like she intended to do, no matter what anyone said.

Chapter Twenty-six

Maddy had been working in the shop for three months when Lily Green gave birth to a baby girl. And any hopes Ann had of getting her daughter to night school to prepare her for a better future went out of the window. Maddy loved her job from the first day she started. Although there was the odd customer who could be awkward, on the whole they were easy to serve, pleasant and always ready for a laugh. And she got on well with Bert, proud that he felt her capable of doing the job without him keeping an eye on her all the time. She looked forward to the tea breaks, when Lily would come down and they'd share a pot of tea and a gossip while sitting on the upturned orange box. The day the baby was born in the upstairs bedroom was the most exciting day of her life. Bert had been on edge for hours, as she herself had been, and when the midwife came down and said he was the father of a beautiful baby girl, he waltzed Maddy around the shop before flying up the stairs. When he came down he looked the happiest man in the world, and he told Maddy she could go up and see the baby, but only for a few minutes because Lily needed to sleep. The midwife let her hold the baby for a minute, and it was a wonderful feeling to look down on that tiny face, which was red and wrinkled but beautiful. And the girl fell in love with her. A very weak and tired Lily told her that they were going to have the baby christened Marie, and Maddy could come to the christening.

When she got home that night, all Maddy could talk about was the baby. And the family shared her pleasure and said they must buy a present for the new arrival. 'I can't wait to tell James,' she said. 'Fancy them letting me hold her!' She saw James nearly every night, and he'd either come in and have a game of cards, or they'd go for a walk. He had asked if he could take her to the pictures, but Ann said she would prefer them to wait until her daughter was at least fifteen.

A few days after the baby was born, Tess had her own good news. The magazine which had printed her first short story was going to print the one about Mrs Lizzie and her talking rose. And once again they were going to pay Tess the handsome sum of five shillings. The day she found out about that, she was eager to tell Jack and waited for him to come home from work. He was pleased for her, she could see that, and she asked him to promise he'd tell his mother. Whether he did or not was hard to say, because Nellie's attitude towards the girl was the same as it was to all her neighbours. She either ignored them completely, or was rude to them. She was never rude to Tess, but was never friendly either. Jack said his mam was over the moon for her, and that she must be very clever, but it was hard to believe he was telling the truth.

With only a few weeks to Christmas, Ann was keen to start buying clothes and presents for the girls and George. So, arm in arm with Dolly and Bridie, she set off for a visit to Paddy's market. And true to form, Dolly's gift for haggling with the stallholders not only gave them a good laugh but saved them money into the bargain.

'It's a genius yer are, me darlin',' Bridie said after buying three shirts at thruppence each less than the man was originally asking for them. She thought they were cheap to begin with and would have willingly handed over the money, but haggling was part of the fun for Dolly and she couldn't resist. And she had an answer for everything. When the man on the stall asked if she'd like to take the eyes out of his head, she shook her head, saying she didn't like the colour of them.

Ann had no money worries these days, with George being paid the wage he was on before the accident and the rent being six shillings a week less. And Maddy was bringing a few bob in now, which made a difference. But old habits die hard, and she was still practical with money, putting a few shillings aside each week. So she was able to splash out on skirts and blouses for the girls, and a shirt and pullover for her husband. Next week she'd buy herself something nice to wear over Christmas and start on the presents for her family and friends.

Feeling pleased with herself, and light in heart, she suggested, 'How about me mugging you to a cup of tea in that café in Scotland Road?'

'No, let's go back to my place and we can sit and talk in peace over a cuppa.' Dolly glanced around before adding, 'Besides, I'm dying to go to the lavvy, I've been crossing me legs for the last half-hour.'

'Same here,' Bridie admitted. 'It's meself that's getting desperate.'

So without more ado they left the market and sighed with relief when a tram came along handy. 'You two go straight up,' Ann said, as they stepped off the tram. 'I'll call into the corner shop and see if they've got any decent cakes in.'

'Make mine a cream slice,' Dolly called over her shoulder as she made good time up the street. 'And Bridie as well.'

'You'll be lucky, they don't get many cream cakes in,' Ann shouted after them. 'And I don't fancy walking down to Sayer's either, so you'll have to make the best of what Bert's got in.'

Maddy's face lit up when she saw her mother carrying quite a few parcels. 'Did you get what you wanted, Mam?'

'Yes, I'm feeling quite chuffed with my little self. But don't ask me what I've bought because I'm not going to tell you. Me and Bridie are going to Dolly's for a cuppa, and I want to mug them to a nice cake. I suppose it's too much to ask if you have three cream slices left?'

'I know we haven't got three slices left, but have a look for yourself, Mam. Unless Mr Green has sold any in the last ten minutes, we've got one slice, a cream bun and an éclair. Oh, and a few iced buns.'

'I'll take the three cream cakes, love, beggars can't be choosers.' While her daughter reached for a bag to put the cakes in, Ann crossed to the long counter where the shopkeeper was serving. 'How's the baby, Bert? Well, I hope?'

Bert included his customer in the conversation. 'Ladies, she's got a pair of lungs on her like nobody's business. When she's hungry or wants her nappy changing, she soon lets us know.' All the love he had for the baby was there in his eyes to see. 'She's getting spoilt too, 'cos Lily spends most of the day nursing her.'

'She'll rue the day she did that,' the customer said. 'Once babies know they only have to cry to be picked up, yer'll never have any peace.'

'I've got a feeling Bert's jealous because it's not him nursing the baby.'

'Ye're right, Ann. I don't get to spend much time with her because she's usually been put in the cot by the time I close up in here. And Lily won't let me disturb her.' He grinned. 'I've tried to get Lily to swap places so the baby gets to know me, but she's not having any. I've told her the child will be growing up not knowing who her father is.'

Maddy came to stand beside him with the bag of cakes carefully balanced on her palm. 'I think the baby takes after you, Mr Green. She's got your colouring, and your nose.'

'Then heaven help her,' he laughed, 'if she's as ugly as me.'

'She could do a lot worse,' Ann said, putting the shopping on the floor between her feet so she could get to her purse. 'How much do I owe, Madelaine?'

'Sixpence, please, Mam.'

After passing the money over, Ann said, 'Now let me get organised. They'll have my guts for garters if I squash the cakes.' After weighing up the problem, she put her handbag in the crook of her arm and the cakes in her hand, leaving one arm and hand free. 'Madelaine, put some of the bags under my arm and the biggest one in my hand. And then be an angel and open the door for me.'

'If you leave some here, Mam, I'll bring them home with me, save you struggling.'

'Not on your life! These won't be seeing the light of day until

363

Christmas morning. Now open the door, please.' When she felt the bags were safe, she called, 'Cheerio, Bert! Give Lily my kind regards.'

Ann was halfway up the street when she could feel one of the bags slipping from her arm. And the only person in sight who could help was Nellie Bingham, on her way to the shops. 'I wonder if you'd help me, Mrs Bingham? One of the bags is slipping and I'd be grateful if you'd push it back in for me.'

Without saying a word, Nellie weighed up the situation. Then, spotting the wayward bag, she pushed it to safety before going on her way. Ann stared at the retreating back and shook her head. Nellie really was a difficult person. Still, that was no reason for Ann to be rude as well, so she called after her, 'Thank you, Mrs Bingham.' But for all the notice Nellie took, she might just as well have not bothered.

Dolly opened the door and grinned. 'I nearly got caught short there, girl, I just made it in time.' She stood aside for Ann to get past. 'Saved by the bell I was.'

Ann deposited the bags on the couch. 'Can I ask if you'll put these on top of your wardrobe, Dolly? Otherwise the girls will be snooping.'

'Yeah, leave them there, girl, and I'll take them up when we've had a drink.' Dolly eyed the cake bag. 'Me mouth is watering.'

'There's only one cream slice, so two of us are going to be disappointed. Shall we draw lots for it?'

'Not at all!' Bridie said. 'Sure, it's meself that'll be thankful for a cake of any kind.'

When Dolly laughed her whole body shook. 'I'm not as generous as her, girl, I'll fight yer tooth and nail for the cream slice.'

'No need to, you can have it. After all, your cheek saved me a few bob today, so it's the least I can do.'

The three women sat around the table discussing the coming festive season. 'You had the party on Boxing Day last year, Ann, so I'll have it this year,' Dolly said, her plump elbows resting on the table. 'That's only fair.'

'No, we'll do as we did last year, shall we? Me Boxing Day and Bridie New Year's Eve. That's if it's okay with you?'

Both women nodded. 'The children can have their own little party in my house,' Bridie said. 'They'd enjoy it better than being with us grown-ups.'

Dolly nodded, looking decidedly happy. 'That didn't take long, did it? Our Christmas parties organised in five minutes! Yer can't beat that!'

'Hardly organised, Dolly, but I know what you mean.' Ann glanced at the clock. 'It's time to start thinking of putting the dinner on. But I've enjoyed myself today, thanks to you two. And if you feel like it, we can go again next week and get the rest of the presents.'

'Suits me, girl!'

'And me,' Bridie said. 'Sure, wouldn't I rather be out in good company than sitting in me house looking at four walls?'

Ann pushed her chair back. 'Come on, Bridie, we'll leave Dolly to get on with her dinner.'

'So you had a good day?' George said, contented to see his wife looking so happy. Moving to Willard Street had been the best thing that could have happened to her. She laughed more easily, even telling jokes herself, and was far more relaxed. And of course the improvement in their younger daughter's health was a big worry off her mind. 'Did Dolly have the stallholders tearing their hair out?'

'Not quite. One said that because of her his children would be having bread and dripping for their tea. And he didn't know how she could sleep at night taking the food out of the mouths of children. But it was all in fun, they seemed to enjoy her haggling.'

'You've made some good friends in the short time we've been here.'

'Yes, I feel very lucky. We've even arranged the Christmas parties, as we did last year, with the children having their own party in one of the houses.'

'Oh, goody,' Maddy said. 'I hope I can ask James and Billy.'

Tess was quick to say, 'And I'd like Jack and Willy to come.'

Ann shook her head. 'No, Theresa, definitely not!' She went on to tell of the encounter with their neighbour. 'Not one word out of her, even when I shouted after her to thank her. She's impossible, there's no getting through to her.'

Tess could keep quiet no longer. She was sorry to break her promise to Jack, but she couldn't sit and listen to his mother being criticised by someone who didn't know what Mrs Bingham had suffered. 'Mam, what would you do if I died? Or Maddy died?'

'What a terrible question to ask, Theresa! What made you think of such a thing?'

'I want to know what you would do, Mam, if I died? Please tell me.'

Ann looked to her husband for help, but George too was at a loss and shook his head. 'I can't imagine anything so terrible, Theresa, but I think I'd want to die too. I would surely go out of my mind with grief.'

'Like Mrs Bingham did?'

There wasn't a sound, not even of breathing, for several seconds. Then George asked, 'What are you saying, Tess? Your mam and I would like to know.'

'Mrs Bingham had a little girl, Enid, and she died when she was five. Jack told me ages ago but asked me to promise not to tell. They only moved here because his dad thought it would be better for his mam. You see, she went out of her mind, Mam, like you said you would.' The tears were rolling down the girl's face, and Maddy put her arm around her and held her close. 'She never used to be like this, Jack said, she was always happy and laughing. And his dad never used to drink either.'

'Oh my God, the poor woman!' Ann was racked with guilt. 'I don't know what to say, I feel devastated for her. And her husband and the boys. If only I'd known I would have tried harder, as I'm sure the other neighbours would. But we weren't to know.' She was sobbing when she turned her face to her husband. 'George, that's why she searched for little Emma Wilson when she went missing. We all searched, every woman in the street, but it was Nellie who found her and brought her out of that entry to safety. And she wouldn't let anyone thank her. She must have been thinking of her daughter then.'

George nodded before turning to his younger daughter. 'What else did Jack tell you, Tess? Did he say why the little girl died?'

Tess sniffed up. 'His mam thought it was only a cold, but it turned to pneumonia and the little girl died. Jack and Willy loved their little sister, and they still think of her. But they were too young at the time to help their mam and dad.' She drew a hand across her tear-stained eyes. 'You mustn't tell anyone, 'cos I gave my promise to Jack, and he wouldn't be my friend if he knew I'd told you his secret. And I wouldn't have broken my promise to him if everyone didn't keep on calling Mrs Bingham bad names.'

'I think this is one promise you were right to break. Only good can come of it, Tess, so don't fret that you've told us.' Once again George was struck by his younger daughter's understanding. She'd said all along that Mrs Bingham couldn't help what she did, and except for the first week or two after they'd moved into this house, she'd never failed to stick up for the woman. It was as though she could sense things that other people missed. And she could be as stubborn as a mule in her loyalty. 'Now we know, we can try to build bridges.'

'You mustn't tell anyone, or I'll never speak to you again.' And the expression on their daughter's face told her parents she meant every word.

'I certainly won't go shouting it from the rooftops, Theresa, but I have to make amends for being so wrong about Mrs Bingham. I've said some wicked things and I'll never forgive myself. In her shoes, I would probably have behaved a lot worse than she has.' Ann looked down at her hands, where the fingers were pressing hard on the skin around her nails. She could feel the pain but told herself it was God paying her back. She felt like rushing upstairs, throwing herself on the bed and sobbing away her sadness. Losing a five-year-old girl didn't bear thinking about. But how to help someone who didn't want help? 'Theresa, do you trust Mrs Lizzie?'

'Of course I trust Mrs Lizzie, she's my friend.'

'Then let me tell her what you've told us. You know Lizzie is very wise, and she wouldn't ever hurt anyone. So let me ask her advice on how we can best help Mrs Bingham?'

'You can tell Mrs Lizzie as long as you don't let on to next door. It would bring it all back and Mrs Bingham would be very hurt if she was reminded about little Enid.'

'I give you my solemn word that we will never tell her what we know. Hopefully the time might come when she feels able to tell us herself. She has to learn to trust us first.'

'I know that, Mam, and I have tried to get her to like me, but I can't get anywhere with her. And I feel sorry for Jack and Willy, 'cos they lost a little sister that they loved.'

'Well, I'm going to leave you to clear the table and wash up, while I go down to see Lizzie. I don't want to leave it, because it's Christmas in three weeks and it would be nice to be friends with our neighbours by that time. I don't mean close friends, that can't be done in such a short time, but it would be something to build on.'

'It's all right for me to invite Jack and Willy to the Christmas party, then?' Tess asked. 'I'll be seeing Jack later when he goes for his dad's cigarettes.'

'Can I ask you not to mention it tonight, Theresa, please? It might be the opening I need to approach Mrs Bingham.'

'You mean you would ask her if the boys can come?'

'It's just a thought at the moment, so don't mention it until I've thought it through. Best to take things slowly or we may make matters worse. I'll see what Lizzie says, she's usually got an answer for most things, and two heads are better than one.'

Norman opened the door and smiled a welcome. 'Come in, Ann. Lizzie's in the kitchen washing the dishes and asking why someone couldn't invent plates that we could throw away when they've been used. I explained the difficulty of putting scouse on a paper plate, but she said it was all right for me, I didn't have to wash the bleedin' things.'

'Blackening my name again, are yer?' Lizzie came through from the kitchen wiping her hands. 'So help me, he's worse than a woman for tittle-tattle.'

'I hope he's going out then,' Ann said. 'Because what I've come to talk about isn't to be repeated to a living soul.'

'In that case I'm not going out.' Norman plonked himself in his favourite fireside chair and reached into his pocket for his cigarettes. 'Mind you, it'll have to be juicy gossip for me to miss me beer.'

'Take no notice of him, queen, he can't stand gossip. And he'd never repeat anything 'cos that would mean talking, and it takes me all me time to get a word out of him.'

'Lizzie Ferguson, yer exaggerate more than anyone I know. Why, only this morning I said ta-ra to yer when I left for work. And I'll be saying it to yer again pretty soon when it's time for me to go to the pub. That's twice in one day, Mrs Woman, so don't be telling people I don't talk to yer.'

'Well try and keep yer trap shut while Ann tells us what she's come for.' Her eyes narrowed, Lizzie gazed at her friend. 'Yer look pale, queen, is something wrong?'

'I've had a shock and it upset me. I'll start from the beginning, when I went to the market with Dolly and Bridie, but I must stress that this is strictly between ourselves.' When Ann came to the part where Theresa had asked if she could invite the boys next door to the Christmas party, her eyes filled up. 'I said she couldn't because their mother was impossible, there was no getting through to her.' By the time she came to the end of the tale, the tears were running freely. 'I feel terrible because while Theresa has been sticking up for Nellie all along, I haven't had a good word to say about her.'

Lizzie digested the news in silence, gazing down at her clasped hands. 'Ye're not the only one, queen, no one in the street has a good word for her. Some of them have come to blows with her, me included! Oh, dear God, what a terrible tragedy! Can yer imagine how she felt, losing a five-year-old child? It's enough to send anyone round the bend. And the father and Jack and Willy, they must have suffered agonies too!'

'It's no wonder Joe Bingham drinks himself soft every night,' Norman said. 'It's probably the only way he can cope with it.'

'Jack told Theresa his dad never used to drink before the girl died.' Ann pinched hard on the bridge of her nose, hoping the pain would take away the pain in her heart. 'And he said his mam used to be always happy and laughing. Those two boys would only be eight or nine, and it must have been awful for them, not knowing how to show their grief.'

'We can't let it carry on,' Lizzie said. 'The family need people around them to take their minds off it. They'll never forget it, or stop grieving, but having friends around them would ease their suffering until such time as they could remember their little girl without it breaking their hearts. The trouble is, Nellie is very difficult, she seems not to want friends.'

'I've got an idea, and I wondered what you think about it, Lizzie.

Theresa wants to invite the boys to the children's Christmas party, that's how all this started. And I thank God now for her obstinacy and her loyalty. She's got a damn sight more nous than I've got. Anyway, I've told her not to mention the party to the boys, because it might be an opening for me to get on speaking terms with the parents. I could knock and pass the invitation through Nellie. I don't think she'd begrudge the boys being asked, she seems to care for them. What d'you think, Lizzie, is it worth a try?'

'I think it's a bleedin' good idea, queen! It's no good being too eager and pushing ourselves on to her, that would only get her back up. I'll pass the time of day if I see her, and I'll keep on doing it even if I don't get an answer. If we do it gradual, like, we'll get there in the end.'

'We've got to,' Ann said, rising from her chair. 'Or I'll never know a minute's peace. I'll give Nellie a knock tomorrow and see how I get on.'

'Will yer let us know, queen?'

'Of course I will. Come and throw me out. Ta-ra, Norman.'

'Ta-ra, girl, and the best of luck.'

Ann stood in front of the mirror and spoke to her reflection. 'Don't stand there dithering, get on with it! She can't eat you!' She gave a nod of determination and made for the door before she could change her mind. But by the time she lifted the knocker on the Binghams' door, her determination had turned to apprehension.

There was no smile of welcome on Nellie's face. 'Yes, what d'yer want?'

'We're having a party for a few youngsters on Boxing Day, just some of the neighbours' children, and I wondered if you'd allow Jack and Willy to come?'

That put Nellie in a quandary. She didn't want to get pally with the neighbours, but she had to think of her boys. They didn't get much pleasure out of life, and she was well aware that she was to blame for it. And she knew they'd be tickled pink to be invited to a party. 'Yeah, they'd like that.' Then, as an afterthought, she mumbled, 'Thanks for asking.'

'It's a pleasure, they're nice boys.' As she turned away, Ann said, 'I'll let you know the details in a day or two. Ta-ra, Nellie.'

Back in her own house, she flopped in a chair and let out a long sigh of relief. She'd done it, and it hadn't been so bad after all. And at least Nellie had spoken to her, that was a start. Then she frowned as a knock came on the door. She wasn't expecting anyone, but it was probably Bridie or Dolly come for a cuppa and a chat. Thank goodness she'd bought a pound of mixed biscuits when she was at the shops.

The smile dropped from Ann's face when she saw Nellie standing outside. Right away she thought the woman had changed her mind, but she was wrong.

'This party ye're having, do the boys have to bring presents, and how many?'

'Good heavens, no!' Ann held the door wide. 'Come in for a minute, we can't talk properly with me up here and you down there.'

'No, I won't come in, just tell me about the presents.'

'Stand inside for a minute. There's no one in but me. As long as you don't look at the state of the room, I wasn't expecting visitors.' Ann walked back into the living room, giving the woman no alternative but to follow. 'There's about ten children, Nellie, far too many to buy presents for. But a Christmas card for each of them would be nice.'

'Yer'll have to give me their names.' Nellie was eyeing the open door and would be glad to be walking through it. 'Can yer let me have them?'

'I'll write them out and give them to you when I call to tell you the arrangements for the party. It'll either be in Mrs Flannery's or Mrs Hanrahan's, we're not sure yet. But there'll be plenty of time for the boys to write the cards out.'

Nellie took to her heels. 'I'll buy the cards tomorrow. Ta-ra.'

George's look was one of disbelief. 'You called next door about the party, and then Nellie Bingham was actually in this house? You've done wonders, love, and I'm really glad the ice has been broken.'

Tess came to give her mother a hug. 'Thank you, Mam, you've made me very happy.'

'I think you've been very clever, Mam,' Maddy said. 'Just a simple thing like the invitations, and it seems to have worked wonders.'

'I wouldn't go as far as to say it worked wonders, or that the ice has been broken.' Ann was optimistic but didn't want to build her younger daughter's hopes up. 'But it's a small step in the right direction.'

And on the other side of the wall, Joe Bingham and the two boys were surprised but very cheered by what Nellie told them. Was this the start to a new lease of life for his wife? Joe was asking himself. He said a silent prayer, please God, let it be so. While Jack and Willy were overjoyed by the invitation to a party, they didn't say much in case it was the wrong thing. Nellie had been very matter-of-fact about it and didn't seem fussy one way or the other. She was happy for the boys but she wasn't thinking of any change in her life.

'It's very nice of next door to think of the boys again, they seem decent people,' Joe said. 'And yer went in their house, did yer?'

'Only 'cos I had to know whether the boys had to take presents, that's all. And I wasn't in the house more than five minutes,' Nellie said. 'Anyway, they don't have to take presents, just Christmas cards. There's about ten children going, so yer'll need to write cards to each of them, Jack.'

'But how will I know their names, Mam? I'll have to put who they're to.'

'Next door's going to write them down for me and pass the list in.'

'Her name's Mrs Richardson, Mam, and she's very nice.' Jack's hopes had never been higher. 'I hope yer don't fall out with her.'

'Of course yer mam won't fall out with her, why should she?' Joe asked. 'Yer don't fall out with anyone when they're being sociable with yer.'

Willy had a wicked glint in his eyes. 'Our Jack's got his eye on Tess.'

His face the colour of beetroot, Jack kicked his brother under the table. 'Don't act daft, she's not thirteen yet.'

Nellie gave them all another surprise when she said, 'She's a nice kid. Not cheeky or forward, just a nice kid.'

It was rare to hear laughter around their table, but Joe chuckled loudly before saying, 'She'll grow up, and two years' difference in age doesn't mean a thing. I'm two years older than yer mam and it's never done us no harm.'

'Don't you start, Dad,' Jack said. 'Or I won't go to the flippin' party.' It was an empty threat, because nothing would keep him away.

Ann waited two days before taking the list of names to Nellie. She wasn't asked in, but she got something she thought she'd never see, a half-smile on her neighbour's face. 'As I said, there's ten names, but I forgot Jack and Willy won't want one for each other, so there's only eight cards to write out.'

'Do they write a card each, or put both their names on the one?'

'Oh, both names on each card, otherwise it would run too expensive. And by the way, the party will be across the road at Mrs Hanrahan's. We'll be popping over to make sure they're all right, and you'd be welcome to do the same.' Ann smiled, thinking she'd gone far enough for one day. 'I'll see you, Nellie, ta-ra.'

'D'yer think yer've made any progress with Nellie?' Lizzie asked as she sat facing Ann across the table. It was a Saturday afternoon and they had the house to themselves. George had taken Tess into Liverpool to help her buy her presents, and Maddy was at work, so they could talk in peace and quiet. 'I've said hello every time I've seen her, and although she nods, that's all I get. Mind you, I never even got a nod off her before.'

'I get a bit more than a nod, I get a smile and we pass the time of day. But at this rate we'll be years trying to break down the barrier.' Ann tilted her head. 'There's one thing I would like to do, and that's go the whole hog. But to do that I'd have to tell Bridie and Dolly what we know about Nellie. And George's brother and his wife, 'cos they're coming too. But it would mean breaking my promise to Theresa, and if she happened to find out she'd never trust me again.'

'She'd never find out, queen, 'cos yer can trust Bridie and Dolly not to breathe a word. Neither of them are gossip-mongers, they never stand jangling with the neighbours, as yer well know. I'd trust them, but yer have to make yer own mind up about that, 'cos you're the one who'll have it on yer conscience.' Lizzie was too curious to leave it at that. 'What did yer mean by going the whole hog?'

'It's a bit devious, and it might not work, but this is what I've been lying in bed at night thinking about.' Ann explained the plan she had in her mind, and when she'd finished Lizzie's head was nodding and she had a smile on her face.

'That's well worth a try, queen, and it could well work. But yer'd have to let Bridie and Dolly know or it would spoil the whole thing. And ay, that's not devious, it's clever! Me now, I can be real devious, but not you, ever.'

'I wonder if Dolly and Bridie are in now? If I keep putting it off I'll never do it.'

'They do their shopping Saturday morning so they should be in. D'yer want me to give them a knock, queen, and find out?'

'If you would, please, and I'll put the kettle on while I'm waiting.'

It was Christmas Eve, and the room looked very festive, with paper decorations criss-crossed from wall to wall, bunches of coloured balloons brightening up each corner, and the tree festooned with silver balls and tinsel. The only thing Ann had to do now was hang some presents from its branches. But before finishing it off, she had a job to do first.

'I'd better get it over with now because my nerves are getting worse by the minute.' She crossed two fingers. 'Wish me luck.'

'You'll be all right, love,' George said. 'I've got every faith in you.'

Tess gave her mother a hug. 'You've tried hard, Mam, and I love you for it.'

'And I love you, Theresa.' Ann took a deep breath. 'Here goes.'

She was expecting Nellie or one of the boys to open the door and was taken aback when she saw Joe. 'Is Nellie in, please?'

'Yes, come on in.' Ann wasn't to know it, but he too would like to build bridges and was heartened when he saw her. 'Nellie's in the kitchen.' He stuck out his hand. 'I'm Joe, by the way.'

'Yes, I know, and I'm glad to meet you, Joe. I'm Ann Richardson.'

The two boys were wide-eyed. Nobody ever came to their house. But Jack pulled himself together and said, 'Hello, Mrs Richardson.'

Nellie came in from the kitchen, and the expression on her face could have been surprise, shock or dismay. 'Did yer want me?'

'I want to ask a favour of you, Nellie. Remember I told you we would be popping over the road during the party to check on the children? Well, I was wondering if you and your husband would take a turn, save me being on edge all the time. It's only to make sure they're not pulling the wallpaper off the walls, or playing catch-as-catch-can with Bridie's best ornaments. Not that they're likely to be doing either, they're well-behaved, sensible kids. But you know how mothers worry.'

'We'll be glad to do it,' Joe said, his voice booming. 'Won't we, Nellie?'

His wife wasn't so keen. 'We'd only have to look in, wouldn't we? I mean, we wouldn't have to stay?'

'No, of course not! I'll be helping Bridie with the sandwiches and setting the table, and I'll stay until the guests arrive at seven. So if you and Joe could pop over about eight, that would be a help. We'll manage after that.'

'We'll be happy to.' Joe followed Ann to the door, and when she stepped down on to the pavement, their eyes met and he said, 'Thank you, I'm beholden to yer.'

'If our children can be friends, Joe, I don't see why we can't.' Ann waved goodbye and reached her doorstep to find George by the open door. 'Did you think I'd been kidnapped?'

'No, love, I just felt like a breath of fresh air.'

Ann shivered as she crossed to the fire. 'Breath of fresh air! It's freezing!'

'It was a joke, love! I was keeping watch so I could rescue you if need be.'

'Actually it went a lot better than I'd dare hope.' Ann held her hands out to the flames, and when she felt warmed through, she sat at the table and recounted every word that had been said. 'I might not even have got over the doorstep if Mr Bingham hadn't opened the door. He was more than friendly and I believe it's through him we'll get to Nellie.'

'"If our children can be friends, I don't see why we can't."' George reached for her hand. 'I think that sums it up beautifully.'

'That was a lovely thing to say, Mam,' Tess said. 'And very kind as well.'

373

'Let's just hope that Boxing Day's plan goes as well as tonight's. We can only wait and see.'

'Come on, love, it's eight o'clock, let's go over.' Joe eyed his wife's new dress. 'Yer look lovely, Nellie, I could fall for yer all over again.'

'Never mind that, Joe Bingham, just remember we're just popping our heads in, we're not stopping.'

'Seeing as our two sons are there, I think we can at least say hello to everyone. Otherwise we might embarrass the boys.' He cupped her elbow. 'I don't know what ye're so nervous about, they're only kids and hardly likely to eat yer.'

The youngsters hadn't been told the whole story, just that the Binghams would be showing their faces to see if all was well, so there was no surprise when they turned up. No surprise for them, but a big one for Nellie. For Tess left her chair like a spring and put her arms around the little woman's waist. 'Oh, I'm glad you came, Mrs Nellie.' The woman's body bent backwards and her arms were raised so as not to come into contact with the girl holding her close. To six of the children around the table it meant nothing, but to Maddy, and Joe Bingham and his sons, it meant a great deal. This was the biggest test ever, and from the look of almost horror on her face, Nellie wasn't ready for it.

It was only a matter of seconds, but it seemed as though time stood still for Joe Bingham. He'd been hoping against hope that this Christmas was going to be a turning point. The Richardsons offering friendship was a way forward. But it wasn't to be, for his wife couldn't even bear to touch the young girl. Then, as he watched, his wife looked at the head resting on her breast, and slowly her hands came down to touch it and stroke the mousy hair. Then she was holding the thin body close. To her husband and two boys it was a miracle, the best present anyone could have given them.

There was a catch in Nellie's voice when she said, 'Go and sit down, pet, before the others scoff the lot.'

Just then Ann came in, missing the emotional scene by seconds. She waved a bottle of lemonade in the air. 'Mrs Hanrahan was afraid she hadn't got enough lemonade in for you, so I've brought this to make sure.'

The three grown-ups didn't stay long for fear of putting a damper on the kids' party. And outside, Nellie was quick to cross the road to her own house. But Ann was out to stop her putting the key in the lock. She knew there'd be faces watching them from her front window, faces of people wanting to make Nellie and her husband welcome. 'Why don't you come next door for a drink? There's only a few neighbours there, nothing exciting.'

'That would be nice,' Joe said. 'Better than sitting on our own twiddling our thumbs.'

'No, Joe, I've got a bit of a headache. But it's nice of Mrs Richardson to ask.'

'Oh come on, Nellie, it's Christmas, for heaven's sake! A time of celebration and getting together with family and friends.' He put his arm around his wife's back and steered her away from her front door. 'We won't stay long if yer're not feeling well.'

Ann didn't bother making proper introductions, seeing as the Binghams had lived in the street for over five years and probably knew everyone's names anyway. It was only Ken and Milly who needed a proper hand-shaking introduction. They were greeted with warmth and friendliness, but none of it was overdone. Everyone had agreed beforehand to act natural and not allow their heartfelt sympathy to show. Tess's secret would be safe with them.

'You and Joe sit on the couch, Nellie,' Ann said. 'I'll sit on George's knee. That's something I haven't done much of since we were courting.'

'We won't be staying long, we don't want to interrupt yer party.' Nellie was looking very uncomfortable and it was plain she didn't want to be there.

'Ye're not interrupting the party,' Ken said, ''cos it hasn't started yet. Half an hour we've been here and not one of us has had a drink!'

'Take no notice of my brother,' George said. 'If he hasn't got a glass in his hand he thinks there's something missing. Paddy is in the kitchen now seeing to the drinks. Is it a sherry for you, Nellie, and a pint for Joe?' He passed on without giving Nellie time to shake her head.

'Sounds good, George.' Joe felt as though he'd been given a new lease of life. There were few men in the room he hadn't picked a fight with at one time or another, but now he and Nellie were being treated as friends. 'And the wife's partial to a glass of sherry.'

Half an hour later, Nellie was more relaxed and was answering when spoken to. She could hear Joe laughing at something one of the men had said and the sound struck a chord. She didn't give him much to laugh about these days, or Jack and Willy. Hadn't done for the last five years in fact. Had she been right to make them suffer so much, and for so long?

'Here, let me fill yer glass, Nellie me darlin',' Paddy said. 'Sure, I wouldn't like yer to be the only sober person in the room.'

'Certainly not,' Dolly said. 'I'll be singing me party piece soon, and yer have to be drunk to put up with it.'

Lizzie was in the kitchen helping to fill the glasses. 'D'yer want another sherry, Ann, or d'yer fancy a milk stout?'

'It's immaterial, Lizzie.'

Lizzie came through with a glass in each hand and walked across to the couch. She gave a gentle kick on Nellie's foot, and when the woman looked up she handed her a glass and gave her a huge wink before turning to Ann. 'I didn't know yer could make clothes, queen, yer never mentioned it. A bleedin' dark horse, that's what yer are.'

'What are you on about, Lizzie? I can't make clothes!'

'Then what are yer buying material for, queen?'

'Who's buying material?'

'You are, yer've just said!'

'I never said any such thing, Lizzie, you must have been hearing things.'

At this, Lizzie got on her high horse. Shoulders back and bosom hitched high, she circled around Ann like a boxer circles his opponent. She looked so comical there were smiles on all the faces, including Nellie's. 'Are yer telling me I'm going daft in me old age, queen? 'Cos if yer are, I'd have to take exception to that and clock yer one.'

'I never said you were going daft, I said you must have been hearing things.' Ann had learned a lot since she came to live in this small house, about good neighbours and friends, about love, and also how to enjoy life. And she was really enjoying this little spat with her best mate. Pushing her nose close, she said, 'I didn't say I was buying material, you soft nit, I said it was immaterial whether I had a sherry or a milk stout.'

'And what does that mean when it's bleedin' well out?'

'It means it doesn't matter, it doesn't make any difference.'

Many eyes were on Nellie, as she edged forward on the couch. There was a grin on her face as Lizzie hitched her bosom higher and snarled at Ann. 'Yer mean we've been arguing about something that means sweet bugger-all?'

In for a penny, in for a pound, Ann thought, before swearing for the first time in her life. But it was in a good cause. 'Sweet bugger-all, sunshine, sweet bugger-all.'

There were roars of laughter, the loudest being Nellie's. And looking at her now, it seemed her headache had miraculously disappeared, along with the burden of sadness she and Joe had carried for such a long time.